I0706066

FULL CIRCLE

A CINDERELLA RETELLING

SAMANTHA GAIL

DSTAR PUBLISHING LLC

Copyright © 2024 by Samantha Gail

Editor: Lea Froelich

Cover Design: Kate Farlow, Y'all That Graphic

All rights reserved.

No part of this book may be reproduced in any form or by any electronic or mechanical means, including information storage and retrieval systems, without written permission from the author, except for the use of brief quotations in a book review.

For author B. Celeste;
Because kindness always comes full circle.

CONTENTS

TRIGGER WARNINGS

Please proceed with caution as the following book contains content that may be triggering for some readers. Your mental health matters.

Triggers include:

-Death

-Loss of a parent

-Suicidal thoughts and ideations

-Emotional abuse

-Physical abuse

-Teenage pregnancy

-Arson

-Depression

-Anxiety

-(On page) attempted sexual assault

The themes, content, and intimacy depicted in this book are suitable for readers 18+.

PROLOGUE

Celeste

Mama always used to say that life comes full circle. Some of my earliest memories are of her explaining that what goes around comes around because my mama believed in the power of karma. It made her feel better to imagine rude customers at The Comfy Cushion, our family's restaurant, stubbing their toe or having an umbrella turn inside out than for her to reply in kind. Poor manners were inexcusable, according to Mama.

She didn't live long enough to explain the concept of soulmates to me, but I'd like to think that she and Daddy were destined to be together. They used to turn up the old jukebox at closing time after all the customers left and slow dance right there in the middle of the dining area.

I know it devastated him when Mama passed, called too soon by the good Lord. At least, that's what the preacher said. Daddy didn't abide much by the church, but my nana said her daughter wasn't a heathen and wouldn't be buried like one, so the preacher man came out and said his piece. Daddy was a blubbering mess by the end of it, so who's to say really? I was twelve years old when Mama died, too angry at the world for taking her away from me to care one way or another what the preacher said. He would forevermore represent the day we buried my mother's body in the ground, and it was a grudge I felt I'd hold til my last breath.

"We've still got each other, sugar bee," Daddy said that night as he cuddled my sob-wracked body to sleep. His words comforted me, my child naivete convincing me that my daddy could never leave me like my mama did. Boy, how wrong I was.

It would be years before I ever felt the kind of eternal love Mama gave me from another person. Wesley Madden blew into my life like a hurricane, all roaring winds and crashing waves. Receiving his love was like swimming in the ocean for the first time—you wanted to open your eyes and see everything even when it burned like hell. I used to wonder if Mama sent Wesley to me because she knew I needed saving or if she recognized the good I could bring out in him. Our opposition became the perfect balance, our personalities clashing in ways that could only complement one another. But when you've only known suffering and loss, the glimmer of light shining through the cracks can petrify you. That's a lesson I learned the hardest way possible.

Life comes full circle, huh? Fate must've missed the mark with me.

PART ONE

"What one loves in childhood stays in their heart forever."
   -Mary Jo Putney

CHAPTER 1
LET THE GOOD TIMES ROLL
CELESTE

THE GRASS HAD BARELY BEGUN to sprout on the ground above my mama's grave, but I ignored the damp soil underneath my bottom. Nana would probably tan my hide when she saw the muddy patches on my jeans. It was worth it to have the quiet moment with Mama.

I had gone to the cemetery to visit her grave every day since we buried her seven weeks ago, shortly before my thirteenth birthday. Talking to her headstone was a crappy replacement for seeing her beautiful smile or feeling her warmth as she held me an extra second longer for a hug, but nothing else brought me any comfort. Missing her felt like a phantom limb; how could I go on in a world without my mama? She had been the center of my world, my very best friend, and my heart ached with the sting of her loss. The future stretched ahead like a barren, arid desert—dusty, painful, and empty—without her bright laugh or delicious cooking.

A car horn honked behind me and I turned abruptly to see Daddy's truck outside the gate. He had the windows rolled down and could have just hollered my name, but we were both stuck in our own downward spirals of grief. Nana figured Daddy didn't know what to say to me to make me feel better, so he stuck to not saying anything at all. Whether that was true or not, even I recognized he would be wasting his breath to try to get my mind off things right now.

Rising slowly, I wiped as much of the debris off my bottom as I could before heading forlornly over to him with my head down. The twinkle had gone from his bright blue eyes and I hated to see yet another reminder of what Mama's death had done to our family. "Good Times Roll" by The Cars echoed faintly from his stereo as I approached, and I stopped next to the driver's side door rather than get in the truck with him.

"Why don't you go hang out somewhere other than the graveyard, sugar bee?" Daddy asked. He always called me sugar bee because he said I was sweeter than honey but buzzed about more than a bumblebee. Normally it gave me all the warm fuzzies on the inside to hear the term of endearment in his gruff voice. Today it merely reminded me of the void I felt.

I shrugged rather than answer him. If we weren't both still reeling, the action would have fired him up because he considered it poor manners not to respond when someone spoke to you. Mama's death meant manners went out the window.

He sighed heavily. "Hop in. I'm gonna take you over to the park." His firm tone warned me that he'd brook no argument.

Neither of us said another word as he followed the gravel path of the cemetery out to the main road. It was late spring here in Georgia, and the sun was bright and high, making the temperature quickly yield to the heat. My tank top was already sticking between my shoulder blades, making me wish I would have worn shorts along with it instead of jeans.

The park was a joint playground and baseball diamond near the town square. Mama and Daddy had always let me play there on days when I didn't have school because it was located across the street from The Comfy Cushion, Mama's restaurant. People came from miles around to eat her recipes, though I always thought she charmed the customers just as much with her flattering words and pretty smiles. Daddy handled the books and all the ordering, a job he took on because he saw how happy it made Mama to cook for everyone. It was the only real restaurant in town, unless you counted the fast food joints right off the highway, but given how my mama's meals always stuck to my ribs, I didn't see how they could hold a candle to her.

On a Saturday afternoon without a cloud in the sky, the park was jampacked with kids. The problem was, I hated being around them now. None of them knew what it felt like to lose someone so special and since everybody in town adored my mother, it rankled me to see their pitying looks. Their eyes followed me as soon as I set foot in the park. Eyes that all held relief that it was my mama and not theirs mixed with uncertainty over what to say to me.

"I'll be in the office for a bit longer," Daddy told me through the car window again. "Just head on over when you're hungry. Marla will whip something up for you." He didn't give me a chance to respond before pulling away to park his truck in his usual spot across the street.

I sighed heavily again. Marla was my mama's best friend who had stepped in to help Daddy with The Comfy Cushion. She seemed to think the only way I could heal was being force fed large casseroles. Even if it was Mama's recipe, it never tasted the same. My stomach wouldn't accept anything Marla made me choke down. The prospect of being made to swallow anything at the moment filled me with dread.

Following the path around the dugout of the baseball diamond where a pickup game was in full swing, I trailed behind the bleachers until I reached the edge of the woods at the back of the park. There was a small dirt trail into the trees that was mostly overgrown with bushes and moss, but I had been down there so many times that the growth didn't bother me. It led down to a small creek where there was a good climbing tree, full of shade with wide branches. I liked to hide up there among the foliage so that the other kids couldn't stare at me, the girl with the dead mama and no friends.

"Hey!" a voice snapped as I hauled myself up to the lowest branch.

It startled me to the point where I misjudged my hand placement and went tumbling face first over the branch and down onto the creek bed below. I was instantly covered in mud and felt a sting above my right eye from where my face landed on a rock. My knees took the brunt of my fall, however, and I cried out in pain on impact.

"Oh my god, are you okay?!" The same voice as before hollered over me. Gentle hands pulled at my shoulders to roll me onto the creek bank and I made eye contact with what must have been an angel. It was a boy around my age with sandy blonde hair and the bluest eyes I had ever seen. A small halo of light shone around his head, making me pinch my leg to check that I wasn't dreaming. People didn't die from falling out of trees, right?

The boy grabbed one of my hands and hauled me to my feet, helping me to wipe off all the mud on my shins. "I'm so sorry! I didn't mean to scare you!"

My cheeks burned with embarrassment. "It's fine. I'm not hurt."

He brushed the hair away from my face. "Yes, you are. This cut is bleeding."

Having a stranger's hands on my face made my heart race in a way that spooked me. I took a step away from him, backing myself up against the tree. "It's fine. Just a scratch."

The boy smirked at my retreat and stuck his hand out as if to shake mine. "I'm Wesley. Wesley Madden."

Staring blankly at his offered hand, my mind went through a rolodex of Smithson County. I knew every child in our small town of River's Run, Georgia. This boy did not belong here. He had to be a tourist. "Where are you from?"

He smiled, a megawatt smile that made my heart race again. Stuffing his hand back in the pocket of his cargo shorts, he explained, "Originally from Atlanta, but I live here now."

That didn't make sense. Marla was the gossip queen of our county and she hadn't said anything about a new family moving here. Whose house did they buy?

Wesley must have recognized the look of puzzlement on my face because he clarified, "I moved in with my great-aunt Shirley."

I nodded. Miss Shirley Jones was a regular down at The Comfy Cushion, although she had to be pushing 85. "Ain't she a little old to be taking you in?"

He shrugged. "My dad works too much and my mom took off when I was a baby. I hated all of the nannies, so he reached out to my mom's family. Shirley was the only one who offered."

It took everything I had to hold back a snort. What kind of family used a nanny? Was he some rich, spoiled brat?

Rather than responding, I turned and started to climb

back up the tree. This boy, no matter how sweet he seemed, wasn't my problem and I was still too depressed to care.

"Wait!" Wesley grabbed onto the leg of my jeans as I paused on the lowest branch. "We need to go get your eye cleaned up. It could get infected."

"How would you know?" I scoffed.

He smirked again. "Let's just say, I've gotten into my fair share of fights."

The retort on the tip of my tongue died with his statement. He looked too scrawny to be much of a fighter to me, but maybe he was just a bully.

"How old are you?" I asked instead.

"Twelve. Thirteen in June, just a couple weeks from now." His blue eyes twinkled as he perused my body, still hoisted onto the lowest branch. "What's your name?"

A warning bell was ringing somewhere in the back of my mind that befriending Wesley Madden would be a bad idea, but there was a gleam in his eye that reminded me of my mama.

Hope.

He looked hopeful, and that was something I didn't have in me to crush.

"Celeste Hendricks," I finally offered.

His megawatt smile returned. "That's a pretty name."

As if sensing my hesitation, Wesley leaned forward with an outstretched hand, waiting for me to accept. Despite myself, I couldn't help but give him a soft smile in return as I enclosed my hand in his. With one tug I was out of the tree and standing next to him, peering up into his crystal blue eyes. Even though I was a few months older than him, Wesley towered over me. He held my gaze far longer than was necessary and I felt something shift inside me, something I couldn't quite put my finger on. I wondered errantly if it would ever shift back.

For the rest of the afternoon, Wesley and I walked around the park and the playground, telling each other more about our lives. I let him do most of the talking, still too in awe of this angelic boy who paid me this kind of attention. He told me that his dad owned a big corporation and had plans for Wesley to take it over one day, but Wesley kept getting into trouble and fighting at school. I gasped in shock as he described the number of fights he had won, supposedly against much older, bigger kids. It never crossed my mind to question him. Wesley didn't seem too keen on the idea of joining his father's company, but when I asked what else he would want to do with his life, he merely shrugged. "That's a long ways off," he said. "I have plenty of time to figure it out."

We had circled the area more than five times before he threw himself down on the edge of the field beyond the base-ball diamond, yanking me down to join him.

"Look at all the clouds! That one kinda looks like a rabbit," he said, pointing upward.

I flopped down so that my head lay right next to him, my body extending in the opposite direction. We were so close that his stray hair tickled my ear. If I turned my head to the left, my face would collide with his.

The shapes he saw in the clouds became increasingly ridiculous, with elaborate back stories that he swore were Native American legends, and I couldn't stop giggling. I never offered my own interpretation of the shapes, content to let him continue talking. After several minutes, his voice faded away and we laid there quietly.

"So how come you aren't with other friends today?" Wesley suddenly asked.

Perhaps it was easier because I couldn't see him, just feel his warm presence, but for once I answered honestly, "I don't really have any. Mama was my best friend."

There was a pregnant pause before he replied softly, "'Was' your best friend…?"

I gulped, tears threatening to spill over. It was the first time I admitted it out loud to someone else. "She died a few months ago. Heart disease."

Wesley leaned up on one elbow to look down at me. "Then I get to be your best friend now." His eyes held no pity, only friendship, for which I was grateful. The assurance in his voice made me feel safe, something I had only ever felt in Daddy's presence. I was reminded of the cosmic shift in my soul from earlier when he shook my hand.

"CELESTE RENEE HENDRICKS, WHERE ARE YOU?!"

Jumping up like my pants were invaded by fire ants, I saw Marla at the park entrance, her hands on her hips. Anger lit up her face. She still had on her work apron, scanning the park for me.

Dang it, I never went back to The Comfy Cushion to eat like Daddy said. Now Marla was gonna scold me til the cows came home.

"I've gotta go," I said to Wesley.

He stood up, too, brushing grass off his tan legs. "Who is that?" he asked, nodding towards Marla.

I sighed. "That's my mama's best friend. She helps Daddy at the restaurant now." Slowly I walked towards her, not in any hurry for the verbal whiplash I knew was coming my way.

Wesley fell into step beside me. "Does your dad manage a restaurant?"

Nodding, I couldn't keep the pride from my voice as I explained, "We own it. It was my mama's restaurant." I pointed across the street to The Comfy Cushion, the outside lights now on from the timer. It must be a lot later than I thought.

Marla finally took sight of me and although I could tell Wesley's presence by my side surprised her, she continued to frown at me. "Care to explain where you been?!" she snapped. "Had me worried sick! Goodness me, what happened to your eye?!" She gruffly turned my chin upward so that she could examine the cut near my eyebrow.

Before I could respond, Wesley shocked me by saying, "It's my fault, ma'am. I'm new here and I asked her to show me around."

If he had announced he was the fifth member of the Beatles, I don't think Marla could have looked more surprised or confused. Her eyebrows receded towards her hairline as her warm brown eyes darted between the two of us. "Celeste..." she clarified, "...showed you around. Willingly."

Wesley didn't skip a beat. "Sure did. She's the only friend I have in the world right now."

I could tell Marla was fighting the urge to smile because she wanted to stay mad at me, but she couldn't hold back. Long before my mother fell ill, I avoided kids my own age, preferring to cook in the restaurant or learn how to manage the books with Daddy. Friends weren't really a thing on my radar.

"Well, as nice as it is to meet you, Celeste needs to come eat something before she passes out," Marla replied, giving me less of a stink eye than usual. "Why don't you come, too? I've got a slice of pie with your name on it."

My heart leapt, hopeful he would accept.

Wesley smiled at me but shook his head. "I should probably get back. My aunt Shirley didn't know I was leaving."

Marla's jaw clenched, warring over his polite decline and his obvious disrespect to his aunt. "Would that be Miss Shirley Jones over there on Houston Street?"

He nodded. "Yes, ma'am."

It was the "ma'am" that redeemed him, I could tell. She finally dropped her stiff demeanor and nodded. "You give Miss Shirley my best now, young man." Marla gave him another once over before turning back towards The Comfy Cushion. "Say good-bye to your friend and get inside," she called over her shoulder.

I gave him a half-hearted smile as I toed with a small rock at my feet. For the first time ever, I felt a real connection with someone outside of my family, and I didn't want to leave. "Sorry about that," I offered.

"Meet you here after lunch tomorrow?" Wesley asked.

He might as well have handed me a four leaf clover. I tried not to make it too obvious as I beamed at him, nodding and wrapping my arms around my own waist to try and contain my joy. A friend—I had finally made a friend.

Spinning on my heel, I started humming along to the song from Daddy's radio. Maybe, just maybe, I could let the good times roll.

CHAPTER 2
IN THE NAME OF
FRIENDSHIP
CELESTE

THE NEXT DAY I was up before the sun rose. I could barely sleep for thinking about Wesley. He actually helped me forget some of the loneliness and he didn't look at me like I was the strange girl who lost her mama. He didn't have one either.

Daddy blinked rapidly when he shuffled into the kitchen and found me sitting at the breakfast bar next to a plate of steaming pancakes, bacon, and fresh coffee. The pancakes were one of mama's recipes and I imagined the lumps I worked out in the batter were the same as the lump I felt in my throat when I pictured her. How many mornings had we spent together cooking a piping hot breakfast before heading into the restaurant? How many times had she kissed the top of my head after whispering the secret ingredient to me?

"It's that extra sugar you give because you're so sweet!" she would say with a proud smile.

This was the first time I had attempted to make anything since she passed.

Daddy looked behind him as if he was confused. "What happened? Where did that food come from?"

I rolled my eyes. "From me, Daddy, obviously!" The last

word stretched out of my mouth, bordering on sassy. Without coffee yet, I knew Daddy would let it slide.

He did. "You cooked all that? For me?" His navy terrycloth bathrobe hung open over pinstripe pajama bottoms and an old concert t-shirt. Thick brown hair stood up in odd tufts, a speckle of gray mixing in at the roots. Watching Mama succumb to her illness had taken its toll on him.

Pulling another plate over with a couple pancakes and fruit, I shook my head. "For me, too. When can we go to the restaurant?"

Daddy shuffled over and drank deeply from the coffee mug in his daze. "You wanna go with me today?"

"And it's about time, too!" Nana shuffled into the kitchen, her too big house shoes smacking hard against the linoleum floors. "Been hidin' out in this house way too long!"

Nana lived in a small cottage about twenty yards behind our house. The property both houses sat on had been in Daddy's family for six generations, and when Nana's knee started giving her trouble, Mama and Daddy insisted on building a small place for her so they could "keep an eye on her." If you asked me, Nana was the one always doing the spying. Nothing ever got past her.

Although she slept in her own place, she spent most of her days in our living room watching soap operas and eating peanuts that she had to wash down with a Coke. She would fill an entire grocery bag of shells in a single episode. Yet you would never know it because soaking wet, I doubted Nana could hit the ninety pound mark. She was a tiny, little spitfire—full of quick quips, wild stories, and firm beliefs.

Despite the early morning hour, Nana had on her usual pair of sweatpants and baggy t-shirt, large bag of peanuts in hand. "Now what's gotten into you?" she asked, eyes squinting in my direction.

As excited as I was feeling, I wasn't sure how Nana would react to news of Wesley. She was old school and maintained that boys and girls couldn't be friends because boys were always up to no good.

"Um…I just wanted to help out today," I hedged. It was a feeble excuse at best and one that she immediately saw through.

"Help out?" Nana cackled. "Girl, you ain't been in a helping mood in months. Wallowin' around, feelin' sorry for yourself! Now come on, out with it."

I glanced over at Daddy for help because he usually intervened when Nana got too pushy, but right now his attention was focused on me, too, his eyebrows arching up towards his hairline. "What is it, sugar bee?" he asked gently.

There would be no distracting them. "I made a friend, that's all." Shrugging, I kept my eyes on my plate, fiddling with my fork as I tried to find the right words. "Thought I might be able to play at the park again."

"Is this that boy Marla told me about?" Daddy inquired.

"A boy!" Nana spat. "Don't you go getting caught up with some little hooligan, Celeste! What's this boy's name, huh? Who's his mama?"

It took every ounce of restraint I had not to roll my eyes. While it might be too early for Daddy to notice my sass, Nana had the beady eyes of a hawk and would waste no time in boxing my ears.

"He's new in town, Nana. I was just tryin' to be nice."

"Bein' nice, my foot! Now you listen here—"

"Suzanne," Daddy cut her off, his tone firm. "That's enough."

Nana's face twisted. She had always been respectful of my father and treated him like he was her own flesh and blood. But this was one subject for which she could not budge.

"Mark my words," she warned, pointing a finger towards in my direction. "This girl's gonna get her heart broken! Boys ain't worth a lick!"

Daddy winked at me before saying, "Hey, now, what about me?" He held his arms out as if to invite her to say anything derogatory.

Nana leaned back on one foot, a fist planted on her hip. "If Celeste wants to wait until she's thirty and found a man who's matured some like you, then she can be my guest!" With that, she opened the fridge behind her and snatched out a Coke bottle, shuffling into the living room as she muttered under her breath.

Daddy couldn't help but smile at me as I repressed a grin. We both knew Nana would cool off after a while. She didn't believe in holding grudges.

"Your nana's got a bit of a point," he hedged, patting my knee. "We don't know much about this boy."

I took a large bite of my pancakes, knowing the sight of me eating would sway him. "I can get to know him, Daddy. He's new here and all alone."

He took a large bite of bacon and chewed for a moment while thinking carefully. "Just be cautious," he finally said.

That was as much of an approval as I would ever receive from him. I couldn't hold back my smile as I took a long drink from my glass of fruit punch.

❦ ❦ ❦ ❦ ❦

"Has Miss Shirley arrived yet?" I asked Marla for what felt like the millionth time. Miss Shirley was normally like clockwork, walking through the door at exactly quarter til noon for the daily lunch special. It never mattered what the special was, that was her order. She hadn't opened a menu for The Comfy Cushion in my working memory.

However, it was now five past and there was no sight of Miss Shirley…or her great-nephew.

"Maybe they decided to head down to Savannah for the day," Marla offered. She stuck paper orders in the ticket window for Jesse, the cook, who did his best to keep up with the demand without Mama's help. Business hadn't slowed down and for that I was grateful. It kept Mama's memory alive.

The Comfy Cushion looked like a diner straight out of a movie. A shiny red countertop wound all the way around the back wall where the kitchen window opened to the line cook. There was a swinging pony door at the halfway point so servers could get in and out, but the rest of counter was circled with vinyl barstools. Big booth tables with Tiffany glass pendant lamps curved around the outside perimeter next to the windows. Every pendant was unique; Daddy said he and Mama found them at an antique shop on their honeymoon and Mama wouldn't leave the shop without them.

There were several tables spaced out on the floor in between, large and made of solid wood by Ol' Man McInworthe down at the lumberyard. He still wouldn't eat anywhere else because he was so proud of his contribution to Mama's restaurant. We could count on his presence for dinner every day of the week.

Best of all were the big, fluffy cushions that Nana and Mama stitched by hand for every booth and chair in the place. There was no rhyme or reason to the fabric, it was just whatever scraps they came by. It created a mismatched sense of whimsy that somehow made the place feel just as cozy and inviting as home. If I really thought about it, the air of the place was one hundred percent Mama, which was why I couldn't imagine a better restaurant anywhere. A large jukebox—still operational—sat in the corner leading towards the bathrooms and Daddy's office. It cranked out an old crooner from Loretta Lynn at the moment, *Don't Come Home a-Drinkin' (With Lovin' On Your Mind)*.

I was perched on the last stool of the counter in perfect view of the only doorway in or out. As soon as Wesley stepped through that door, I would know it. Mama's book of recipes was sprawled out on the counter in front of me as I helped Daddy pick out the menu for fall. It was difficult to even look at her tiny writing in the giant scrapbook she kept, but I didn't want anyone to realize how intensely I watched for a certain someone to walk through the door.

The bell over the door clanged again and despite the sinking feeling in my gut, I sat up higher in my seat, straining to see over the diners seated at the counter across from us. My hopes were quickly doused as Jimmy and Bill from the mechanic's shop down the road came in.

My shoulders visibly sank as disappointment weighed them down. Where was Wesley? I knew I hadn't imagined him because Marla met him, too.

Ever in tune with my emotions, she plopped a warm slice of strawberry pie in front of me. "You just get your mind off him and then see how fast he walks in," Marla suggested. She started to roll silverware into napkins as I morosely pushed the pie around on my plate. Marla thought everything could be fixed with a slice of pie. She had an uncanny knack for guessing everyone's favorite flavor.

"Miss Shirley always comes here for lunch, though," I huffed out.

Marla nodded. "That she does, but it's not every day you take in your great-nephew. Maybe they're just settling in."

I rolled my eyes. "Wesley doesn't need to settle in." His presence was already too overwhelming. I couldn't picture him settling into anything.

One of the customers called out a request for a refill on their lemonade and Marla acknowledged them with a wave and a smile. "Comin' right up, sir!" She dropped the smile as she took in the remnants of smashed pie before me. "You take a bite outta that, you hear? Gonna turn into skin and bones if you keep this up."

If I didn't eat something, she was liable to tell Daddy, or worse—Nana—and then I really wouldn't be allowed to do anything with Wesley. I shoved a forkful into my mouth and did feel a slight lift in my spirits to taste Marla's little slice of heaven. She was a great baker like my mama was a great cook.

The bell clanged loudly as one of the diners exited, but I didn't bother to crane my head this time. Clearly Miss Shirley was dining elsewhere today.

I wasn't aware of a presence next to me until a voice commented, "That sure looks good."

Wesley.

My eyes darted to my right where he sat grinning at me like a Chesire cat. He had on a clean white T-shirt that high-lighted his angelic features and a pair of camo cargo shorts. Somehow my brain short circuited at the sight. Kids our age weren't supposed to look that good, right?

That had to be why it took me a full two minutes to formulate something to say. "You shouldn't wear white if we're gonna play outside," I said.

Oh my word, I did not just say that!

Wesley's smile widened like he found me entertaining, but he didn't contradict me. "What else is there to do around here?"

I frowned at the question. What else was there to do anywhere on a warm spring day in Georgia?

Thankfully I was saved from voicing my ignorance out loud when Marla returned. "Well, hello there again, Wesley," she greeted him. Her sharp eyes were still sussing him out. "Wouldn't you rather sit with Miss Shirley?"

Marla gestured over his shoulder to the booth by the door where Miss Shirley usually sat. She occupied it now across from a man who could not have looked more out of place if he had green skin and a second head. He was impeccably dressed in a crisp gray suit with a white button down and lavender tie. He even had a matching pocket square, something I thought only men in the movies wore. The man's dark hair was slicked back away from his face, but his features weren't discernible behind the large sunglasses he wore. He was talking rapidly with someone on a cell phone, a large silver watch catching sunlight on his wrist. It was the first time I ever saw someone actually use a cell...nobody in River's Run owned one.

"Who is that?" I asked Wesley.

He reddened. "That's my father." Marla was too busy staring at the man to catch the way Wesley's shoulders hunched at the admission, but I saw it. It made me want to give his hand a comforting squeeze.

"Your daddy isn't from around these parts, is he?" Marla

commented quietly. She shot me a look that conveyed how amusing she found the man to be as she poured Wesley a glass of water.

Wesley snorted. "My father has never stepped foot outside of a major city until yesterday when he brought me here. He'll be leaving in a few minutes to head back to Atlanta."

"Then don't you wanna go sit with him?" I asked curiously. If my daddy were leaving, I would want to soak up every minute with him I could.

My friend just shook his head. "It's better if I don't."

The statement didn't make sense to me and I looked to Marla for clues as to what to say. Her shrewd scan of his face as her mouth formed a thin line told me that whatever her thoughts were, they weren't something she was willing to voice at the moment.

Wesley didn't seem to mind, however. He grabbed the discarded half of the sandwich Marla had provided me for lunch an hour ago and took an enormous bite. "This is good," he complimented her, holding up what now amounted to a quarter of a sandwich.

His topic change wasn't going to deter her. "What's your daddy's name?"

He swallowed thickly and kept his eyes trained on the sandwich in his hands as he replied, "Benedict Warner Madden the Third," through gritted teeth.

Marla's eyes widened. "As in Madden Markets?" she asked.

Wesley dropped the crust of the sandwich back on the plate as he ground out, "Uh huh."

Normally Marla would scold someone for responding so rudely, but she looked dumbstruck at the moment. And with good reason. Madden Markets was a chain of general stores that was taking over the South, becoming the biggest rival to Wal-Mart in the country. They were known for their bargain bins that had new deals each morning, sometimes marking the particular item down over 75% off. Marla loved shopping at the one outside Savannah on Sunday mornings when she had the day off from the diner.

It meant my new friend was the heir to a gold mine, in her eyes. I could practically see the gears shifting in her head as she tried to process this information. For once, she was left speechless, no doubt too stunned by the revelation to know the appropriate thing to say.

As impressive as his daddy's job was to adults, I only cared about Wesley. Who cared that he owned a bunch of stores? We owned a restaurant and nobody acted like that around us. Although we didn't annoy people by arguing loudly over the phone in the middle of The Comfy Cushion like Mr. Madden was doing now. More than one customer was turning in his direction to shoot him a warning glare.

"Come on." I pulled Wesley off his bar stool and made to head for the door.

"Wait!" Marla said. She whipped a plate out and slid a slice of strawberry pie on it before setting it at the place Wesley just vacated. "Have a slice, young man."

He smiled at her, the megawatt smile I wanted him to turn back on me. "No, thank you, ma'am. I don't like strawberry pie."

For the second time in just a few minutes Marla was left with her mouth hanging open. No one ever refused a slice of her pie. *No one.*

I couldn't help but chuckle at her face. "Let's go or she'll never let us leave," I whispered conspiratorially as I pulled him by his sleeve towards the door again.

"Celeste Hendricks, you better stop and introduce your-self, now!" came Marla's reprimand.

Since we were going to pass Wesley's daddy and Miss Shirley going out the door anyway, I figured she was right. I walked up to the edge of their booth and nodded to his great-aunt.

Miss Shirley Jones had resided in River's Run her entire life, like most of the folks here. Her late husband passed away young, more than thirty years ago, followed ten years later by her only child. She lived alone in a big house on Houston Street that had long since been considered rundown. A tiny thing, Miss Shirley resembled a fourth grader in size and stature, but insisted on wearing a dress with pantyhose and kitten heels each day like she was dressed for church. Her iron gray hair was pulled back into its signature bun, but she gave me a friendly smile now, eyes holding the same pity I expected from everyone.

She grimaced, however, when she looked across the table at Mr. Madden, who was still having a rather heated discussion with someone on the boxy cell phone. Now that I was closer, I realized how stern his face looked, even behind the glasses. His body language suggested he was not someone to be trifled with.

Wesley cleared his throat loudly and gave his father a pointed look. Mr. Madden nodded and barked out an order to the caller before ending the call in a huff.

"You wouldn't believe the nightmare China is becoming with these imports!" he snapped. With a sharp tug, he removed his glasses to reveal cold, black eyes staring at me. "And who is this?" he demanded of Wesley.

"This is the girl I told you about," his son began. "Celeste Hendricks."

Wanting to reflect well on my parents, I smiled brightly at him and held out my right hand for him to shake. "Pleased to meet you, sir."

Mr. Madden merely glared at my hand before turning back towards Miss Shirley. "I want weekly updates on his activities. Wesley will maintain perfect grades or I will be forced to send him to Montmeri."

His rudeness rankled me. I had never met a man with such horrible manners before. Mama would have given him the burnt bacon.

"What's Montmeri?" I asked Wesley. My friend's face had turned to ash, his back ramrod straight.

"Don't you worry, Ben, dear," Miss Shirley cooed. "I'll make sure Wesley is well taken care of."

Mr. Madden didn't look as if he believed her, but he snorted his acceptance. Turning to Wesley, his face turned even colder. "Stay out of trouble this time, Wesley, or so help me, I will drag you on that plane myself. This is your last chance."

Wesley didn't say a word. He nodded once before turning abruptly on his heel, catching my hand in his as he stepped towards the door.

Ever my mama's daughter, I couldn't help but add, "It was nice meeting you, Mr. Madden. Good afternoon, Miss Shirley," as Wesley yanked me out the door.

Once outside, Wesley's feet pounded the pavement so fast I expected sparks to fly. He made a beeline across the street for the park, following the path down to the creek bed where we met the day before. Other kids stopped and pointed at us. The fact that I only cared about Wesley's feelings rather than their stares should have been a wakeup call, but at the moment I was too consumed with concern for him to care about anything else. When we reached the edge of the woods, he picked up his pace even faster, practically bolting to the tree. I had to run just to keep up with his long legs. As soon as we reached the safety of its branches, he spun abruptly on his heel and brought me up short with his cowering glare.

"Go ahead," he snarled. "Tell me how I'm a spoiled, rich kid with a prick for a dad! And how you don't wanna be my friend!"

I gaped at him, my brown waves flying loose around my face. "Wesley," I whispered, "that thought never crossed my mind."

His face contorted into an ugly sneer of anger, his startling blue eyes intense with rage. "Then tell me how you feel sorry for me, for being dumped on some old lady's doorstep because my rich daddy doesn't want me!"

My mama was probably rolling in her grave hearing him refer to his elders like that, but I recognized his true feelings. They laced right through his fury. Wesley wasn't angry—he was hurt. He wanted to lash out at the world the same way I had after I lost my mama. Only Wesley's daddy chose to do this to him.

I shook my head slowly, keeping my gaze trained on his so he could see my sincerity. "The only one I feel sorry for is him because he's missing out."

Wesley's entire face crumpled as he struggled to contain his feelings. I recognized that look because it was the same mask I had been wearing for weeks now. Without giving it a second thought, I rushed forward to throw my arms around him. It took a few moments of stunned silence before he awkwardly returned the embrace. He hugged me as if the gesture was foreign to him, like no one had ever held him when he fell asleep at night, or when he scraped his knee, or when he won the school spelling bee.

Realizing that made my heart break for him. Obviously, his mother hadn't been around and it didn't seem like his daddy was someone who took the time to hug him. I couldn't imagine a world where Daddy and Nana wouldn't hold me. Even Marla pulled me in for a squeeze at the end of the day. Poor Wesley had never known a family like that.

I stepped away and brushed the hair out of my face, trying to nonchalantly keep my eyes on the ground so he didn't feel embarrassed if he needed to dry his face. Hastily, I saw a quick swipe of his forearm and knew I made the right call.

Wesley needed me. He deserved to know what it felt like to have someone care for you, to have someone cheer you on and call you out on your sass just like my mama and daddy always did for me. If I could do that for him, maybe that would be a good thing. It's what Mama would have done, and that gave me the desire to try.

Besides, I had a feeling that befriending Wesley Madden was about to be the biggest adventure of my life.

CHAPTER 3
SOUTHERN GENTLEMAN I AM NOT
WESLEY

I HAD KNOWN her for only a day and Celeste Hendricks was the most important person in my life. We might as well be permanently joined at the hip; there was no breaking away even in wind, rain, or burning sun. She had already shown me more consideration and compassion than anyone else, even those stupid shrinks my father made me see for a while. Turns out, all you needed to make me believe in myself were light green eyes and hair like a lion's mane.

Everything I said seemed to impress her. I could tell by the way she hung on to every story, asking for details and reacting to all the best parts. I might've embellished just a tad, but who wouldn't if someone admired you? Aunt Shirley hadn't reacted to anything I'd said the night before other than to tell me she'd wallop me with her wooden spoon if I didn't behave. There was no way Aunt Shirley could catch me if it came down to it, so I couldn't say her threat really worked.

All I was good at was getting into trouble. That's what my father always said, with my teachers in agreement, and all the school administrators had finally washed their hands of me at my fifth school in 18 months. One nanny after the other, even the most highly established from international agencies, ran from our penthouse screaming. When money thrown at Atlanta's finest shrinks didn't solve my "problem," my dad threw down the gauntlet and said I would have to go to a strict boarding school in Switzerland called Montmeri since I couldn't get my act together. The school sounded horrible from reviews I read online, enforcing strict curfews and enough rules to make military boot camp look like summer vacation.

I threw a fit big enough that our housekeeper, an older Puerto Rican woman named Mrs. Aguilar, called the mobile crisis line. Being placed under the microscope made my father reconsider his decision to send me to Montmeri, but I was on my last chance. Even I could tell by the determined set in his jaw. My mother's aunt was the only family member willing to help, though I had no idea how she was even in contact with my father. She didn't own a computer or a cell phone and still had an old satellite dish for her dilapidated television set.

River's Run, Georgia was nothing like my old home. Atlanta was a city always on the move, which was ironic considering how jampacked traffic always was. Everyone there was hustling to be somebody and the atmosphere had a crackle of energy to it. Here, everything took its own sweet time, and people's family connections meant more than anything else. It was all just...different.

Celeste made different good. There was a hollowness to her that I could already sense, an echo of loss that matched my own. It sounded like her mom's death really hurt her. Since I didn't have any memories of my own, the thought of her death didn't matter. Like picturing the death of a stranger. You might say a kind word out of respect, but there wouldn't be any real feeling behind it. Celeste's mother must've been something really special, though, for her daughter to hang on to her memory like she was. Mourning the loss of anyone was a foreign concept to me, and in many ways, I envied Celeste for knowing a love like that.

We spent the rest of that afternoon sitting in the tree by the creek and swapping stories. She made it so easy to forget everything with my father. Today was Celeste's turn to share, although I had to ask questions to get her to open up. She said all of the kids in town were awkward around her since her mother died and she didn't really hang out with anyone anymore. I offered to throttle anyone who crossed her. Her smile was so soft and sweet. Like she knew she shouldn't be happy about my threat, but she couldn't hold the smile in. I found her shyness to be endearing, a kitten too weak and new to walk on its own, and I vowed to protect her for as long as she'd let me.

Lightning bugs were out in full force before she squealed and scrambled out of the tree. "I'm gonna be in so much trouble! I never went in for supper!" Celeste took off down the path without a backward glance.

I shuffled out of the tree after her when I heard her distant cry. "C'mon, Wesley, we can't miss supper!"

Marla was just getting ready to lock up when we tore back inside. Her lips were pursed so tightly that I couldn't help but wonder if they would fall off. *Falling For You* by Colbie Caillat played faintly on the jukebox. Celeste hung her head as she waited for Marla's reprimand. I stopped just behind her, uncertain how to proceed. I didn't really care if I upset Marla, but clearly Celeste did, so I guess I would have to.

"I'm so sorry, Marla," Celeste said quietly with her head down.

"It was my fault," I insisted. "I didn't wanna leave the creek and I made her stay, too."

The look on Marla's face warned me that she didn't believe me. Her stern expression darted back and forth between us before she finally released a heavy sigh.

"Look, I'm gonna let this slide once, but that's all you get." Marla pointed a finger at us in warning. "Wesley, if you're gonna be around much this summer, you better learn my rules. Lunch is at 11 before the rush. Supper at six. Y'all are always welcome to come by and get a snack or I'll pack something up for you. D'you hear me?"

I risked a glance to my left and saw Celeste was still hanging her head.

"Don't you look at her, Wesley! You're dealing with me!" Marla snapped. "It ain't her place to save you."

I frowned at her, unwilling to yield to someone without any authority over me. "I hear you loud and clear." Turning on my heel, I stormed out the door, allowing it to slam behind me as I sped down the street. I couldn't even remember where Aunt Shirley's house was.

A few minutes later, a large pickup truck pulled up beside me and rolled down the passenger window. The man had a neatly trimmed beard and the same facial features as Celeste.

"Are you Wesley?" the man asked.

I didn't say anything, though my hands balled into fists at my side. He continued to creep next to me in his rusty red pickup.

"The name's Doug Hendricks. I reckon you and I need to have a little chat," he said.

So he was Celeste's father. That brought me up short.

Mr. Hendricks stopped and unlocked the door so I could climb in. I was still too irritated to look at him, but I knew Celeste would never speak to me again if I disrespected her father. Even in the short time I had known her, I already gathered that her family meant everything to her.

He headed to the outskirts of the main street where River's Run's lone traffic light blinked red. There would be next to no traffic at this time of night. This town had a 9 o'clock curfew because everything closed by 8 p.m.

"Listen," Mr. Hendricks began, "I don't know you and you don't have to explain yourself to me. You're not my kid, so it's not my place. But I expect certain manners and courtesy for me and my family. That includes my daughter and my wife's best friend."

I could feel his stare boring into the side of my face, a look I refused to acknowledge.

"Are we clear?"

Swallowing hard, I let out a deep breath and nodded. All my anger dissipated.

"What was that?" he asked gruffly.

"Yes, sir," I replied.

From my peripheral I saw him nod his approval. "Then we have no hard feelings. We'll get a fresh start tomorrow. I'm assuming I'll see you tomorrow?"

Mr. Hendricks pulled up to Aunt Shirley's house where all the lights were on downstairs. She had probably fallen asleep in front of the tv like she did last night.

Despite pulling up, Mr. Hendricks put the truck in park and turned to face me. His eyes were kind, reminding me of Celeste's even though they weren't the same color as hers. "Now I'm sure that things are a lot different here than what you're used to. It'll get better if you really give this place a chance. Celeste has her mama's big heart. She'll help you so long as you let her."

I could detect the sorrow in his voice when he spoke of his wife. I felt sorry for him in a way that I never felt for Celeste when she talked about it. Her grief was still fresh. Mr. Hendricks' sounded like it was embedded in his bones. How would it feel to love someone like that?

How would it feel if someone loved *me* like that?

I tried to let his words sink in as I nodded. "Yes, sir. I can do that."

Mr. Hendricks offered me a small smile that was so reminiscent of Celeste's I couldn't help but grin back.

"Thank you for driving me home, sir," I said, climbing out of the truck.

As I rounded the front end, Mr. Hendricks rolled down his window and leaned one elbow out. "There's good people around here, son, so don't take so much to heart."

The moniker he chose instantly rubbed me the wrong way and I felt my hackles rise. In the back of my mind I knew he didn't mean anything by it, but I hated being called "son." My own father never called me that, and he was the most condescending person I knew. I didn't belong to anybody— that much had always been clear—and I refused to allow a stranger to think he could talk down to me because of it.

There was an edge to my voice that I knew Mr. Hendricks didn't deserve as I ground out, "Don't call me that! You're just a shitty old man!"

I dashed into the house, slamming the door loudly behind me. From the corner of my eye I saw Aunt Shirley jump in her armchair in front of the television, blinking rapidly in her sleepy daze. I bolted up the stairs to what had been assigned as my room and threw myself onto the old quilt covering the bed, making sure I stomped loudly on her hardwood floors along the way.

Everything about the room was off, from the lumpy mattress and flattened pillow to the slanted wooden ceiling and solitary window. Even though my father's penthouse felt more like a showroom than a home, I suddenly missed my king size bed and floor to ceiling windows looking down on the bright city lights below. It was so dark and quiet outside here in River's Run; I had no idea how anyone was supposed to sleep here.

As my racing heart began to settle and I felt some of the anger ebb out of my system, I flipped onto my back and settled my hands behind my head, glaring up at the rickety ceiling above me. I was nobody's son, at least not anybody worth mentioning. Although a small part of me knew I owed Mr. Hendricks an apology, it felt good to lash out at someone. One of the therapists had suggested I should get involved in some kind of sport in order to better channel some of my rage, but my father had scoffed at the idea that I had any rage to work out. All the fights I got into at school were the only time I ever felt some of my anger go away. It was always burning just below the surface, like it flowed in my bloodstream.

Celeste was the first real friend I'd ever had. There were lots of kids back in Atlanta who wanted to hang around me because of my father, but I wasn't close with any of them. All it would take was the right piece of gossip and they'd turn on me in the blink of an eye. I knew they were after power and influence, all the stuff my dad's money could buy. I couldn't even say why things were different with Celeste; I just looked in her eyes and knew. Maybe that was how it worked. Maybe friends were something stronger than soulmates, where the connection ran so deep that it defied logic or reason.

Sleep came over me as I mulled over the possibility of that kind of connection with a girl who had pretty green eyes like Celeste Hendricks.

CHAPTER 4
A LESSON IN SOUTHERN HOSPITALITY

CELESTE

I COULDN'T EVEN BRING myself to sit in the dining area at The Comfy Cushion the next day. Marla had been appalled by Wesley's behavior and warned me after he stormed out that I was never to sass anyone like that. I knew manners meant everything to Marla and Daddy, but after seeing how Wesley's father acted, I wasn't too sure that Wesley understood the difference. Even still, I wanted him to apologize to Marla, which was something I expected him to refuse. It was easier to avoid the entire situation by hiding out in Daddy's office.

It wasn't much of a surprise when Daddy came around the corner just before 11 a.m. and told me Wesley was out front asking for me.

"He's your friend," he reminded me firmly. "You don't ignore your friends, especially when they come to ask forgiveness."

My ears perked up at that and I walked down the hall and into the dining area with bated breath. Wesley stood next to the jukebox, a look of deep contrition on his face, holding a bouquet of light pink orchids and wildflowers. Marla stood just behind him clutching a bouquet of her own, bright red cardinal flowers.

I stopped when the toes of my sneakers were just a few inches away from his. My face flushed all the way to my hairline when I asked, "Are those for me?" No one had ever given me flowers before, not even Daddy.

"Celeste, I'm really sorry for storming out like that yesterday. I apologized to Marla, too." Wesley shuffled his feet and pulled at the bottom of his shirt, his fidgeting letting me know that he was just as uncomfortable with our exchange. "Can you forgive me?"

"Let's just forget the whole thing ever happened," I offered. I accepted the flowers from him and inhaled deeply. They smelled sweet, fresh out of the ground.

He shook his head. "My housekeeper always said that I can't forget or else how can I do better next time?" Wesley's corresponding grin told me he knew the effect his apology was having on me. I wondered if the butterflies were located in my heart or stomach because at that moment, they felt one and the same.

I glanced at Marla and saw she was smiling at both of us. That was all I needed to see to know she had already forgiven him, too. Offering him a small smile of my own, I nodded.

"Go on back and whip up something for y'all to eat," Marla directed me. "Jenny was too busy last night to properly restock all the condiments on the tables, so if I don't get something out there soon, they're gonna run me ragged over some dang ketchup!" She shooed us away towards the door that led into the prep kitchen.

"What do you like to eat?" I asked Wesley as I crossed the

threshold to the large steel prep table that dominated the tiny room behind the grill line.

Wesley hovered near the doorway, his eyes as round as saucers as he took in the tall shelves filled with baskets of fresh vegetables, dry pantry items, and pre-made jars of sauces. Everything was lined up and neatly labeled, with a dry erase board on every section to write down due out dates.

"Aren't we just gonna have a sandwich or something?" he asked.

I shrugged and went to the small sink in the corner to wash up. "I can make you a sandwich if that's what you want." Drying my hands, I grabbed a cutting board and large knife from the rack of clean dishes and returned to the prep table.

"Do you know how to cook?" he asked incredulously.

I laughed at the surprise in his voice. "Of course I do, silly! How else are you gonna eat if you don't know how to cook?"

Wesley's ears went red. "My father always insisted that we go out for dinner. Our housekeeper made my breakfasts and lunches."

His revelation was equally surprising to me. I couldn't imagine being nearly thirteen and not knowing how to make my own meals.

"Didn't you ever help the housekeeper in the kitchen?"

He shook his head.

"So you can't even make a grilled cheese? A peanut butter and jelly? A bowl of cereal?"

Wesley smiled sheepishly as he continued to shake his head with every question.

Mama never would have allowed him to leave until she taught him how to cook everything from scratch! She had forced Daddy to learn, too, though she hardly ever let him.

Said it made her happy to serve him a hot meal filled with love.

"Well, I'm in the mood for a chicken quesadilla, so that's what I'm gonna make," I announced. Turning, I grabbed the clear plastic container holding the fresh bakery items and withdrew a large flour tortilla that our neighbor, Mrs. Hernandez, made from scratch for us every few days. I entered the large, walk-in refrigerator and pulled out the blocks of cheese, a tomato, an onion, and cilantro. After I placed them back on the cutting board on the table, I pulled out a plate and placed the tortilla on it to keep it out of the way, but also make it easy for Jesse to throw on the grill. Dicing the tomato and onion carefully, the pieces were placed on the corner of the cutting board. I returned to the rack of dishes near the sink and grabbed the grater so I could grate fresh cheese onto the tortilla before adding the tomato and onion. When I was satisfied with everything, I returned to the fridge to grab the plastic bin with pre-grilled chicken pieces and a bottle of our homemade chipotle ranch dressing.

Wesley watched me with his mouth hanging open. He moved closer after I started dicing the onion, but his eyes tracked my every movement as I went about my work. After I squirted some of the dressing across the tortilla, I couldn't help but squirt some onto my finger and lick it off. It was a recipe I had created with my mama, and even now I could see her face beaming at me as she swore up and down it was the best she had ever tasted.

"What is that?" He nodded towards the bottle as I squirted more on my finger again.

I tried to laugh it off when I realized I must look like a nutcase to keep putting a condiment on my finger and eating it. It was good enough to eat with a spoon. Or so Mama and Daddy told me.

"It's my homemade chipotle ranch," I explained. "I made the recipe a couple years ago with Mama, so now we always keep it on hand as a condiment."

Maybe my mind was playing a trick on me because it almost looked like Wes was impressed.

"What kind of food do y'all serve?" he finally asked after several moments of considering my answer. Only he over pronounced "y'all" like the Yankees who came to visit on vacation.

I laughed at that. "A little bit of everything. Mama always said that her kitchen was her canvas, so she wasn't following a recipe, she was making art. It was amazing to watch an entire meal come out of thin air! And she made it look so easy!" My voice dropped off as I lost myself in her memories. "I wish I could grow up to be like her," I added quietly.

Wesley brushed the hair away from my face, staring directly into my eyes. "I bet you already are," he whispered. Just the feather-light touch of his fingers on my skin had the butterflies return to my stomach.

I knew a thing or two about what happened between boys and girls. Mama had started giving me The Talk at a very young age because she said it was important for me to feel comfortable with my own body and to handle myself with grace whenever I was attracted to someone down the line. Wise words that all dissipated into smoke in that moment.

"You're awfully pretty," he whispered, his voice barely loud enough for me to hear.

I gulped. "You're really pretty, too," I breathed.

Wesley's eyes sparkled with mirth as he laughed. He

dropped his hand from my face in that same instant and took a step away from me.

The pull of gravity shifted with him. I shook my head and returned to my quesadilla, taking far longer than necessary to fold it over and center it on the plate.

Sensing the tension in the air, Wesley stepped closer and slid the plate in front of him. "Can you show me how to make one now?" His smile was rich and warm, reminding me of an angel again. "I wanna be a good cook like you."

I snorted and rolled my eyes. "My mama was a good cook, not me."

The blue in his eyes reminded me of a photo I saw at school once of the Caribbean Sea, bright and crystal clear. They didn't waver from mine as he said quietly, "She's not the one standing here to cook for me."

Ice glazed over my heart at his words as the overwhelming sense of loss hit me again. It was like a freight train barreling down a hill towards me at the bottom, stuck on the tracks. Mama was *supposed* to be here. She left me and I wasn't ready for her to go. Although even with his poor manners, something told me that my mama would have loved Wesley.

"Um, you can just have that one. I'm not really hungry." I snatched the plate from him and brushed past him to round the corner and placed the plate at the end of the grill line. Jesse would know from its placement that it was something I cooked up, then pass it through to Marla when it was ready. We had a routine down after all these years. As I turned back around, my eyes were too blurred with tears to see and I slammed into Wesley's hard form.

He grabbed me by the shoulders and soothingly rubbed

his thumbs. "Don't cry, Celeste. I don't wanna make you sad."

Whether he intended to or not, I didn't want to ruin the moment. I nodded and hastily wiped the tears from my eyes. "Come on," I offered. "Let's make one for you, too."

Wesley and I spent the rest of the afternoon together. Teaching him to make a quesadilla took three times longer than it should have because he had never held things like a knife or grater before. I had to show him how to properly dice the vegetables so his fingers were tucked in, reducing the chance of accidentally slicing one open, and then I had to explain the importance of washing all the dishes properly afterwards. Apparently, it never occurred to him that any dishes he used were actually washed by his housekeeper. I sent Mama a mental prayer asking her to bless the poor Mrs. Aguilar Wesley described.

He told me about some of the various five star restaurants he had eaten in while traveling to places like New York City, Paris, and Shanghai. I had never traveled further out than Tybee Island, roughly two hours away. Mama rarely ever wanted a break from the restaurant, so we didn't really take vacations. It fascinated me to hear about the white gloved service and crystal dishware at the fancy places he had been.

When Wesley started describing the tiny servings, where food tended to pile up vertically rather than being spread out on the plate, my belly ached from laughing. He said there were several courses, so it wasn't like anyone went hungry, but there was no such thing as a second helping. I couldn't imagine a meal like that.

"I hope I can travel like that someday," I commented suddenly. "Go to all those exciting places and try new foods!"

"You will, because I'll take you!" Wesley vowed.

My cheeks burned at his promise. All I could offer was a shy smile of thanks in return. I hoped he kept his word.

We ended up spending most of our time perched on barstools in the back corner of the dining room, sharing more about our lives. I wanted to hear all about his life in Atlanta, which sounded like something out of another world. His father had more money than God (his words, not mine) and loved to show off his wealth with extravagant parties, enormous houses, and flashy cars that Wesley said his father never drove because he had a driver who worked for him 24/7. Marla popped in and out of the conversation between customers, chiming in that Wesley was gonna have to lower his expectations if he expected to live comfortably here in River's Run.

He grinned sheepishly at me every time she said it. I doubted Wesley had ever been around folks who lived a lot simpler than he did, but I got the impression that I was happier with my life than Wesley had ever been with his. The blue in his eyes dulled whenever he talked about Atlanta and the penthouse he described sounded cold to me.

"Kiddo, it's about time you returned home to your aunt Shirley," Marla interrupted us.

A glance out the window told me the sun had set, meaning it was close to nine pm and The Comfy Cushion was about to close. We spent another afternoon doing nothing but talking. When had I ever talked that much to anyone, let alone a boy?

"I'm sure you've gotta get up for school tomorrow, too," she prompted again when neither of us moved.

Ever since Mama's death, I had struggled to remember the days of the week. It was hard to keep track when they all blended together from the blur of grief. I hadn't been back to school since it happened; Marla and Daddy had worked something out with the principal, who was an old friend of Daddy's, to let me finish up the year with a home school program. As long as I had all the work turned in by July 1st, I would be allowed to progress to seventh grade.

Wesley's ears reddened again and he became fascinated with his shoelaces. "I'm actually not going to school yet," he admitted quietly.

Marla's eyes widened. "Oh?"

He glanced up at me with a face pleading for a way out of the conversation, but I was just as curious. Did rich kids not have to go to school either? Was that a thing?

Finally, Wesley sighed in defeat. "I got kicked out of all my other schools for fighting and there's an issue with my transcripts not being completed." He shrugged like it was no big deal, but the embarrassment still lingered on his face at the admission.

"Transcripts not being completed? Like you're missing a few credits?" Marla asked. Her lips were starting to purse again and my hackles rose in his defense.

"I can help you," I offered. "I'm not in school right now either, but I have workbooks and things I have to turn in to finish all my credits for the year. We can do it all together."

Wesley's blue eyes flooded with hope. "You'd do that for me?"

"Of course. We're friends, aren't we?"

His smile lit up his face. "Best friends," he affirmed.

Marla smiled at the exchange between the two of us. "Looks like you're finally gonna get some work done yourself, Celeste," she commented playfully. She knew I hadn't touched any of the work the school sent home with Daddy.

"It might be kind of distracting for me to work on school stuff here…" Wesley's voice faded off in uncertainty.

My mom's best friend shook her head firmly. "Oh no, y'all'll work at Celeste's house. Nana can keep on eye on y'all." She began wiping down the counter tops and resetting the clean drinking glasses as if the matter was settled.

I, however, groaned. "Not Nana!"

CHAPTER 5
A SCHOOL MARM FROM HELL

WESLEY

AUNT SHIRLEY whole-heartedly approved of the plan to work on my missing school credits at Celeste's house under the watchful eye of her grandmother. Ms. Suzanne Moffitt, otherwise known as Celeste's nana, was not someone to be trifled with, Shirley warned me as she glided her sleek Oldsmobile down the county highway to the Hendricks' property.

This part of Georgia was unlike anything back home. Trees stretched towards the sun like skyscrapers, competing with one another to spread their thick branches. The earth was red from a clay-like dirt that Aunt Shirley said was great for growing crops. Periodic pools of green, swamp-like water dotted in between the vegetation, and she cautioned me more than once to be wary of the water because we weren't too far north for gators to build their homes.

Celeste's house was nestled behind a thick tree line with a dirt driveway. The house was a single story with a giant wrap around porch, perfect for shade in long afternoons spent in rocking chairs, according to Aunt Shirley. Flowers were everywhere around the outside; fat begonia bushes with bright pink blossoms and thick foxgloves towered along the porch railing. A yard was cleared around the house, although an enormous flowering dogwood tree reigned over everything on the righthand side. The lowest branch was wider than a grown man's torso and sported an old tire swing. The dirt drive swung around the house to the left where other outbuildings were visible.

Aunt Shirley said the property had been in the Hendricks family for generations. I didn't doubt that because why would anyone want to leave a place like this? It looked like a slice of heaven.

Celeste was waiting for me in a rocking chair by the front door. She gave her usual shy smile as Aunt Shirley and I climbed the porch steps. It was then that I noticed a figure behind the screen door. The door popped open with a snap and it had to be Celeste's nana who stepped out.

Her nana wasn't much bigger than poor Aunt Shirley, but her features were far more severe. She glared down her nose at me, although I was just a fraction of an inch taller than her. Her petite frame was swallowed up in an oversized t-shirt bearing The Comfy Cushion logo and sweatpants that must have been blistering once the heat set in for the day. She eyed me up and down like I was the devil incarnate, and for once I wondered if maybe in fact I was.

"You'll call me 'Ms. Suzanne' or 'ma'am,' you got that?" she snapped at me. The burn from her gaze made me leery.

Aunt Shirley gave me a gentle push to acknowledge what was said.

"Yes, ma'am."

"You'll stay outta the living room," Ms. Suzanne continued. "I like my shows and there's no need for you to be interrupting me."

I shook my head and stood up a little straighter, hoping she took it as the sign of respect I intended. "No, ma'am. I'm here to work."

She nodded, still eyeing me with a face full of suspicious dislike. Celeste told me the night before that her nana didn't think boys and girls could be friends and she didn't trust anyone who didn't grow up in River's Run. I didn't want to give the old lady any other reasons to hate me.

"Go on and take him up to your tower," Ms. Suzanne directed Celeste.

Celeste's eyebrows rose, surprise evident across her face. "You'll let me take him there?" she asked incredulously.

Ms. Suzanne rolled her eyes as she barked out, "I just said so, didn't I? There's a double episode of *Fear the Wicked* today and I'm not gonna miss it 'cause of y'all. Git on into work!"

My aunt wished her a good day and thanked her again for her hospitality. "I'll collect you around 5 o'clock for supper," Shirley reminded me before hobbling down the stairs to her car.

Celeste grabbed my hand and dragged me around to the right side of the house before her nana could say another word.

"*Fear the Wicked*?" I repeated in a whisper.

She snickered into her free hand. "It's a soap opera about witches and vampires that Nana's obsessed with!" We both shared a quiet chuckle.

"What's she mean 'your tower'?" I asked in confusion. Her hand felt warm and soft in mine, and it was oddly soothing. I'd never wanted to hold someone's hand before, but Celeste's palm fit in mine as though it belonged there. I quite liked the idea of that.

As we rounded the corner to the back half of the house, I

realized there was a second story to the house that wasn't visible from the front. The branches from the dogwood scraped along the porch roof back here, blending into the side of the house so that it resembled a treehouse. Another screen door faced the tree directly and it was through that door Celeste directed us.

A steep set of wooden stairs led upward. We had to hold the railings on both sides to climb safely. We emerged in a room that reminded me of movies I'd seen where the kids had a club in a treehouse. String lights crisscrossed the ceiling, hanging low enough that I could reach up and touch them. If I grew much taller, they would hit my head. There were several mismatched bookcases with chipped paint along two walls. Some held old books with cracked spines and peeling bargain stickers, others held board game boxes held together with packaging tape. One of the taller bookcases had a bunch of craft supplies like paints, construction paper, and those funny scissors that cut things in different shapes. There was one window each on the walls to my back and right hand side facing out into the flowery branches of the dogwood tree. You could barely see anything through the foliage, although streams of light snuck through.

A weathered wooden table sat closer to the bookshelves with a couple rickety wooden chairs to match. Flecks of paint from old art projects dotted across the surface. Using the stairwell as a divider, the other side of the space, closest to the windows, had a bright area rug. There were beanbag chairs and giant floor cushions all around. A small table sat in the corner with a record player and a crate of old vinyl records leaned against it.

The best part about the space was all of the photographs,

though. Unframed photographs lined most of the walls and slanted ceiling. Some even hung from wire down between the string lights. I approached the one hanging closest to me, held up by a paper clip, and observed what looked like a candid shot of a much younger Celeste—maybe four or five—in a ruffly Cinderella two piece bathing suit standing in an inflatable kiddy pool. She was smiling so wide that her eyes were squinted shut, wet hair plastered around her face. A young woman sat on the ground next to the pool. The photo caught her mid-laugh, her dark hair piled high as her head tilted back in the joy of the moment.

It was Celeste's mom; I could recognize her without hazarding a guess.

I cut my gaze to some of the others and realized many of them were far older. There were several polaroid shots of people wearing clothing from the 70's or 80's. A few clearly had Mr. and Mrs. Hendricks when they were first dating judging by the youthful face of Celeste's dad. Most of the photos were candid shots of people, with the occasional beach view peppered in here or there. I didn't see any of Celeste with other friends her own age, though. It was mostly just her with her parents.

"So we call this my 'tower,'" Celeste explained. There was a hitch to her voice that indicated she was nervous about my judgment. "It's just a place for me to hang out. Daddy and Nana don't ever come up here."

"It's amazing," I said fervently. This room held more memories than I could recall from my entire life. I turned around again and realized there was only a single stairwell in or out. "Was this meant to be a room? Where are the other doors?"

She giggled and my stomach lurched with how much I enjoyed the sound. What the heck was wrong with me? "It was meant for pantry storage when the house was originally built 150 years ago. This is directly above our kitchen," Celeste explained. "But as different generations updated the house, it kinda became like an attic space. After Mama and Daddy found out they were expecting, Mama wanted to turn this into a cool place for me." The words caught in her throat.

I knew Celeste well enough by now to know that she found it difficult to talk about her mother, so I hastily changed the subject.

"What do you wanna start on?"

For the next few hours we pored over worksheets from her school together. She said her father was good friends with the principal at what would be my school here and he was going to talk to him about letting me turn in work just like Celeste's to help get me caught up. She had used the copy machine at the restaurant to make a second set of the packets Smithson County Schools had allocated for her.

As much as I appreciated Mr. Hendricks and Celeste looking out for me, I was immediately bored out of my mind.

Celeste's patience eventually ran out as she looked over a sheet of pre-algebra equations I filled out. "Wesley, you're giving me the wrong answers on purpose."

I was currently leaning back in my chair, trying to balance the pencil on the tip of my nose. Her accusation brought me up short, and I slammed the front two table legs back down.

"No, I'm not!"

She shoved the paper across the table at me, pointing at the problem on top. "Then why is all of your work right, but the answer is wrong?" Her Southern drawl was a lot heavier when she was mad. Her green eyes drilled into me, daring me to contradict her again.

I rolled my eyes and shot out of the chair. Ten paces away, in the middle of the area rug, I whipped my hands around and faced her. "It's just school! Nobody cares!"

She was immediately crossing over to me, stopping just as her sneakers hit the toes of mine. I expected her to yell at me, to make me feel like an idiot the way all the other tutors my dad hired always had. Everyone always acted like grades were some sort of definitive proof of the future, and my future was chosen for me, so what did it really matter? Whether I was a total idiot or a prodigal genius, I was going to take over Madden Enterprises. I had no say in the matter.

Instead, her face was utterly sincere as she whispered up to me, "I care, Wes."

Her faith in me was heavy, a burden I needed to take seriously. Life had already given her far too much disappointment for me to add to it. If she needed me to do better, then I would. That's what best friends did for one another, right?

Except I was reminded again how much she didn't feel like a best friend. Celeste felt like a soul mirrored to my own. Letting her down was therefore like letting myself down, and my dad already did enough of that. I wouldn't do that to either of us.

"Fine, I'll redo it." Shrugging in defeat, I crossed over and sank down into my seat.

Celeste struggled to keep the smug look off her face. She resumed her seat across from me and pushed the worksheet towards me. "Why do you downplay how smart you are?"

I snorted. "I'm *not* smart."

"Um…yeah, you are."

I refused to answer her, keeping my eyes trained on the paper in front of me.

"Seriously, Wesley," Celeste continued. "All of these problems were meant to be a placement sheet for math class next year. Some of them are pretty advanced, and you solved them perfectly. Why would you change the answer?"

As good as I'm sure her intentions were, I hated being called out. It felt like an attack, despite her having never made it one. "I just don't care about any of this! I don't want to be some nerd who gets perfect grades. It never makes any difference to my dad anyway." Unwittingly, I flexed my hands into fists on top of the table as I tried to get a grip on my rising temper.

She shrugged. "I guess that's one way to look at it," Celeste said thoughtfully. "I just always wanted to know that no matter what I decide to do as an adult, I have plenty of options to get there."

Her words confused me. "What are you talking about?"

"Well, think about it. If we get good grades in high school, we can probably get into any college we want. That means we could study pretty much anything we want, which leads to whatever job we want. Seems like an awful lot of freedom just for answering some questions on a worksheet." Celeste flipped her long, bushy hair over one shoulder and began scribbling answers down on the assignment in front of her.

"I guess I never really thought of it like that," I admitted. But dang, who would?

Celeste, that's who. Why wouldn't a girl who could make up a recipe from thin air also plan her future ten steps ahead?

"You can do what you want," Celeste added. "I'm never gonna tell you what to do."

Her idea of freedom as an adult was awfully attractive,

though. What I wouldn't give to someday tell my dad he could piss off, that I had a scholarship to a college I chose, not one he donated a million dollars to in order to get me in. Picturing his angry sputter of disbelief made me smile.

Correcting the answers gave me a lot more confidence than I thought it would.

CHAPTER 6
SUMMER NIGHTS
CELESTE

Wesley and I very quickly fell into a routine after that. Three days a week Ms. Shirley drove him out to my house so we could work on school stuff. We managed to only take short breaks most days, so even with me explaining things to Wesley, both of us were caught up in no time. Principal Roberts met with Daddy and Ms. Shirley and got the green light for the same work to count towards the missing credits on Wesley's transcripts. Wes tried not to get teary eyed when I told him how Daddy had gone to bat for him, swearing to the principal that our family was going to do right by Wesley, but it was hard not to notice the moisture building up. I conveniently needed a pencil sharpener on the other side of the room when that happened.

On the days when we weren't working on school stuff, I would join Daddy at The Comfy Cushion in the morning. Wesley would come with Ms. Shirley for lunch and we would all eat a meal together before Wes and I crossed over to the playground in the town square to spend the afternoon. Half the time was spent down at the creek, though. We both became bolder in our attempts to climb the tree, challenging each other to go higher and higher. When we encountered a wasp that Wes swore was big enough to saddle up and ride, we both agreed it was in our best interest not to climb too high anymore.

As the weather grew insufferably hot, we began to live in our bathing suits, dashing into the creek every so often to cool off. Wesley found a deck of cards on one of the shelves in the tower and started teaching me how to play poker. He said it was "scandalous" that I didn't know how to play. In between dips in the creek, we would sprawl out under the branches of the old oak and play for hours. No matter how many times he explained the rules to me, I always got confused and had to fold. We only bet wood chips and pebbles anyway. I couldn't exactly consider it a loss.

On rainy days we would hitch a ride from Daddy down to the only movie theater in the county, just a few streets over from The Comfy Cushion. It only had two different theaters and the movies were often out on DVD before the theater could get the film in, but at only $3 a ticket, it was a cheap way to spend the afternoon. The owner, Mr. Custer, was a regular down at The Comfy Cushion, so he often let us stay and watch the same movie twice. Wesley and I would mimic the characters the second time around to change their lines into something far more entertaining. We cracked up every time.

Wesley's birthday was a special treat to both of us. Marla helped me bake a two tiered cake from scratch. I spent three long nights in our kitchen at home practicing with fondant so that I could decorate it all by myself. Nana commented that my flowers looked like they were wilting, but Wesley's face lit up like a Christmas tree when we all surprised him at The Comfy Cushion with the cake and a few presents. Daddy and

I had gone into Savannah the day before to buy Wes a real Polaroid camera since I always caught him staring at the photographs lining the walls of the tower. He laughed in delight as soon as he tore the wrapping paper off and immediately ripped it out of the box to take a photo of the two of us next to his cake. Wesley's tan face was beaming down at me rather than looking at the camera, slightly blurring his face, but he swore it was his favorite picture ever.

Mr. Madden sent a check for $10,000 that Wesley shredded into a dozen pieces with a frown. Marla said he was going to bring Jesus down from Heaven with his attitude.

I found myself laughing most days like I used to before Mama's death. The dark cloud that always circled around me felt lighter every day until one day towards the end of June I realized I hadn't felt the sadness at all in a few days. Part of me felt guilty, like I was forgetting about Mama, but whenever I voiced my concern to Wesley, he asked me to tell him more stories about her. It helped keep her memory alive in a good way. I liked the way Wesley asked questions about the things she liked and the way she handled the restaurant because he always made it sound like she was still with us and he was just summoning up the courage to meet her. It helped ease the loss that hovered because I knew if she had still been here, Wesley would have made quite the impression on her.

Whether we were at my house or at the restaurant, I continued Wesley's cooking lessons. He mastered basic things like pasta and casseroles so we started progressing to things that took more skill like homemade sauces, jambalaya, and handmade meatloaf. Wes preferred the meals where he could get his hands dirty and make a mess. I expected the novelty to wear off after he realized how much work went into cleaning it back up, but it never happened. He continued to spread debris all over the kitchen no matter where we were or what we were making.

Nana and Marla were both growing fonder of him by the day. His use of "sir" and "ma'am" increased exponentially in their presence, and he learned to hold open doors for others, to stop and pick something off the ground for someone when they dropped it, or simply to put something away because it needed to be done. Wesley admitted to me that he liked how appreciative Nana was when he placed an ice cold Coke bottle on her side table when she watched her shows, but he also thought it was hilarious to try to figure out the storyline on her soaps. Marla said we'd make a Southern gentleman out of him yet.

The fourth of July was around the corner before I knew it, and The Comfy Cushion was in a flurry of activity as we prepped for the annual county barbecue. Our restaurant had catered everything but the meat for the event since before I was born. Most of the people in town competed in the Grill Off to present the best meats for everyone in town to eat. Daddy was excluded from participating, but when Wesley saw the flyers posted, he insisted on entering the grilled chicken category. I had taught him a couple different marinades that the restaurant used for meals and he felt confident that he could make up a recipe on his own. He worked on it for days leading up to the fourth.

"Trust me, Celeste," insisted Wesley, "it's in the bag!"

The restaurant closed for the day as the town gathered in the square for the Fourth of July celebrations. There were cornhole tournaments and a volleyball net set up, and the baseball diamond was packed with spectators. Everyone started off with a home run derby before switching to the annual fundraising game for the Smithson County High School athletic boosters—teachers versus students. Both teams always wore comical uniforms to bring more fun to the game.

Wesley and I laughed in delight as one of the teachers came out in red clown shoes to match his American flag tank top and short shorts, then fell repeatedly while trying to run the bases. Wesley admitted he didn't think high school would be that bad here in River's Run if those were the kinds of things teachers would do for their students. It made my heart skip a beat to hear that he wanted to stay long enough for high school. Although we never discussed it after that first encounter, I couldn't forget Mr. Madden's threat to send Wesley away to boarding school.

When the game wore down, Wesley jumped up and raced over to the grilling area. People brought their own grills, sparking heated arguments about the merits of charcoal versus gas, and lined them up around the edge of the town square. Daddy let Wesley borrow our old charcoal grill and helped him get the hot coals going.

I beamed at Wesley as we dragged the heavy cooler across the street from the restaurant to the lawn where his place was set up. He wore an apron with an American flag on it and the words "Grill Master" emblazoned on the chest. Marla laughed at how long the apron was and placed a snow white chef's cap on his head to wish him luck.

Wesley expertly pulled on a pair of rubber cooking gloves and used tongs to remove the chicken from bags inside the cooler. They had been marinating in Wesley's special recipe for roughly 48 hours, and the smell alone when he opened the bag was enough to make my mouth water. Contestants in the grilled chicken category had to cook three breasts for entry, but were welcome to make more if they wanted to serve the meat to others. Wesley had enough for me, Daddy, Marla, Ms. Shirley, and Nana to eat, but he made us promise that we wouldn't give him any reactions until after the judges made their verdict.

Wes looked studious and contemplative as he hovered over the chicken. In his mind, this was a battle to the death; he was determined to win first prize. When I asked him the day before why it mattered so much to him, he said, "Because I've never won anything on my own before. It's always been whatever my father could buy."

Nana sat in a folding chair underneath the tent Daddy erected for Wesley and lounged with her legs out in the sun. For once she had on a light cotton dress, making her look ten years younger, but almost overdressed compared to her usual garb. She leaned her head back and dozed while I sat on the cooler next to her, anxiously biting my nails and watching Wesley like a hawk.

His determination never wavered as he carefully turned the chicken breasts. After another four minutes, when the skins were golden brown, Wesley moved them to the outer edges of the flame, just like Jesse and Daddy had recommended. I felt on edge enough for both of us because I didn't know how Wesley would react if he didn't win.

The county mayor, head of the school board, and deputy sheriff comprised of the judge's panel. They were older men whose families had lived in the River's Run area for generations, just like Daddy. Jonah Hillsborough, the sheriff, had a family tree that stemmed all the way back to the Revolutionary War. As they made their way down the line with a clipboard where they marked notes based on each person's entry, my nerves only worsened. Daddy and Marla joined us under the tent.

"Wesley, why'd you wanna win this so badly?" Daddy asked, probably to lighten the mood. Daddy hated any kind of tension or confrontation.

I assumed Wesley would give him the same answer he gave me about winning something without Mr. Madden's money, but he surprised me by telling Daddy something different. "Figured it would make me really belong here." He shrugged and kept his eyes on the judges as they approached.

My heart leapt up in my throat at Wesley's admission. It was too easy to forget that Wesley didn't feel as though he had anyone who cared about him when all he had known was distance and coldness from his father.

"You belong here in my book," Nana commented in her usual sullen tone.

We all grinned at one another right as the three judges stepped up to Wesley's grill.

"And now who is this?" Mr. Wyatt, the county mayor, asked jovially. He looked as out of place as Nana in his checkered button up, red suspenders, and light blue jeans. Puffs of white hair stuck out from under his baseball cap that was too bright and stiff to have ever been worn before. He was almost always dressed in a gray suit, so today's ensemble felt at odds with his personality.

With an encouraging nod from Daddy, Wesley held out his hand to Mr. Wyatt. "My name is Wesley Madden, sir. I moved here to live with my great-aunt Shirley a couple months back."

Mr. Wyatt shook his hand while Dennis Hildebrandt, the school superintendent, merely smiled and let his eyes roam.

He had to be 90 years old if he were a day, but he simply refused to retire. I doubted he even knew what was going on.

It was Sheriff Hillsborough who made me question if something was wrong. He glared at Wesley, gripping his duty belt tightly where his badge hung at his hip. I had only ever had a reason to greet him or wish him a good evening when he stopped at The Comfy Cushion with his family, but the look he seared Wesley with in that moment made me wonder if I really knew him at all. Wesley was a problem to be eliminated immediately in his eyes, and I did not like it one bit.

When Wesley went to shake the sheriff's hand, the deputy merely glared at it before adjusting the toothpick clenched between his teeth. He ignored Wes' outstretched hand completely without saying a word.

I saw my friend's smile falter for a moment, but he managed to brighten as Mr. Wyatt moaned in delight from his first bite of Wesley's chicken.

"My word, this is positively delightful!" Mr. Wyatt crowed. "What is this marinade you have?"

Had Wesley not looked directly at me when he said it, I might not have believed it. "It's an old recipe of Rachel Hendricks' that I changed up for the grill." The blue in his eyes was brighter than I remembered seeing, his megawatt smile back in place so Wes perfectly embodied the angel I knew him to be.

"Jonah, you've *got* to try this!" Mr. Wyatt beamed and held out a plate with a plastic fork and knife for his co-judge.

Deputy Hillsborough wouldn't take it. "He cheated. He's disqualified," the sheriff declared.

"What?!" squawked Marla and Nana.

At the same time, Daddy said, "How do you reckon?"

The chief stood taller and crossed his arms across his

chest. "I heard him say he used someone else's recipe. That means he cheated."

"Jonah, every person here used someone else's recipe," Daddy countered. "There isn't a rule against that."

Mr. Wyatt looked intimidated as he glanced between the two of them while Mr. Hildebrant smiled and watched the entire scene with a bemused detachment.

"Now, Chief, we don't have a set rule about these things," Mr. Wyatt began, but the sheriff cut him off.

"I say we do." He took a large step towards Daddy, squaring up with him.

Wesley's face was crestfallen. Without a word, he threw the tongs down on the ground and ran into the crowd, heading in the same direction as the old oak tree.

"Jonah, your daddy would tan your hide for hurting a kid like that!" Nana sputtered at him. She leapt out of her lawn chair in a fit of anger.

The chief took a step back and gave a curt nod to her, ever the Southern gentleman respecting his elders. "My daddy wouldn't want a little hothead punk from Atlanta to bring trouble into this town," he challenged. "I did some digging on that brat as soon as I heard he stepped foot in my town. He shouldn't be here, and the sooner we get that through his head, the better."

The injustice of it all made my blood boil. It was just a silly contest at a local party, but I knew Wesley wouldn't see it that way. He would internalize it as another way he was different, another justification for why no one wanted him, only now he would believe that of River's Run just as much as Atlanta. It wasn't fair for anyone to do that to him.

For once I didn't care about my manners. "You're just a big, ugly asshole!" I had never used a swear word a day in my life and I imagined my mama rolling over in her grave from hearing that word come from my lips.

Except I couldn't bring myself to care. Whirling around, I ran into the crowd, pushing people out of the way as the tears streamed down my face.

CHAPTER 7
BONFIRES AND BREAK INS
WESLEY

I HATED EVERYONE HERE. No matter what I did, I was never going to fit in. They didn't like anyone who couldn't trace their ancestors through the graveyard on Church Road. I was so tired of everyone looking at me like some worthless punk who threw around his daddy's money.

Except they were right about half of it—I was a worthless punk. Wasn't that why my mother left? She didn't love me enough to take me with her or keep in contact? Wasn't that why all of my teachers gave up on me if I challenged them? Okay, maybe "challenged them" wasn't exactly what I did, but it's not like I was the only kid ever to have gotten in fights or messed up school property. They didn't think I was worth the dirt on their shoes, as Nana would say.

Oh, I could bet what Nana would have to say to me now that I had run out on them like that. She was finally growing to like me and I just ruined it all over again. Probably with Marla and Mr. Hendricks, too. Celeste had promised to always forgive me, but everyone else always broke their promises to me, so why wouldn't she? My dad promised to call me every week, but I had been here for close to eight with radio silence from Atlanta. Nobody cared about me.

Then fuck them! My rebellious heart sang. *Fuck them all!*

I threw myself down onto a large rock in the creek bed a few feet away from where our favorite tree was. It only took a minute for me to hear Celeste's feet pounding behind me. I knew it was her just based on the sound alone, that was how in tune with her I had become. But now that connection felt spoiled. Tainted. How could she be friends with someone worthless like me?

"Don't you listen to that," Celeste said quietly behind me, stopping short. I couldn't see her face, but her voice was low with what sounded like sorrow.

I snorted. "Listen to what? All the people who don't think I belong here?"

"The voice in your head that's telling you they're right."

I shot up and turned on her. "You don't know anything about it! You've lived here your entire life surrounded by the same boring people, all set to grow up and have more boring babies to keep this stupid town running! I hate it here! I hate all of them!"

Celeste nodded. "'Kay."

Her monosyllable response made me angrier. "That includes your family! Everyone here is just a dumb, redneck hick! I wish this whole town would burn to the ground!"

Round green eyes filled with tears, but that was the only reaction I got from her. She didn't say a word, didn't move to walk away, or anything. Seeing one trail down her cheek made all the rage burn out of me.

"I'm sorry, Celeste." I pulled her into a hug, throwing my arms around her tightly. Being the one to make her cry made me feel like the world's biggest prick. She should never have to cry over me.

She instantly molded into the hug, wrapping the arms I pinned to her side around my waist. "I'm sorry, too," she whispered into my shoulder.

Of course she was. Celeste was too good not to apologize on behalf of those idiots.

"I didn't mean what I said," I promised her as I pulled away. "You're my best friend in the whole world, Celeste. I don't hate you or your family."

She sat down on the rock I had been perched on and patted the small space beside her. "I know that, Wes. Mama always said people say hurtful things when they're mad because they want others to join them in misery. I'm already upset at what they did to you, so nothing you say can hurt me right now."

More of her mother's logic to save the day. I would need a book someday to keep up with that woman.

I squeezed into the small space next to her on the rock, our sides pressed together as our bodies fought for nonexistent space. Feeling her touch calmed me even further. Things were just simpler with her. Easy in a way that I couldn't understand but didn't want to question.

Suddenly, Celeste started giggling. She tried to cover it up with her hand, but I could see her full set of teeth from how big her smile was spreading. Her whole body racked with laughter and even though I couldn't see the joke, I joined in at the sight of her losing it.

"What's the matter?" I asked.

She could barely stop laughing long enough to admit, "I called the sheriff an *asshole*!" before she lost all hold. She was laughing so hard she was wheezing, clutching her side like it hurt.

"No way!" I cried incredulously. We both lost our minds at the image. Celeste said her first swear word and she said it to the county sheriff in front of her father! I laughed so hard that tears ran down my cheeks and I fell backward onto the mud in the creek bed.

She joined me, her bushy brown hair falling into my face. I didn't mind, though. I loved her crazy hair. Really, I loved everything about Celeste. The loyalty she had shown me by calling a respected town official a cuss word had me buzzing like the pot kids at my old school smoked in the bathroom.

"You deserved to win that barbecue," Celeste assured me. "There's no way Mr. Wyatt would have gone on like that unless you made up something really special."

I shrugged. "I just wanted to surprise you by bringing a bit of your mom here today," I admitted.

She snapped her head over to look at me, her gaze critical as she scrutinized my face. "You did it for me?" she asked in a small whisper.

It seemed like the right thing to do to brush my fingers along her cheek. Her skin was always so soft even though she didn't use any of the millions of moisturizing creams I watched women like Mrs. Aguilar and Aunt Shirley apply.

"This is the first holiday without your mom here, and I wanted you to be okay."

Her face crumpled, as I expected it to, and I sat up, pulling her with me by wrapping an arm around her shoulder. She buried her face into my collar bone as she cried.

"It's okay," I tried to soothe her. "I'm here."

Celeste's mother meant everything to her, and although it was a love I couldn't really understand, I had learned enough by now to know that her grief always made her emotional. She needed me to be strong for her in moments like this.

After a few minutes, her cries subsided and she pulled away to dry her eyes on the palms of her hands. "You know what, I hate all of them, too!" Celeste burst out. "I hate everyone who was ever mean to you, Wesley, because I think you're perfect."

I grinned at her, a little cocky from her assessment. It certainly didn't hurt to have your favorite person in the world feel that way about you.

"Come on, we should get back." Celeste stood up and did her best to wipe the mud and grass from her red jean shorts. Then she held out a hand to pull me up.

"Do you really think that's a good idea?" I hedged.

She made a show of looking around the creek. "Or what? You're gonna stay out here forever?"

Rolling my eyes at her sarcasm, I grabbed onto her outstretched hand and hauled myself up. "I really don't want to go back yet."

Celeste looked thoughtful for a moment before nodding. "There's another path a little ways up that will lead us back into town by the school yard. There probably won't be anyone that way since everybody's at the town square. We can just walk around for bit."

She led the way along the creek, both of us trying to avoid the mud. The dirt path through the trees she pointed out was definitely not as well used as the path we frequented behind the baseball diamond, but we soon found our way back into civilization. It deposited us behind the elementary school, just like she said, and we walked in companionable silence to the front of the building, then onto the main road. We could either turn right and head back towards the town square and

The Comfy Cushion or go left and walk through one of the small residential areas in River's Run.

I made the decision for her. "Let's go this way," I prompted, turning towards the houses with their fenced in yards and concrete driveways. None of the houses were very big or imposing, certainly nothing my father would ever deem appropriate, but they were all clean and well maintained. There was plenty of space between them for big yards and swing sets unlike the suburban neighborhoods I'd been in outside Atlanta where the massive houses sat so close to one another that you could hear when the neighbor's phone rang.

Celeste kept a running commentary of who lived where and what they did or which scandal was attached to their family name. I guess growing up in the town's only restaurant gave her access to all the gossip. She drew up short when we reached a square brick house towards the end of the lane.

"This is Chief Hillsborough's house," she said quietly.

I grinned wickedly at her. "Come on!" Without a backward glance, I darted up his driveway and climbed the chain link fence into his backyard. Mercifully, I didn't see any sign of a dog.

"Wesley!" Celeste hissed at me, standing right at the fence line. "What are you doing?"

The chief's house was one of the last on the street and had a large backyard that curved into the forest at an angle. There was a small concrete patio with a glass table and chairs, but otherwise the yard looked empty and mostly unused. A secondary detached garage was at the very back of the property, where the yard met the trees.

"What do you reckon is in there?" I asked her with a wolf's grin.

Celeste's face was red and frantic. "Wesley, get out of there this instant! We're gonna get in so much trouble!"

I rolled my eyes at her. "How are we gonna get in trouble if everyone is at the party?"

Celeste shook her head. "Please get out of there!"

"Guess you're gonna have to come in and stop me." I shrugged and headed towards the detached garage. It was only big enough for a single car, but there was no driveway to it, making me assume it was meant for a riding mower.

Sure enough, the window on the side of the garage revealed a gleaming riding mower that looked far too big for the square backyard the chief owned. The rest of the garage looked like a small woodshop, with tools hanging from pegs and pieces of unfinished wood leaning against the back wall. There was a large saw table in the space behind the mower, but I couldn't see more from the angle of the window.

The urge to see what else was inside was too strong for me to ignore and I found myself shoving the window open. Nobody ever locked things around here. They were all too trusting.

A warm hand clamped around my elbow as I reached my hands inside the window to haul myself up. Celeste's eyes were pleading with me as she tried to pull me away. "We're gonna get caught!"

"Then keep a look out," I instructed her. "I just wanna take a look around."

Celeste continued her quiet protests as I stumbled down into the garage. It was mainly used for outside storage, metal shelves holding gardening equipment and more tools for the woodshop. There was nothing out of the ordinary, although what I was expecting to find, I had no idea.

"Wesley Carter Madden, you get out here this instant!" Celeste's tiny voice came through the window.

I rolled my eyes again even though she couldn't see. "Marla's lines won't work on me," I called out to her.

My eyes fell upon two large portable gas caddies when inspiration hit. Both were full of gasoline that I began pouring over every surface in the garage. They were heavy, full enough to douse the floors, the saw table, and the shiny riding mower. Chief Hillsborough probably thought highly of himself for having a monstrosity like that. I imagined that was the kind of things hicks like him cared about. So I'd take it from him, just as simple as that.

I grabbed a dirty rag from the tool bench and a glass bottle from what looked like a recycling bin. A box of matches sat on one of the shelves next to the grill equipment and I felt the wicked grin return to my face. It had to be karma, right, if I torched this garage like the grill master I wanted to be?

I climbed outside, much to Celeste's relief, though she was practically hyperventilating by now.

"We're gonna get in so much trouble!" she whined. As soon as both my feet hit the ground, she took off running towards the fence. "Come on, Wesley, we've gotta get out of here!"

She hadn't seen the objects in my hand or else she would have stayed to take them from me, I was sure of it. However, I knew how dangerous this could be and I didn't want Celeste anywhere near this building with what I was about to do.

I shoved the rag into the bottle and used a match to light the portion hanging out of the top. Since the window was open and I had only poured the gasoline on the ground, I was betting on having the extra few seconds I needed to run away even though I had no idea if science backed up my logic.

Setting the glass on the window ledge, I simply pushed it over so that it rolled down onto the random pieces of lumber beneath the window and ran like hell away from the garage.

The sound of flames erupted behind, but nothing was strong enough that I could feel the heat from an explosion. Celeste was sputtering and pointing at the garage as I hopped the fence.

"Did you just set the building on fire?!" she screeched. I had never heard her voice so high pitched before.

I gave her a one arm shrug as I laced my hand through hers. "I was just manning the grill," I countered innocently. With a quick smile, I took off down the street, keeping a tight grip on her hand in mine.

It couldn't be too obvious that we were leaving the scene, so when we got to the cross street that could take us back past the school and towards the town square, I veered to the left as if we were going to the movie theater. That was my destination at the moment before we got a couple blocks away and Celeste dug in her heels.

"We have to alert the fire department!" she insisted.

"What?!" I snapped at her.

She was breathing heavily, trying to get the air in her lungs to function after the adrenaline wore off. "That garage is right next to the forest line and could start a huge fire. We can't just let it go, Wes."

She had a point, but that didn't make it irritate me any less. "So what? You're telling me to turn myself in?" My hands balled into fists that I clamped on my hips.

"No!" Celeste leaned forward, her hands holding onto her bent knees. She pointed down to the grocery store that still had one lone employee inside. "I'm gonna go call the fire department! You have to get home!"

"Get home?" I repeated in confusion.

"NOW!" she screeched again, louder this time.

I didn't argue with her at that volume. Turning on my heel, I sped down through the parking lot of the movie theater, behind the town florist shop, and into the alleyway. If I followed it down to the end, there was a fence missing a couple boards that I could only just squeeze out of that would deposit me one street over from my great aunt Shirley's. Ever since going to Celeste's house, I had learned that it was rude to cut through people's yards, but I took that chance today since everyone was still at the Fourth of July party.

I didn't stop until I reached my bedroom, the patchwork quilt still disheveled from where I forgot to make my bed that morning. Pacing the small space did nothing for my rattled nerves, so I pushed open the lone window and climbed out onto the gabled roof.

The sky was starting to darken and stars were beginning to twinkle as I plopped down on the brown tiles, warm from the day's sun. In the distance I could hear the sound of a siren, which I hoped meant Celeste was successful in contacting the fire department. It hadn't occurred to me in the heat of the moment that the garage was next to a flammable forest.

I tried to use one of the breathing techniques a therapist taught me to regulate my heartbeat and calm myself back down, but after two attempts, I gave up. My nerves were like a live wire, my ears listening for the police that were sure to be approaching the house soon to arrest me. Wouldn't that make my father proud?

"Wes?" I heard Celeste call from my window.

"Up here," I replied.

Her tan legs swung out and she slowly climbed the slope

of the roof towards me. Her eyes were still as round as saucers and her hair was starting to slip out of its ponytail.

"Don't you ever do something like that to me again, y'hear?!" She was trying not to shout, but her anger was written all over her face. "Best friends don't scare each other!"

Scared? I hadn't meant to scare her. I opened my mouth to say so, but she held up her hand to stop me.

"I ran into the store and told the clerk I had been out looking for you," Celeste explained. "Said I saw smoke coming out of someone's back yard on Main Street and needed to let the fire department know. The clerk pulled up the phone and called them. I ran back out as soon as I heard him talk to someone." She pulled up her knees and rested her forearms on them in front of her.

"Thank you," was all I could think of saying.

She smirked at me, throwing me a sideways glance. "I'm still mad at you, but I have to forgive you."

I grinned. "Didn't you give me that lesson on what poetic justice means?"

Celeste snorted, trying to hide her amused smile. "I'd hardly call setting his garage on fire 'poetic justice.'"

We grinned at each other, then both snapped our heads up to the sky. Fireworks were going off, painting the dark night with dazzling colors. She scooted closer to me and pointed out all the shapes. Her face was alight with wonder and awe, highlighted with the greens, blues, and purples as the world exploded above our heads.

I couldn't even look at them because I was so mesmerized by her face. The way her mouth sloped with her smile, the straight edge of her dainty nose, the way her wild brown mane surrounded her in a halo of frizz, even when she tried to contain it in a ponytail. She had called me perfect earlier, but she was the perfect one. My best friend...but also the reason my heart now skipped a beat.

She turned to look at me, no doubt noticing my lack of response, and I don't know what came over me at that moment, but I kissed her. It was the first kiss for both of us, I knew, and I had zero idea what I was doing. Yet when I felt her soft lips against mine, when I felt the way they kissed me back and held the moment, with all the fireworks still lighting up the world around us, I knew I was a goner. Celeste Hendricks might be my best friend, but she was also the love of my life.

CHAPTER 8
CRUEL SUMMER
CELESTE

Two years later

LOCKER DOORS SLAMMED all around me in the wild craze that comes at the end of the school day. Summer break was just around the corner and my entire eighth grade class was eagerly awaiting its arrival. We were at the point in the school year where pretty much everyone had stopped caring about homework and grades because freedom was tantalizingly close. Even I found myself wistfully staring out the window at the bright sun and budding flowers during most of my classes. I was ready to have another perfect summer with Wesley before the daunting fear of high school crashed into reality.

"I swear, Mrs. Gallatin hates me!" Maggie whined as she slumped one shoulder against the locker next to me.

Maggie moved here in the middle of our seventh grade year after her parents divorced a couple counties over and her mom wanted a fresh start. Everybody looked at her like she was an alien simply for being new, so I had made it a point to befriend her. Wesley told me I needed to stop adopting lost puppies, but when I pointed out that included him, too, he merely grinned at me and swore he was different. Maggie and I had been practically sisters ever since.

"What happened?" I asked as I swapped out books from the locker shelf to load into my backpack.

"I was five minutes late to class because I had a bathroom emergency and she gave me detention!" Maggie threw up her hands in frustration.

Laughing, I clarified, "An *actual* bathroom emergency?" I already knew the answer because Maggie was obsessed with two things, makeup and boys. For all the times she claimed to have a "bathroom emergency" with me, I had yet to experience one that didn't have something to do with one of the two.

She rolled her eyes at me but joined me in laughing. "Max Daniels was tooootally checking me out! I had to make sure my lipstick was on point!"

"Max Daniels is a douchebag," Wesley said from behind me. "You can do better."

I turned and flashed him a smile. He had grown a few more inches over the course of the past couple years and it felt like he towered over me now. Puberty was still as foreign to me as ancient Greek, so despite my recent 15th birthday, I retained my child-like figure and flat chest.

Maggie had already started blossoming what looked to be a good size set of boobs and more of an hourglass figure that I envied. We could no longer share clothes like we had only a few months ago because her shape was changing so rapidly. It seemed like all of my peers were lightyears ahead of me in maturity and development, and I tried not to feel embarrassed at the prospect of being left behind.

"Be nice, Wes," I reminded him. Since Maggie had become friends with us, he was very protective of her.

Maggie just shrugged, though. "As long as he can give me my first kiss, I don't really care. It's gotta happen sometime, and I refuse to start high school with that kind of innocence!"

I chanced a quick glance over my shoulder at Wesley and found his bright blue eyes burning into mine. His smirk grew wider, and I diverted my eyes as I felt my cheeks start to redden. We had never told Maggie about our first kiss, almost two years ago now, that had never been repeated. I wasn't sure why I wanted it to be a secret, but I loved having that remain a special moment between Wesley and me. Something only we could share.

"So you're staying now for detention?" I asked Maggie in order to change the subject. I could still feel Wesley's gaze boring into the back of my head.

She nodded glumly. "I'll meet you over at the diner afterwards."

The three of us had started walking over to The Comfy Cushion after school and taking over one of the bigger corner booths to work on homework while Marla supplied us with snacks. Wesley took his studies very seriously now, and after we had explained our philosophy on future freedom to Maggie, she did, too. Which was just as well because with how often Wes received in school suspensions for fighting in the boys' locker room, he was liable to be expelled. No matter what kind of influence my family had over him, Wesley's rage never dissipated and only worsened as we got older.

Wesley reached down and grabbed the handle to my backpack, tossing it over his shoulder like he did every day. "We'll see you in a bit then," he agreed.

Maggie turned and had only taken a few steps when she

suddenly spun around and added, "Oh! I almost forgot! Hillary was talking about you in the bathroom earlier!" She winked at him and continued down the hall to detention.

Her words sent a slither of dread down to my stomach. It was common knowledge that Hillary Stanbrooke, the most popular girl in school, was obsessed with Wesley, yet he always tried to change the subject or ignore people's remarks. He claimed that he wasn't going to date until he was a little older, but I was pretty certain he only said that to make me feel better since Daddy said no daughter of his was allowed to date until high school. Given how crazy hormones had turned some of my classmates, his ultimatum never bothered me.

None of it meant that Wesley didn't like Hillary, though. We had never even talked about our kiss under the fireworks the summer before last, just continued with our friendship as we always had, so I had no idea if it meant anything to him at all. He had become so engrained in my family that Nana and Daddy even permitted him to stay the night in the guest room a few times—conveniently located directly across the hall from Daddy's open bedroom door. We were inseparable like all best friends were inseparable. So the possibility of ever being something more was only a vague dream in the deep recesses of my heart. That didn't mean I wanted to see him with a girl as vapid and cruel as Hillary Stanbrooke, though. She made a rattlesnake look like a labrador puppy.

We walked in companionable silence up Main Street towards the restaurant. It was already hot, despite the early spring season, and within minutes I was piling my hair on top of my head to wrap a hair tie around it just to get the sweaty mess off my neck.

River's Run Primary School, as it was called, housed

grades K-8. There was one other primary school on the other side of the county, roughly a 35 minute drive away, but Smithson County High School was smacked directly in the middle and we would have to take a bus starting our freshman year. I was filled with dread at the prospect of a new school with more kids, but also at the possibility that Wesley might not be allowed to return with me.

His father had only come down to visit once in the nearly two years Wesley lived here, with inconsistent phone calls here or there, but Mr. Madden communicated heavily with Wesley by email. Wesley was the only person I knew who had a satellite cell phone with reception that worked even in the deepest part of the Georgia woods. Mr. Madden had insisted on it and continually warned Wes that the phone had a GPS tracking device that could pinpoint the exact room he stood in at any given moment.

I thought it was rather odd for Mr. Madden to track Wesley's whereabouts so closely when he couldn't even bother to call, but Wes shrugged it off. The past several emails had contained pointed advice about Wesley "living up to" the Madden family name and that now was the time for him to start taking his future seriously. He had even emailed a brochure for some fancy college preparatory academy that he stated had a reputation for producing the "leaders of the 21st century." Wesley had punched a hole through the wall of the cafeteria in his rage, thereby earning another in school suspension. Daddy, Marla, and his great-aunt Shirley continued to smooth things over and prevent him from getting expelled, but it was only a matter of time before their pleas and promises ran dry.

From the corner of my eye, I caught Wes staring at me and glanced over with a smirk. "Can I help you?"

"I really like the way your hair curls when it's wet," he replied instantly.

I scrunched my nose in disgust at the compliment. My hair was only curling because I was getting sweaty, which was not something I wanted him to notice. "Don't be gross!" I shoved him playfully.

He laughed and came right back to my side, standing closer this time, so that our hands were almost touching. It would have been the easiest thing in the world to lace his fingers through mine as we had done so many times. Yet it felt different now in a way that made my heart skip a beat, and I chickened out at the last second.

"It's not like you can help it, Celeste," he said. "I know it's the Georgia heat. I'm just saying, you wear it well."

I groaned. That compliment was just as awkward as the first!

Wesley's face dropped for a split second as embarrassment flooded his features, but in a flash, he returned to his megawatt smile. "Geez, next time I'll just ignore you."

That didn't make me feel any better, however. I didn't want him to ignore me; I wanted him to think I was beautiful. Letting him fall a half step ahead, I followed him into The Comfy Cushion.

Marla was already setting a tall pitcher full of ice water and three glasses down on the table when we walked in. "Now, don't let this sunshine stop you from acing those finals!" she chirped.

Wesley and I slid into opposite sides of the booth before she asked, "And where is Maggie? She better not be out with some boy!"

He grinned at me as he replied, "She got in trouble over one, so she's stuck in detention."

Marla sighed like the indiscretion offended her personally. "Lord, that girl's gonna wind up pregnant before she gets her driver's license."

I rolled my eyes at her theatrics, but for once, Wesley frowned. "We would never let her get into that kind of trouble, Miss Marla," he said firmly.

His answer must have somewhat appeased her because Marla dropped the subject. "I'll bring over a veggie platter in a bit."

"Only if it's got Celeste's chipotle ranch, please!" Wesley called after her retreating form. Marla merely held up a hand in acknowledgement.

The condiment had become Wesley's favorite, but for some reason, hearing him say it now made my skin flush again. That was the first time I felt butterflies over a boy. I never had the courage to ask if Wesley felt them, too.

I shook my head against the memory flooding my thoughts. Is this what all crushes did to people? No wonder the kids in my class turned into morons when they discovered the opposite sex. "Let's focus on our geometry, please," I said curtly.

Before long, Maggie slid into the booth next to me, swearing that Mrs. Gallatin was secretly a witch who flew around on her broom at night. She made a dramatic show of slumping against me with a heavy sigh.

"Maggie, it's just detention," I reminded her. "Which you earned from being late."

"Yeah, stop wasting your time on the likes of Max Daniels," Wesley ordered. There was a clip to his tone that for a moment sounded like jealousy. The recess of my heart holding onto hope all but died out. Wesley had never had that tone with me before. Did he like Maggie? Was that the problem?

"Oh yeah? And who should I go out with instead?" Maggie countered.

Wesley nodded across the restaurant towards a table where some of the school baseball players were filing in after practice. "Cameron Wyatt," he said, his voice low.

Maggie and I both turned to crane our heads over our shoulders and give Cameron a once over. He was pretty good-looking, actually, in a nerdy sort of way, with thick, black glasses and dark, curly hair. He was the great-grandson of the school superintendent and tended to lead all the academic clubs. I had overheard him once say that he hoped to attend Harvard University and study law.

In a way, I kind of agreed with Wesley's assessment. "You could do worse," I offered with a shrug.

Wesley shook his head. "His parents were high school sweethearts and his father always holds open the door for her anytime they're out together. They look like two people still lovestruck, which means they're teaching their son how to properly love someone. Don't take that for granted."

Maggie nodded her understanding and turned back around to assess Cameron with far more interest, but I kept my eyes on Wesley. His reasoning intrigued me because it must have taken some intentional observations on his part.

"Are you taking notes or something?" I joked.

Wesley grinned at me, a wicked smirk that made me forget to breathe. "Maybe."

Suddenly, the door to The Comfy Cushion flew open with a bang and a harried looking aunt Shirley swept inside. Her snow white hair was flattened on one side, no doubt from falling asleep in her armchair like she did most afternoons, and one leg's pantyhose had rolled down below the hem of her dress.

She scurried over to us with her wicker handbag fluttering at her elbow like a broken wing. "Wesley, your father is on his way! He'll be in town within the hour!"

Maggie and I both turned to stare at Wesley. My mouth felt dry as I watched his face instantly pale with apprehension. Mr. Madden's visit couldn't be a good thing, especially when it was unannounced.

Daddy rounded the corner from his office and headed our way with a smile. He greeted all of the customers as he passed before joining us with his hands on his hips. The smile slowly fell as he took in all of our stricken faces.

"Who's been summoned to Hell?" he teased.

"Mr. Madden is coming," I said after a moment. Daddy and Ms. Shirley had tried to talk to Mr. Madden once after Wesley first got in trouble, but he couldn't be bothered to answer his phone or return their voicemails. They never tried to discuss Wesley's school antics with him again, but I could tell how little respect Daddy held for him. Family was the most important thing in the world to Daddy.

"You didn't get in trouble again, did ya?" he asked Wes.

Wesley shook his head.

"Then what the devil is he coming for?" Daddy inquired.

As if on cue, the restaurant door burst open again and Mr. Madden walked in wearing a navy suit perfectly tailored to his body. His eyes were covered by aviator sunglasses, but even from across the dining room I could see the frown lines marring his forehead. He looked more formidable than I remembered, and now that Wesley had told me so much about his old life in Atlanta, I noted the diamond encrusted

Rolex, solid gold cufflinks, and Italian leather shoes. Money was power, and Mr. Madden had more than anyone.

"Why did I know I'd find my son here rather than the home I pay you to provide for him?" Mr. Madden snapped at Ms. Shirley.

Her cheeks reddened and Daddy instantly glared. It was unusual to see Daddy frowning at someone, which must have drawn Marla's attention from behind the counter because she immediately wiped her hands on a towel and came to join us.

"Looks like we've got a party goin' on right here!" she commented in a vain attempt to diffuse the situation.

Wesley nodded once at Mr. Madden. "You found me anyway, Father."

His dad whipped a cell phone buzzing from his pocket, not even bothering to look up as he replied, "We're leaving in an hour, Wesley."

My best friend leapt out from his booth seat as I scrambled to follow, grabbing his bicep to hold him back from doing something he would regret. His anger was another beast entirely and it seemed his father had forgotten or simply didn't care.

"Like hell I am!" Wesley barked out.

I glanced at Maggie, but she looked as stunned as I felt. We both gaped at Mr. Madden in horror.

Mr. Madden didn't react. "I'll wait in the car. Go collect your things," he ordered without looking up from his phone.

Daddy shared a bewildered glare with Marla and Ms. Shirley, all of them equally as surprised, though I couldn't tell if it was from Mr. Madden's indifference or sudden appearance. It was obvious Marla was trying to bite down on the inside of her cheek and I could see a tick in Daddy's jaw that let me know he was fixing to say something that could get ugly.

"Now wait just a minute here, sir," Daddy said. "The school year isn't even over yet. What's the rush?"

The tone in his voice must have caught Mr. Madden's attention because he leaned back on one foot and stopped typing on his phone to gaze at Daddy. He pulled his sunglasses off and fixed Daddy with a stern expression, sizing him up.

"And you are?" he asked.

"Doug Hendricks, sir. I've been helping Ms. Shirley here take care of your boy for almost two years now. Wesley's like a part of my family."

My heart threatened to burst from the pride in Daddy's voice. I felt Wesley relax in my hand and snuck a glance up at him. His eyes were on my daddy, trying hard to block the tears brimming along the edge.

I knew instantly from Mr. Madden's face that this was the wrong thing to say. His eyes darkened with anger and he straightened his back to exaggerate the couple inches in height he had on Daddy.

"Well, Mr. Hendricks, your services are no longer required. Wesley is *my* son and it's not *your* place to decide what happens to him. Shirley, if you weren't up to the task, you only had to say so."

Mr. Madden turned abruptly and started back towards the door, sliding his aviators onto his face in one fluid motion.

Wesley stayed rooted to the spot, my hand still holding onto his arm. His face had the same intense determination as his dad's as he glared at him, the blood now completely drained. No one else could tell, but I knew my best friend like I knew myself, and he was terrified of leaving right now.

"For how long?" Wesley snapped.

"Excuse me?" Mr. Madden turned back, his phone once again in his hand and posed to type.

His son didn't flinch at his father's harsh tone like I did. Mr. Madden wasn't used to being questioned, especially by Wes.

He held his ground, though. "For how long? I want to come back here. I am not returning to Atlanta permanently."

Mr. Madden shook his head. "Of course not. You'll be attending Montmeri Academy in the fall."

"No." Wesley's voice rang out angrily through the restaurant, making the other diners turn and face our way. All other conversations died out and I saw one of the guys from the baseball team hold up a cell phone so he could record the exchange.

The billionaire business mogul must have noticed it, too, because he blanched before nodding at Wesley. "Then you'll join me for the summer. I'm going on a tour through South America for Madden Markets; it's time you start learning the ropes and preparing for your role in the business." He didn't give Wesley a chance to respond as he swept out the door towards the shiny black Rolls Royce Phantom idling in front of the restaurant.

Wesley exhaled loudly from holding his breath in anticipation. I could feel the tension leave his body as mine began to tremble. He was *leaving*…for the entire summer. The next few months suddenly looked bleak as the prospect of not spending every day with him loomed imminent. What if he couldn't come back? What if I couldn't ever see him again?

He turned to me with his megawatt smile, grasping both of my shoulders so I faced him. "It's going to be okay, Celeste," he promised, rubbing soothing circles with his thumbs. "We have him on camera promising that I can come back. It's only for a few months."

The tears started to fall despite my desire to rein them in. My upper lip quivered because no matter what Wesley said about the situation, I didn't feel it was as likely. A teenager with a cell phone in River's Run was hardly going to be enough to change Benedict Madden the Third's mind.

"Wesley's right, sugar bee," Daddy said. He and Marla both looked somber while Ms. Shirley was on the verge of tears herself. Maggie was speechless for once, eyeing us with her mouth agape. No one really knew what to do or say.

"I'll write and call as much as I can." Wesley leaned down so he could hold my gaze and indicate his sincerity. My heart was breaking, but I couldn't let that be Wes' problem. He didn't have a say in this anymore than I did.

I settled for hugging him fiercely, my arms locked around his neck as he pulled my waist into a vicelike grip against him. The tears kept falling as I buried my face into his neck but I managed to choke down my sobs. I would save those for later in my tower with Maggie.

"Come on, now, honey, your daddy's waitin'," Marla chided us. She pulled Wesley away to give him a tight hug herself. Daddy clapped him on the shoulder.

"Mind your manners," Daddy reminded him. "Just because your daddy lets things slide doesn't mean you can forget what we taught you here. Respect goes a long way."

Wesley nodded and shook my daddy's hand. "I won't let you down, sir," he promised. He pulled his great-aunt Shirley into a hug as she tearfully swore to keep his room just the way he liked it. With a final smirk and a wink for me, Wesley followed his father outside and into the car.

I couldn't hold back anymore and a strangled cry escaped

my throat. I sank into the booth beside Maggie as she wrapped an arm around my shoulder from behind.

"We'll get through this summer together, Cee," she whispered. I nodded and squeezed her arm in thanks, but inside it felt like I was dying. Wesley had become like a shadow for me and I didn't want to face three whole months without him. If Mama's death had taught me anything, it's that a lot could go downhill in 90 days.

CHAPTER 9
ALL THE CHANGES
WESLEY

Three Months Later

STEPPING off my father's private jet in Savannah felt like stepping back in time. The air was clearer here, smelling of fresh mown grass and the rainstorm that passed through every afternoon in southern Georgia. The plane had only barely stayed behind the dark clouds on the way from Atlanta. Summer felt agonizingly long but now that I was on my way to River's Run, I could breathe a sigh of relief on returning home.

Home. I hadn't realized how much I had grown to love everyone in Smithson County, although Chief Hillsborough might be excluded from that list. My heart raced at the prospect of enveloping Aunt Shirley in a bear hug, eating dinner at The Comfy Cushion while Marla forced me to eat seconds, and telling Mr. Hendricks about the different restaurants I visited while on tour with my father.

Most of all, I couldn't wait to see Celeste. I tried to send her postcards whenever I could with a phone call sprinkled in here or there. My father always had a pressing need for me to attend a meeting or photo opportunity with him whenever I managed to get Celeste on the phone. His pompous behavior grated my nerves the entire trip and I struggled to keep my anger in check. It was only by picturing Celeste's green eyes, kind and hopeful, that I managed to bite my tongue. She saved me from more than one outburst over the past three months.

I was about to surprise her by arriving two days ahead of schedule after an unexpected disaster in the Hong Kong market sent my father in a tailspin and he headed over to China to sort it all out. We had barely spoken more than ten sentences during our visits to Brazil, Argentina, and Chile. The only time he found me useful was when I was able to serve as an interpreter for those speaking Spanish in his presence, something he reminded me was only possible because of the private education I had received in Atlanta. He made it clear that his expectation was for me to attend Montmeri Academy and that my time in River's Run was an indulgence that would soon be coming to an end. I dreaded the day that happened.

Phillip, one of my father's assistants, was charged with delivering me back to Aunt Shirley and it was evident how annoyed he was at the task. He followed me off the plane and all but gagged in disgust. "They call this an airport?" he asked, his British accent dripping with disdain.

"You really don't have to go with me the rest of the way," I offered, silently praying he would take it.

He frowned at me, his bushy brown eyebrows angling in a way that made his face comical. "Your father would be most displeased with me."

I shrugged. "Dear old Benny boy isn't here, now, is he?"

Phillip's face registered shock at my disrespect. He could

give Mr. Hendricks a run for his money when it came to manners and etiquette. "I gave Mr. Madden my word that I would safely deliver you to your aunt, so deliver you I shall."

Rolling my eyes, I continued along the tarmac to a waiting Cadillac with a paid driver standing next to the back passenger door. The man nodded curtly to Phillip and me before holding open the door for us. A male airline attendant carried my duffle bag over to the trunk that the driver opened remotely. As soon as we pulled away from the plane, Phillip pulled out his phone and started responding to emails and calendar notifications to manage my father's schedule. He didn't say another word to me for the entire drive to River's Run, which was fine by me. We could both be irritated with the other's presence in silence.

The familiar sights of Smithson County came into view and I found myself bouncing on my seat as we turned onto Main Street. "Just pull up here before we get to The Comfy Cushion," I instructed the driver.

I jumped out of the car before the driver could make it around to open the door for me and snatched my duffle out of the back, slinging it crossbody over my back. My mind was whirling with imaginings of this moment, of seeing Celeste's face light up, how she would run into my arms, and the next few days we would spend swapping stories of our long summer apart.

The bell chimed over the door as I entered the restaurant and Marla squealed in delight as soon as she laid eyes on me. "Wesley Madden, you didn't tell me you were coming early!" she cried, coming around the counter to fold me into a warm hug. "Why, you've grown another four inches!"

A few other patrons called out hello's, along with Jesse on the grill line, but I didn't see the one smiling face I expected.

My eyes darted around for her, standing on my toes to peer into the back kitchen.

To my surprise, Marla's face dropped slightly. "You won't find her here," she said. Her voice was barely above a whisper as though she didn't want to be overheard.

"What? Where is she?"

Marla pursed her lips and glanced behind her before nodding towards the door. "She got a job as a lifeguard this summer down at the pool. Just head on over."

A lifeguard? *What?*

I was so confused as I shuffled out the door in a daze. Why would Celeste work anywhere other than The Comfy Cushion? She loved that place more than anything since it represented her mother. Besides, we were too young to start thinking of jobs, right? Why was she working in the first place?

The River's Run community pool was a couple blocks from my aunt Shirley's house, only a five minute walk if I cut through back alleys like Celeste taught me. It was normally packed all summer long as people tried to beat the stifling heat but didn't wanna risk the ticks and leeches that thrived in the creek. If you were under 16, you had to have a parent or guardian present so Celeste and I had avoided it in the past. Her dad was too busy at the restaurant and Nana and Aunt Shirley were too old to lay out in the sun like that every day. Still, it was a decent enough place, with an end deep enough for a diving board along with a kiddie pool that led into a splash pad.

I arrived at the pool and Travis Emerson, a boy from class who didn't typically annoy the hell out of me, was manning the entrance. He greeted me cheerfully, squinting up at me from under his bright red hat.

"Yo, Wes, my man!" He held up his hand to slap a high five with me. "Haven't seen you all summer! Cee said you were going all over the world or something."

Cee? Only Maggie ever called her that. I tried not to grind my teeth in irritation, but his overfamiliarity with Celeste felt like a torrent of ice water shooting down my spine.

"Yeah, dude," I sighed. "Where's Celeste?"

Travis turned and pointed towards the small shed that served as the lifeguard headquarters. "She should be in there. Hey, man!"

I didn't wait to pay him the entrance fee or get a designated wrist band to indicate my age before I took off across the concrete patio. The rules were already broken anyway since I still had on my sneakers, jeans, and polo shirt my father insisted I wear to travel. Travis could go ahead and suck a fat one if he thought I was going to wait another minute to see Celeste.

A tall girl with long brown hair and the perfect sun-kissed tan was walking out of the shed in a tight red bikini that perfectly displayed her round breasts and perky ass. She had a pair of black sunglasses tucked into the hair on top of her head, and it felt like a Baywatch rerun as I watched her pull the glasses down to shake out her hair before sliding the glasses onto her face. The closer I got to her, the more familiar she looked…

"Oh my god, WESLEY!" the girl shrieked before hurtling herself at me.

"Celeste?!" I didn't remember my voice getting so high pitched, but maybe that was what happened when shock turned on the autopilot function.

She pulled away from me beaming while my mind felt like it was being twisted by a corkscrew. "What happened to your hair?" I finally managed to ask. It sounded so stupid to say out loud that I nearly kicked myself.

Celeste only laughed before pulling the long locks over one shoulder. "Maggie and I went to Savannah for the day and paid to have it chemically straightened, just for fun. Don't you like it?"

What had once been a wild mane reminiscent of a bison now resembled the wannabe models that hung out around the rich men at my father's parties. Celeste's hair had a shine to it that I had never noticed before, and with it being so straight, the length was approaching her waist. It looked incredible, drawing even more attention to her high cheek bones and dainty nose.

"You…you look…" I stammered. She had grown a few inches over the summer, bringing the top of her head to my chin. And her curves…

Celeste had always been beautiful to me. This was something else entirely. She looked like a woman. The word "sexy" flashed across my mind and I felt my ears redden as though Celeste was going to read my thoughts.

"It's not permanent." She shrugged as if my reaction didn't really matter. "Desiree told Daddy it cost too much for me to maintain, so I doubt I'll be able to do it again."

My mind was still trying to force my body to deposit blood somewhere other than my dick and it took a minute before I registered what she was saying. "Wait—who is Desiree?"

At this, her entire face fell. "We have a lot to talk about, Wes."

Celeste talked to Travis and another lifeguard before slipping on a pair of tiny black shorts and a thin white tank top. Rage boiled through me as I caught Travis eyeing her backside appreciatively and I nearly clocked him across his jaw to make him stop, but I was too caught up in the view myself.

She had changed so much in the three months I had been gone. Even her body language was different, like she was surer of herself and confident in who she was. Yet there was a nagging feeling in my gut that she was holding something back. Our connection had changed, and I wasn't sure I could handle that.

We fell into step quietly as we exited the pool. A million questions were buzzing in my head and I didn't know where to begin. Meanwhile, Celeste seemed content at my side, her shy smile in place as she looked at everything but me. I realized belatedly we were walking in the opposite direction of The Comfy Cushion and started to turn around, but her hand darted out to grab my elbow.

"Don't," was all she said. Celeste turned down my aunt Shirley's street and greeted my aunt, who was sitting in a rocking chair on the front porch with her Bible.

"Why, Wesley!" Aunt Shirley crooned. "You're home early!" She stood up to give me a hug and I tried not to show my surprise at how frail she felt. Had this summer been that hard on everybody?

"Couldn't go another day without seeing my favorite auntie," I teased her. She had never given up on me, even with all the trouble I seemed to cause at school, and that made her rank a lot higher on the list than anyone I knew back in Atlanta. Poor Aunt Shirley was too old to pay attention to the little things, though, which made sneaking over to The Comfy Cushion or Celeste's house the easiest thing in the world. I would never get a better set up than this and I didn't want to risk losing it.

"I'm gonna go on up and show him his surprise!" Celeste announced with a grin.

Shirley smiled airily as she sank back into her rocking chair. "Oh yes, dear, go on up!"

"My surprise?" I repeated as I climbed the stairs after her. I had to keep my eyes on my shoes because the sight of Celeste's round ass that close to my face had me fighting a semi, which probably wasn't the best way to greet the girl I had been dreaming about all summer.

She led the way into my room and I was brought up short. It had been transformed. There was a new queen size bed with a metal bed frame and huge down-filled pillows. The bedding looked brand new, replacing the weathered quilt that Shirley had on the old bed. The dresser had a facelift and was no longer chipped with peeling lacquer, but instead boasted a bright red color that matched the stripes in the bedding. A desk replaced the nightstand with a single door on the right hand side that resembled a locker.

The best part was all the black and white photographs hanging on strings from the ceiling. Celeste had recreated her tower and showcased all the memories we had made in River's Run since my arrival. There was a photo of me with her family at the first Fourth of July barbecue, another of us sitting at the counter of The Comfy Cushion drinking out of a milkshake with two straws. I stepped further into the room, examining every photo. Some were candid shots we had taken with Maggie. There was one from the eighth grade dance, our first formal school dance, where I had my arm around Celeste's waist and Nana could be seen in the corner raising a finger at me in warning. She had all my favorite moments on display and it took away my ability to speak.

"Do you like it?" Celeste asked tentatively from the doorway. Her green eyes looked apprehensively around the room at all her handiwork.

"You did this…for me?" I gulped, feeling too many emotions at once to articulate where my mind was.

She nodded. "Maggie and Daddy helped, of course. They'll both want to have a party to celebrate now that you're back."

Without thinking about it, I crossed the room in two strides and kissed her. My hands circled her tiny waist and molded her body to mine, and I was lost in how perfectly her lips aligned with my own. Celeste didn't hesitate, wrapping her arms around my neck and pushing her breasts into my chest. I could feel her nipples starting to pebble through her bikini top, creating a tender friction against my chest. Wild images rioted through my head about taking them in my mouth, laying her down on my bed to cover her body with mine. Nobody would disturb us up here because Shirley hadn't stepped foot in my room since the day I moved to River's Run.

Celeste moaned and I used her open mouth as an advantage to invade my tongue against hers. Our kiss deepened as I pulled her tighter against me, wanting to memorize the way her body felt when it pressed against me. Letting one hand slowly sink down, I cupped one of her ass cheeks in my hand, firm and tender at the same time. There was no hiding the erection I was sporting now, but Celeste didn't seem to mind. Her hips grinded forward before she suddenly gasped and broke away, breathing heavily.

"I'm so sorry!" she whispered. Her face registered horror and guilt, like she couldn't believe what had just happened between us.

"This has been a long time coming, don't you think?" I

asked. Air was finally returning to my lungs and I panted like after one of my locker room brawls. A stiff tent had formed in the front of my jeans, like it had almost every night the entire summer, only now the girl of my fantasies was finally in front of me and her kiss was a million times better than anything my dreams invented.

Celeste looked dumbfounded. "It has?"

My cock softened as my heart bottomed out. "Celeste, you have to know how I feel about you! Do you honestly think I could ever like another girl more than you?"

"But we're best friends!"

"I don't just wanna be your friend!" I burst out angrily. "I've always wanted more than that!" Shaking my head in frustration, I slumped onto the bed, my shaggy hair falling down in front of my eyes as the shield I needed it to be. Nowhere had it ever crossed my mind that Celeste wouldn't feel the same way. That she didn't feel the same deep-seeded connection I had since the moment we met. No matter how I tried to frame it in my mind, I always came up empty because the possibility of me without Celeste couldn't possibly exist.

Her rejection *hurt*.

From the corner of my eye, I could see Celeste cross and uncross her ankles. Her fidgeting feet gave away her anxiety. "Hillary won't like it," she finally said, her voice small and apologetic.

"Hillary?" I repeated in confusion, jumping back to my feet. "Like Hillary Stanbrooke? What the hell does she have to do with this?"

Celeste's eyes were round and filled with tears. She had never been on the receiving end of my rage before and although I knew somewhere deep down that I needed to get it in check, I was too hurt and pissed off to care.

"She's about to become my stepsister," confessed Celeste.

My jaw dropped as I tried to process that information. "Your dad is…" I trailed off, the statement too ludicrous to fathom.

"Marrying Desiree Stanbrooke in a few weeks," she finished for me.

So that was the Desiree she mentioned back at the pool. Hillary and her twin brother Jeremy were treated like royalty at our school. She had won several beauty pageants, including Miss Georgia Peach Teen, and her brother was the all-star of the eighth grade football team. He was already slated for varsity when our freshman year started next week.

"But he wasn't even dating her when I left!" I cried.

She nodded tearfully. "I know. They went on their first date the day after you left. Daddy hasn't…been himself." Her voice cracked as her words dropped off.

None of this made any sense. I couldn't get my mind to catch up. Mr. Hendricks was the most careful, considerate person I had ever met. He hadn't expressed any interest in dating again after losing Celeste's mom. Well, that I had heard anyway. I guess a grown man wouldn't have to admit something so personal to his daughter's best friend. But still, there was a small part of me that felt just as betrayed. I respected the hell out of her dad, which was more than I could say about most other adults in my life. It was really out of character for him to do something so impulsive.

I slammed my fist on top of the dresser, making Celeste jump. "Hillary can fuck off! I don't like her, Celeste. We'll deal with her and your dad, I don't care!"

She gave me her usual small smile, albeit a bit more watery than usual as she brushed the tears from her cheeks. "Let's go find Maggie and head back to the restaurant."

This wasn't at all how I pictured this moment going. I expected the same kind of fireworks as our last kiss, for her feelings to be as powerful as mine. This was all wrong. I grabbed her hand and pulled her back against me, tilting her chin up to force her to look in my eyes.

"Tell me you don't feel the same as me," I snarled. "Tell me you haven't wondered how kissing me again would feel since that first time in July."

A twinkle sparked in her eyes as the arm I wasn't holding snaked around my waist and sealed our bodies together. My cock was starting to get hard again. She felt so warm and so *right*.

"I would never lie to you like that, Wesley," she murmured. "You're my person, right?"

Her soft smile tugged at my heart and I felt instant relief. I gently ran my fingers along the side of her face to weave them through her hair and pull her closer. Placing a tender kiss on her forehead, I whispered, "For my whole life."

She looked up at me and nodded. "For my whole life. But things are different now. You'll see."

I opened my mouth to argue, but thought better of it. Celeste wasn't the type of girl you rush things with. Just like everything else with her, she threw me off kilter. But this discussion was definitely going to be revisited later. I wouldn't take "no" for an answer.

We left the room and said our goodbyes to Aunt Shirley on the front porch, who reminded me to call if I ended up staying over at Celeste's for the night as I had in the past. The prospect was something I was eager to explore, but from the way Celeste's face fell, I knew that was no longer an option. Still, she didn't stop me as I wove my fingers through hers, walking in companionable silence side by side.

Maggie had found a job babysitting this summer, which she hated, but Celeste said they paid her a lot more than what Celeste made as a lifeguard. They spent a lot of their free time over in Savannah, the closest city to River's Run, since Maggie's mom was dating a man who lived out that way. Celeste said their original plan was to start saving up for a car, but after they both started earning money, they found it far more enjoyable to spend it on clothes and makeup.

I tried to laugh with her as she told me stories of their shopping excursions, but I only felt guilt eating away at the pit of my stomach. My dad had given me two new credit cards with unlimited credit at the start of the summer in addition to the access I had to my checking account with an obscene amount of money from being a stock shareholder in Madden Enterprises since birth. My father had never even so much as batted an eye when I bought something, no matter the price. Why would you when money wasn't an issue? I had no idea what it meant to live on a budget or have to save up for anything. It had never occurred to me to save up for a car because I fully expected my dad to provide one as soon as I got my learner's permit. He might be a douchebag, but he never withheld from me financially. Money was his solution to every problem, and his wild son was his biggest problem to date.

"Wesley!" Maggie squealed as she threw her arms around me in the backyard of the Ross family. They lived one street over from Aunt Shirley and were one of the few families in Smithson County who had a lot of money. Both Mr. and Mrs. Ross were attorneys who preferred country living and wanted to restore an old house in their spare time. They commuted to Savannah a few days a week for court, but predominantly worked from home in their crumbling southern farmhouse. They had three kids who howled as they chased each other around the yard while we stood there talking to Maggie.

I laughed as I hugged her back. "This doesn't really seem like your scene," I joked as I dodged a Nerf bullet that hit her square on the head.

She shrugged. "Turns out, anything with money is my scene. Hammond, STOP EATING GRASS!"

Celeste and I both exchanged a look, mine filled with alarm while hers was full of mirth. She tried to hide her laughter behind her hand, but Maggie joined in right away.

"They're heathens, I swear!" she sighed dramatically. "So are y'all heading over to the diner?"

We nodded and she promised to meet us there as soon as the Rosses returned. Celeste and I started to walk back towards the gate when Maggie called me back to her.

She leaned in really close and poked me in the chest. "If you hurt her, I'll kill you and make it look like an accident!"

My eyes widened, not at her threat but the fact that she knew something. "How did you know?"

Maggie rolled her eyes and clutched a hand over her heart. "You wound me! You seriously think I wouldn't notice the hearts in the eyes of my best friend?!"

Jealousy made me bristle a bit. "She's *my* best friend," I corrected in a huff.

She quirked an eyebrow in a way that told me how stupid she found the statement to be. "Not if you're gonna go making her fall in love with you!"

It was my turn to roll my eyes. "It literally just happened!"

All I got was a swat to the arm in return. "Don't hurt her!" Maggie warned again before pushing me towards a confused-looking Celeste.

As much as I didn't want it to, Maggie's shrewd assessment burgeoned a bubble of hope in my chest. We might only be starting high school, making it way too early for us to fall in love, but sometimes you just know. High school sweethearts stayed together all the time. And one thing was for certain—I was in this for the long haul.

With that happy thought in mind, I clasped Celeste's fingers through mine again, beaming at her. *For my whole life*, I vowed to myself.

CHAPTER 10
HEARTACHE AND HOPE
GO HAND IN HAND
CELESTE

WESLEY LOOKED *hot* with his dark tan skin and tight polo shirt. He had grown bigger over the summer, not in height, but in width. His shoulders were broader and his arms looked more muscular in a way that made me do a double take. I could tell he noticed the changes in my body right away (thank you, puberty, for FINALLY showing up!) and it would be a lie to say it didn't make me feel a bit full of myself. I liked the way his eyes roamed my body, the smolder he started to give me when I caught him staring…it was a heady rush to know that I had the power to bring out that reaction in him.

But then when he kissed me, it was like a rocket shot me straight to the stars. My body was no longer my own, fully prepared to do something reckless and crazy, because nothing could be reckless or crazy with Wesley Madden. Our bodies fit together like Legos, perfectly aligned and contoured to one another, and it made me want to shout to everyone in the River's Run town square: WESLEY LIKES ME BACK!

Had I not remembered Mama's warnings to always keep it slow with boys, things might have really escalated in there.

I was aware how much his body wanted me since it definitely wasn't a tv remote pressing against his jeans, but we still needed to take things down a notch. Stepping away from him felt like backing away from a hot grill; there was so much cold air all at once that you felt even more cautious of the flames in front of you.

I meant it when I said Hillary wouldn't like it. She made no secret out of her intent to pursue him once he returned to River's Run, and had pestered me with questions all summer long. Crossing the line from best friend to romantic relationship sounded terrific in theory, but in actuality, wasn't practical. Hillary tended to always get her way, and Mama had never advised me on what to do about that.

Now, though, with his hand laced through mine on the way to The Comfy Cushion, it was hard to remember why Mama warned me off boys in the first place. I knew my bubble of happiness was about to burst when we arrived at the restaurant and Hillary set her eyes on Wesley again, but it didn't seem right to let the opportunity pass by. Knowing what it felt like to hold Wes' hand in mine was something she didn't deserve to take from me.

As we got nearer, my anxiety began to grow and I dropped his hand before he could feel the sweat gathering on my palms. I stopped a few feet away and turned to face him, my back to The Comfy Cushion.

"Desiree will probably be there because she rarely lets Daddy out of her sight," I explained quietly, looking at the ground. Seeing his anger would only make it harder to accept something that was already crushing my soul. "Hillary usually hangs out in the corner booth with all of her friends. Jeremy might be back from football practice by now, too."

Wesley leaned down to capture my gaze, tilting my head up once again to face him. It was just as awful as I imagined it would be, his face already contorting with anger mixed with a heavy dose of confusion. "And all of this happened in three short months? I wasn't gone all that long, Celeste…"

I nodded, sucking in a shaky breath to stop myself from breaking down. "Daddy's been doing a lot of weird things lately. He even let them move in already even though they aren't married yet."

While that probably didn't sound like a big deal to most people, for someone as traditional as my daddy, it nearly made me choke on my breakfast when he told me a few weeks ago.

"You don't have a guest room anymore?" Wesley asked in surprise. He had slept in that room often enough that we used to keep a drawer of pajamas for him in the dresser.

I shook my head sadly. "When Daddy let Desiree and the kids move in, he gave Jeremy your room…and Hillary took mine." I paused knowing this part was going to make Wesley's anger flare.

Right on cue, he choked out, "So where are you sleeping?"

"We moved all my stuff up to the tower." I shrugged like it was no big deal, but deep down inside, it still broke my spirit to admit out loud. It shouldn't have meant so much to me but that had been my bedroom since the day I was born. My mama and Nana had hand painted the flowers on the wall in anticipation of my arrival, and on a single Saturday, Desiree and her daughter covered up every one. The whole time I kept reminding myself that Mama said to sprinkle kindness around like confetti, and that I should be excited at the prospect of siblings, but it was hard to bear that in mind as the ugly mint green paint Hillary selected buried the reminders of my mama's love from view.

Wesley was indignant on my behalf. He was breathing heavily, his nostrils flaring, and his hands became fists at his sides. The veins popped out on his forearms as he tried to control his temper.

"What is your dad thinking?!" he burst out angrily.

I just shrugged my shoulder before turning back to the restaurant. Wesley was immediately at my side and tried to lace his fingers through mine again, but I dropped them like I had been burned, crossing my arms across my chest. Hillary would be on the war path if she realized anything had developed between Wesley and me, and if the past summer had been any indication, Desiree always took her daughter's side. As much as I loved Wesley, I didn't want his homecoming to be ruined with a fight.

Just as I predicted, Hillary and her followers were all huddled in a corner booth, jabbering loudly over one another and filming videos on their cell phones. Several of her friends were already high school sophomores and juniors who flocked to Hillary's side because of her beauty pageant titles. She was Queen Bee, and The Comfy Cushion now served as her royal court.

Hillary's eyes lit up the moment Wesley stepped through the door behind me.

"Wesley Madden, is that you?!" She pushed two of her friends out of the booth so she could rush over to him and throw her arms around him, a fake smile frozen on her face.

Or at least, she attempted to. Wes caught her wrists as they neared his neck and halted their trajectory.

"Don't touch me," he warned her firmly.

Hillary's face dropped instantly, a flare of anger flashing

in her eyes before she quickly schooled her features into an exaggerated pout. "Didn't you miss me, Wesley? I've been thinking about you all summer! Celeste wouldn't give me *any* details!" She shot a glare my way as if I had done something wrong.

Wesley gave her a cruel smirk. "That's funny since Celeste had to remind me of your name." He threw an arm around my shoulder and led me around the table to my left so we could go down the other aisle, away from Hillary.

"Wes!" I whispered furiously. "You know that's not true!"

He shot me one of his megawatt smiles. "But she doesn't, does she?" he whispered back.

Right as we reached the hallway entrance that would lead to the back kitchen and my father's office, Desiree came into view. She was several years younger than Daddy, having had her kids early in life. Her dark brown hair was nearly black, falling in a thick bob around her face. She and Hillary went to Savannah at least twice a month to get heavy eyelash extensions, and their eyebrows were waxed to perfection. They both kept their makeup impeccably pristine, regardless of weather or time of day. Desiree usually wore light pencil skirts or dresses with high stiletto heels that made her tower over me. She was very attractive in a way that I had come to associate with city life, but looked pretty out of place in River's Run.

Now, she arched one carefully manicured eyebrow at me before looking back at Hillary. "And what have we here?" she asked.

"We're just going back to see Daddy," I explained.

Desiree's lips pursed. "He's got another migraine and will be heading home for the evening." Daddy's migraines were becoming almost a daily occurrence. Most of the time they were so bad that he lost vision and became sensitive to light and sound.

I nodded and Wesley's arm slid from my shoulders to my waist. Desiree's eyes zeroed in on the movement like lasers, making me take an awkward step away from him.

Wesley didn't skip a beat, however. "Guess we better catch him before he leaves, then."

Desiree crossed her arms across her chest, glaring down her nose at him. "I don't believe I know your name," she responded coldly.

Hillary's voice came from behind me. "That's Wesley Madden, Mom."

She surveyed Wesley again, this time with newfound interest. Her gaze softened as she noted his designer apparel and expensive watch. "As in Madden Markets?"

Beside me, Wesley stiffened at her inquiry. He clenched his teeth and eyed her with disdain. "My father's business is exactly that—*his*." Without another word, he grabbed my hand and pulled us both around her towards my daddy's office.

Wesley's audacity never ceased to amaze me. I never would have had the gumption to speak to an adult like that, particularly one as scary as Desiree. She was so stern, full of hard angles and harsh lines—the kind of customer who wants filet mignon at a place like The Comfy Cushion.

I heard Wesley's sharp intake of breath as we walked into Daddy's office. He was packing up for the day, powering off the computer, and shuffling papers into the appropriate place on the bookcase behind his desk. With my best friend by my side, it made me realize how pale Daddy was starting to look, and how the round belly that had always crushed me in a bear hug was starting to disappear. As much as I hated to accept it, Daddy didn't look like himself either, which was just as upsetting as his behavior.

"Wesley!" Daddy boomed out in surprise when he saw us. He held out his arms, and as he wrapped them around Wes, I suddenly noticed how loose Daddy's shirt hung on his frame and how sharply his elbow popped out now. "It's so good to see you! We weren't expecting you around here for a few more days."

Wes nodded. "All part of my master plan to surprise Celeste." He flashed me his megawatt smile, his tongue just barely poking out between his white teeth, and my heart leapt.

"Desiree said you have a migraine again?" I inquired.

Daddy grimaced before shrugging his shoulders. "It's not that bad. It'll pass, sugar bee. Are you gonna come over for dinner?" he asked Wesley.

Desiree's voice barked out from behind us. "Doug, you have to put your health first!"

She shuffled past us, all but knocking Wesley out of the way, and made a big show of fussing over Daddy, smoothing back his hair and rubbing his back. A flash of a glare in our direction told me she blamed me for Daddy's selfless behavior.

He offered her a soft smile in return. "Now, honey, Wes is practically a member of the family. It wouldn't be right not to celebrate his return." As Daddy wrapped his arm around her waist, a surge of fury shot through my body, and I had to actively stop myself from ripping Desiree away from him. She would never be my mother, so she had no business at Daddy's side.

"Tell you what—I'll plan something for later this week!" Desiree beamed like it was the best idea in the world, though the smile didn't quite reach her eyes. "We want you to feel better before we celebrate, dear!"

I stole a glance at Wesley and found his face pinched in concentration. The gears in his head were turning as he watched the exchange, no doubt taking notes on their behavior like he seemed to do with everyone else. Judging by the scrunch of his nose, like he smelled sour milk, he didn't like what he saw.

Daddy sheepishly looked at Wesley with an apologetic smile. "How does that sound to you, Wes? I'm sorry, I've just been getting these headaches here and there. Today's not a good day."

"Of course, Mr. Hendricks," Wesley replied. "Celeste and I will have dinner with Aunt Shirley tonight so we can catch up and you can rest."

"Oh, now that just won't do." Desiree tsked and shook her head, looking wide-eyed between the two of us, then back to Daddy. "Ms. Shirley can't be expected to run Celeste back out to our place later this evening, and I'm gonna have to go home now with you, Doug. She'll have to come home now, too, and see you another time, Wesley. In fact, y'all are getting to the age where it's not decent for a girl to spend so much time with a boy. People might talk."

My head was spinning at her words. Wesley and I had done this over 100 times in the two years we had been best friends. Ms. Shirley never once protested giving me a ride, nor had Daddy ever refused to come get me. He knew it wasn't my fault that our family's land was too far out of town to walk.

And as for people talking about us, the idea was laughable in my mind. No one had ever said anything about that, even when Wes spent the night at our house. We spent every day together from sun up to sun down from the day he moved to River's Run to the beginning of this summer. Even on days we were sick, we spent hours on the phone until we badgered one of the adults in our lives to have pity on us and let the other one go take care of the sick one. It was just how things were between Wesley and me.

There were tears in my eyes as I waited for Daddy to say as much to Desiree, to remind her that I was his daughter, not hers. Daddy held my gaze for a moment before averting his eyes to his desk. He let out a long sigh.

"Perhaps you're right, honey," he finally agreed. "I don't know nearly as much about raising a teenage daughter as you do."

"But Daddy!" I protested.

Desiree held up a hand. "Your father is sick, Celeste! How can you be so selfish?"

A lone tear escaped, something I didn't want Desiree to see, but Wesley grabbed my hand again and started pulling me out of Daddy's office. "We'll just step outside to say our goodbyes," he told them.

Daddy nodded. "Meet me at the truck in five minutes, sugar bee."

Wesley wound his way through the dining tables in the front of the restaurant, ignoring Hillary's tittering call for him, and dragged me outside around the corner to the extra parking spaces on the side of The Comfy Cushion. Once we were safely outside of anyone's earshot, he dropped my hand and began furiously kicking the side of the restaurant.

"That stupid fucking bitch!" he seethed with each kick.

"*Wes!*" There was no telling if she could hear us or not, and we certainly didn't need more trouble.

"I've been waiting all summer to see you and she's taking that away!" he yelled. "Don't you see what's happening?"

His anger left me speechless, opening and closing my mouth like a goldfish as I tried to find the right words to calm him down. Instead he slammed his palm into the wall between us.

"She's trying to keep me away from you so that I focus more on her ugly ass daughter! Like I'd ever look twice at Hillary!"

I shook my head. As much as I loved hearing that he didn't care about my new stepsister, I didn't think Desiree would sink that low. Daddy certainly wouldn't be attracted to her if she was that mean of a person. "That's not what she's trying to do, Wes," I insisted. "You heard her—people will talk. I don't want to start high school already having a reputation."

Wesley's blue eyes seared right through me. "I'd beat the shit out of anyone who tried to say something about you. Don't drink her poison!"

Instead, I pulled him in tightly, my hand tucking his head in above my shoulder. His arms instantly wound around my waist and I stroked his shaggy hair soothingly for a few moments before I finally heard Wes' loud sigh of relief. The fight had gone out in him.

As I leaned back to look at his face, Wesley's soft lips pressed against my own. This kiss was sweet—tender, even—and didn't last nearly long enough. He stood straighter to place a gentle kiss on my forehead. "For my whole life," Wesley whispered, making me smile against his throat.

The sounds of Daddy and Desiree's voice drifted around the corner, breaking the spell of the moment. Begrudgingly, I pulled away from Wesley and walked sadly towards their truck. Wesley followed closely behind.

"You have a good night, Wes," Daddy said. "It's good to have you home."

Wesley smiled tightly and nodded at him.

Daddy had already shut the car door behind him when Desiree turned to us with another cold smile. "Since you're such an upstanding gentleman, Wesley, why don't you join Hillary and her friends inside. I'm sure they would all appreciate a fine young man walking them home."

"Hillary doesn't have to come home now?" I tried to ask casually, but my voice shook a bit. Was Wesley right? Did Desiree want to keep us apart?

Desiree's face tightened. "Some of her friends are already licensed drivers. She'll be along after a while."

My best friend shrugged one shoulder, leaning back and fixing my soon-to-be-stepmother with a glare that should have incinerated her on the spot. "I've got better things to do."

He didn't wait for her to respond before pulling me into a one-armed hug and whispering, "I'll come get you first thing in the morning." Wesley flashed me a wink that sent a bolt of lust right through me, and sauntered off down the street.

I couldn't help the flush that heated my face and it was apparent that Desiree saw. "Your father and I are going to have a little chat about this," she hissed at me. She climbed into Daddy's waiting truck and slammed the door.

My heart felt torn as I wistfully watched Wesley head down towards the alleyway that would serve as a shortcut to Ms. Shirley's. Yearning for what was just out of reach was hardly a new concept, but it wasn't a struggle I was familiar with. Daddy and I had been a team for so long now, with

Wesley always caught up in the mix, that it made my entire body tremble to see him walking away from us. I doubted Desiree would let this go; she wasn't the type of person to allow Wesley's rude behavior go unnoticed.

Sighing heavily at the barren night that awaited me, I climbed into the tailgate of the pickup and knocked on the window to let Daddy know I was ready to go home.

CHAPTER 11
THE VOW

WESLEY

I *HATED* walking away from Celeste like that. She looked so small and helpless, two traits I had never associated with her before. No matter what any of them said, there was no way I was ever going to be polite or respectful to that Desiree woman. She reminded me of the women who hung around my father's country club in hopes of catching a rich man's attention. They never minded being wife number three or four as long as there was an unlimited credit card attached. Desiree was the last person in the world I would have picked out for Mr. Hendricks.

Seeing Mr. Hendricks like that had been an even bigger blow. He looked like he was sick with more than just migraines, but I didn't know how to approach that subject without upsetting Celeste. She had enough on her plate now that she was facing a new stepmother and stepsiblings. Mr. Hendricks must have the patience of a saint because hearing Desiree's clacking heels would drive me downright batty.

"He'll need it now," I muttered under my breath.

I was nearing the community pool and a group of

teenagers was walking out through the gate. Travis was with them, still in his red lifeguard swim trunks. They were all laughing as they tried to enjoy one of the last few nights of summer break. I envied them because they didn't have their friendships hanging on the whim of a stranger. Desiree had known me all of five minutes and possessed the power to keep me away from Celeste.

It was therefore rather stupid on Travis' part to nod in my direction and ask, "Wes, my man! How was that action with Celeste?"

"Excuse me?" I paused, waiting for him to reword his question and for the morons he was with to get rid of their shit-eating grins, like they knew a secret I didn't.

Only Travis made it worse.

"C'mon, man, you're trying to tell us that you got a glimpse of Celeste in that bikini and didn't try to lay some pipe?!" All three of the boys cracked up, slapping hands and exchanging whoops. It was the dumbest display of small dick energy on this side of the Mason-Dixon.

My jaw clenched. "Wow, I hope someday I can be as clever as you," I quipped.

"Huh?" They looked like Neanderthals as they exchanged confused looks.

It was all the more satisfying when my fist cracked Travis across his nose. The crunch that echoed, followed by blood spurting everywhere momentarily diffused some of my anger.

"Whoa, man, what the hell?!" One of his friends pulled Travis out of my reach before they ran off down the street, shouting over their shoulders about me being a lunatic.

"KEEP HER NAME OUT OF YOUR MOUTH!" I screamed after them.

There was a black cloud of anger and despair circling in my vicinity as I walked into Shirley's house and slammed the door behind me. She jumped awake from her spot in the armchair, her knitting needles clattering from her lap to the wood floor. "Wesley?" she called at my retreating form. "Is that you?"

"Who else would it be?" I snapped back. There was no way she could hear me above my stomps upstairs and my low voice, but I still felt a twinge of guilt. Celeste's nagging voice reminded me that Aunt Shirley didn't deserve to be on the receiving end of my frustration when she hadn't done anything wrong. But at the moment, it was hard to care.

This was not how I pictured my first evening back in River's Run. My homecoming was supposed to be a surprise, but the whole Hendricks family had dropped some bombs on me that far outshone my arrival. Part of me was pissed off that Celeste hadn't told me anything. She didn't need to suffer alone all summer. But I also knew Celeste better than I knew myself, so I knew without a doubt that she stayed silent because she didn't want to ruin my trip. In spite of everything she knew about my dad and I, she still believed that someday we would be able to reconcile. As if I would ever let that happen.

Pacing back and forth in the small space made me feel like a caged tiger, but I didn't know what else to do to calm myself down. I had been looking forward to this night all summer and the reality of the night was completely wrong. Rage was simmering just below the surface, a tea kettle about to blow right under my skin. Squaring up to Travis hadn't taken the edge off. If I stood still for a moment, I could almost see my skin vibrating from the restraint.

"Oh, fuck this!" I ground out after ten minutes of no reprieve.

The way I thundered down the stairs should have been enough to wake up Aunt Shirley, but her snores drowned out any noise I made. Without giving it a second thought, I snatched her car keys from their hook by the door and took off into the night. Technically I didn't have my permit yet, but my dad's driver had given me enough lessons to understand the basics. It was a summer night in River's Run, so it wasn't like traffic would be busy. A high speed chase with the sheriff sounded appealing with the mood I was in anyway.

Driving to Celeste's was as easy as I expected; there wasn't another soul on the road. As I got closer to her drive, I killed the lights on Shirley's Oldsmobile and let the full moon guide my way. Parking the car behind a grove of evergreens near the road, I circled the house and kept to the tree line. A lone light was shining from Celeste's window while the rest of the place was ensconced in darkness. For the first time ever, a sliver of trepidation trickled down my spine from being on the property. Desiree and her uppity attitude changed things, but at that moment, it wasn't enough to stop me from seeing my girl.

Massive tree branches brushed against the side of the house from the old dogwood, creating an easy route to her window. I didn't want to chance the door because I knew how often the old wood stuck. It would cause a ruckus that would wake the whole house if I tried to shove it shut when that happened. Better to go for the window and slip inside.

Celeste was visible through the glass lying on her stomach on a tiny bed that had been shoved into the far corner of the room. It barely qualified as a twin, sending another irrational shock of fury through my system. How could Mr. Hendricks let Celeste sleep on something that small after having an entire room to herself her whole life? The choice was so out of character for him that I almost wanted to go wake him up and make him justify it to my face.

She shifted, tucking her hair behind her ear and turning the page of the battered novel open on the pillow. Her ankles crossed in the air over her ass, drawing my attention to the round curve of it. Booty shorts of some sort of spandex material hugged the cheeks. How pathetic had my life become that I was jealous of a scrap of material for clinging to Celeste's body when I couldn't?

The window was already ajar in a vain attempt to lure a nonexistent breeze inside. It only took a quick jerk of my arm to open it wide enough that my body could slide through. Celeste's head darted up in surprise, her mouth forming a round O of alarm. She swung herself upright, tugging a blanket over her body to shield it from view. I frowned at her reaction.

"Wesley Madden, what on Earth are you doing here?!" Celeste panic whispered.

I dug at the heel of one shoe to pull it off before repeating the action on the other and joined her on the tiny bed. It was as hard as a 2x4 and could not possibly offer any kind of comfort conducive to sleep.

"Did you really think I was only gonna see you for a few minutes on my first night back?" I asked with a smirk. She glanced towards the door, keeping the blanket high along her collar bone, which bugged me to no end.

I yanked the blanket away from her and crumpled it into a ball that I placed behind my head as I leaned back against the wall.

"Hey!" she cried, lunging and failing to take it from me.

The sports bra Celeste wore left little to the imagination, causing me to draw my knees up so she couldn't see the wood I was instantly sporting. Round breasts were ready to fall out of the cups that dipped far too low to be of any use to a girl actually playing sports. Part of my mind registered that it was rude and downright disrespectful to stare at her chest like a vampire aiming for the jugular, but I found the cleavage too distracting to stop.

Celeste's cheeks reddened but she didn't make a move to cover herself again. "It used to be Hillary's," she offered by way of explanation.

My eyes snapped up to meet hers. "She never could have looked as good in it as you do."

Her eyes softened as she smiled at me. "Pretty sure Daddy would whip you if he saw the way you're looking at me right now."

There wasn't a shadow of a doubt that was true. "Pretty sure he'd have good reason." My breath caught as I waited for her response. For her to finally admit what I had wanted to hear from her since that first day in River's Run.

The blush that brightened her cheeks urged me to trace its descent down to her collar bone with my tongue. While I was just as much of a virgin as she was, Celeste maintained an innocence I had never possessed. Growing up as the shadow of all my father's raucous parties meant I had seen more adults having sex and snorting lines of coke than a porn star. Right now my urges were all primal instinct because I was desperate to connect with Celeste on that level. All of her firsts belonged to me just like mine belonged to her. We were soul mates, and my need to know if she recognized that was greater than my need to breathe.

In a move I couldn't have predicted, Celeste leaned

forward, drawing herself up on her knees, and kissed me. The shock lasted for all of a millisecond before I drew my arm around her to pull her body down on mine. My erection was a steel rod inside my jeans, pushing at the zipper with enough force that it might actually break through. She didn't acknowledge it, however; didn't do anything more than kiss me fervently. A happy sigh escaped her lips and she settled onto my chest, tucking her head just under my chin. Her tan legs wove around mine as I pinned her to me with both my arms. It was such a natural position that my mind checked off another box on my internal checklist of signs that Celeste Hendricks was made for me.

"I love you," I whispered without thinking. My voice was barely audible, and for a split second I hoped she didn't hear me because it was such a huge thing to say out of nowhere.

Instead she turned her head to look up at me, the small smile that I loved clinging to her lips, and warmth radiating from her eyes. "I love you, too, Wesley."

If I hadn't aced my anatomy test in health, I would swear that hearts could shatter with joy. Mine may have stopped beating altogether with her admission. "We're together now, okay? Not just as best friends. You're more than that to me, Celeste."

She didn't say anything for a moment, contemplating my words with a tilt of her head. "Do you mean that?"

I kissed the top of her head and squeezed her tighter against my chest. "For my whole life."

Celeste giggled. "People don't fall in love when they're fifteen years old, Wes."

Shrugging, I countered, "Well, I fell in love with you at thirteen, so I guess we're both a little different."

With another happy sigh, she burrowed her face into my

chest. I closed my eyes in rapture, never wanting to leave the blissful bubble we were in right now. Laying on the rock hard cot up in her tower with Celeste in my arms was the most peace I had ever experienced.

CHAPTER 12
DARKEST BEFORE
THE DAWN
CELESTE

"W HAT IS THE MEANING OF THIS?!"

Desiree's shrieking was not an ideal way to wake up, having become the sound of my anxiety, and I bolted upright. Or at least, as upright as I could considering Wesley's arm circled my waist in a vice grip for dear life. He was spooning me, his front pressed so snuggly against my back that we might have been wearing the same clothes.

Uh oh.

"Desiree, this isn't what it looks like!" I stammered. In vain, I tried to pry Wesley's arm off me or at least jostle him awake, but he only let out a soft snore and tried to burrow deeper into my back. My body was coated with a thin sheen of sweat from his body heat and I realized belatedly that having on only a pair of workout shorts and a cast off sports bra of Hillary's was not winning me any brownie points in this scenario.

My soon to be stepmother snorted derisively. "I know very well what this is, little girl. This is exactly why I told your father that you needed to be separated from him!"

How can Wesley sleep through this? I thought frantically. Not that any argument from him would help the situation.

"Get up, you little hussy, and get downstairs immediately!" Desiree turned on her heel, black bob spinning, and climbed down the steep stairs, stiletto heels clacking the entire way. No doubt on her way to get the hose.

"WESLEY!" With a violent shove, his arm flew off my torso, rousing him enough that his eyes sleepily blinked open. It would have been adorable were it not for the steaming pile of shit I knew we were both in. Already Desiree's frantic shouts were starting to echo up from the screen door below.

I leapt up and pulled a random t-shirt from the floor, too scared to care if it was dirty or clean. Yanking open a drawer, I searched for a pair of regular shorts while haphazardly throwing the rest of the drawer's contents about the room.

"What's going on?" Wesley's voice was thick and still laced with sleep.

"Desiree found us!" I hissed at him. "Get up--NOW!"

That made him spring into action. He leapt off the bed to scramble into his shoes, chucking a pair of paint splattered cloth shorts at me from under the bed. I didn't have time to argue as I pulled them on over my spandex bottoms.

We were both shuffling like maniacs as we tried to adjust our shoes and clothes while clambering down the stairs. Wesley's shaggy hair was sticking out at all angles, and the wrinkles in his polo and jeans were a dead giveaway of just how long he had spent in the position where Desiree found us. There was no way we were going to come out of this in one piece once Daddy and Nana got a hold of us.

The screen door to the kitchen slammed behind us as we entered, Daddy and Nana both standing at the island with their mouths hanging open as Desiree loudly proclaimed me a harlot and a jezebel for sleeping with a boy at only fifteen. I turned my head to glance down the hall and found Hillary's crestfallen face taking in the sight of Wesley and me, disheveled and half asleep. Her expression quickly morphed into one of pure loathing that promised revenge, which would have been far more concerning if I wasn't certain my daddy was about to bury me alive.

Daddy's shocked face turned to both of us, his mouth agape as he took in the state of our appearance. "Sugar bee…" he murmured in a daze.

"Oh no!" Desiree argued, pointing a finger at him across the island. "Don't 'sugar bee' her and let her out of this, Doug! I caught her with a boy in her bed AT FIFTEEN."

Wesley shook his head as his face flushed with anger. "Nothing happened, Mr. Hendricks, I swear on Rachel's life!"

Nana gasped at his choice of words while Daddy's mouth snapped shut. He peered at Wesley with newfound scrutiny as if he could laser the truth out of him with a single look.

Desiree continued to prattle on, however. "Of course you would say that! Nothing ever happens to a boy's reputation! You just want her to be another notch on your belt! How many girls were you with this summer while you were out trotting the globe, hmm?!"

Although I should have known better than to rise to Desiree's bait, her accusation gave me pause. Wesley and I had barely spoken all summer. What if he had been with another girl? Loving me didn't mean he wasn't pressured into hooking up with someone because of his lecherous father. Out of the corner of my eye, I saw Wesley puff up in rage.

"Nothing happened this summer other than me missing Celeste like crazy!" Wesley barked. "Just like nothing happened last night other than *you* interrupting my first night back with her!" He turned towards my father, all anger gone. "I absolutely swear to you, Mr. Hendricks, I would never disrespect you or your home like that. I came over to see Celeste last night and we just fell asleep. Nothing more than that."

Desiree snorted as she folded her arms across her chest. "Yes, that's obviously why I found Celeste half naked next to him this morning!"

Sparks were flying from Wesley's eyes and I had to grab onto his wrist as he lunged forward. "She was wearing a sports bra and shorts because you make her sleep in an *attic* with no air conditioning in *summer*!"

"ALL RIGHT, THAT'S ENOUGH!" Daddy's bellow rang out through the room with enough force to rattle the cupboard doors. He sent a piercing glare to Desiree and to Wesley before demanding, "Desiree, go to the living room. Wesley, step outside. I want to talk to my daughter."

His fiancé immediately started protesting, citing again how she had more experience raising teenage daughters than he did. Daddy was not to be trifled with, however. "I am more than capable of talking with my own daughter, Desiree. Leave. Now." Ice dripped from the coldness in his words.

With one eyebrow cocked, Desiree sent a glare my way that made me wish the ground would swallow me whole. She sauntered out of the room with her nose in the air, hips swaying in her tight pencil skirt.

Nana walked over and put an arm around Wesley's shoulders, guiding him back towards the door. His bright blue eyes bored into mine, turning around to stare at me over his shoulder, fear written all over his face. Daddy had the power to keep us apart permanently and Wesley knew it.

"Daddy, I—" I started to say, but he held up a hand to silence me.

His shoulders sank wearily, making the gray hair stand out noticeably in the morning light. He lost weight over the course of the summer and suddenly appeared far weaker than I ever remembered seeing. It was my fault, too; my carelessness did this to him.

"Celeste, I am going to ask you one time what happened, and you're going to give me an honest answer. You're my daughter and I trust that you wouldn't lie to me. Liars are the worst sort of people," Daddy said. He kept his gaze trained on my face, which did nothing to assuage my burning shame. "What happened?"

My cheeks should have been combusting by now from how red they felt. "Nothing happened, Daddy. I swear it. Just like he said, he came over, we talked, and we must have fallen asleep. It wasn't intentional. Wesley never would have broken your trust like that."

He continued to stare at me while he considered my words. The hairs on the back of my neck were standing straight up as I waited for him to say something in response. Guilt was going to make me suffocate, I just knew it.

After a long, pregnant pause, Daddy sighed. "Tell Wesley to get in here. You wait outside with Nana."

It was so much worse than if he were to scream at me or punish me in some other manner. The resigned calm with which he spoke had my knees trembling and my palms sweaty. This wasn't the reaction I anticipated and that only made my anxiety go into overdrive. But Daddy had to believe me. He wouldn't really take Desiree's word over mine, would he?

The bright sun outside was poking through gaps in the

tree branches while the heat already indicated today would be a scorcher. I had the afternoon shift at the pool since I requested tomorrow off in anticipation of Wesley's arrival. At this point, it was entirely likely that I wouldn't be allowed out of the house again, even to go to work. I gulped to fight back the sobs threatening to burst as I made my way over to Nana and Wesley at the tire swing.

"Daddy asked you to go talk to him, Wes," I instructed. My voice warbled from the tremor.

Wesley stepped up and placed a quick kiss on my forehead. "It's gonna be fine, Celeste," he assured me. "We didn't do anything wrong."

Nana harumphed loudly, her hands fisted on her hips, as he briskly walked inside. An odd part of my brain imagined this was what it must have been like in the olden days to watch someone you loved walk to the gallows. I turned back to Nana and hung my head.

"Celeste Renee Hendricks, what *were* you thinking?" she chastised me.

A tear leaked out from the corner of my eye. This entire scenario was Nana's worst nightmare come to life, and was exactly what she had an issue with when I met Wesley two years ago. It seemed surreal to have felt so loved and important last night only to wake up scared and ashamed.

"We didn't do anything, Nana, I swear it on Mama's grave. We just fell asleep."

Her lips were a firm line as she scrutinized my face. "What's done is done now. I don't know how your daddy will react."

More tears fell as I climbed into the tire swing, wrapping my arms around the rope to bury my head in my elbow. I hated disappointing everyone. After a moment, Nana's bony hand settled on my shoulder, offering comfort I wasn't wholly sure I deserved. Nothing had happened, but that didn't mean we hadn't broken everyone's trust. Wesley would likely not be allowed over anymore. The coward in me was grateful Daddy didn't want to talk to us at the same time because the thought of listening to him yell at Wesley was enough to turn my stomach. Desiree was blowing the whole thing way out of proportion, and for the life of me, I couldn't figure out why she was in my room to begin with. She never braved the tower steps because of her ridiculous heels.

None of that was enough to dry my tears, however. I didn't dare tell Daddy or Nana how I really felt about Wesley, but I also didn't want to lie to them about the change in our relationship. There was no way Desiree would allow me to have a moment alone with him if we admitted we wanted to date. Daddy had already started changing the rules and Wes had only been home for 12 hours. Maintaining our friendship on Desiree's terms was the only route I could see that wouldn't result in the loss of his presence in my life, too.

Nana cleared her throat loudly and gently tapped my shoulder. I whipped around to find Daddy and Wesley walking towards us with Daddy's arm around Wes' shoulders. That had to be a good sign, right? I couldn't imagine Daddy doing that if he was going to keep us separated.

As they drew nearer, I saw Daddy give Wesley an encouraging smile and nod towards me. Wesley came over to the tire swing and lightly cupped my cheek. "It's okay, Celeste," he whispered.

I was so confused. Clambering out of the tire swing, my face blotchy and wet from crying, I turned to Daddy expectantly. He slid his hands into the pockets of his robe, leaning back on one foot. Just over his shoulder, I saw Desiree come outside, slamming the screen door behind her as she stood with her arms folded tightly across her chest. Her glare was enough to power the sun, even from several feet away.

Daddy sighed. "Wesley and I had quite the chat just now," he began. "I believe both of you when you say nothing happened, so I'm not going to punish either of you."

"What?!" Desiree cried from behind him, dropping her hands into fists at her sides.

Hope burgeoned in my chest.

"But," continued Daddy, "we all have to acknowledge that things have changed between you two. Things I could stomach when y'all were thirteen aren't gonna fly now that you're going on 16 and entering high school. Wesley and I agreed that he is no longer going to go into your room without a chaperone. The same goes for you with his room, Celeste. Hang out in common areas only. We clear on that?" His blue eyes were watery as he leveled me with a pointed stare.

His restrictions were more than fair. "Yes, Daddy!" I agreed, hugging him around the middle. What was once a bone crushing hug was softer now, but just as welcoming and assuring as ever. I opened one eye to see Wesley standing with his hands in his pocket watching us wistfully. When our gazes locked, he gave me an overconfident wink.

Stifling perfume clouded my nostrils as Desiree hobbled near, her high heels sinking slightly into the soft dirt. "Perhaps it would be best if Hillary hung out with them, too," she offered. "After all, there's strength in numbers!"

For a brief second it looked like Daddy was considering it. "Wesley and Celeste have always done their own thing," he finally said. "I think it's best we leave 'em to it and trust that their bond is something special."

My heart leapt up to my throat. It was the first time since Desiree entered the picture that Daddy had spoken up for me like that. Without even looking at him, I could sense the smug satisfaction rolling off Wesley in waves. He definitely didn't like Desiree.

And apparently with good reason. As I extricated myself from Daddy's embrace, Desiree was glaring daggers at Wesley, her mouth pursed like she swallowed a sour lemon. It was a look that promised there was more to come.

"Come on, dear," she said, winding an arm around Daddy's waist while simultaneously still glaring at Wes. "Let's get ready to head into the restaurant."

"You go on ahead. My head is already starting to hurt and I don't know that I'm gonna make it in today," Daddy said. It was then that I noticed the way he grimaced from the sunlight, his eyes squinting as though it was too bright for him to handle.

"Darling, never without you!" Desiree cried. She was suddenly overcome with concern for him, rubbing his back and leading him towards the house. "You go right back to bed. I'll just grab your wallet real quick and head over to Savannah for that homeopathic remedy you like so much!"

They shuffled into the house together, taking all of Daddy's warmth with them.

Nana snorted behind me. "'Homeopathic remedy' my foot! She just wants to go spend his money!"

Wesley's head whipped back to her. "What do you mean, Nana?" he asked.

She rolled her eyes. "Just what I said, lovebird! The only thing that woman has managed to do since the day she batted her eyes in Doug's direction is dwindle his savings account!"

He shot me a quizzical look as though waiting for confirmation. I minutely shook my head to indicate he needed to leave it alone.

"I'm going back to my place to watch my shows," growled Nana. "You two try to keep your hands off each other. I don't care how good you look together!"

I let out a shaky laugh. "Yes, ma'am."

With that, she stomped off towards her cabin behind the main house.

Wesley looked on with confusion. "Since when does she watch her shows at her place?"

I shrugged. "Ever since Desiree moved in and told Nana that her shows didn't belong in a good Christian household. Nana called her a hypocrite and started spending more time in her own place."

He nodded before languidly drawing my arm through his elbow and meandering towards the front of the house. We walked in companionable silence for a couple minutes while my mind tried to process everything that had happened in the past hour. There were so many emotions lacing through me that I might end up with whiplash.

"Where are we going?" I finally asked with a laugh as he steered me up the dirt driveway, away from the house.

He grinned sheepishly at me. "I may have stolen Ms. Shirley's car last night to come here," Wes admitted.

My jaw dropped open, caught between laughing and screaming. "Please tell me you're joking."

"Now, why would I joke about something like that?" Glancing up the drive, Wesley leaned down to pull me in for a kiss. It was tender and emotional, something he let his whole body sink into, making mine respond in kind. Everything between us felt so natural, so easy…almost like it was too good to be true.

At that thought, I broke away, tucking my head under his chin and wrapping my arms firmly around his waist. Tears were threatening to spill over again, and I knew if I saw the hurt in his eyes from what I was about to say, I wouldn't be able to do it.

"Wes, we can't be more than just friends," I said into his collar bone, like the coward I was. "You saw how Desiree acted. It's only going to get worse."

He tried to use both hands at my shoulders to peel me away, but I tightened my grip with both arms to the point of pain.

"Please," I whispered. My voice started to warble on the verge of tears.

There was a long pause before Wesley sighed and hugged me back, resting his cheek on the top of my head. "Celeste, I'm not gonna lie to you, your family, or myself. Your daddy and I just had a talk about my feelings and intentions, and nothing or nobody is gonna change them. I love you. Period."

Part of me wanted to sigh with relief at the assurance he gave while another part of me wanted to stomp my foot in exasperation. It wasn't about lying to anybody, it was about self-preservation. Neither of us could face Daddy or Nana's disappointment if something got out of hand, and I was no longer entirely sure that I trusted Desiree enough to let things be. As much as I wanted Wesley the boyfriend, it wouldn't be worth a lick of Marla's cake batter if I couldn't keep Wesley the best friend. I needed him, plain and simple. This summer without him was proof enough.

"Wes, she'll try to keep us apart." There was no reason to clarify who as we both know exactly who I meant.

He snorted and withdrew himself from me. "She's welcome to try, but that's never going to happen." The intensity in his blue eyes would have frightened me if there was any indication he was angry or upset. But this was sheer determination, an ironclad stubbornness that I was never going to break. He cupped both of my cheeks with his hands as he swore firmly, "You're. It. For. Me."

I let the tears flow freely because who was I kidding now? His words turned me to mush. They didn't seem to faze him as he gently pressed his lips to mine once more.

"Nothing has to change, except I'm gonna hold your hand and kiss you any time I want." Wesley grinned down at me, his tongue poking out slightly between his gleaming white teeth. "Now get back in there before your daddy changes his mind."

I rolled my eyes but turned to walk back towards the house. A strange sense of foreboding settled in my gut because I knew Wesley's assertion wasn't true. Everything had to change now.

CHAPTER 13
EVIL STEPMOTHERS AND WICKED STEPSISTERS
CELESTE

I IMMEDIATELY WENT INSIDE to take a shower before going to check on Daddy. His migraines were becoming more and more frequent and it was high time I put my foot down that he go see Dr. Atkins over at the clinic. I was also itching to know what the conversation with Wesley consisted of, but all the begging and bribery in the world wouldn't make him tell me about that. Daddy was just as stubborn as Wesley about certain things.

As I got out of the shower and headed into the kitchen to grab a bottle of water on my way to Daddy's room, however, I found Desiree, Hillary, and Jeremy in a flurry of activity. My soon to be stepsiblings were both cramming clothes and towels into duffle bags on the kitchen table while Desiree was blubbering fake tears to someone on the phone. I paused in the doorway, unsure of what to do or say.

"Look who finally decided to show up!" Hillary's nostrils flared in the most unladylike fashion I had ever seen from her. Her expression was full of disdain and disgust. "Guess we know who she *actually* cares about!"

Normally her comments rolled off me, but after the

emotional turmoil I had already experienced today, I wasn't in the mood to take anything from her. Blood coated the inside of my mouth from how hard I clamped down on my cheek to prevent saying something that would land me in deeper trouble.

"What's going on?" I asked Jeremy, nodding towards the bag he was zipping shut.

My almost stepbrother was normally very quiet, preferring to keep to his room or go to his friends' houses. While we never acted friendly towards one another, I couldn't say it was an antagonistic relationship either, more like that of tolerant acquaintances. He avoided conversations with Daddy and Nana like the plague, only speaking to his mother or sister whenever they were home.

Now, however, he cast me a glare so reminiscent of his mother's that I took a partial step backwards in surprise. Pure loathing was all that could be seen in his features as he let out an exasperated sigh.

"We're waiting on the ambulance to get here to take your dad to the hospital," Jeremy explained, the words laced with venom. "*We* are taking care of him since *you* never do. Maybe you should stop worrying about your boytoy so much and start focusing on the man who raised you!"

A slap to the face would have hurt me less. I had done nothing but try to take care of Daddy since the day Mama died and I couldn't imagine anyone accusing me of less. Daddy and Nana were the only family I had left, and before Wes came into the picture, they were all I had. Jeremy Stanbrooke had been in school with me since kindergarten. He knew me well enough to know that my whole world was tied up in my parents and our restaurant. How could he say such a thing?

I prepared to turn on my heel to go check on Daddy when Desiree's sharp nails dug into my elbow. "Don't you go bothering him and make it worse!" She snapped the cell phone closed and laid it on the counter. "No doubt your whore antics this morning are what caused him to be in so much pain!"

The entire thing was so unjust and simultaneously terrifying that I burst into tears as I wrenched my arm from her grasp. Blinded by my sobs and fears, I let habit guide me out the back door towards Nana's cottage. She jumped up in alarm when I crashed inside and slid to the ground with my back to the door, clutching my knees to my chest as it wracked with howls. Daddy was in pain and it was all my fault.

"Now, what's all this?" she crooned. She crouched down in front of me, her knees popping on her descent, and gently placed her hands on my shoulders.

"Desiree is takin' Daddy to the hospital!" My voice was so warped from crying and anxiety that I hardly recognized it to my own ears. "She said it's my fault he's in so much pain after what I did this morning!"

Nana grimaced and wrapped an arm around my shoulder to tug me to her chest. "It's not your fault, Celeste. Pain isn't gonna come on because a man's daughter falls in love."

My head snapped up in shock. "I—Who said--?" I stammered.

She rolled her eyes at me in a scoff. "Girl, do you think I don't have eyes?! That Madden boy has been in love with you since the day I met him! You just took a lot longer to catch up!"

Automatically I shook my head, disliking how uncomfortable it felt to have my Nana pick up on something so intimate about me.

"Oh, hush! Ain't nothing wrong with being in love. If I know one thing about your Daddy, it's how much he loves you. He'd be happy as pie over you and Wesley finally getting together now that you both are old enough. Don't let that devil woman poison your happiness!"

Nana never spoke so poorly of Desiree before. While I always suspected she wasn't fond of my stepmother-to-be, she never outright expressed any dislike. Had I not seen Desiree's comments in action about Nana's shows, I wouldn't have understood why she started watching them from her own television instead of ours. Manners were everything to Nana, and she never would have disrespected Daddy in his own home by voicing disdain for his marital choices.

"I'm scared, Nana," I whimpered. "None of us have been to the hospital since Mama died. What if Daddy never comes home either?" A weight lifted off my shoulders from admitting that awful thought out loud as I began to tremble. I didn't want to see Daddy in a hospital bed like Mama, hooked up to a bunch of wires and tubes, a shell of who he used to be. And despite the comfort she offered, I didn't entirely believe Nana that I hadn't been the cause of his pain. It was all too coincidental for him to wind up in an ambulance not even an hour after finding a teenage boy in my bed.

She pulled me closer, gently running her fingers through my hair as she rocked me. There was nothing she could say in that moment that would make me feel better because we both knew from Mama's illness that health could turn in the blink of an eye. One day you're fine and the next day you're gone. Life was kind of bittersweet like that.

When my sobs turned to light tears that finally descended

into sniffles, Nana gave me one last squeeze before hauling herself up off the floor. "You've let it all out, so now it's time to get to the hospital and be the rock your daddy needs. We'll get some answers about what's going on." She held out a hand to pull me up, which I took gratefully. "Go grab a book or two and meet me at the car."

Nana might be a spitfire, but she always showed up when I needed her.

Smithson County General Hospital was just off the highway on the edge of the county line. Even seeing the sign at the road was enough to make my heart skip a beat. I vividly remembered the day we rushed Mama to the hospital when she woke up clutching her chest because she couldn't breathe. Even though she was meticulous about my own doctor's appointments and checkups, Mama never went to the doctor herself and hadn't mentioned to any of us when she started having chest pain and heart palpitations. Although we all noticed when she started feeling fatigued more often, she chalked it up to the busy holiday season we had at The Comfy Cushion that year. By the time she woke Daddy up because she was unable to breathe, the doctors said she was already too advanced in her heart failure to do much of anything. Turned out she had been diagnosed with dilated cardiomyopathy, a somewhat rare complication from pregnancy and childbirth, shortly after I was born but hadn't done any follow up with the cardiologist like the hospital advised. Mama wanted to put blinders on and will the problem away. By the time she realized she couldn't rely on a miracle, it was too late.

The hospital was still as cold and sterile now as it was then. Stark white walls coupled with the bitter chemical smell of cleaning solvents made the atmosphere unwelcoming.

Everyone in the lobby looked as though they were waiting for bad news, their faces drawn and haggard in the harsh fluorescent lights. A shiver ran down my spine, from fear or from nostalgia. Nana tucked her arm through mine and navigated us to the front desk where she asked for Daddy's room.

Daddy looked every inch a corpse when I drew back the curtain in the emergency room bay, laying with his back flat on the bed, eyes shut and face gray. All the lights were off and the steady beeps from the monitors were low and faint, although it was hard to hear much of anything over Desiree's shrill voice at the nurse's station where she was arranging for Daddy to be admitted. For all their vitriol back at the house, Jeremy and Hillary were nowhere to be found.

Nana pointed to a chair just outside the doorway and indicated she was going to sit there so I could have a moment alone with him. I crept in as quietly as I could, scared to disturb him, but also desperate to have his soft eyes crinkle with a smile while he looked at me.

All the memories of Mama's final days came flooding back, her too weak to even turn her head as I clung to her, begging her not to leave me. I hated seeing him like this and the wave of helplessness that washed over me—again—from the sight of a parent hooked to monitors. It was all too much, and I desperately wished Wes was here to lend me some of his indomitable strength. Daddy had been my rock for so long that I took it for granted I would ever be in this position again.

As gently as I could, I wrapped my hand around his, finding his skin cool to the touch. His breathing sounded shallow and labored, like it hurt even to expel the air. Tears leaked out of the corners of my eyes despite how hard I tried to hold them back. Crying didn't do anything for Mama, so there was no way they'd do any good now for Daddy, but I was too overcome with fear to do anything else.

"I need you, Daddy," I whispered, leaning down close to his ear to ensure Desiree didn't hear me. "Please be okay."

The curtain swung back loudly and Desiree stalked in, followed by two people in scrubs and my stepsiblings. Nana's worried frown was visible in the doorframe behind them. The hospital workers started to adjust wires and lock the steel rails on both sides of the bed to prepare him for transport.

"Is it a private room?" Desiree barked at the gentleman closest to her.

"Room 615, yes, ma'am," he replied anxiously. Both of them were scrambling about like their livelihoods depended on it.

We followed them out and turned to the right towards a larger hallway where the elevators were located. I planted myself at Nana's side and swiped the tears from my cheeks as quickly as I could. A private room sounded expensive and unnecessary, but perhaps that was Desiree's way of coping with her own anxiety. Glancing at Nana, I noted her forehead was wrinkled in concern and her lips molded into a firm line. I decided it wasn't worth asking and worrying her further.

Once we got settled into Daddy's new room on the sixth floor with a large window, en suite bathroom, and full couch, there was nothing to do but wait. Desiree stayed on her phone, only pausing to occasionally glare at me. She and her children claimed the couch, which made my blood boil. Nana didn't have the best knees and didn't deserve to stand. I flagged down a nurse outside and requested a chair for her after a while. Without anywhere else for me to go, I slid onto the floor to sit across from Daddy's hospital bed.

Hours passed and although none of the alarms went off from the many monitors, Daddy's breathing didn't improve and he didn't wake up. I started to nod off against the leg of Nana's chair when a tall doctor swept into the room with a clipboard and Daddy's chart.

"I'm Dr. Nielsen," he said, speaking low so as to not disturb Daddy. "Who all do we have here?" His eyes were kind, but there was a weariness to his expression that told me he had long since accepted the sadness of his occupation.

"My name is Desiree Stanbrooke, soon to be Mrs. Hendricks." Desiree held out the hand with her engagement ring as if the doctor needed proof of her statement. "These are my children."

Nana cleared her throat loudly, sending a stern glare my stepmother's way. "This is Celeste, his daughter. I'm his mother."

"Former in-law," Desiree interjected quickly.

Nana drew herself up to her full height, all five feet two. "He's been like a son to me since he met my Rachel almost 25 years ago," she retorted. "He hasn't even known you six months."

Dr. Nielsen glanced uncomfortably between the two women, sizing up who it would be best to address. The tension was thick enough to suffocate a cat, both Nana and Desiree shooting each other looks meant to incinerate. He swallowed thickly before continuing.

"I am going to run more tests," explained Dr. Nielsen. "Given the frequency and the potency of these migraines, I have some concerns and want to rule out anything more severe."

"More severe?" I echoed as knots twisted my stomach.

He winced and wouldn't meet my eyes fully when he replied, "There could be other causes of pain this bad."

The rest of his words were drowned out by the roaring in my ears. I remembered the doctor saying something similar about Mama when she was first admitted to the hospital. It was all too reminiscent of her downward spiral and the de ja vu I was experiencing made the walls cave in. The air in the room was suddenly stifling as cold sweat trickled down my back. I needed to escape, needed to breathe, needed to go back to last night before any of this happened and I was safe in the rapture of Wesley's puppy love.

I could hear Nana's voice calling my name from a distance, but it sounded muffled, like it passed through a series of air vents to get to me. Nothing could make me stay in that room a second longer. Frantically, I ran down the hall, dodging nurses along the way, before bursting into the small waiting area next to the elevators and emptying my guts into the small trash can there. Since I had barely eaten anything in the past 24 hours, it was mostly acidic bile that burned its way up my throat.

When it turned into a sputtering cough, I dropped into a plastic chair and wiped my mouth on the back of my hand. My hearing returned to normal, so when a nurse with a look of concern came to ask me questions, I assured her I was fine. More than anything, I wanted Wesley's megawatt smile to shine on me and take the pain away. Even though he had never been through anything like this with a parent, Wes was the only person who would understand how this shook me to my very core.

My legs were wobbly as I slowly walked back to Daddy's room. Nana was talking to someone in scrubs at the nurse's station in the center of the hall and did not see me as I skirted past. Just outside of Daddy's door that was cracked open an inch or two, Desiree's steely voice wound through.

"That good for nothing, little brat is the reason he's in here and then she doesn't even have the decency to stay!" my stepmother hissed.

"Where did she go? It's not like she can drive," Jeremy asked.

A snort that sounded like it came from Hillary echoed from the room. "Probably out with Wesley Madden again. He has a chauffeur to drive him around, doesn't he?" There was more than a hint of jealousy in her tone.

"I'll make it clear to the staff that Celeste and that meddlesome old lady aren't allowed in here anymore," Desiree huffed. "And I'll make sure Wesley keeps his distance from her. It's all about *who* you know, Hillary. Remember that. Celeste Hendricks will be nothing but a distant memory by the time I'm done."

The injustice of it all rankled beneath my skin. At fifteen, I had no authority over anything and there was nothing I could do. Even Nana couldn't push the issue too much, if she even believed me in the first place. My stepmother-to-be had all the power right now, and she knew it.

My shoulders slumped as I leaned back against the wall. I had nowhere else to go.

CHAPTER 14
PROBLEM SOLVING FEELS GOOD

WESLEY

THE GLASS DOOR to The Comfy Cushion all but swung off its hinges with the force of my entry. Blinds rattled against the metal frame, but I didn't bother to shut it behind me. I hadn't heard from Celeste in over 24 hours and I was prepared to wait in the restaurant all day in order to speak to her. Today might be the first day of school, but I wasn't going without her at my side.

There wasn't a doubt in my mind that Desiree was the one keeping us apart. She was just like every other slimy woman who saw dollar signs whenever she looked at my father. The only difference was that Desiree had her claws hooked into Mr. Hendricks, which made no sense to me. Although The Comfy Cushion was always swarming with people, the Hendricks family certainly didn't live the high life like my father did. It was unlikely they had the kind of money a woman like that coveted.

Still, Desiree's act didn't fool me. She was cashing in on poor Mr. Hendricks somehow, it was just a matter of discovering it. Regardless of her interactions with Celeste's dad, I'd be damned if Desiree kept me from Celeste. We had been apart all summer; there was nothing that was gonna come between us now. I had done my fair share of the respectful schtick that Celeste insisted upon, but everyone in this town was in for a rude awakening if that spiteful bitch tried to keep her from me. River's Run wouldn't just get a scene, they'd get the whole Broadway musical.

Feeling particularly feisty from my built up anxiety, I slammed my hand down on the little counter bell to alert everyone in the back of my presence. Marla's head poked out from the kitchen, shooting daggers at me before she stomped out.

"Did you forget your manners while you were out globe-trotting, Wesley Madden?" she hissed through her teeth. "Don't you dare come barging in here and causin' a ruckus like that!"

Marla was actually pretty great, one of those rare adults where her sass meant she well and truly cared about you. She had given me more than a handful of verbal lashings since I first landed in town, and I had come to value her opinion nearly as much as Nana's and Mr. Hendricks'. My conscience —which I had come to picture as a Jiminy Cricket version of Celeste—was screaming at me for talking to Marla like this, but my rage was drowning it out.

"Where. Is. She?" The glare I served was intended for someone else, but Marla was the only one available.

Her jaw popped open as her eyebrows receded under her bangs. *Yeah, my audacity was surprising me, too, Marla.* She came out from behind the counter and yanked on my elbow so that I was forced to follow her over to the corner of the restaurant, away from the other patrons who were looking on with unabashed interest.

"I don't know what you're trying to pull here, Wes, but it

ain't gonna get you what you want!" Marla whisper-shouted at me.

I rolled my eyes and looked away from her. At that moment, I'd look at just about anything if it meant I didn't have to see her disappointment at my behavior. Jutting out a hip, I folded my arms across my chest and huffed out a long breath. The lie I was about to deliver already tasted sour in my mouth. "I don't really care what you think, Ms. Marla," I ground out. "Where is Celeste? That bitch is keeping her from me!"

Marla's body visibly softened, enough so that I dared to look her in the eye. Her look of pity was so reminiscent of all my old shrinks back in Atlanta that I turned and slammed a fist on the counter just to let out a fraction of the wrath overtaking my common sense. From the corner of my eye, Marla startled at my outburst, one hand clutching her chest.

Pacing like a caged bull, I didn't offer her an apology, only an explanation. It was hard enough to admit the thoughts out loud that my voice broke at the end. "Desiree found me in bed with Celeste. I swear on my life that nothing happened! We just fell asleep! But Desiree flipped her lid and swore she was gonna keep us apart, and now I haven't been able to get ahold of Celeste all day. Something's wrong, Marla, I can feel it."

She frowned at me. "It's never okay to speak about an adult like this, Wesley. Doug would be downright insulted to hear you talk about his future wife that way! Just because you got in trouble doesn't give you permission to carry on like you're a king! However…given the circumstances…" Marla trailed off and noisily cleared her throat. It was then I noticed her eyes were welling with tears and I felt like the world's biggest douchebag. I never wanted to make Marla cry.

It brought me up short. "I'm sorry, Marla!" I said in a panic. "Please don't cry!"

She shook her head as she wiped a tear from her cheek. "It's not you," she replied tearfully. "Doug has been in the hospital since yesterday morning. Celeste is still there right now."

The rest of the world faded to black in that moment. It was sad that Mr. Hendricks was sick, I admit, but it didn't hold a candle in comparison to what I knew Celeste had to be feeling. She needed me, and that was the only thing I could focus on right now.

"What hospital are they at?" I demanded, my voice thin and tight like even that was stretched to my breaking point. So much rage swirled beneath the surface that I might detonate like a bomb.

"Smithson County General," Marla said. "You should know, it's…it's where Rachel died."

I let out a bellow of frustration as I turned on my heel to storm out of the restaurant. Someone should have told me the minute Celeste had to step foot back in that building. Nothing good could ever come from her reliving that trauma. Everyone around us might be adult in age, but they were infants in maturity and understanding when it came to that girl.

Aunt Shirley might not be willing to take me since it was the first day of school, but I would charge whatever an Uber driver requested on my dad's credit card if it meant they got me to the hospital.

It took me less than half the time it normally did for me to storm inside Shirley's house. She popped up from her recliner in alarm. I must have been terrifying because she drew back from me with a gasp.

"Wesley! What's happened?"

"I need a ride to the hospital. *Now*," I added pointedly. "If you don't take me, I'll find another way to get there."

"But why? Are you hurt?" She squinted as she checked my body for open wounds or visible bones.

I shook my head. "Celeste is, so I need to go. Right now!"

Aunt Shirley jumped again at how loudly I cried out the last part, but she immediately grabbed her old purse and car keys from their table by the front door. I followed her outside and dove into the passenger seat behind her. The downside to her transportation was that Aunt Shirley could barely handle driving the speed limit and frequently had cars go around her because she was so slow, but I needed that extra couple minutes to get a grip on my feelings. While Celeste would be glad to see me, she wouldn't take too kindly to a rage-induced outburst.

That didn't stop my head from sending me horrible ideas at lightning speed the entire drive there. Images of Celeste huddled and scared in the corner of a hospital room. Montages of her crying next to her dad's bed. I was sure Desiree was there, too, meaning Celeste probably had to deal with her nastiness in addition to worrying over her dad. However, I made her dad a promise yesterday, and I intended to keep it.

When Aunt Shirley pulled up in front of the hospital, I didn't even wait for her to stop before I was barreling out and through the glass doors. A receptionist at the desk raised her eyebrows at me when I yelled, "Doug Hendricks' room, now!"

The smiling ducks on her shirt mocked me, their cartoon eyes bright and cheerful. Who wore ducks as a grown woman anyway? Her name badge was partially covered by a lumpy sweater that looked to be two sizes too big.

"Sir, that's not how we do things at this hospital," she said firmly. "You don't get to yell at any of our staff."

I rolled my eyes and plastered on a fake smile that was probably equal parts smile and sneer. "I need to know which room Doug Hendricks is in."

"Are you family?"

I blinked at her like she was an idiot. Which she was. "I'm his daughter's boyfriend. She needs me."

The woman's entire disposition changed and she gripped her hands to her chest while making gooey eyes at me. I drew back in disgust as she cooed, "Aww! That's absolutely adorable!"

"Yeah, call it whatever you want, lady, I just need to know where she is." My irritation was spiraling.

She gave me a saccharine smile that she must have stolen straight from the HR training video on difficult patients. "I'm sorry, I can't give you that information. Family only."

Both of my hands smacked the counter at the same time, startling her and wiping the sadistic smile off her face. "Did you not hear me? I am dating his daughter! I *am* family! Where is the room?!" My voice echoed off the walls, making more than one person stop and stare.

The lady's eyes were about to pop out of her head if they got any wider. "Sir, I need you to keep your voice down or security will have to be called."

"So call 'em! Hell, call the damn hospital director and let them know that the Madden Enterprises will be making a generous donation as long as you tell me where my fucking girlfriend is!"

The woman opened her mouth to give me another de-escalation tactic before a tiny, fragile voice cut through them all.

"Wes?" Celeste's eyes were rimmed with red and entirely gaunt in her face. She was holding a paper coffee cup and looking at me in a way that said she wasn't sure if I was corporeal or a hallucination. There were several feet between us as she stood off to my left in a lobby area of sorts, but I crossed the distance in two strides to scoop her up into my arms. Only once I could feel her arms wrap around my neck did the vice grip of rage loosen on my heart. Now everything was right with the world again. And if I needed to call the damn Georgia Surgeon General myself to oversee Mr. Hendricks' care and ease a bit of the tension I could feel in Celeste's tiny frame right now, I would do so happily.

Drawing back, I gently kissed her forehead and took the hand not holding coffee in my own. "What's going on, Celeste? I've been calling you all night, scared out of my mind. Marla told me y'all were here."

She nodded, but the halfway vacant expression didn't leave. "Yes, Daddy's sick." She began walking slowly towards the elevators, pulling her hand from mine to grip the coffee cup tighter.

Okay, what the fuck was going on? Celeste *never* dropped my hand. The situation must be a lot worse than I thought.

"Sir, you need a visitor badge—" Happy Duck Lady called out from behind the receptionist desk.

"Yeah, thanks for the offer. Catch you next time!" I snapped back, rushing to catch up with Celeste.

She moved as if in a daze, waiting for the full elevator to evacuate passengers before getting on and pressing for the sixth floor. Her eyes were staring off into space and it was then that I noticed her wrinkly clothes and messy hair, indicating she had, in fact, been here all night. I wondered if I could give Marla enough of an apology over the phone that she'd run fresh clothes and toiletries out here.

"Celeste, please tell me what's going on." I hated the pleading tone in my voice, but this was beyond my range of comprehension. Celeste was always smiling and full of life. I didn't know how to interpret this shell of herself.

"Um…it might be easier for Nana to explain," she offered. "I'm not sure I totally understand yet myself."

Shit. That couldn't be a good sign.

On the sixth floor, we found Nana in a small lobby area near the elevators. Celeste handed her the cup of coffee, which she accepted with a wane smile. She didn't say a word against my presence, only nodded to me in greeting.

Celeste sat down in a hard chair on her left, but I kneeled down in front of Nana and tried my best to keep my face kind. "Can you tell me what happened? Celeste didn't know how to explain."

Nana sniffled. "They think Doug may have a brain tumor. Their imaging isn't too great here, so they're seeing about sending him to the bigger hospital in Savannah, I think. It all sounds expensive and scary." She absentmindedly rubbed Celeste's knee and offered her a small smile of reassurance, as if any could be found.

Expensive and scary, huh? I could fix that. Without a word, I stood up to kiss Celeste on the forehead and went out into the hall towards the bathrooms I spotted in an alcove opposite the elevators. The men's room was empty, not that I gave a shit, but then again, Mr. Hendricks wouldn't want anyone to know what I was about to do.

"Phillip," I barked out as soon as I heard the line click. "I need you to make arrangements for a patient named Doug

Hendricks to be moved to Emory University Hospital. I want the best doctors they have. Pay them to give all their other patients to someone else. Mr. Hendricks is the only one they care about until he's better, understand?"

He sighed on the other end of the line. "Your father isn't going to like this, Wesley."

I snorted. "My father isn't even going to notice, but nice try on the guilt trip. Just make it happen. I want transportation arrangements from Smithson County General to Emory within the hour. Oh, and we'll need the jet to get his family up there, too."

"Gee, anything else?" The sarcasm in his voice made me want to throttle him.

"Yes, they'll need a VIP suite at the closest hotel to the hospital. Anything they want or need. This is important to me, Phillip." The gravity of the situation finally hit me and I choked up a bit on his name, trying to hold back what felt like tears. I hadn't cried since the Fourth of July when I shared my first kiss with Celeste.

His sigh this time was a bit softer, as if he actually cared about my feelings. "I'll make it happen, but Wes, I can only keep your dad out of the loop for so long. I can't throw his name around without it getting back to him."

"Yeah, well, when have I ever asked for anything?" I argued. "I'll be coming with the Hendricks family, so he can tell me off in person. That oughta make it worth his while."

Phillip snorted and tried to cover it up as a cough. "The jet is on its way to the Savannah airport now to pick everyone up. I'll text you info on Emory within the next 30 minutes."

"Good." I didn't bother thanking him as I hung up.

Out in the waiting room, Celeste was still sitting next to

Nana, her eyes glossy and vacant. I squatted down in front of her, gently cupping her cheek to force her to look at me.

"Hey, Lovebug," I whispered with a soft smile. "I'm gonna take care of this, okay? Your dad is gonna get through this, and I'll be with you every step of the way."

This was enough to finally get through to her and she returned my smile with a watery one of her own. She looped her arms around my neck, taking a deep inhale against my shaggy hair, and whispered, "I love you."

My sap of a heart melted at those three little words. It meant something when they came from Celeste's lips. She said them with conviction, like every fiber of her being believed in their absolute truth. I would drain every penny from my dad's bank account if it meant I could show her just how much I loved her in return.

"Come on, let's go see your dad and let him know he's gonna be moved." I laced my fingers through hers and pulled her up beside me. From the corner of my eye, I swore I saw Nana grin at the sight of our hands, but she dropped it too quickly for me to be sure.

"Am I invited, too?" Nana quipped.

I held out my other arm for her. "You get my best side," I offered.

The three of us went down the hall towards what must have been Mr. Hendricks' room. Desiree and her two kids were inside, Hillary perking up and fluffing her hair as soon as she saw me. Mr. Hendricks was sitting up in bed, with a wire looped into his nose to help him breathe, and an IV plugged into his right elbow. A doctor stood on the other side of his bed, who glanced at us briefly before turning back to Desiree. She looked flustered and angry.

"I don't understand!" she whined. Actually whined, like a

damn toddler. Jesus take the wheel because my patience left the car. "What do you mean 'there's been a change in plans'? Why isn't he being sent to Savannah?"

"Because I want the best care possible for Mr. Hendricks and that ain't gonna happen in Savannah," I interrupted snidely. Unlooping my arm from Nana, I held out my hand to the doctor instead. "I'm Wesley Madden, Benedict Madden's son."

The doctor's eyes widened in surprise and he vigorously shook my hand. "Please thank your father for his generosity to our hospital. All of Mr. Hendricks' files have already been sent to Emory. The helicopter should be here shortly for transport."

I smirked at the gaping hole Desiree's mouth made as her jaw dropped. Her shock quickly morphed into something else, a mix of jealousy, anger, and resentment. She regained her composure enough to smooth back Mr. Hendricks hair.

"Wesley, *you* did this?" Mr. Hendricks asked.

Leveling him with a look, I replied, "I keep my promises, sir."

Realization dawned and Mr. Hendricks nodded slowly. "Thank you, Wes. Hopefully I'll have a chance to thank your dad, too. I don't mean to be so much trouble."

"Of course you're not any trouble, darling!" Desiree cooed, mussing the pillows behind him. "Everyone wants to take care of you!"

The doctor looked uncomfortable as he shuffled on his feet. "Well, I'll send the nurse in with the paperwork to sign off on the transfer. The paramedical flight staff should be here shortly to prep you. I assume other transportation arrangements have been made for family?" A glance to Desiree and then to me left the room in an awkward silence.

If there was a perfect moment to exemplify just how much Celeste Renee Hendricks changed me as a person, this was it. Every bone in my body wanted to drop Desiree like a bad habit and let her fend for herself. She didn't deserve to fly on my father's private jet, nor receive any of the accommodations Phillip made at what was sure to be a five star hotel suite. I wanted nothing more than to throw in her face the fact that I had the money and means to take care of Mr. Hendricks while pampering Celeste in the process. The idea of Desiree cursing my name as Celeste, her nana, and I drove off in a sleek car that left her in the dust sent physical jolts of joy to my chest.

But as I looked down at Celeste's sweet face, her eyes brimming with hope and tears, I knew I couldn't do that to her. As much as I wanted to drop Desiree and her annoying daughter into a twelve foot pit filled with venomous spiders, Mr. Hendricks chose to make her part of his family. And that meant Celeste considered them family, too.

My jaw clenched together as the two sides of my brain warred with each other, all while keeping my eyes on Celeste. She must have read the change in my expression when one side finally gave in to the other because she offered me a grateful smile as she assured the doctor, "Yes, travel arrangements are made."

Was it my fault if I gave Desiree a smug smirk afterwards? Yeah, probably.

The doctor nodded as though everything was settled and swept from the room, clipboard in hand. Tension wove through the space for a moment. Hillary's eyes were growing wider by the second, darting back and forth between her mother and me in abject horror. It was sickening how she didn't even try to hide her crush. Why were teenage girls always so desperate?

Now, though, all of my attention needed to be on my girlfriend. She looked nearly dead on her feet and even though she would always remind me of an angel, the heavy bags under Celeste's eyes and messy hair couldn't be a good sign. I would make her take a nap on the plane, but for now we could at least run out to her house so she could grab a quick shower and some clothes. Nana, too.

"Mr. Hendricks," I said, letting go of Celeste's hand to step closer to his bedside, "I'm going to take Nana and Celeste home to get ready for the trip to Atlanta. We'll meet you at Emory after you arrive. Have a safe flight, okay? I've got our girl."

Doug's face brightened with a wane smile. "Thank you so much, Wesley. This takes a real load off my shoulders." He tried to shake my hand, but his grip felt weak in mine where the effort to do so taxed him.

"Be sure to thank your father for us, too," Desiree cut in, her voice hard as nails. "After all, he is the one footing the bill for all this, right?" A heavily manicured eyebrow arched in challenge.

Bitch, I thought.

Celeste stepped up to take my place at her daddy's bedside. "I love you, Daddy," she croaked in a whisper. Tears were cascading down her cheeks again, though she tried to brush them away. "You're gonna get better, okay? I just know it!"

He pulled her hand up and placed a soft kiss on top. "From your mouth to God's ears, sugar bee!"

Nana stepped up to say her goodbyes, so I used that as a

reason to grab Celeste's hand again and steer her out into the hallway. Hillary's voice echoed behind me in a panicked whimper, "Mother, I thought you said she had to stay away from him!"

Loud clacking heels sounded behind me as we whirled around to face an incensed Desiree. "You two won't go anywhere without a chaperone *and* Hillary!" she snarled.

From the corner of my eye, I could see Celeste visibly wilt as Desiree's words were enough to squeeze the air out of her. My rage boiled over. Rather than cracking her across her makeup-caked face, however, I rocked back on my heels and poked my tongue out through my cheek as I sized her up.

"So you're willing to let your daughter—who is no blood relation of Mr. Hendricks' *at all*," I emphasized the last two words in case my point didn't come across, "miss her first few days of school because of his illness? What makes you think the school board will allow that?"

Desiree's nostrils flared as her skin grew blotchy. "You two—"

"—Have both had to make up schoolwork for things like this before and have special arrangements in place with the superintendent," I finished smoothly. "He won't bat an eyelash to our request. But for Hillary to do that for a man her mother isn't even married to yet..." I let my voice trail off, wincing for effect. "People are definitely gonna talk. And the rumors won't be pretty. What if the rumors get to the judges of her next pageant?"

I was a dead man, that much was obvious on that hateful witch's face. An angry flush coated her face and neck, and her glare made me think of Medusa. She pointed a long, manicured nail in my face and opened her mouth to deliver another weak threat when Nana came out of the room and joined us at Desiree's side.

"Now, what's all this?" Nana asked. Her gaze locked on me as if she already knew I was the culprit.

This was my saving grace, however. I gave Nana and Desiree both a cocky smile, drawing Celeste's and my clasped hands up across my chest. "Nothing. Celeste and I were just making our way to the car. See you soon, Ms. Stanbrooke."

Once again steering Celeste away, we both power walked to the elevators as fast as was socially acceptable. Nana stayed to talk to a screeching Desiree, so we were able to get in the elevator car without anyone else. Celeste let out a boom of raucous glee the moment the doors closed behind us, then slapped a hand over her mouth.

"Wesley Carter Madden, you are evil!" Her peals of laughter filled the space and I willed myself to commit the sound to memory. A grin spread across my face as I pulled her to my chest, wrapping my arms around her waist and burying my head in her hair. She sighed in contentment as her arms folded around my neck. It was probably the first time she had been able to let go of her fear in the past 24 hours. I wanted to always be the reason she could let go of her heavy feelings. To always be the one she could hold onto with a deep sigh because I was her anchor in the storm. That's what loving her felt like for me.

"We'll get through this," I promised her, pulling back enough to kiss her forehead.

Instantly, her smile melted into a frown and I internally kicked my own ass for spoiling the moment. I pulled her closer to me, one hand gently rubbing her back. The tension in her body softened and by the time the elevator landed on the ground floor, Celeste appeared more relaxed. We walked hand in hand out to the parking lot, pausing only so I could wave at Happy Duck Lady scowling at me from reception.

All I wanted to do was make everything better for Celeste. The helpless feeling was foreign to me; for so long, all I had to do was smile and be present—Celeste was simple like that. A million times better and easier than someone as high maintenance as Hillary. But a serious illness wasn't something I could solve for her by my presence alone. Hell, I didn't even have the right words to say because this wasn't something I had ever experienced before. It wasn't right that the Universe would make someone like Celeste suffer twice with a deathly sick parent, but then again, you can't always escape bad luck. If she was going to have to go through this again, the only thing I could do was make sure she didn't have to go through it alone. And I would damn sure get her father the best medical care my family had access to because Celeste and I both needed Mr. Hendricks around for a good long while yet.

CHAPTER 15
ATLANTA AIN'T FOR THE FAINT OF HEART
CELESTE

THE REST of the day passed in a whirlwind. Nana, Wes, and I went home to pack for a few days in Atlanta, though we weren't entirely sure how long we would be staying. Today should have been the first day of school, but if Daddy was going to be undergoing treatment so far away for the foreseeable future, I had no idea how I was supposed to concentrate on school back home. Nana said we would figure it out once we knew more. She also had the wherewithal to call Marla at The Comfy Cushion with an update. Marla swore up and down it was no trouble, that she would take care of the restaurant for the next few days until we had more answers. She promised to talk to the other waitresses to see if they could pick up more hours this week, too.

"Worst case scenario," Marla added, "we can always change the operating hours and close on the weekends."

My heart dropped to my stomach at the suggestion. Could we afford for the restaurant to be closed like that? Before I could ask Nana, however, Wes chimed in.

"It's normal for business owners to take time off, Lovebug. Your customers aren't going anywhere else."

I cocked my head to the side, peering at him quizzically. "Why do you keep calling me 'Lovebug'?"

Wes shrugged. "If you can be your daddy's sugar bee, you can be my lovebug."

That was another thing to contend with. Desiree was going to lose her mind if she heard Wesley speak to me like that. Not to mention how catty and cruel Hillary could be. I had already fallen out of their good graces, but this seemed more like I was stoking the fire.

Yet feeling love and cherished during something so horrible was also like a lifeline. It kept the darkness at bay that had been gone since I met Wes after Mama's passing. I could see it swirling off in my periphery, waiting to swarm over me and suffocate me in its depths. And I refused to live like that again.

The flight to Atlanta was quick, but mottled with tension. Hillary went into a total meltdown when Desiree told her she wasn't coming with us. She threatened to trash all of Desiree's things while she was gone, screaming and stomping like a toddler. More than once I heard Nana muttering that some kids deserve whippings and Wesley outright labeled Hillary as a diva. I had secondhand embarrassment from watching her.

Oddly enough, though, Desiree stuck to her guns and stated Hillary couldn't come. She made arrangements for Jeremy and Hillary to both stay with their grandparents on their daddy's side until we got back. It gave me a sliver of hope that perhaps something good would come of this as far as Desiree was concerned. Maybe she and I could find some common ground if Hillary wasn't there to make everything a contest.

That all disintegrated the moment Desiree's hateful gaze

fell on me, however. She glanced at Nana as though considering her words with care before whispering, "I'm watching you, Celeste. Never forget that," and then taking a seat in the back of the plane.

I had never been on a plane before to compare it to the Madden family jet, but it was surprisingly spacious and comfortable. We discovered that Nana was a nervous flyer as she white-knuckle gripped both her armrests for the duration of the flight. One side of the plane had seating similar to a couch, which Wesley made me use to nap while using a pillow on his lap. His long fingers stroked my hair the entire time, soothing me enough to actually fall asleep. Wheels up to wheels down (a term I learned from the jovial pilot I met upon boarding) was only 45 minutes. Much faster than we ever could have made it by car.

A sleek black Cadillac Escalade met us right on the tarmac when we landed, complete with a red carpet at the foot of the stairs. Several skyscrapers could be seen in the distance, which already looked intimidating from so far away. There were far more trees than I imagined for a big city, but the airport loomed enormous and imposing ahead of us. Wesley laughed at how big my eyes widened trying to take it all in.

One of Mr. Madden's drivers opened the doors for us, with Desiree insisting on getting in first, and he then loaded our bags into the back. The drive from the airport to Emory University Hospital should have been short given its proximity, but traffic was backed up for several miles. The highway was the largest I had ever seen and there were so many cars on the road that I felt anxiety for the first time in my life from being inside a vehicle. It seemed impossible we wouldn't be involved in an accident from one of the numerous drivers weaving in and out of lanes far too quickly for everyone's own good.

I tried not to gape at it all. I didn't want Wesley to notice my rising panic.

Desiree complained the entire drive. The car was too hot, then it was too cold, and then the high population of the city was the root of all evil in the world. She spoke as if she frequented the area and knew firsthand what went on inside the city limits. Mr. Madden's driver never said a word in response beyond a polite "yes" or "no, ma'am." It made me wonder if he was paid to be silent or if he was so used to someone like Wes' daddy that Desiree's whining rolled right off him like butter. I made a mental note to ask Wesley about it at some point.

When we arrived at the hospital, a man with gorgeous terra cotta skin in a three piece navy suit waited for us at the entrance to the hospital. He had a blue tooth device hooked onto his ear and a tablet in his hand.

Wesley greeted the man with a sardonic smile. "Phillip, you didn't need to spy on me, too. Surely the hospital staff will do enough of that."

Phillip rolled his eyes. "Your father demoted me to being your PA since we are apparently 'so close.'" He used finger quotations as he said it. "Do me a favor and let him know what excellent service I provide you so that I can return to my original position, please."

No one else could have picked up on the faint blush of shame that bloomed across Wesley's cheeks, but I noticed it right away. Taking his hand in mine, I gave it a gentle squeeze of comfort.

"I'm Celeste," I introduced myself, holding out my other hand to shake Phillip's.

That helped bring Wesley back into focus. "Yeah, sorry, I had a brain fart for a second. Phillip, this is my girlfriend, Celeste, and this is her grandmother, Suzanne, and her daddy's fiancée, Desiree." The way he said Desiree's name reminded me of how a child reports finding dog poop in the yard. I had to fight the urge to laugh.

My soon to be stepmother pushed between Wes and me to stand directly in front of Phillip, though she eyed me as she corrected, "Celeste is not his girlfriend. She's not allowed to date. We can do introductions later; I need to see Doug right away."

Emory University Hospital Midtown was bigger than any building I had ever seen. Hallways went on forever, turning into different wings, and there were signs indicating special clinics and medical disciplines for as far as the eye could see. It was overwhelming to take in, especially given the hundreds of people that were hurrying along. And everyone seemed to be hurrying, lending to an atmosphere that felt like its own electric pulse. Thankfully, Phillip knew how to efficiently get to Daddy's room and I didn't need to interrupt the flow of traffic by asking for directions I'd never be able to follow.

Once inside, we found Daddy already sitting up with another IV hooked into the vein in his elbow. The lights in the room were dim, but I could tell it was significantly bigger than Smithson General. There was a separate seating area that had a kitchenette along one wall and an enormous bathroom with a marble tub. Everything looked sleek and modern, more high tech than anything I had ever seen. The flat screen tv's (yes, there were multiple) were all bigger than the television we had back home. Floor to ceiling windows provided a panoramic skyline of downtown Atlanta, but there was some sort of screen behind the glass that darkened the view. A woman in a plain gray dress was holding a tablet in front of Daddy and explaining the different functions as we entered.

Desiree's eyes narrowed on the woman, who looked to be approximately 25 years old or so, and had very pretty curls cascading down her back. The woman did not look back at us or stop her explanation. Desiree made a great fuss over clearing her throat and adjusting the neckline of her top before she rushed to my daddy's side with an emotional, "Darling!" She all but cooed as she rounded the bed to stand across from the woman and pepper his face with kisses. I noticed with disgust that they left lipstick residue on his cheeks.

"And...you are?" Desiree coldly asked the woman.

Wesley snorted low beside me, shaking his head in disbelief.

None of it seemed to phase the woman, however. She flashed Desiree a bright smile and held out her hand. "As I was explaining to Mr. Hendricks, my name is Willow and I am his personal concierge for the duration of his stay. I will attend to anything and everything Mr. Hendricks needs so that he can focus solely on feeling better. There's no need to fret when I'm around!" Willow turned her bright smile on Daddy and if I knew how to gamble, I'd be willing to bet that Daddy blushed a little in response.

Pure, unadulterated hatred spread across Desiree's heavily manicured face. "We won't be needing your services," she seethed. "Doug has me...his fiancée." Ever so casually, Desiree's diamond ring slid down Daddy's arm until it was front and center in Willow's face.

I've seen dogs and cats piss to mark their territory more

times than I could remember. It never occurred to me that humans needed to do the same thing.

Willow's smile never broke, though, I'll give her that. She nodded and enthusiastically gushed, "Congratulations on the upcoming nuptials! However, I will be staying until Dr. Hassan says otherwise as my services are required by the Madden family." She turned to give the rest of us a friendly wave, nodding to Phillip as though they were already acquainted, then provided Daddy with another even brighter smile. "I'll be right back with some refreshments for you and your guests, Mr. Hendricks!"

As soon as the door closed behind her, Desiree's eyes flashed. "Douglas Hendricks, were you just *flirting* with that simpering idiot right in front of me?!"

For once, Daddy didn't rise to her screeches and instead turned towards me. "Sugar bee! I've got a hug here with your name on it!"

A sob involuntarily escaped my throat as I threw myself into his waiting arms. I let the smell of Daddy, that Georgia pine flavor, wash over me and allowed myself to hope for just a moment that everything could be okay. Yes, we were in a fancy hospital in a big city to seek treatment for a brain tumor. But in that hug, I could pretend to be six years old again and allow my daddy's presence to assure me that we were all safe.

"Mr. Hendricks, if it's alright with you, I'd like to take Celeste back to my house so she can get some real sleep in one of our guest rooms. Nana, too," Wesley's voice cut in.

I pulled away to look at him in surprise. "We don't have to stay here at the hospital?"

Phillip held up the tablet. "I have made arrangements for the family to have the penthouse suite at the Four Seasons hotel nearby, and I am available to take anyone there whenever you would like. Dr. Hassan is scheduled for Mr. Hendricks' consultation at 4 p.m. after Emory has completed all of their initial testing so there are updated results for Dr. Hassan to examine."

"He already had tests done!" snapped Desiree. She looked angry almost, enough that I took a step away from Daddy. What had her so wound up?

"Oh, but our machines are much more advanced!" Willow announced as she returned to the room with a rolling cart covered with finger food on a white linen cloth. She wheeled everything closest to Daddy and whispered conspiratorially, "I'll make you a plate first since you're the man of the hour!"

Daddy giggled. My grown father actually *giggled*.

Desiree started to open her mouth, but Daddy cut her off. "It's okay, sweetheart. Let Willow ease some things for us. And Wes, I think that's a great idea, as long as Nana can chaperone."

"Doug!" Desiree scolded in alarm.

"Honey, you heard Phillip. I'm about to go sit through a bunch of tests anyway. All of you should go get some rest. You can't do me a lick of good pacing in here like a caged lion." He took her hand in his and gave it a reassuring squeeze. "I'll be okay for a few hours. And then you can come back in time for the doctor, right, Phillip?"

The assistant nodded. "Absolutely. I will ensure all your needs are met."

Desiree huffed in annoyance, but didn't say another word. Her eyes were calculating as they swept up and down Willow's form before planting a deep kiss right on Daddy's mouth. I gagged in response and turned to join Wesley. Nana followed close at my heel, mumbling about jealous women.

We made our way out to the elevators and down through the labyrinth of hallways to the same black Escalade waiting by the curb. Once again, the driver opened the door for us, nodding to Wesley.

"Don't we need to wait for Desiree?" I asked as we pulled away from the curb.

"Phillip has his own car that he'll transport her in," Wesley assured me.

I realized belatedly that our hands were still intertwined and resting on his knee. Nana already looked to be half asleep in the seat beside me. She leaned back against the headrest and allowed her eyes to close, a soft snore confirming my suspicions.

The sights of downtown Atlanta could wait. The chance to see Wesley's home was what excited me at that moment. While he had never sounded particularly fond of it, I knew Wesley spent most of his time there alone since his father was always gone on business. His life before River's Run fascinated me and I hoped to learn more about it while we were here. It was a welcome distraction from what awaited us back at the hospital later.

Wesley didn't wait for the driver to open the door when the Escalade pulled up in front of a shiny black skyscraper that stretched towards the clouds. Even with my neck craned all the way back, I couldn't see the top. He led us through glass doors that two men in crisp white jackets held open for us. Three other men in similar jackets were stationed behind a desk made of black, jagged granite. A glass mosaic with a waterfall cascaded behind them, identifying the building as the M Tower. Although I could see a lobby with four elevators just behind the waterfall, Wesley turned to the left and went through a door that blended in perfectly to the wall.

A sleek gray vestibule surrounded us in front of another elevator. This one had a blue screen on the wall next to it, but no buttons to go up or down. Nana hovered in the doorway behind me, her eyes as wide as mine surely were, too.

"Sorry, Nana, I can't scan us up if that door is open," Wesley told her apologetically. She scooted in closer, firmly closing the door behind her, and Wesley let go of my hand to place his on the blue screen. It scanned his entire palm and then the doors opened to an elevator with wood paneling, carpet, and a loveseat.

I gave Wesley a side eye of inquisition before he grinned sheepishly at me as Nana settled into the seat behind us. "It's a security measure," he explained. "My father didn't want anyone to have access to our penthouse. No one can scan in if the door is open because it would be all too easy for someone to sneak inside and jump on the elevator uninvited."

Nodding as if it made sense, I glanced back at Nana and found her just as awestruck as I was.

The ride to the top was otherwise silent and quick. I never would have known it was an elevator otherwise. I assumed all of them were as clunky and loud as the ones back in River's Run, but this was efficient and quiet. When it stopped, we stepped out into a similar gray vestibule as below, only larger with a small seating area and a few flower arrangements on glass tables. Another scanner was on the wall next to a sleek wood panel door that opened after Wesley placed his hand on the screen.

Stepping into his home caught me off guard, though I had no idea what to expect. None of it looked real. We walked into a three story living room of glass and white. Windows on both sides were so crystal clear that I was momentarily afraid someone could fall out to their death. A white marbled fireplace roared to life as Wesley stepped further inside, which would have been cozy had it been surrounded by furniture that looked lived in. The circular couch was white leather with a glass coffee table in the middle. Far beyond, I could see an enormous kitchen that opened into the joint dining/living area. The cabinets were all sleek white, shiny enough to reflect the lights hanging from the ceiling, and I knew my mama would have put the stainless steel appliances to good use. The white marble island was large enough to seat ten people, as evidenced by the white leather barstools perfectly posed around it.

As I took it all in, I realized there were no photographs or paintings. No shirts or shoes anywhere, no blankets to curl up with, or any real signs of life. While the entire ambiance was imposing, it grew less impressive as I looked around. It almost felt sterile, like a scene from a catalog meant to feature the items displayed. There were no movie nights or family board games going on in a room like this.

Wesley looked nervous, worrying his bottom lip in a way I rarely saw. He turned around with his arms spread out, half-heartedly explaining, "So this is it."

Nana had the good grace to pat him gently on the shoulder. "It's very nice, young man, but I'm gonna fall asleep standing up soon, so why don't you show me where I can hunker down for a bit."

Wesley smiled warmly. "Of course, Nana. This way."

He led us down a hallway behind the kitchen that followed a line of clear windows. I realized as we walked that there was actually a glass encased terrace outside, with small glass tables and chairs place periodically along as if at any given moment someone would want to step out to admire the view. As he walked, Wesley gestured to closed doors to say things like, "Here's the gym," or "This is the game room."

At the end of the hall, it opened into what Wesley called the den. This area looked far more lived-in, with a plush couch, a large screen television mounted on the wall, and several candles that already had burned wicks. A small side table had a display of trophies while a few plaques hung on the wall above it. There were four closed doors along one wall, and a black spiral staircase to my left led up to another level of the penthouse.

"It's only my dad's stuff up there, so I wouldn't bother with it," Wes offered when he caught me peering up the stairs. "This is primarily the area I stay in whenever I'm here. Nana, you can rest in here."

Wesley opened the door on the far left and my jaw dropped. It was a bedroom bigger than the entire downstairs of my house. The four poster bed actually had silk curtains hanging that perfectly matched the silk bedspread. It faced out towards another wall of windows that had a matching private terrace. On the opposite end of the room, I could just make out a large bathtub beyond the open doorway.

"There should already be fresh towels and things in there," Wes said, gesturing towards the bathroom. "And feel free to hang anything up in the closet or put things in the drawers. If you'd like to watch tv, you can press this button and the tv will come up." He picked up a tablet from the nightstand and showed Nana the icon to press. What I had assumed was a hope chest at the foot of the bed opened up and a flat screen tv rose out of its depths.

Nana whistled. "That's all too fancy for the likes of me, Wesley. Is there a way to put up some drapes or something? It's almost blinding in here."

He grinned at her and pressed another button on the tablet. The windows immediately darkened to almost black, blocking out any view or light from outside. A small row of low lights came to life around the bases of all the furniture, including the bed, making it just enough that you could see where everything was located in the dark. Wes hit a button and the windows returned to normal, flooding the room with sunshine.

"If you hit the button twice, the furniture lights will go out, too." He enveloped her in a hug before retreating towards the door.

I followed, unsure of what to do. Wes said this was Nana's room, implying I would have a room of my own.

Nana noticed my hesitation and put her hands on her hips. "I'm telling y'all right now, there ain't gonna be any funny business, you hear? I'm dead tired and don't want to stay up to keep my eyes on you. Be respectful and don't get into any trouble!" She pointed a finger at me in warning. "I mean it, Celeste. Be a good girl."

I nodded and smiled softly at her. "Of course, Nana. We're all just gonna get some sleep."

"In separate rooms," Wesley added from the doorway.

Nana snorted like she didn't believe us, but turned towards the bathroom anyway. I joined Wesley at the door and my heart did the fluttering thing again when he returned his hand to mine. It was like they were meant to be joined. Lacing my fingers through his felt was a natural extension of myself.

"Now be a good girl," he whispered mischievously. My stomach did a somersault at his words.

Wes pulled me to the door on the opposite end of the wall, furthest from Nana's. "This is my room," he said quietly. He paused just at the threshold, his shaggy blonde hair enveloping him like a halo as he leaned down to kiss me. His lips were firm, but soft, cutting off the kiss before it could deepen into anything more.

I, on the other hand, was barely keeping a grip on my composure or my sanity. My pulse was racing to the point where I wanted to clock it against a metronome. Nana was only a few doors away, so why did it feel like once I crossed through his door, I would be stepping over the line into something far more serious? Wesley's bedroom here was almost sacred, the place where he spent the majority of his time, if his recollections were accurate, and it was the most intimate place I would ever be with him. The walls here were way too thick and if Nana was the only adult in the place, we were basically about to be on our own. Nana slept like the dead on a bad night, and given the emotional chaos of the past couple days, I had no doubt that it would require a nuclear missile to wake her up now.

He opened the door, then stood back to allow me entry first. A light switch flicked behind me and I gasped in shock. The entire right side of the room was floor to ceiling windows, but this room was two stories tall. An oversized red sectional dominated the front half of the room, with a projection screen on the wall in front. Glass stairs led up to a loft area in the far corner and an office set up occupied the space beneath. It was all an open concept, but the office and loft both felt like separate rooms within the room. Tall bookcases lined the wall across from me until it reached a door that opened into a bathroom or closet, I couldn't tell which. The wood floors were so shiny, I could see my own reflection, and when I stepped farther into the room and looked out through the windows, I realized the terrace here was big enough to boast an outdoor kitchen and a rooftop pool. Cabana chairs lined the perimeter that wasn't encased in glass like the others, but had a wall of ivy for privacy.

It took me several moments to catch my breath. "What's up there?" I whispered, pointing to the lofted room at the top of the glass stairs. There was no good reason to be whispering, yet I was too awestruck to speak at a normal register.

Wesley came to stand in front of me, all once awkward and unsure. His voice sounded too throaty and deep as he gulped and replied, "My bed."

My feet moved on their own accord. I could hear the soft pitfalls as he trailed behind me, but I climbed the glass stairs and my heart caught in my throat. The pseudo room was also surrounded on three sides by glass, but it was a white glass you couldn't see through. A bed larger than any I had ever seen was centered in the space, leaving enough room only to walk around the bed with a nightstand on either side. But that wasn't the part that had me stunned. Dozens of our photographs, just Wesley and me, hung from wire and twinkling lights along the ceiling. It looked so much like my tower —even like Wes' bedroom at Aunt Shirley's—that I wanted to cry.

"I just wanted it to feel like home," said Wesley from behind me. I turned to find him standing a respectful distance behind me at the top of the stairs, both hands in his pockets. "And well, anywhere you are feels like that. When I first came home for the summer, I asked Mrs. Aguilar to put this together for me."

That was all it took for my brain to turn to mush and my hormones to throw caution to the winds. I threw my arms around his neck to pull him in for a savage kiss. My fingers threaded themselves through his hair, locking him to me. His resistance dissolved with a groan and he opened his mouth to allow my tongue access. We were in a frenzy of emotions and desire, and when Wesley's hands slid down to grip my backside, I didn't hesitate. My hips pushed into his, craving some kind of friction, and it took an extra few seconds to register the hard length I felt in his jeans.

Before I knew it, my knees were hitting the edge of Wesley's bed and we both fell onto the sheets in a tangled mess. Our lips never broke apart, only sought comfort from the other. Kissing Wesley Madden was like getting to have dessert for dinner. You had to go back for seconds.

One of his warm hands worked its way under my shirt and splayed his fingers across my abdomen. He pulled away just enough to look me in the eye as he asked, "Can I touch you?"

It was barely louder than a breath, but it made my ears roar. My body was no longer my own, so alive from all the fantasies in my head of what I wanted Wes to do to me. I finally understood why Mama said girls could lose their minds over boys...what girl wouldn't go crazy over him?

I nodded frantically and pulled my shirt over my head in one swoop. For a split second I worried that my boobs were too small and disappointing, or that my simple white bra from Madden Markets wouldn't be sexy enough, but as soon as Wesley's eyes landed on my chest, all my insecurities vanished. His pupils were practically blown out as he gazed in wonder at my newly budded breasts.

"Is this okay?" he inquired in a reverent tone as his hand cupped the outside of my bra.

It wasn't enough. I needed more. The heaviness of his hand on the outside would never satisfy the raw ache building in my core. Leaning up to kiss him again, I guided his hand inside my bra to feel my erect nipple. He moaned into my mouth, using his long fingers to caress and then pinch my pebbled point.

"Okay, this has to come off!" Wesley pulled the straps off my shoulders, which made me giggle. The boy didn't have a clue how bras worked. I sat up and twisted my arm around to unhook the clasps, letting the bra slide off.

If Wesley looked enraptured at the sight of the bra, he looked damn near mesmerized at the sight of my breasts without it. I could almost see him salivating like the Big Bad Wolf. He pounced on me, kissing me so hard that I fell back onto the bed, both of his hands lacing his fingers through mine as he pinned them above my head. Shifting forward so he was straddling me, he trailed the kisses down my neck and onto my chest. Without warning, I felt his warm tongue twist around my nipple. He opened his mouth enough to suck my entire breast into his mouth before releasing it with a loud pop! and repeating the actions on the other breast.

There was so much wetness gathered between my legs that it should have stained through my jeans. Every part of me felt like it was being traced with a livewire, the electricity jolting with his touch. My hips instinctually rose up, seeking some sort of friction for the feeling building between my legs. His lips on my skin were enough to make me pant and writhe, yet I wanted more.

Wesley peppered his kisses back up to my mouth, letting go of my hands so he could lay down on his side and pull me tight against his chest. I loved the way it felt for my sore nipples to press against his muscles, though I wished he didn't have a shirt on to block the sensation of his skin on mine. He nuzzled his nose against me, letting the kisses grow softer.

"Do you know anything about sex?" he asked me gently.

I frowned. We were nowhere near having sex in this moment, although if it would do something about the sensation growing down there, I wouldn't necessarily be opposed to it.

"This isn't sex, Wes," I reminded him.

He rolled his eyes with a grin. "I know that, Lovebug, but do you know why people have sex?"

My eyebrow arched. His line of questioning didn't make any sense. "Because they love each other?"

Wesley smiled. "When we have sex, it will always be because we love each other."

The certainty in his voice made my heart soar. Like there was never going to be a possibility of us *not* being intimate, it was just a fact of life.

"But you know what an orgasm is?" he continued.

Oh.

"I know people have them when they have sex," I admitted, blushing profusely to be discussing something so personal with Wesley. It was beyond embarrassing. "And according to all of Maggie's magazines, women don't have them as often as men do."

That definitely piqued his interest. "Oh, really?" he said, his voice filled with excitement.

Too uncomfortable to reply, I merely nodded.

Wesley unleashed his full megawatt smile on me, the brilliance of it causing my stomach to bottom out and my knees to quiver. "Challenge accepted," he murmured against my mouth before planting his lips on mine once more.

His fingers started trailing their way down my stomach, firmly, as though he wanted to memorize the way every inch of skin felt beneath his touch. When he got to the waistband of my jeans, there was no hesitation. His hand continued the descent under my panties and I felt a gush of wetness between my thighs. Wesley was going to touch me *there*.

Mama's words from so long ago echoed in the back of my mind. "Your body is rare and delicate," she had told me. "Someday people will want your body. It's important to wait for the person who wants all of you."

Well, Mama, mission accomplished.

I kissed Wesley harder, my tongue roving into his mouth on a breathy exhale as his long fingers parted my pussy. Spreading my knees wider to give him more access, I panted a desperate, "*Yes*," against his lips, making him smile. His pupils were blown out with desire and happiness...and love. So much love.

"I want to have all your firsts," he declared as he sank one digit inside me up to the knuckle. My pussy walls contracted, from the intrusion or the rush of emotions at his words, I had no idea. "Your first kiss, your first boyfriend, your first love," he continued. "And someday, as soon as we're old enough, the first dance at our wedding. Our first baby. All of it. I get them all."

He began a rhythmic circular motion with his finger that felt divine in time to his words. A future with Wesley sounded like heaven. And the fact that he already knew he wanted that kind of future with me—one that included things like marriage and babies—made my heart soar. I knew we were too young, that it was foolish to fantasize about something so far off. But Wesley had a way of making everything seem possible.

His finger pressed further inside me and a second finger joined the first, bringing my thoughts back to the heat of the moment. The wet sounds coming from my pants mortified me on a certain level, but I was too far gone with love and lust to care. Besides, Wesley didn't seem to mind one bit.

"You can have all my firsts," I promised him, pulling his mouth back to mine for another kiss. He increased the tempo, the palm of his hand pressing down on my clit and creating a delightful friction to ease the ache rising from my core. Pressure was building and building until suddenly, his hand slid out one last time and I felt a release so strong I cried out. It was an out of body experience; a subconscious part of me could see the ecstasy on my face as Wesley crooned, "That's it, Celeste! I love you so much!"

I was floating and never wanted to come back down. My body would never be my own again. From here on out, it could only belong to him. Wesley, who wanted me in every way, just like Mama said.

Perhaps that fact sobered me up because I couldn't stop myself from bursting into tears.

"Whoa!" Wesley said in alarm. "What's wrong? Did I hurt you, Celeste?!"

Traitorous tears continued to fall as I shook my head. My cheeks burned with embarrassment, but I couldn't stop. "No," I assured him. "I just wish my mama was here. I want to talk to her about you."

Wesley gave me a tender smile and pulled me into his chest, tucking my head just under his chin. The hand that had just been inside me was now tracing a comforting path up and down my spine. "D'you think I would have your mama's approval?"

A watery laugh slipped out at his question. "Mama would have loved you."

He held me for a couple minutes more before softly whispering, "Then maybe she sent me to you."

CHAPTER 16
A NEW NORMAL MEANS WAR

WESLEY

ONCE CELESTE'S tears turned into low snores, I slid my arm out from under her and found a blanket to cover her. I was glad she was finally getting some real sleep after the turbulence of the past couple days, but my body was poised and ready to strike for no reason whatsoever. Too frazzled to sleep, that was for sure. I headed into my bathroom to take a shower and jerk off some of the incredible energy pulsating through my body.

What we did in there was pure magic. Instinct took over the moment I saw Celeste's permissive smile. A small part of me felt guilty for already breaking a bit of my promise to Mr. Hendricks, but he was a teenager once, too. He couldn't honestly expect that I was going to keep my hands off his daughter when she looked like an angel freeing me from the gates of Hell. Everything with her was so right, so natural, and I didn't care that I sounded like a lovesick idiot when I told her I wanted all of her firsts. It was true. Most important was the fact that she agreed. Celeste Renee Hendricks loved me and we would always be together. It had to be fate because there was no doubt in my mind, even at almost sixteen years old, we were meant to be together.

Handling my father's rage for the large hospital bills that were headed his way was microscopic in comparison. Nothing was going to bring me down right now. It didn't even bother me that I hadn't finished. We had our whole lives ahead of us for that. Celeste needed to know I worshipped her now, before Desiree could mess with her head and make her believe the bullshit that Celeste needed to stay away from me.

After a shower hotter than Satan's ball sack and rubbing out the fastest jerkoff session I've ever had (come on, I saw Celeste's gorgeous tits for the first time), I returned to my room as quietly as a mouse to place a change of clothes next to a fluffy robe and towel on the bedside table for Celeste to find when she woke up. There were a dozen texts from my father on my phone, but I ignored them all to set an alarm for her and left that charging on the table as well since Celeste still didn't have a cell phone.

Stepping out into the hall, I found Mrs. Aguilar, our housekeeper, dusting in the den. She jumped when the door closed behind me and waved the rag in my direction. "Wesley, you scared me!"

"Sorry!" I held up my hands in truce before she sprayed me with the Pledge can.

She eyed me suspiciously. "Did you get kicked out of school again?"

"No! Of course not!" It probably should've bothered me that her automatic reaction to my presence was a school expulsion, but then again, she was always the one who had to go pick me up whenever the principal called. Mrs. Aguilar earned the right to be suspicious. "My girlfriend is in there sleeping. Her grandmother is in the guest room at the end. Her dad had a medical emergency, so I'm just trying to help them out."

Mrs. Aguilar had been with us since I was six years old. While my father never took the time to learn my nuances, she could read me like a book. A fact I was reminded of now as she pinned me with a look that clearly said I needed to have my head examined. "Does your father know you're here?" she asked.

I shrugged, agitated that she would ask. "Wouldn't make a difference if he did, would it?"

She started mumbling under her breath in Spanish about how I was playing with fire as she turned her attention back to the bookcase she was dusting.

"You know I can understand you!" I sighed. "You're the one who taught me Spanish!"

Nodding in agreement, Mrs. Aguilar continued to clean as she replied, "Yes, and I also taught you not to let your guard down with your father. He doesn't like to be crossed!"

My jaw clenched in aggravation, mostly because I knew she was right. "I've got it all under control. He won't even notice they're here."

She nodded in time to the strokes of the cleaning rag. "Just like he won't notice the medical bill? I bet you took it upon yourself to pay?"

Why were all of my father's employees so concerned with him getting the bill? He owned a billion dollar company. It wasn't like paying for Mr. Hendricks' medical care would break the bank.

"It's gonna be fine, Mrs. Aguilar," I insisted.

She folded her arms across her chest as she turned around to stare me down. "It's just the one day?" she pressed.

The question filled me with dread. "Not exactly..." I trailed off, knowing damn well it would be a lot longer than one day.

Hunching her shoulders, Mrs. Aguilar draped the rag over her arm and grabbed the bottle of Pledge before plunking it down in the bucket of cleaning supplies at her feet. "Next time you declare war with your father, you tell me ahead of time. I'll use my vacation days."

As much as I hated to admit it, my housekeeper had a point. There would be a price to pay if I expected my father to hand over the funds. He never did anything for me without strings.

Yet as I glanced back at my closed bedroom door where Celeste could finally sleep soundly in what had to be her worst nightmare, I couldn't summon an ounce of remorse for my actions. Dear old dad would just have to deal.

CHAPTER 17
ROCK BOTTOM AIN'T A
TRAVEL DESTINATION
CELESTE

Sitting up abruptly, it took me a moment to remember where I was. All the photographs looked different and it was probably the most comfortable mattress ever created. A cell phone I recognized as Wesley's continued to ring out a shrill alarm until I hastily crawled across the bed to hit the button. Wes was nowhere that I could see, but that was just as well because I needed to get a handle on myself before I laid eyes on him again.

I meant every word of that promise to let him have all my firsts. Daddy and Nana would both say we were too young and shouldn't be making such promises to each other, but they would be wrong. Young love didn't cancel out true love, and what I felt for Wesley Madden was as true as the stars in the night sky.

My heart ached to share these feelings with Mama. It had been a long time since her ghost haunted me the way it was right now and I wondered yet again what she would have thought of Wes. His statement earlier of Mama sending him to me brought fresh tears because I could definitely see her doing something like that, then teasing me about not letting it go to my head because all her heavenly gifts couldn't be as great as him.

More than anything, though, I yearned for one of Mama's hugs as I spilled my heart over Daddy. If she got to pull strings up there, couldn't she do me a solid and keep his health in check? I kinda needed at least one parent, after all. The thought of losing Daddy now wasn't even worth entertaining. He *had* to get better.

Wesley was considerate enough to leave me a fresh change of clothes and I realized with crippling embarrassment that I never put my shirt back on to sleep. Memories of where his hands had roamed my body made my cheeks burn pink. And as much as I knew it would land me in trouble if any of the adults found out, I didn't regret a single moment of it. I finally understood why Maggie wanted to read every article on tips and tricks for great sex she could get her hands on; I was just as eager to experiment with Wesley's body as I was for him to explore my own.

The thing was, it didn't feel sinful or wrong to share something so intimate with him. He made me feel beautiful, important, cherished, and what could possibly be bad about that? Nana would say that we had our whole lives to go down that road, but between the curveballs from both my parents' health crises, it was pretty obvious to me that life could change in an instant. No point in prolonging a sure thing, in my opinion.

I dressed quickly, stopping in the bathroom to brush my teeth and tame my hair into a top knot. Wes still hadn't reappeared, and although I knew he wouldn't mind, I resisted the urge to poke through his drawers and inspect his shelves. The rumbling coming from my stomach reminded me that what little food I had consumed was thrown up hours ago, so I decided to head to the kitchen first.

Nana and Wesley were both sitting at the immense kitchen island before a platter of giant subs and bowl of cut up fruit. A Hispanic woman wearing an apron was on the other side of the island, rubber gloves up to her elbows as she washed dishes by hand in the wide sink. Wesley's laugh echoed in the large space as I came around the corner.

"Welcome back to the land of the living," he teased me with a grin as I slid onto the barstool beside him.

I glanced at the woman washing dishes who was peering at me with a knowing smile before answering him. "Yeah, that nap was very much needed. Thank you."

Wesley waved a hand towards the woman. "Celeste, this is Mrs. Aguilar. She's our housekeeper."

The woman's smile widened. "Buenos dias, senorita," she said.

I nodded to her with a shy smile. This was the woman who cooked all of Wesley's meals and spent the most time with him as a child. She had the wherewithal to call Mobile Crisis when he freaked out over being sent to Montmeri, from what Wesley told me years ago.

"Hurry up and shove a sandwich down," Nana ordered. "We need to get to the hospital. I wanna know what's going on with your daddy."

By the time I finished eating, there was a buzz at the door that Wesley said meant the driver was ready for us downstairs. This time the drive to the hospital had my stomach twisting in knots, making me clamp my mouth shut in case Mrs. Aguilar's sub made a second appearance. My knee bounced from the restless energy the entire ride, and more than once Wesley placed a gentle hand over mine to urge me to calm down. It didn't work, but I appreciated his efforts.

Nana actually looked worse. Her arms were firmly crossed under her chest and she faintly rocked back and forth in the front seat. She snapped at the driver twice to pick a faster lane, something that was very out of character for her. Both times she apologized to him afterwards and he assured her it was fine. He maintained the same detached composure as he had with Desiree, so it definitely had to be part of his job description.

Desiree was already back inside Daddy's hospital suite when we arrived, wearing far more makeup than normal and a dress that bordered on indecent. While she typically wore dresses and skirts tighter than I thought comfortable, the black number she had on molded to every curve of her body and sported some serious cleavage. Maggie would die to get her hands on that kind of outfit.

"My, my. Look what the cat dragged in," she mocked.

Nana settled into a leather armchair with a loud sigh. "Are we going to a dinner party after this, Desiree? That dress hardly seems appropriate."

My stepmother flushed. "I think I have a far better grasp on what's appropriate here, Suzanne."

Willow swept into the room then, followed by Daddy in a wheelchair pushed by another hospital worker in scrubs. She began adjusting the blinds through the same tablet she had earlier, drawing down the lights so the room was much dimmer. Daddy was slumped over, his head propped up by one hand, and in much lower spirits than when we left him, if his grimace was any indication.

"Oh, Doug!" Desiree cooed, jumping up to fuss over him.

"Don't just stand there!" she barked at the employee behind the wheelchair. "Get him into bed!"

The worker scrambled to obey, hastily putting the brakes down on the chair and guiding Daddy up. He placed one arm against Daddy's shoulder blades when he started to sway.

Willow turned toward Desiree with a frown, hesitating for a moment before she stated, "Ma'am, our staff has everything under control."

Desiree snorted. "Hardly."

She tucked the blankets around Daddy, snapping for the employee to grab another since the ones on his bed were too ragged. They looked more like a duvet than any other hospital blanket I'd ever seen.

"Sweetheart, these people are takin' good care of me," Daddy assured her. His voice was weak and he squinted his eyes when he spoke. "Can we just keep it down? The noise really hurts my head."

"D'you hear that?" Desiree fumed. "You're hurting him!"

Willow gaped at her, at a loss for words.

I glanced at Wesley and found the annoyance clear on his face. He cleared his throat loudly and said, "When is the doctor going to be here? Let's focus on Mr. Hendricks."

Right on cue a short man in a white doctor's coat strolled inside. "Sounds like I am here at the perfect time," he announced jovially. Most of his head was bald except for a ring of gray, closely cropped hair around his ears, and I had to bite back a laugh from the lights reflecting off his scalp. Poor Daddy wouldn't be able to look at the man without it hurting his eyes.

"I am Dr. Hassan," the man continued. "Unfortunately, you will come to hate my name because I come bearing bad news.

Mr. Hendricks, you have what is called a glioblastoma, which is very rapidly growing brain tumor. It originated in your prefrontal cortex, based on your scans, and the growth trajectory is unlike anything I have ever seen. If you take a look here…" Dr. Hassan opened his own tablet to a 3D rendering of Daddy's brain, color coding different parts, but by that point the roar in my ears had returned and rendered my hearing useless.

It couldn't be real. This was the kind of news you heard on a *Grey's Anatomy* episode, not something your family member actually suffered from. Every fiber of my being went numb because the only thought I could form was that my daddy was going to die. Dr. Hassan might be the best doctor on Earth, yet I knew in my bones he couldn't save him.

"What's that all mean, Doc?" Nana cut in. Her voice had a hard edge to it.

Dr. Hassan sighed and shook his head sadly. "It means that our goal is to extend the time you have left to be as comfortable as possible."

Daddy's face fell. "How long?"

The air was somewhat sucked out of the room as I waited for the doctor's answer, a response that would determine the course of my life. Unless he predicted Daddy had a lifetime ahead of him, it wouldn't be nearly long enough.

"As much time as I can buy you, Mr. Hendricks. In a perfect world, as long as a year, if our treatments are successful."

This was another one of the moments that become a core memory. Time stopped so that the only thing that could be heard was the off-brand Muzak playing in the hallway. I wanted to be anywhere but here. None of it could be real.

"Breathe, Lovebug," came Wes' faint voice. "I need you to breathe."

His face was now all I could see, pressed close enough to mine that if I lifted my head a fraction of an inch, we would kiss. It took me an extra few seconds to register that he was tapping his hand on my cheek to get my attention. I was lost in a haze of confusion and disbelief, but my faithful Wesley was out here trying to be an anchor.

Desiree was wailing, overexaggerated laments that would have been expected from Meryl Streep herself. Nana sank into a chair and let the tears stream down her face. Even Daddy was crying, a sight I didn't think I'd see again after losing Mama. Somehow, I wound up on the floor, swaying like a drunken sailor, with Wesley kneeling down to check on me.

"I'm going to give you some time to process everything. No doubt you'll have questions, so I'll check back after a little while." Dr. Hassan swept from the room, gesturing for Willow to follow him out and give us privacy.

His footsteps had long since died down the hallway before I was able to whisper, "Daddy?"

"Oh, sugar bee!" Daddy whimpered, holding his arms wide for me. I dove into them like I was still a five year old little girl who needed her father's presence to scare away the monsters.

Only this monster wasn't one my daddy could slay.

CHAPTER 18
THE EYE OF THE STORM
WESLEY

THIS HAD to be what heartbreak felt like. Mr. Hendricks was going to die and there wasn't shit I could do about that. All the money in the world couldn't make him better, nor could it make Celeste hurt any less. It couldn't make me hurt any less, for that matter. Doug had been more like a father to me in the past two years than my own father had been since conception. He encouraged me to be a better person, guiding me towards good choices, but never once lost faith in me when I lost faith in everyone. I owed him so much that a few hospital bills felt paltry in comparison.

The only brief spark of joy I found in this moment was that he immediately turned to Celeste, not Desiree. His fiancé looked somewhat stunned at this turn of events, no doubt calculating her next step of revenge. It was obvious from a mile away that Desiree viewed Celeste as a threat, not a daughter, and right now it was clear why. At the end of the day, if it really came down to it, Doug would always choose his daughter over her, always put his daughter first, and a woman as jealous and shallow as Desiree couldn't stand it. She needed attention like fish needed water.

Nana stepped up to the hospital bed and took Mr. Hendricks' hand in her own. "Let's hear the doctor out. There's always hope, like the Good Lord says. This is a time for prayer and faith."

Celeste turned towards Nana, her back to Desiree, and added her hand over their clasped hold. "We'll get through this together," she whispered tearfully. Her poor face was blotchy and tear-stained.

Turning slightly, Nana shot me a look over her shoulder. "C'mon over here, Wesley! You gotta do your part now, too, since you got us into this fancy joint!"

Doug and Celeste both let out a watery chuckle as I joined them, adding my hand to the pile. These people right here. This was my family.

I wrapped my other arm around Celeste and pulled her into the crook of my arm, kissing the top of her head. "I'll do anything I can," I promised, looking Mr. Hendricks in the eye. "For all of you."

Desiree sniffed dramatically, and it was clear from the way the four of us jumped that we had all momentarily forgotten her presence.

"Isn't this just a little picture?" she sneered. "I guess it doesn't matter that I'm your future wife, Doug!"

Mr. Hendricks sighed heavily and leaned forward to place a hearty kiss on her cheek. "Of course it does, sweetheart! I love you!"

Her eyes flashed dangerously. "And yet you didn't turn to me at all! Can't you imagine how this feels for me, Doug? The perfect wedding I was planning is now up in smoke! It's so unfair!"

The bitch had brass balls, I'd give her that. Imagine being told that your fiancée was dying from a brain tumor and being more concerned with the wedding you'd have to cancel. I wasn't sure how Mr. Hendricks could stomach having her in the same room, let alone offer her comfort like he was trying to do now. Desiree continued her crocodile teared, woe-is-me act, so I pulled Celeste away from the pair of them and crushed her to my chest.

She clutched to my shirt like a lifeline as I stroked her hair and murmured assurances in her ear that everything would be okay in the end. It was an empty promise because how the hell did I know how anything would turn out, but I felt better offering it to her all the same.

Nana came to stand beside us, gently rubbing Celeste's shoulder as she cried into my shirt. It took mere seconds for the front to feel wet, but I didn't care. If all I could be in this second for her was a snot rag, so be it.

After several tense minutes, all of the tears in the room ran dry. Desiree's pouting apparently made her ruin her make up and she shuffled into the bathroom to fix it. Celeste drew back from me, hastily wiping her face with the back of her hand, and nodded when Nana asked her for assistance in locating the doctor out in the hall. That left Mr. Hendricks and myself alone in the room together.

He eyed me wearily. "I'll never be able to thank you enough for all this," Mr. Hendricks said quietly.

I shook my head, trying to ignore the burning in my chest. "You'll never have to, Doug. I'm just so sorry. You don't deserve this."

As much as I hated them, my own tears began to fall. I quickly brushed them away with my shoulder, turning to look out the window in hopes of hiding my emotional turmoil from him.

"Just keep your promise to me from the other morning,"

Mr. Hendricks reminded me. "That girl is my whole world. That's how you can thank me."

I nodded. He didn't ever have to worry about that from me.

"Well now!" Desiree loudly burst into the room from the bathroom, with a fresh coat of red lipstick and a calm expression. "It's time to plan ahead!"

Once the doctor returned, things started happening in hyper speed. Dr. Hassan explained that tumor's location effected Mr. Hendricks impulse control and emotions (I tried so hard not to glance at the ring on Desiree's finger), but it was starting to branch out into other areas of his brain. The doctor's main concern was a part of the tumor that could potentially take away Mr. Hendricks' eyesight. He wanted to begin an aggressive combination of Tumor Treating Fields therapy and chemotherapy before attempting the surgical route because of the size and location of the tumor. The hospital needed to monitor its growth closely, so Dr. Hassan advised it would be best for Doug to remain hospitalized for the time being while receiving treatment.

After an hour long discussion where the doctor used a series of computer renderings and videos to explain the treatment plan, Mr. Hendricks signed off on everything and shook Dr. Hassan's hand in thanks. The doctor paused at the doorway, awkwardly shuffling the tablet in his hands.

"You may also want to consult with an attorney," Dr. Hassan advised. "Patients often wait until it's too late and their lucidity becomes an issue." With a final nod, he swept from the room.

Nana shot Mr. Hendricks a stern look. "Before we do that, we need to figure out what's gonna happen with these youngin's while you're up here getting treatment. Can't have them failin' school 'cause of you."

Desiree immediately drew herself up to her full height. "I need to take Celeste home to chaperone her. We can't just let her run around with a teenage boy unsupervised."

"And leave your beloved fiancé here fighting cancer by himself?" I asked, filling my voice with alarm. I knew she would take the bait and I was handsomely rewarded when Desiree paled and glanced at Doug in a panic.

"Yeah," Nana chimed in next to me, no doubt catching on, "sounds kinda fishy, Desiree. Wouldn't you want to stay by your man's side as he fights for his life?" She gave me a wink so fast that I might have imagined it.

Desiree's mouth open and closed as the gears in her head tried to work through her predicament. Did she want to play the role of loving bride-to-be or doting stepmother more?

Doug rubbed a hand over his eyes as though the conversation pained him. "Suzanne, would you be alright staying with Celeste back home? I know that's asking a lot, but I'm not sure that it's Desiree's place to mind my daughter like that."

"Darling—" Desiree started to protest, but Nana beat her to it.

"Celeste is my own flesh and blood! Of course I'm gonna do right by her!" She huffed at the suggestion she would do anything less.

He looked over to Desiree, the question clear in his eyes. "Des, are you gonna stay here with me or do you need to go back for Hillary and Jeremy? You're their mama first and foremost." It sickened me to see the uncertainty on his face as he asked the woman he pledged to marry to stand by his side.

For her part, Desiree still looked torn, weighing her options between what she wanted most. It was a calculated move because she needed to ensure she kept Mr. Hendricks roped in while also ensuring Hillary stayed right under my nose.

"I'll call and see if my ex's folks can keep Jeremy and Hillary a little while longer," she finally said. "But we are absolutely getting a lawyer in here first thing, Doug Hendricks! There's so much to consider in all this!"

He nodded gratefully and drew her hand up for a kiss.

"But what about what I want?" Celeste asked hysterically. Her voice was in the shrill octave I only ever heard her use once before when Desiree found us in bed together. "I'm not leaving you, Daddy!"

"Sugar bee," he replied softly, "you have to. We need to focus on your schooling and your future."

"No!" she sobbed, throwing herself back in his arms. "What if I leave and don't get to say good-bye to you?!"

The sound of her sobs drew tears from my own eyes. It was sheer agony to witness someone I loved in so much pain, let alone a pain I couldn't stop. There was no happy ending to this scenario, only a hope that she would come out okay on the other side. Given how early Celeste's mother left her, it made perfect sense to me why she would be afraid to leave her dad for even a bathroom break.

"I'll fly us up here every weekend," I found myself offering. It was an insane thing to promise because my father used his jet all the time and it was pure luck that it had been available earlier today. Flying commercial wasn't nearly as fast or comfortable, but if I had to buy tickets from Savannah Express every weekend, I certainly would without batting an eye. "And we can be here for any surgeries or scheduled procedures. That way you don't miss any of the important stuff."

Celeste sniffled. "Really? You promise?"

I couldn't help but smile at her. "For my whole life."

Her face crinkled into a watery smile in return before rounding on her father and pointing a finger in his face. "I want to be notified of everything!" she warned him. "I'll call Willow five times a day for updates if you try to get on the phone and tell me everything's fine. You can't brush this off, Daddy. I won't let you."

Doug chuckled. "No, I don't suppose you will. Might as well buckle down and get you a cell phone, too, while we're at it. Suzanne, think you can handle that for me? That way I can call y'all at the drop of a hat."

Nana nodded. "As long as I don't have to finagle with the damn thing," she muttered.

"I'll go make the arrangements for us to fly home," I offered.

Stepping out into the hall, I let out a shaky exhale. Today was fast becoming the world's curviest emotional rollercoaster and I was ready to get off the damn thing. Going back to River's Run without Desiree would definitely help. Nana would never keep me and Celeste apart, that much I knew. For all the hassle she gave me in the beginning, I was pretty sure Nana was one of my biggest supporters.

Phillip answered on the first ring. "Your father is back in town," he said, "and he wants to have dinner with you and your girlfriend tonight."

Fuck.

"I'm not sure that's such a great idea, Phillip," I groaned. "We found out her dad has an incurable brain tumor. Kinda bad timing. Why don't you add it to his calendar a year from now and see if he remembers?"

"He means it, Wesley," Phillip countered, lowering his voice. "He's already made a call to Montmeri today to see if they have a room available."

"Damn it!" I kicked the wall next to me in frustration, creating a small dent in the drywall. "Fine. Have the car pick us up in an hour."

"You got it, boss." The phone clicked and I kicked again. The hole was definitely noticeable now, but they could add it to the fucking bill. Now if I could only figure out a way to explain this to Celeste without her freaking out over a meal with my old man.

And that's exactly what she did. She frantically ran to the bathroom to try and smooth down her hair, lamenting over the fact that she hadn't borrowed any makeup from Maggie or brought a nice dress. I offered to buy her a dress on the way there and she almost bit my head off.

"I'm not asking you to buy me stuff, Wesley! I want your dad to *like* me!"

I didn't bother telling her no dress in the world had that kind of magic. If my dad could barely tolerate me, there was no way he would ever like my choice in partner.

Celeste gave her father a tearful goodbye, swearing up and down to return Friday night, before I gave him a firm hug. He felt so fragile in my arms, which was the polar opposite of my impression of him, that I had a sudden urge to stay. If something were to happen with Mr. Hendricks before Celeste had a chance to make it back here, I could never forgive myself. Nana followed us a minute later, asking if it would be too much trouble for the driver to take her to the airport to wait. Although she didn't say it, I strongly suspected she was just as eager to get away from Desiree as I was.

The ride to the restaurant was tense with only the periodic snap of my neck to break the silence as I tried to force myself to relax. I was on high alert, too suspicious of my father's unusual dinner invitation to focus on Celeste in the seat beside me. She hadn't said a word, not that I blamed her, merely looking out the window with her arms crossed over her chest. I knew I should be saying something to comfort her, but it was hard to give something I couldn't feel at the moment.

As always, Benedict Madden the Third chose one of the swankiest restaurants in downtown Atlanta, Magnifique. The driver dropped us off at the door to a white gloved doorman and I thought Celeste was going to have a stroke from how loudly she sputtered. Guests were exiting the place in crisp suits and sparkly cocktail dresses, and I knew her well enough to know she deeply regretted blowing off my offer to stop and buy her a dress.

I, however, could not care less. It was so second nature to me to arrive at these types of places in ripped jeans and crumpled shirts just to piss off my dad that I didn't hesitate to grab her hand and drag her inside. Another doorman scampered forward to hold open the door, but I brushed him aside to open it for Celeste.

My poor girl looked like she had been through the ringer and then some. Her face was ghostly white, with dark circles under her eyes. Sleep would probably avoid her for a good long while now that she had a cancerous tumor to worry over at night. Her clothes were clean, but very clearly from the bargain bin at Madden Markets, something that might make a normal businessman proud but would only make my father snort in derision. If you didn't have money, you weren't worth his time, and nothing was going to change his mind.

Yet another attendant stepped forward to politely inform me of Magnifique's strict dress code. "I am so sorry, sir," the man said, his French accent heavy. "You and your guest are not permitted here."

His condescension made me want to strangle him. However, I would never embarrass Celeste in that manner, so I settled on smirking at the poor fool. He was about to be toast.

"I am the son of Benedict Madden," I replied in flawless French, "He will not take kindly to you insulting me, so unless you prefer to be unemployed after tonight, you'll take us to his table."

The man visibly shuddered. He waved over another host, whispering something in his ear that caused the host to beam at us and grandly sweep us forward.

"You speak French, too?" Celeste whispered. She was clutching my arm, out of support or nerves, I wasn't sure.

I shrugged. "A few things were bound to stick from my other schools."

The host led us to a private booth in a separate lounge of the restaurant. All of the tables here were far more intimate, with candlelight on each linen tablecloth and heavy curtains surrounding each booth. My father was the only person seated in this particular area, which was probably intentional, but gave me an impending sense of dread. Judging by Celeste's hard gulp next to me, she sensed it, too.

"Father," I greeted him as we drew up to his table. A gentleman would have stood up to welcome the new guests to his table, but I could already tell my father's rage was simmering just below the surface. Maybe I did inherit something from him after all.

Rather than responding, he shot a pointed look at the seat across from him. I guided Celeste in first, scared she would be ordered to leave if I let her sit on the end. She was practically trembling under the disdainful look he gave her and I had to sit on my free hand to stop myself from smacking him across his pompous face. My other arm wrapped around her shoulders, drawing Celeste as close to me as possible. My father read into the gesture, casting a furious gaze where our bodies connected, before turning his hateful black eyes on me.

"So my assistant tells me there's been a substantial sum deposited to two different hospitals in my name today," he began. "Care to explain, Wesley?"

I rolled my eyes. His version of a "substantial" sum was probably barely one fifth of one percent of his wealth, something he would make back by the end of the night tonight.

"It's…it's my fault, sir," replied Celeste, her voice small. "My daddy is real sick."

The way his expression changed at her words had me justifying a prison jumpsuit for a few seconds. "And—you are?" he demanded coldly.

She glanced at me, her eyebrows raised in surprise. "I'm Celeste Hendricks, sir. We met at The Comfy Cushion down in River's Run a couple years ago."

My father snorted and didn't acknowledge a word she said. Turning back to me, he fumed, "There's better pussy out there, Wesley! I'd expect you to know that by now. Fuck her and move on with your life! I'm not paying millions of dollars for you to get your dick wet."

Pain flared across my knuckles as my arm snapped back.

Blood from my father's mouth coated my hand before I could think about what I had done. My chest was so tight I could barely breathe. "Don't. Ever. Speak. About. Her. Again." I pronounced each word as distinctly as possible, my voice like ice.

Two of my father's bodyguards stepped forward, their black sunglasses shielding their faces. I knew both of them carried guns and neither would hesitate to use them, even on me. My father didn't give two shits what happened to me. He stood up, wiping the blood from his mouth and glowering at me.

"This ends now, boy," Father growled. "I've indulged your bullshit long enough."

"The money can come out of my trust, which is money you and I both know you can't take away," I replied coolly. "Mr. Hendricks has taken care of me for two years now and is the only adult who has ever cared about me. I *will* help him for as long as I need to." I dared my father to contradict me, but he didn't comment.

"And what will I get in return for paying for all this?" he countered instead.

It threw me for a loop. Father had never negotiated with me before. "What do you want?"

"You to start acting in a way that reflects on the Madden name. Earn your place in this business," Father replied instantly.

Because it was always about the business. His bottom line never went beyond that. I ceased to be a person as soon as he had to write the first check for my care. I resented him more in that moment than I ever had in my life.

"Fine." As much as I wanted to stab a stake directly into his cold, dead heart, it would never outweigh my desire to take care of the girl beside me. A girl who I realized too late was absolutely petrified right now.

"We're leaving now," I snapped, grabbing Celeste by the elbow. "See ya around, Benny."

Moving faster than was socially acceptable, I pushed past the maître d' and kicked open the door to the restaurant before the doorman had a chance to get there. Celeste panted half a step behind me, struggling to keep up as I all but dragged her out to the sidewalk.

"Get me a taxi, stat!" I shouted at the valet. It would take too long to call my driver and by this time of night, it could be hours before he made it back from the airport. What a rookie mistake not to have another on standby for when shit hit the fan with my dad. It was never a matter of *if*, but *when*.

"Wesley, you just punched your father!" Celeste yelped.

"Sure did."

"In the face!" she protested.

"I was there."

"Wesley!" She gave my arm a good shake, forcing me to stop and look at her, green eyes wide with anxiety.

It was enough to douse the flames roaring inside of me. I slumped forward, all the adrenaline draining from me, and pulled her into a tight hug. Apologizing would be a lie because I wasn't sorry, but I hated that she had to witness something so ugly when she was already going through Hell.

"Next time I'll make sure you leave the room first," I decided.

She giggled into my neck, and just like that, we were both lost in our laughter. I doubled over, clutching my side, as she dropped onto the sidewalk. Her giggles were so deep, they led to snorts, which had us laughing all over again. Strangers passing by were blatantly gawking at us and the valet came over to offer assistance.

I waved him off with another laugh. "Just the taxi, please."

It was so good to see a smiling Celeste looking up at me that I temporarily forgot about the world around us. Her dad's illness, the stepmother from the Black Lagoon, my father's crazy ultimatums—what did any of it matter? We had each other, and in that moment, that was more than enough.

Pulling her up from the sidewalk, I couldn't help but remind her, "I love you."

She stood on tiptoe to press her lips to mine, which was the best response she could have given me.

CHAPTER 19
A NEW NORMAL
CELESTE

THE NEXT SEVERAL months went by in a blur worthy of a rom com montage. I honestly couldn't tell what was going on day to day, nor could I keep a single thought in my head. The school board agreed to let me attend a four day school week as long as I gave up my study hall period and devoted it to another subject. It meant way more homework for me, but getting to have three days in Atlanta every week with Daddy was more than worth it. Plus it kept me busy enough during the beginning of the week that I didn't spend all my time dwelling on his latest scan or whether or not he was in too much pain. There probably wasn't another girl around who could say it, but all that homework might have saved my life because I would've driven myself insane without it.

Wesley was there by my side for every minute of my unraveling. Sometimes I wondered if he'd grow sick of me, if at some point my depression and anxiety would be too much for both of us, and he'd walk away rather than watch my downward, self-destructive spiral. I wouldn't have blamed him if he did. That day never came, however. No matter what my temperament was or how short I was with him, that megawatt smile stayed firmly in place followed by a forehead kiss to remind me how much he loved me. There was no way I deserved that kind of love given my poor attitude, but I was eternally grateful to him just the same.

His horrendous father made Wesley live up to their bargain. The moment the plane touched down on Thursday evenings in Atlanta, Mr. Madden already had one of his assistants waiting at the gate with a change of clothes and an event invitation for Wes to attend. Most of them were social galas with paparazzi, celebrities, and other so-called elite members of society, and Wesley made it crystal clear how much he hated the lot of them. His photographs started to appear in every gossip magazine across the country as more than one teenage girl noticed how gorgeous his tan skin, long blonde hair, and angelic blue-eyed combo could be. Mr. Madden wanted Wesley to become the new face of the company, a golden boy that everyone loved, adored, and recognized.

While the recognition part was in full swing, Wesley's surly attitude and volatile temper were more likely to land him on a TMZ report than anything else. I didn't have the guts to voice it out loud, but I was of the opinion that Mr. Madden was one of those people who didn't believe in bad press; as long as their names and his company were in the media, he was satisfied.

As much as I knew he hated going, Wesley never once complained. He would return to the hospital as soon as possible to check on Daddy, Nana, and me, then assure us all that we didn't need to worry about a thing because all our bills and needs were taken care of. At the end of every night, one of the Madden family drivers would come to collect us from the hospital and drive us back to their penthouse to sleep before waking up the next day and doing it all over again. Never once did I see Mr. Madden himself, not even in their home, and from the photos I saw online, it looked like Wesley always attended the events alone. He said his father was too busy "brokering deals" to actually go to anything. Sure didn't stop him from filling Wesley's calendar, though.

At the suggestion of the school guidance counselor after Wesley got into yet another fight at school ("He shouldn't have been running his mouth about you, Celeste!"), he began training with an MMA fighter to work out some of his aggression. Wesley took to the sport like white on rice, and the muscles he developed would have made any girl stop in her tracks. Pleased with the media attention Wesley's new physique was getting, Mr. Madden invested in a gym back home in River's Run that Wesley was given 24/7 access to use. He even put the business in Wesley's name so that he earned the profit from it. Or at least, had there been any profit, Wesley would benefit. As far as I knew, Wesley, Maggie, and I were the only "members" in town.

The downside to our new routine was that Wesley was not granted the same accommodations from the school board this time around. Mr. Hildebrandt, the superintendent, said that while he appreciated Wes' commitment to our family and that he showed excellent character by flying me back and forth every weekend, it wasn't something that was necessary on his part. Wesley being Wesley meant that he told Mr. Hildebrandt the school board could fuck right off (I literally felt my mama's ghost shake her head on that one) and continued to blow off school on Fridays anyway. After the first semester, he was going to face suspension if he continued, but he insisted I didn't need to worry about it. As if it was that easy for the likes of me.

Whether it was River's Run or Atlanta, Wesley and I were together, and my naïve, little heart loved every second of it. It surprised me that Nana never asked to check the accommodations, but Wesley and I managed to stay in his bedroom together every weekend we visited Daddy. Nana maintained the guest bedroom on one side of the penthouse and slept harder than a rock, her snores occasionally drifting out into the den, leaving us plenty of privacy. Privacy, however, that didn't go to good use. I was a basket case on a good day, and physical intimacy beyond that of make out sessions and spooning in bed wasn't on my radar.

Thankfully, Jeremy and Hillary continued to stay with their paternal grandparents. Jeremy went back to his same old routine of pretending I didn't exist, which suited me just fine, but Hillary made it her life's mission to harass me as much as the school would allow. She started to call me her baby sister (she was older by two months) and constantly felt the need to give me unsolicited advice. None of it was helpful and nearly everything circled back to the premise that Wesley Madden, heir to Madden Enterprises, didn't belong with a poor redneck from the backwoods of Georgia. I didn't want to add anything more onto Nana or Daddy's already overloaded plates, so I ignored her as best I could rather than tell anyone. Since the only thing I could count on was Wes' overreaction, it was easier to keep that secret close to the chest.

Nana had no other choice but to step up at The Comfy Cushion. We simply couldn't afford to hire anybody else, even with the Madden family paying medical expenses. The problem was Daddy had his own particular system at the restaurant, so there wasn't a good blueprint to follow when it came to ordering and balancing the books. Schedules were getting all messed up and Marla was at her wit's end, ranting like a lunatic at Jesse and the other waitresses when nobody knew how to keep it together. By the time Nana got home at the end of every night, she was exhausted and passed out right on the couch.

It only took two months of the craziness before everyone agreed that The Comfy Cushion would need to close on weekends. Nana wanted to be able to visit Daddy, too, and since she couldn't be in two places at once, it was the only viable solution. I cried harder than anybody else when they reached that decision because a piece of my mama's soul died with it.

Surprising no one, Desiree continued to be just as awful and ambiguous as she ever was. One minute she sang my praises to Daddy, claiming to have heard from Hillary that I took top place in the science fair or that I volunteered to help a teacher decorate the school gym for a fundraiser, but then as soon as the nurse came to take Daddy for his next scan, she would lash out at me for wanting too much attention and ruining her daughter's reputation. Supposedly all the kids at school were talking about Wes and me dating (I never once heard or saw anyone care) and it reflected poorly on Hillary to be related to such a jezebel.

And sadly, we were in fact now related. On one particularly good weekend for Daddy, I arrived at the hospital to find Desiree in a white silk dress and a minister at the foot of his bed. She insisted they would have a "real" wedding at some point, but for now, it was most important that they actually be joined as man and wife. Daddy had stars in his eyes the whole time, so who was I to argue? His happiness was all that mattered to me and Lord knew he had suffered enough over the past few years. They both recited their vows back to the minister and that was that. I officially had a stepmother.

Of all people, though, why did it have to be Desiree Stanbrooke? She was as cold and calculating as a viper, and made it clear, in no uncertain terms, that we did not have an affectionate bond as step-relations. The ink hadn't even dried on the marriage license before she zipped out of the room with Daddy's attorney and a shiny new credit card, making Nana purse her lips so hard the skin cracked.

From there on out, any time I came to visit, Daddy was alone. He insisted that it was just Desiree's way of coping and told me to try and imagine how hard it would be to see Wesley suffering in a hospital bed, knowing I couldn't do anything. I didn't have the heart to tell him that there was no version of that scenario where I wouldn't have remained by Wesley's side. When the people you love are weathering the storm, you grab a rain jacket and hunker down so you can ride it out together. Mama never would have left Daddy's bedside, just like he never left hers. Desiree seemed content to shop at all the Atlanta boutiques, only returning to show Daddy all the purchases she made.

I cried inconsolably about it to Wesley more times than I could count. Every time I arrived to find Daddy thinner, paler, and all alone in that giant hospital room, it chipped away a tiny piece of my heart.

It didn't help matters that treatment wasn't going well. Winter break was spent in Atlanta, with Nana doing the unthinkable and closing The Comfy Cushion for an entire week. She said our family had too much going on and needed to spend the quality time together after Daddy's latest scan showed the cancer not only resisted the TTF/chemo combo, but had spread out further into his brain.

On Christmas Day he had his first seizure, right after a bite of Marla's famous apple pie, and I'm still not entirely sure my heart didn't seize up right along with him. I have never felt as helpless in my life as I did sitting next to him, watching his entire body jerk erratically while alarms went off around us like a bad karaoke machine. It was all too soon and crashed into me like the sky was falling: Daddy was going to die.

Dr. Hassan started showing less and less optimism as the weeks went on. Daddy lost a ton of weight and all of his hair, looking downright skeletal. He requested to stay in the hospital bed more and more rather than walking around or even sitting up in a chair. Sleep became his most natural state as he was almost always napping. All of these side effects were normal, Dr. Hassan assured me, but that didn't make it any easier to watch. I wanted Daddy to be strong and cuddly again. Not that I ever let it show. I never wanted him to know how badly his illness was affecting me. He didn't deserve a side of guilt along with his hot plate of pain and suffering.

At night, though, whenever Wesley and I would lay down in his bed, he would wordlessly pull me to his chest and stroke my hair as I bawled everything out. Sometimes he would croon out the lyrics to "See You Again" by Carrie Underwood. I fell asleep every night to his gentle reminders that I was the strongest person he knew and it was okay to break down with him. There wasn't a chance in heaven that I could have gone through any of it without Wesley's steadfast presence. He kept me going when all I wanted to do was curl up in the fetal position and cry my problems away.

We were all making the best out of the worst situation and created our own version of normal. But the thing about normal is that it's constantly changing. And for me, change wasn't good.

CHAPTER 20
SURPRISE, SURPRISE
CELESTE

WHEN I WOKE up on my birthday in April, I found Wesley grinning at me like the Chesire Cat. We were in River's Run that morning and it was impossible for me to find any joy in my sweet sixteen. I wouldn't be able to get my license since I hadn't even had a chance to get a learner's permit yet without Daddy to sign for it. Birthdays were already hard enough without Mama, so the prospect of spending one without either of them kept me from getting out of bed. Wesley was here to change that.

"Happy birthday, Celeste Renee Hendricks, the love of my life and the most beautiful girl in the world!" Wesley crooned. "Hurry up and get ready! We have something extra special planned today!"

I groaned into my pillow. "What do you mean 'we?'"

"He means GET UP!" Maggie yelled, popping out from behind him and waving her arms in excitement. "It's time to celebrate because a girl only turns 16 once!"

Despite my instinct to reject their surprise, I sat up and stretched. "Are y'all gonna make me do this? Even if I swear I don't want to celebrate my birthday?"

Maggie rolled her eyes and looked at Wesley. "I told you she'd say that!" Turning back to me, she countered, "*We* want to celebrate your big day because you're our favorite person. C'mon, you deserve to have a birthday to remember! Up and at 'em!" She proceeded to cross over to the rickety dresser and rummage through my clothes.

Wesley stayed at my bedside and smirked. "I knew you'd say no and I'd cave because I hate not giving you what you want, so I recruited Maggie to our cause because she never cares if it pushes your buttons."

"That's evil!" I whined.

"So is the fact that you sleep in nothing but your panties here, but wear long pajamas when we're alone in Atlanta," Wesley countered, giving my body a onceover that made my skin heat.

It was totally true. "Well, it's not my fault your penthouse is ridiculously cold!" Pulling my blanket over my sports bra and spandex short sleep attire I tried to keep my mind off the memories of Wesley touching my bare skin. It felt like a lifetime ago.

"What about school?" I made my last ditch effort, a feeble excuse at best.

Wesley snorted. "There's a rule that says you can't spend your sixteenth birthday in their building." When I rolled my eyes at him, he held up his hands in surrender. "Hey, I don't make 'em, I just enforce 'em!"

"Here!" Maggie cried triumphantly. "Put these on!" Clothes hurtled onto my lap as she danced in place, unable to contain her excitement.

If my best friend was this worked up, I was in for something completely over the top. Wesley merely continued to grin at me over her head as they both made their way to the stairs so I could change.

"Oh—and wear sneakers!" she called up the staircase. "We're gonna be doing a lot of walking!"

"Ugh!" I groaned again, falling back onto my lumpy pillows in defeat.

An hour later, we exited Maggie's rusty old hatchback at the airport in front of the Madden family jet. My hopes instantly soared. Wherever we were going wasn't here in River's Run.

I recognized Atlanta as soon as the plane began its descent and once again felt my hopes go up. Spending my birthday with Daddy would be the best gift ever, but it certainly didn't involve a lot of walking. Daddy couldn't even handle walking from his bed to the bathroom anymore. My suspicions were confirmed when the waiting car merged onto an unfamiliar highway going the opposite direction from the hospital. Still, it was unlikely that Wesley would bring me all the way here just to keep me from my dad.

"Are you serious?!" I whooped as we drove through the gates.

Wesley and Maggie both nodded vigorously.

We were at Six Flags amusement park, one of the places on my bucket list to visit someday. I had never been on a roller coaster before.

Maggie squealed with delight the moment the car pulled up to the entrance. Before he could get out, I grabbed Wesley by the sleeve of his t-shirt. Concern rimmed his bright blue eyes.

"How did you know?" I whispered.

"Know what?"

"That I've always wanted to come here." My heart was

fluttering again, something it hadn't done in a really long time. For the first time all year, I was actually *feeling*.

Wesley was all smirk. "Because I know you, Lovebug." He kissed me, pulling away before the passion grew, and quickly exited the Cadillac.

I never had so much fun in my life. Wesley pulled some strings with one of the park shareholders, who also happened to be a neighbor at M Tower, and got special passes that let us walk to the front of every line. And not just those line hopper things they advertised in commercials where you got to go in a shorter line with priority seating. No, we were able to flash ours and move directly to the operating attendant. We also had an unlimited food allowance, resulting in Maggie and I stuffing our faces with more French fries, cotton candy, and pizza than a human being should be allowed to consume. Wesley didn't want to ruin his "training" and stuck to light salads throughout the day.

By the time we rode everything three times, including a roller coaster with a 95 foot drop, I was ready to cut my feet off. My entire body hurt from whiplash after being thrown every which way, but I couldn't wipe the smile from my face. Poor Maggie's voice was gone after all the screaming and we had never laughed so hard. I never wanted the day to end.

"Are we ready to move onto the next phase of Operation Birthday Surprise?" Wesley asked, stretching his long legs out in front of him. The three of us had collapsed onto a bench after a fourth ride around on the Georgia Scorcher, which had instantly become my favorite ride.

"I'm not doing a Phase Two!" I shook my head, frowning at both of them. "This has already been too much, y'all! You don't have to go all out like this."

"This isn't even a fraction of what I want to do for your

birthday," insisted Wes. "I love you so much, Celeste, so let me make this day special. Please." His eyes were imploring me to give in, their sincerity so powerful that I had to look away.

Maggie laced her fingers through mine. "She's ready. Let's get to it!"

The sun was already starting to set, giving the air a cool edge. Wesley noticed the shiver that ran down my spine and quickly put his arm around me, rubbing my arm for heat. Somehow his driver was already waiting for us at the gates when we finally walked to the exit. To my horror, Maggie held up a folded bandana and said I had to be blindfolded for the drive to our next stop. No matter how much I protested, she continued to smile like a lunatic and insist. Wes had to pin my arms to my sides for her to wrap it around my head. The shiver I felt after he brushed kisses along my earlobe and whispered, "Be good for me, Celeste," had nothing to do with the temperature outside, however.

I had no idea how long it really took to get to the next place. My anxiety with the blindfold made time stand still as far as I was concerned, and I absolutely hated it. Wesley didn't say a word, but made me settle against him, one arm wrapped around my shoulders. Periodically, he would trace a finger down the back of my neck and there was something oddly possessive about the gesture.

"Ugh, Wesley, you promised!" groaned Maggie to my right.

"Promised what?!" I was immediately on high alert.

Wesley snorted as Maggie replied, "No romantic stuff today! This is for all of us, not just you lovebirds!"

My flush extended all the way to my hairline. "I'm sorry, Maggie." I genuinely was.

"It's fine." She sighed dramatically. "It just gets hard being the third wheel to the world's most perfect couple."

Perfect couple? Was that really what people thought of us? Wesley and I had never had an argument, which was true, but did that make us perfect?

I always used to think Mama and Daddy were perfect. The way he lit up every time he saw her. How she never let him walk by without touching him in some manner, even if it was just brushing her fingers across his arm in passing. Hell, he gave up farming, what generations of the Hendricks family had done on our land, just so that he could help her run The Comfy Cushion. Her dreams became his dreams, and they both worked their tails off for it. That seemed like the perfect couple to me.

It was also drastically different from the way Wesley and I were so wrapped up in each other that you couldn't separate us. Neither one of us knew how to live without the other, and the ever looming threat of Mr. Madden sending Wesley away to a French boarding school kept both of us in that sweet spot between addiction and affection. Was that really how a perfect couple was made?

Before I had time to mull on these thoughts, the vehicle came to a stop and Maggie squealed beside me. "This is gonna be so much fun!" she gushed.

They both held a hand to lead me from the car, warning me when there was a staircase. Wesley let go long enough to open a door for us and then returned to my side. I couldn't hear anything other than Maggie's repeated squeaks of excitement, which had me on edge. It was a relief when they both drew me to a stop.

"Okay, you ready?" Wesley asked. Even his voice had an undercurrent of anticipation.

I nodded and the blindfold fell from my face.

We were standing inside a grand lobby that had aquatic themes and titles over cavernous entryways. Signs indicated different marine life, along with what looked like a cafeteria to my right and a gift shop that stood behind Wesley.

But none of it took my breath away quite as much as the sight of my daddy there in front of me. He was sitting in a wheelchair and the sheer size of the space made him look infinitesimally small, but he was *here*. Desiree was, of course, at his side, trying and utterly failing at keeping a pleasant smile on her face. Nana and Marla were here, too, along with Willow and a nurse I recognized from the hospital. Phillip, Mr. Madden's assistant, stood beside a gentleman in a three piece suit who had a blue name tag on his coat.

"Daddy!" I cried, darting forward to hug him. It was so good to see him outside of the hospital, sitting up and smiling at me like he used to.

"You didn't think I'd ignore my favorite daughter's sweet sixteen, did you?" he teased me. The crinkle around his eyes was just the same as ever, even if his face was a bit paler than I remembered. Seeing him outside of a hospital bed in real clothes made him look more like the daddy I remembered rather than the patient I had come to recognize.

"Where are we?" I asked, though the question was posed towards Wesley.

The man beside Phillip stepped forward. "Happy birthday, Ms. Hendricks," he greeted me, "and welcome to the Georgia Aquarium."

Now the excitement hit. Wesley had told me countless stories of the Georgia Aquarium, a place he visited frequently with his nannies as a child.

"Where is everybody?" I inquired. If it was as popular as

Wes made it out to be, I expected the place to be packed with people.

Daddy chuckled. "We get the place to ourselves! Wesley worked it all out!"

Phillip snorted. "I had a fair hand in it, Mr. Hendricks." We all laughed, including Wesley.

I stepped closer to him, overwhelmed and grateful for the lengths he went to so my birthday could be special. "You did this all for me?" I murmured. It had to have cost a fortune, and I dreaded the favors his father would demand in exchange.

He shrugged. "You deserve to have a special day."

Frowning, I couldn't help but ask, "Won't you get into more trouble for this?"

Wesley gave me a smile that was more sad than happy. "Definitely. But I'll take the punishment for the rest of my life if it means I give you the perfect birthday."

CHAPTER 21
PLENTY OF FISH IN THE SEA
WESLEY

PHILLIP MIGHT HAVE ACTUALLY EARNED the obscene amount of money I paid him by pulling this off. Celeste's smile hadn't left her face, and she clung to her dad like a newborn baby. It irked me to no end that I had to include Desiree, Hillary, and her dipshit excuse for a son, Jeremy, in the mix, but when I first approached Mr. Hendricks with the idea, he was adamant that the "whole family" be included. Blood coated my mouth from how hard I bit down my retort on that one.

Despite their black cloud tainting the event, we had an incredible time. The night started off with a catered meal from a local barbecue place that I thought Celeste would like. The moans that came from her mouth while eating ribs definitely put a tent in my jeans, and I hastily threw a napkin over my lap before her father could see. If I had my way, she'd be moaning like that around my dick by the end of the night.

Everyone tried to keep the conversation light throughout the dinner. No one discussed Doug's deteriorating health or the fact that the nurse who accompanied him had to help him with soft foods because his gums were starting to bleed from all the chemicals in his body. His teeth were so sensitive, he couldn't handle food he had to chew. Thankfully, Celeste was too distracted by Marla's story about a Comfy Cushion regular to notice.

After everyone stuffed their faces (except for Desiree, who did nothing but bitch about the food and the accommodations the entire meal), Mr. Jennison, the director of the Georgia Aquarium, gave us all a tour of the building. He explained the aquarium's conservation efforts, how they acquired all the animals in their care, and the kinds of things we could do to help take care of the ocean. Celeste had stars in her eyes the entire time, gazing at all the animals in rapt wonder. She and Maggie were two bleeding hearted peas in a pod, cooing over all the colorful fish, and swearing they were now vegetarians. We all had a good laugh when we went into the shark area and a large hammerhead swam up to the glass out of nowhere, making Maggie shriek and jump three feet in the air. Hillary rolled her eyes and pouted the whole time because I refused to take any photos with her.

Seal trainers gave us a private show and let us interact directly with the animals. Even Mr. Hendricks yelped with delight when a seal came right up to his wheelchair and rested its head on his knees. Nana wouldn't come within 20 feet of them, saying the way they moved reminded her of a bad horror film she watched in the 70's.

I had such a surge of pride seeing all the people I cared about so happy and carefree, knowing I was able to give them this experience. Just one day without the threat of death and scans and medical procedures hanging over our heads. We all needed it, me just as much as the rest of them. I found myself whipping out my polaroid camera a hundred times to capture the unadulterated bliss on Celeste's face.

The final part of my hat trick was really the biggest risk. I had no idea if Celeste would be willing to do it or how she would react, but I wanted to take the chance rather than miss an opportunity. Mr. Jennison led us "backstage" to see the labs, medical areas, and behind the scenes spots where only employees typically go. When we got to the humungous pool that led into the largest part of the aquarium, I not-so casually sidled up behind Celeste and Maggie, having tried to hold back and let them have their fun throughout the tour. I'd already seen everything a dozen times, after all. But now I needed to be close to her, see her reaction firsthand, and find a way to put a band aid on the situation if she refused.

"Would you like to take a dive in with the fish, Ms. Hendricks?" Mr. Jennison asked politely.

Maggie and Celeste's jaws dropped.

Nailed it.

"Seriously?" Celeste gasped.

"We can do that?!" Maggie was jumping up and down like a cheerleader.

He nodded, gesturing to the wetsuits and scuba gear in an alcove behind us. "With the professionals, of course."

"OH MY GOD!" They screamed in unison and simultaneously made a mad dash towards the gear.

Desiree looked like she was going to vomit. "We're just going to let a couple of teenagers swim in a cesspool of fish droppings, Doug?"

Before Mr. Hendricks could respond, I snapped. "You're not her mother so why don't you take a backseat on this one, Desi."

Marla and Nana both tried to cover their snickers with fake coughs, and I could see Celeste watching the scene like a deer in headlights. Desiree's mouth dropped open, her face contorting in an ugly sneer, when Mr. Hendricks surprised us all by saying, "Stay out of it, Desiree. Wesley went to a lot of trouble to make tonight special for all of us and you're not gonna ruin my daughter's birthday."

The itch to pull out my camera and keep the polaroid of her face was almost too great to ignore. My hand actually snuck towards the device hanging around my neck on instinct, but at the last second, I dropped it. She was fuming, turning red and visibly bristling. Even Hillary and Jeremy looked scared.

"Darling!" she whined. "You can't possibly think I would want to ruin Celeste's special day. I'm only thinking of what's best for her!"

"I'll be fine, Desiree. Thank you for thinking of me," Celeste replied before her father could say anything. Doug looked at her in surprise.

Desiree swallowed thickly, perturbed at Celeste's kindness. But that was my girl. Kind to everyone, whether they deserved it or not.

One of the animal handlers came out from a back room already in their wetsuit and demonstrated to Maggie and Celeste how to put on the equipment and the proper way to use it. While they were distracted, Marla came over to me and whispered with a wink, "This was perfect, Wes. I'm so glad you thought of it!"

Nana nodded. "Rachel would have loved every minute of this," she added wistfully.

Damn it, now I wanted to tear up like a baby.

"Can't I go in, too?" Hillary pled. "Why does Celeste get to do everything?!"

I turned away from them before I lost my shit and therefore all of Doug's respect. Instead I focused on Celeste, who now had on a wetsuit, flippers, and large goggles on her head. Excitement radiated from her. She beamed at me, practically giddy with anticipation.

"Wesley, this is so amazing!"

Grinning, I didn't even care that her whole family could see. I pulled her to me by her waist, locking my lips on hers. Mr. Hendricks cleared his throat loudly behind us, and Celeste giggled as she pulled away.

"Sorry, Daddy!" she called over my shoulder while maintaining eye contact with me. She didn't look sorry, however. She looked happy and carefree, green eyes full of mirth. Just as she deserved to be.

I gestured to Maggie, telling both of them to smile wide so I could take a polaroid of them in their gear. Celeste had never looked more beautiful to me than she did in that moment; her brown hair hastily pulled back into a bun at the nape of her neck, cheek to cheek with her best friend as they sported matching beams and wetsuits.

She needed a day like today. A birthday full of laughter and memories, because that was what the Hendricks family had always given me.

CHAPTER 22

PRESENTS AND PRESENCE

CELESTE

Colors.

Colors were everywhere.

Being underwater, surrounded by a wide array of fish and sea creatures was pure magic. Our guide, Mira, was just up ahead of us, pointing towards the unique fish that were exclusive to the aquarium. She told us before we entered the water that their aquarium housed some of the rarest sea animals in the world. Maggie and I watched in rapture as she demonstrated how to use the scuba gear, then cursed her for how heavy the equipment was. It was a relief to fall back into the tank and let gravity do the work.

Now, I couldn't believe how lucky I was. Wesley had gone out of his way to make my birthday spectacular. It was a day I would never forget, from riding my very first roller coaster to playing with sea lions to seeing my father laughing out in the world like his normal self. I knew the value in memories because someday memories were all you had.

Maggie and I spent an hour underwater, exploring the enormous tank with Mira. I was afraid to even blink in case I missed something. Floating weightlessly made me feel like

Ariel and I found a new dream blossoming in my chest to go out to the ocean and scuba dive for real. Maybe someday. It seemed like the kind of dream Wesley would manifest.

When we emerged back at the surface, Desiree and her kids were gone. Daddy looked crestfallen and Wesley looked furious. Dread turned my skin to ice and I had a sudden desire to go back under the water. I would take any escape, really.

Mira helped guide me to the shallow platform where Maggie and I could take off the tanks on our backs. Clambering off the ladder, I immediately went to Daddy's side.

"What's wrong?" I asked, anxiety spiking.

Daddy just shook his head. I glanced at Wesley, who minutely shook his head.

"I think it's best if we get Mr. Hendricks back to the hospital," Willow announced. She and the nurse hung back from the festivities as much as they could while still monitoring Daddy. Judging by his ashen face, however, I agreed with them.

His departure brought a dark gray cloud over the remaining guests. Wesley had arranged for a custom birthday cake from a famous Atlanta bakery, but their rendition of the happy birthday song was hollow without my daddy's voice in the mix. I wanted to be delighted with the two tiered, sparkly cake, but found myself pushing the slice around on the plate rather than eating it. Whatever made Desiree leave had clearly put everyone in a sour mood, but I was more worried about the effect on Daddy. When I pulled Wes aside to ask him, he simply whispered, "Later."

The night came to a close, and a separate driver pulled up to take Nana, Marla, and Maggie back to the airport. They would be returning to River's Run tonight, but I elected to stay behind. We only had one more day of school until spring break started anyway and at this point, it hardly mattered if I missed another day. My transcripts would look like a joke to college admissions.

My heart was heavy and my mind preoccupied when Wesley and I loaded into another car to head back to his father's penthouse. It wasn't until we walked inside that I realized we didn't have a chaperone. Nana was already on her way back home.

Sensing my thoughts, Wesley offered a slightly sheepish, slightly smug smile. "I told her that my dad was home tonight," he explained. "I just needed a night alone with you. And I didn't want any of them to see your present."

I furrowed my eyebrows in a frown. "Wesley, you spent an obscene amount of money making today happen for me already. I think a physical gift is a little unnecessary at this point!"

He smirked, but didn't contradict me. Instead, he wove his fingers through mine and led me down the hall. Rather than sitting on his bedroom couch or going up to bed, he led me out onto the private pool deck. Hundreds of lights were strung up to create a dimly lit canopy while the pool itself was filled with tiny candles and rose petals. A small, gift-wrapped package sat on top of the table behind him.

My breath caught in my throat. It was gorgeous, far more romantic than I ever anticipated. "Wes..." My voice trailed off, too awestruck to know what to say.

Wesley picked up the package and held it up in the palm of his hand like an offering. "Happy birthday, Celeste Renee Hendricks. I love you."

For some reason, his words felt intimate, like a caress ghosting across my skin. I blushed as I accepted the package and delicately unwrapped the glossy paper. A square blue box marked Tiffany and Co. opened on a hinge to reveal a white gold heart necklace. I squinted as I held the necklace closer to my face.

For my whole life.

"It's actually a locket," he offered after a few moments. I was still too overwhelmed to respond.

Gently he pried the locket from my hands, removing it from the box, and opened it up to reveal a photo of Daddy on one side and Mama on the other. "This way you know they'll always be close to your heart," Wesley explained in a whisper.

Tears sprung to my eyes and I took in a shaky breath. He held up the locket, waiting for permission to put it on. I nodded through my tears, feeling equal measure of love, grief, and comfort when the necklace hit my chest.

"I'll never take it off," I vowed. "I love you."

Wesley's eyes darkened, the blue akin to the thunderclouds that rolled in on a River's Run summer afternoon. "I'm gonna go for a swim," he finally whispered after a long minute.

He took a couple steps back, pulling the t-shirt over his head and dropping it on the ground. His eyes never left mine as he slowly unbuckled his belt, then pulled down the zipper to his jeans inch by inch. My skin grew hot, the prospect of seeing his glorious body igniting something deep in my core. The soft lights were just enough to highlight the outline of his six pack, his biceps flexing as he let his bottoms fall off. Removing his shoes was far less graceful, but I was far too distracted by the sight of his hard cock to care.

A shiver of longing ran down my spine, uncertain of how to proceed, but eager to enjoy the moment.

Wesley smirked as though sensing my inner conflict (which he probably was) and broke eye contact so that he could dive into the deep end of the pool. When he broke through the surface again, sending candles and rose petals flying, he whipped his head backwards, slicking his long blonde waves back. I loved his shaggy, scruffy halo, but seeing his hair pulled away from his face, his steep cheekbones in full focus of the candlelight made me clench my thighs together.

"Just live in this moment, Lovebug," he called softly. "Even if it's just for tonight, let's just forget everything else."

Just tonight, I repeated to myself. *Just let go, Celeste.*

Blocking everything else out felt foreign to me. My heart was pounding damn near through my chest as I grabbed the hem of my tank top with both hands and pulled it over my head. Unclasping my bra gave me more courage because the way Wesley's eyes dilated had my blood heating. There was no way I could be sexy taking off my shorts and sneakers, but Wesley's attention never wavered.

It took tremendous effort on my part not to cover up under the intensity of his gaze. I was completely bared to him, which had happened before all those months ago, but I never felt as exposed then as I did right now. I had to force a deep exhale of pent of up emotion, ignoring him to carefully descend the stairs into the pool, gently brushing petals away as I moved. We met in the middle, the water just high enough to cover my breasts.

Wesley dragged a featherlight trail down my sides with his fingers, making my skin tingle, as he bridged the gap between us. His dick was erect and rock solid as it pressed into my abdomen. It was the lust in his gaze, however, that caused my core to throb with need. His eyes never left my face, a mixture of awe, desire, and love. Always love.

"Thank you for today," I said, aware of how low and seductive my voice sounded. "You made it so special."

A smug grin escaped him and he pulled me tighter against his body. "Can I make you feel special, too?" he murmured against my forehead after placing a gentle kiss against my hairline.

Too aroused to respond properly, I nodded.

He wasted no time in gripping my thighs just under my cheeks, yanking them up to wrap around his waist. The steel ridge of his cock rubbed against my clit to create the most delicious sensation and I was too far gone to wonder if this counted as losing my virginity. It hardly mattered anyway because Wesley Madden could have me, body, mind, and soul.

In the blink of an eye, his lips met mine and I lost the ability to do anything other than move my mouth against his. My hips thrust into him on their own accord, my drenched pussy all but desperate for some kind of friction in the place I craved it most. He set me down on the edge of the pool so that my pussy was at his eye level.

It was the first time he had ever looked properly upon my lower lips, and rather than feeling embarrassed or ashamed as I always assumed I would, the smoldering need lining his face made me bolder than I thought possible. Without pause, I spread my legs wider, leaning back on my arms so he could see everything. I refused to hide myself from Wesley. There wasn't a shred of doubt in my mind that he loved every inch of me.

A moan tore from the back of his throat and Wesley roughly kissed the inside of my thigh near my left knee.

"Celeste, I'm going to taste you now," he declared, his voice full of gravel and hunger. "I'm going to make you feel as special as you make me."

There was no chance for me to respond before his lips found my clit and I transcended into heaven. His tongue, warm and flat, swiped up the entire length of my flesh and Wesley let out another moan. "You're gonna be the death of me," he murmured. Using his tongue to flick my clit, two of his fingers pushed inside me, matching the tempo of his tongue as he worked my clit. It was the best thing to ever happen to me, lighting me up from the inside until I knew I must have been glowing. If this is what happened behind closed doors, why did anybody ever leave?

There was a pressure building in my lower abdomen, gaining momentum as his tongue moved faster, adding a third finger that made my muscles quake. I writhed beneath him, torn between never wanting it to end and wanting to implode.

Instinct had full control over my decisions and I found myself pushing his head closer to my pussy. Wesley growled in response and the vibrations from his lips against my clit sent me over the edge. I was spiraling as my toes crinkled and my body stiffened in shock. The orgasm was much stronger than the last time; either my body had grown used to the sensation or Wesley had been practicing somehow.

Knowing Wesley, it was probably the latter. I wouldn't put it past him to take some sort of class or talk to an "expert" on how to properly make me cum.

Wesley lapped at my release like a dog, panting and all. "You taste so sweet," he groaned, gripping my thighs tightly. "Pretty sure I want to die with my face buried between your legs."

I giggled at the absurd thought before reality came crashing back down. My daddy *was* dying, and he would not be happy with me for spreading my legs so my boyfriend could eat me out. Even Wesley wasn't *that* much of a smooth talker.

"Nope, don't do it!" Wesley suddenly commanded, his voice sterned. He stood up taller, one arm gripping me at the waist to pull me upright. "Don't you dare let your mind wander back to the bad stuff. I told you, tonight is just about us."

I sighed. He made it sound so easy when it was anything but. "I don't do it on purpose, Wesley," I reminded him. "My brain just can't shut everything out like that."

He sighed, too, the romantic moment gone. "I know that. I just wanted to give you a break from your own head for once."

Ugh, he was seriously too sweet for me. Wesley was always going on about how I was the kinder of the two of us, but that couldn't be further from the truth. When Wesley loved, he did so with his whole heart. There simply wasn't any gray space for him—everything was a matter of absolutes.

"Let's go to bed," he offered.

I stood up and grabbed a towel from the basket against the wall to wrap around myself. As Wesley hauled himself out of the water, droplets shimmering between his muscles in all their yummy glory, my eyes zeroed in on his still erect cock bobbing between his legs.

He sheepishly ran a hand through his hair. "Yeah, I'm gonna need a minute," Wesley admitted.

Yearning burned in my lady parts again, a small sign that while my head might be in the wrong space, my body still wanted to be a normal sixteen year old girl driven by her hormones. I tried to listen to his advice and turn my brain off as I gingerly stepped forward and wrapped my hand around the shaft.

"Or I could help," I whispered.

"Yeah?" Wesley asked eagerly.

I nodded quickly. It was time for me to give Wesley just as much as he always gave me.

My favorite megawatt smile returned. "C'mon," he said, taking my hand. "We'll go inside."

Wesley hit the button to darken his window panes as soon as we stepped inside, which left only the string lights over his bed to illuminate anything. It made the entire atmosphere shift to something far more intimate and romantic again. With the press of a button on the tablet that controlled the room, his surround sound speakers began to softly play "Crash My Party" by Luke Bryan. I knew without asking that Wesley chose that song on purpose given the lyrics promised that the man was always willing to drop everything for the woman whenever she needed.

Ever so gently, Wesley dragged the towel around my body down until it dropped in a pool at my feet. His hands were warm as he began to caress my breasts, pinching my hard nipples so that I yelped and then giggled. That was all it took for me to draw him to me, grabbing his firm ass to press his groin tightly against my belly button. We could have been fused into one person and it still wouldn't have been enough for me. Our mouths clashed, tongues warring for control. Wesley reached around my thighs again to lift me up around his waist and deposit me on the bed.

I got up on my knees, shaking my finger in his face.

"Nope," I insisted. "Now it's my turn!" Pointing at his pillows, I raised my eyebrows in challenge.

The megawatt smile returned. "Lovebug, we can role play where you're in charge any time you want." He did as I commanded, however, laying down with his head in his hands and his long legs extending around me.

Wesley would always be cocky enough for the both of us. It would never matter how shy I felt.

I had about as much experience handling a boy's dick as I did sailing around the world. Wesley's, therefore, looked particularly impressive to me, long and pink, with a dark purple vein running along the bottom of the shaft. I knew logistically that whenever we had sex, it would somehow fit inside of me, but I had no idea how to physically make that happen without rearranging my organs. As much as I wanted to experience everything with Wes, his cock was a little too intimidating at present.

Instead, I leaned down and ran my tongue along the exposed vein, tasting his skin for the first time. Wesley's sharp inhale told me I caught him off guard.

Good.

Emboldened by his reaction, I started swirling my tongue, trying to remember all the tips and tricks from the ridiculous Cosmo articles Maggie read as her bible. When I got to the head, the salty, sticky consistency surprised me. I kind of liked the tanginess, though, and wrapped my lips around the mushroom head, popping them off with a smack.

Wesley was so rigid he resembled a corpse. His expression was a cross between blissful and tormented, his lips a thin line while his blue eyes were dilated to almost black. I raised an eyebrow to him in question.

"Don't laugh at me," he said, "but this feels so good and I don't want to blow my load after 90 seconds of a blowjob."

Laughter erupted from my chest, though I tried to stifle it with my hands. For all his embarrassment, Wes joined in.

"There's no way I'm good at this!" I giggled.

"Celeste, it's *you*. The girl I love has my cock in her mouth, and holy fuck do you look sexy as hell doing it. No matter what, you're gonna rock my world six ways from Sunday." The sincerity in his tone left no room for argument.

A surge of warmth spread through my body and the wetness returned between my thighs. I allowed my jaw to relax as I wrapped my mouth around Wesley's shaft again. I only got about halfway down before my gag reflex kicked in, but I let some of my saliva pool down farther. Using my hand, I cupped the base of his cock, letting my saliva act as a lubricant and repeated the motion with my mouth on the top half. As I got used to the movements, I gained momentum, noting that each time I was able to take him just a little further down my throat.

Wesley let out a series of whimpers, biting down onto his fist at one point as though he wanted to muffle the sound. He pulled my hair back from my face, watching me with eyes so blown out from lust I could no longer see the blue in his irises. Seeing his reaction was so damn sexy and intoxicating that I reached down and started rubbing my clit with the hand not on his cock to try and relieve some of the pressure.

As soon as I started touching myself, Wes lost it. "Oh, fuck me, Celeste! I'm gonna cum!" he shouted.

The shot of cum that filled my mouth was fast and salty and…gross. It hit the back of my throat, stimulating my gag reflex worse than Wesley's cock ever had, and without thinking, I leaned over the side of the bed and spit it all out, sputtering like a drowning victim.

Thankfully, Wesley let out a breathy laugh. "That bad, huh?"

Wiping my mouth with the back of my hand, I sheepishly smiled. "Just unexpected. Not sure that I like the taste."

He nodded. "Next time we'll have a towel ready."

His confidence made me snort. "'Next time?'"

Sitting up, Wes cupped my face with both hands. "Celeste, when are you going to stop questioning our future? I love you and you love me, and I'm never going to let anything come between us."

I tried to shake my head, but he wouldn't let me. "We're only sixteen. Nobody finds their soulmate as a child."

"Well we did," Wesley replied assuredly. "For my whole life." His megawatt smile returned.

Every fiber of my being wanted him to be right. I desperately wanted the future he planned, but no matter how much I tried to picture it, everything going forward looked blank. My mama left me and my daddy was about to join her. Why would Wesley be any different?

Not wanting to ruin the moment, I didn't voice that thought aloud. Smiling back at him, I said, "I think we need to shower and go to bed."

Wesley smirked. "Only if we get to shower together."

If Mama was in the heaven Nana talked about, I sure hoped God knew how to censor things. Some experiences didn't need to be shared with your parents, no matter how close you were.

CHAPTER 23
KEEP ON KEEPIN' ON
WESLEY

THE NEXT COUPLE months went by faster than I would've liked. Mr. Hildebrandt dropped the suspension threat when I signed a five year contract allowing all of the high school athletes to use my gym in River's Run for free. All they had to do was show their student ID and they could work out as much as they wanted. I tried to put in an exception for Jeremy Stanbrooke, but for some reason the superintendent didn't find that funny. Rude of him.

My father called me a week after Celeste's birthday to ream me out about the expense of the entire day (after which I called Phillip and tore him a new asshole for not charging things to my bank account instead of my dad's), but it was how he ended the conversation that killed me.

"I have an internship set up with our partner in China," my father snapped. "You'll be leaving for Shanghai the moment school ends."

"No way! What if something happens to Mr. Hendricks?!" I yelled.

My father snorted derisively. "It's cute that you think I give a shit." He hung up.

I threw my phone at the wall in my rage, feeling no relief at all when it smashed into a thousand pieces and left a tiny dent in Aunt Shirley's drywall. How the fuck was I going to leave Celeste to go to the other side of the world when her dad could die at any moment? How was *I* going to miss my chance to say goodbye to Doug?

There was no chance he was going to be around by August. He deteriorated rapidly after Celeste's birthday, like he had been holding on for that occasion and the fight went out of him afterwards. All skin and bones, with pasty white skin and rattly breathing, the poor man looked like a zombie. Not that I'd ever say so to Celeste. She was already a basket case as it was.

Desiree had gotten so much worse, too. After storming out of the Georgia Aquarium when Doug stood up for Celeste, she came back to the hospital the next day, full of contrition and kisses, yet somehow still spinning the line that the entire thing had been Mr. Hendricks' fault because he didn't put her first. It was so fake it would have made a telenovela actress roll their eyes. By that time, though, Mr. Hendricks was already so much worse off (and I'd guess in far more pain), that he bought everything she said, hook, line, and sinker.

And my sweet girl was worse than a shell of herself. Celeste stopped caring about everything, no longer paying attention in class, doing homework, or helping Marla with The Comfy Cushion at all. Maggie and I were both at a loss as to how to help her. What can you do when the person you love is watching their parent slowly, painfully wither away before their eyes? How do you find any comfort at a time like that?

It made me so pissed off at the world. Why did fucktards like Benedict Madden and Desiree Stanbrooke get to live, spreading their malice and ugliness around like black tar, while Mr. Hendricks, the nicest guy I had ever met, had to die from a fucking brain tumor? It wasn't fair and it would never be fair. Nana tried to quote some sort of scripture to me once, but I shot that shit down real quick; I had no patience for a god who stole good people before they were due.

My anger kept getting me in trouble, but that was hardly new. The best fight was when Jeremy himself had the audacity to run his mouth about how Celeste was "pathetic" for not taking better care of her only parent. Rearranging his teeth was the least I could do for him. When you play stupid games, you win stupid prizes. The school board didn't even suspend me for it either. Jeremy got in trouble for bullying, which was the icing on the cake for me.

Pretty sure Desiree would have made it a far bigger issue had I not offered to present her with the hotel bill for the duration of her stay in Atlanta. She kept her mouth shut and avoided me at all costs after that. Color me broken-hearted.

The tipping point came when Celeste stopped eating and struggled to get out of bed. Unless it was a day we were heading to Atlanta, she didn't want to be bothered with it. Nana made the treacherous climb up the tower steps and tried to light a fire under her, but even that failed. Celeste didn't so much as roll over. It terrified me because what if I lost them both? I didn't want to live in a world without Celeste Hendricks.

I was the one who put my foot down, screaming at every adult in our lives that Celeste was going to stay with Doug in Atlanta until she was ready to go. Willow up at the hospital was very accommodating in making a bed for her on the couch in the lounge area. It wasn't like Desiree was ever around to use it.

Because she was so sad, such a ghost of her old self, I didn't have the heart to tell Celeste that I was leaving for China as soon as the school year ended. It felt like every aspect of my life was a ticking time bomb; I was just tiptoeing around trying not to detonate one of them. My temper made that nearly impossible. The only person who could ever calm me down was Celeste, but that only took her away from her dad, which then made me feel like shit. That would then stoke the flames of my fury, and the cycle would start all over again.

I didn't want to feel helpless. I didn't want to accept that there was a problem money couldn't solve—hadn't that been my father's solution for everything? Dr. Hassan was the best neurosurgeon in the world and padding his bank account didn't do shit at the end of the day. Every instinct wanted me to lash out at him, at the rest of the doctors, the nurses—basically anyone who had anything to do with Mr. Hendricks' medical care because it was hard to accept they were doing enough when the results were still the same: Doug Hendricks was dying.

Celeste and I were about to board the plane to fly back to Atlanta. It had been a trying day because the whole school was ecstatic for the weekend because of prom. Maggie was going with Cameron Wyatt, which she was thrilled about, but Celeste only halfheartedly responded to Maggie's questions about dresses, shoes, and hair. Celeste looked ready for three hots and a cot the one time I brought up going, so I hadn't broached the subject again. Although I knew it wasn't her fault and I didn't blame her, part of me was bummed not to take Celeste to prom. With my father constantly breathing down my neck and all of the media coverage on my every move the moment I stepped foot in Atlanta, I had a sneaking suspicion that my days in River's Run were numbered. The likelihood that I would be able to take Celeste to prom next year was dropping by the day.

My mind kept playing games with me, imagining her in a sleek pink dress, her wild hair tamed into long curls that trailed down her back. She would smile coyly at me when I presented her with a boutonniere. I might even consider cutting my long hair for the occasion. Having a polaroid of the two of us in the traditional prom pose would be one of my most treasured possessions.

Suddenly, I had an idea and whipped out my phone to text Phillip. Hopefully, it wouldn't cost a fortune since it wouldn't *technically* be last minute. Even if it was, however, I would take whatever bullshit my father threw my way for it.

On it, Phillip's text read.

Perfect.

⚜ ⚜ ⚜ ⚜ ⚜ ⚜

I tried to stifle a groan when we stepped off the plane and found two cars waiting on the tarmac. Of course there was some function for me to attend. Didn't the rich yuppies ever take a day off? The surge of hatred made me murderous, but I tried not to take it out on the driver when he handed me a brand new Armani suit and said, "There will be senators at this function, Mr. Madden."

For once I turned back to find Celeste in tears. "Can't you stay with me, just this once?" she pleaded, her voice so small and fragile. "I can't shake the feeling that we're getting close to the end, Wes."

She looked so helpless, clinging to me with hope and fear

written all over her face. I hated it, and hated it even more that there was nothing I could do about it.

"I'm so sorry, Celeste, but I can't tonight. I have to go to this thing or it'll just get worse with my dad." It was on the tip of my tongue to add a warning about China, but something held me back. She was already upset enough. Why add that if her mind had started its downward spiral?

Silent tears streamed down her cheeks as she nodded. "I know. It's not your fault."

"But listen." I brightened, trying to sound as cheerful and upbeat as I could in hopes that my surprise on Saturday night might put some wind back in her sails. "I have something really special planned on Saturday night, and your dad is in on it, so you can't say no." In the back of my mind, I prayed Mr. Hendricks had been awake long enough to actually have the conversation with Phillip so that I wasn't lying through my teeth to her. "It's gonna be so much fun!"

"Okay." Celeste sniffled, swiping at her cheeks and backing away from me.

The distance instantly put me on high alert. I had the same panic coursing through my veins; there was something bad on the horizon. While it was only a few steps back, it might as well have been across continents. She was slipping through my fingers and she was right in front of me.

I placed a kiss on her forehead with more force than I meant and abruptly climbed into the waiting Mercedes. I didn't trust myself to look at her again or I would end up telling ol' Benny Madden where and how he could go fuck right off. It was torture, but it had to be done.

CHAPTER 24
TITANIC REFERENCES CAN'T BE GOOD

CELESTE

Sometimes it just sucked being a girl. My emotions were hitting me hard for some reason and I was irrationally angry with Wesley for leaving me. It wasn't like he didn't do the same thing every time we came to Atlanta, but today it hit me like a steel baseball bat. I was so tired of being tired, of feeling overwhelmed, of just being plain sad. Looking in the mirror was the same as looking at a Picasso painting—it made no sense and I couldn't recognize anything. More than anything I wanted to go back in time, back to when it was just Maggie, Wesley, and me, when Daddy was healthy and The Comfy Cushion wasn't on the verge of ruin. Now it seemed impossible that I'd ever be as happy again as I was back then.

When I arrived at Emory, my feet automatically carried me up to Daddy's room. I didn't even need to look where I was going anymore. Dr. Hassan was just stepping out into the hallway when I arrived. He gave me a kind smile, eyes full of pity.

"Do you have a moment, Ms. Hendricks?" he asked softly.

This was it. This was the day he told me that Daddy was circling the drain.

My breath caught in my throat as blood roared in my ears. I had sworn to myself that when the time came, I would be strong and handle it like an adult so that Daddy didn't have his last moments racked with guilt, but now that it was here, I sincerely doubted I could manage anything other than a blubbering mess.

Dr. Hassan led me down to a small kitchenette set up near the nurses' station. He set up the Keurig and hit the button to dispense a small cup of coffee, offering one to me. I mutely shook my head. Coffee wouldn't go down with the bundle of nerves working its way through my body.

"Miss, I feel the need to express my concern for you," Dr. Hassan disclosed. "What you are going through would cause tremendous amounts of stress for anyone, let alone a child who has already lost her mother. While I am certainly not a therapist, I am happy to help connect you with someone to talk to."

The lump in my throat grew. His tone was calm, soothing even, but his words told me that my act wasn't fooling anyone. I was a trainwreck barreling towards certain disaster. But I didn't know any way to cope other than shutting down. That was all I could handle or else I would simply fall apart. So I did the only thing I could. I lied.

"I'm fine," I said quietly. "I talk to my nana, and I've got Wes and Maggie. I'll be fine."

Dr. Hassan shot me a wistful smile. "You are so young to be taking on so much."

There was a pregnant pause as I contemplated how to proceed. Was our talk over? Would it be impolite for me to leave?

The doctor finished his coffee and got up to refill the cup. "You know, being a doctor is the only profession in the world where there is a zero percent success rate. Rewards are so few and far between in this field."

My brow furrowed in confusion.

"It's true," continued Dr. Hassan. "What doctor do you know who has allowed their patient to live forever? Part of the human condition is to die, and no matter what medicines we cook up in our labs, nothing can ever reverse that."

He sat back down across from me, balancing his newly filled coffee cup on his knee. "I have found accepting the fact that at some point, all of my efforts will be in vain is the only way I can live with the outcomes. To remember that I am also human and therefore susceptible to the same conditional flaws." Dr. Hassan met my eyes, the chocolatey-brown color radiating sympathy. "Loss, failure, grief…they are all a part of it."

While his heart was in the right place, I was not in the right mindset to hear it. I nodded as though I understood before standing up, clutching my bag to my chest. "That's a beautiful theory, sir," I murmured. "I'm gonna go see my daddy now. Thank you, Dr. Hassan."

With another soft smile and a nod of his head, I was dismissed. His words circled in my head long after I walked away, however. Everyone kept telling me that grief was a natural part of life, reminding me that all people die, yet they all neglected to mention that most people do so after they've met major milestones. My daddy would never get to walk me down the aisle. He would never see any of my school graduation ceremonies or meet his grandchildren. I wouldn't get to tease him about retirement or hear his words of wisdom as I navigated adulthood. Life wasn't bitter enough from taking away all of those things with my mama, now it had to claim Daddy, too.

Daddy was asleep in his bed when I entered, heavy blankets tucked in tight around him. No matter how much the hospital increased the temperature in the room, the medicine always made him cold. Not to mention he had no insulation now that he was as gaunt as a skeleton. Still, his comforting scent was just the same as I remembered and the rise and fall of his chest served as a reminder that for now, he was with me. I grabbed my own blanket from the cabinet and climbed into bed next to him, resting my head on his shoulder and wrapping the blanket as tightly around myself as I could. The ice lacing my veins had very little to do with the temperature of the room and everything to do with the numbness overtaking my soul.

I woke up several hours later with a stiff neck and sore joints to Wesley jostling me. Daddy was still asleep beside me, although at some point during my nap, he had moved to cradle me in his arms. The morbid thought that it might be the last time I would ever feel him hold me crossed my mind and I had to fight back tears again.

"Come on, Lovebug, I wanna take you back to my place tonight," Wesley whispered.

I shook my head even though the motion made my neck scream in protest. "I want to stay here. What if Daddy gets worse?"

"Celeste, there wasn't a question in there." He was stern, all frown lines and clamped lips. "Now, whether I have to carry you out of here or whether you come willingly, you're going."

A small recess in the back of my mind loved the authoritative tone in his voice even if I wasn't ready to listen. Right now, I hated that he felt he had any right to tell me what to do. Wesley Madden didn't own me and he could exit the way he entered if he thought this was gonna go any other way.

I must've hesitated too long because in the next breath I found myself hanging upside down over Wesley's shoulder. He picked me up as easily as a sack of potatoes and stood upright, turning towards the door.

"Hey!" I protested, pounding a fist into his back. My mama would be sending a demon from the depths of Hell after him for manhandling me like that in public.

My scream woke Daddy up, who jerked awake, and called out in a weathered voice, "Wesley, what on earth are you doing to my daughter?!"

I tried to lift myself so that I could see Daddy, but I had no abdominal strength to speak of and couldn't maneuver my body upwards in the awkward position. Wesley did a half turn so that we could both look over our shoulders at him. Daddy's mouth hung open, gaping at us in shock.

Wesley nodded tersely. "I'm keeping my promise, sir. I'll be taking Celeste back to my place for the night to ensure she gets a solid meal, a hot shower, and a good night's sleep."

To my horror and surprise, my daddy chuckled at him. Actually laughed like anything Wes just said was funny.

Traitor!

"And you couldn't find a way to do that that's a little less 'caveman' and more 'gentleman?'" Daddy asked.

Wes shook his head. "Not when her mama's stubbornness comes out."

Daddy nodded in agreement. "Understood. Carry on."

WHAT?! The nerve of both of them!

"Take care of yourself, sugar bee," he called out with a laugh as the door swung shut behind us. "I love you!"

I was fuming by the time we got down to the car waiting

at the curb. Everyone in the hospital stared at us, appalled and incredulous to see me swinging like a limp rag over Wesley's back. It didn't matter how much I squirmed, yelled, or pounded on his back, Wesley was as immovable as the Pyramids of Giza. Embarrassment burned my cheeks, which I knew had to be as red as a stop sign by the time we got outside. What if one of the paparazzi who liked to follow Wesley around took a photo of him carrying me like a petulant child?

As I tried to wriggle out of his grasp in the humid night air, he unceremoniously dumped me on the floor of the SUV, smirking as he climbed into the seat behind me.

Wesley was gonna get a visit from my mama's ghost tonight, I was sure of it.

"Knock it off, Celeste," huffed Wesley. There was a tick in his jaw that I had never seen before. "Your mama and daddy don't want you to die, too, Lovebug. You've gotta keep on living, even when the bad stuff happens!"

The accusation was so spot on that I burst into tears. "I can't miss a moment with him, Wesley!" I shouted. It echoed in the vehicle like a toddler with a temper tantrum. "What if he dies in his sleep and no one's there with him? What if I don't get to say goodbye?"

Wes grabbed me by my biceps and yanked me onto his lap where my arms instantly wrapped around his neck in a vice-like grip. He gently rocked us, smoothing his hand through my hair and shushing the sobs that wracked my frame.

"Lovebug, what if your dad's last moments on this earth are full of worry and pain over the state he's leaving you in? He's holding on and trying so hard *for you*. All the pain of his treatments, the crazy side effects, they're all worth it *for you.* You owe it to him to live."

It was impossible to hear anything more over the pain ripping from my throat. Wesley's words stung, shattering the fragile wall I built around my heart for protection. But he was one hundred percent right. Daddy's final memories of me would be full of heartache because I couldn't escape the dark clouds long enough to smile, to shower, to just be *me*. He deserved to leave this world with the peace of mind that I would be okay.

Except I wasn't okay, and there was nothing Wesley or Nana or Maggie or anybody else could do about it. Both of my parents were leaving me alone in this world--I was terrified. Nothing would ever be the same, and I was barreling towards that change like a rollercoaster falling off the rails. Even though my daddy was still alive, he was no longer the person he used to be, and I hated the selfish part of me that could only focus on my own misery over that fact.

I was sick of wallowing in my own grief over something that hadn't even happened yet. There was only so long a person could wait for the other shoe to drop before they went crazy, and I was long past that mark. It was exhausting. I didn't want to be strong anymore. I wanted to fold into the fetal position and shake away the nightmare. Because this had to be a nightmare, right? It couldn't possibly be real.

And so the cycle went on in my head. All day, every day, and I was sick of that, too. I didn't know how to make my brain turn off or how to force my heart to feel anything other than fear.

I must have fallen asleep from crying so hard in Wesley's arms because when I woke up, several hours had gone by and I was curled up in a ball in Wes' bed, his arm draped around my belly and his soft snores in my ear. He had stripped me down to a t-shirt and panties, but both clung to my back that was now coated with sweat from how tightly Wes held me. I rolled over to face him, wrapping my arm around his naked torso and tucking my head under his chin.

Our relationship was becoming ridiculously one-sided. I didn't have anything to offer him anymore, what with my heart shrinking and blackening by the day. Clearly, I was too selfish to give him up, but it didn't sit right with me that I could no longer give Wesley what he deserved. Relationships of any kind were supposed to be give and take, let alone a romantic one like we had, yet Wesley continued to give and give with nothing in return. Eventually it would be too unfair and he would leave. I was only prolonging the inevitable by dragging him through my Greek tragedy.

Did it make me the worst kind of person if I admitted I was too selfish to let him go? I wasn't far enough gone in my misery not to recognize how unhealthy my addiction to Wesley had become. I was just as bad as Rose in *Titanic*; I knew Wesley needed to climb on the stupid door to survive with me, but I just couldn't make myself move over. It was sick and selfish, and my mama would have boxed my ears. You know you're in trouble when a death scene is the closest analogy to the current state of your life.

But how could I stop?

CHAPTER 25
UNDER THE SEA

WESLEY

Too excited to contain myself, I woke Celeste up at the crack of dawn the next morning. I was bouncing like a puppy, desperate to execute my plan without my father intervening while also simultaneously allowing Celeste to have another special day. It killed me to see her break down like she had yesterday and now all I could focus on was how to remind her to live. I needed her more than I needed air to breathe, so if she was gonna go on another downward spiral, I wouldn't be far behind.

She blinked wearily at me as I shook her awake and laid on my most charming smile. Immediately, she drew back, eyeing me critically with one eyebrow arched. "What did you do this time?" Celeste asked.

Her insightfulness made me laugh. "Don't be mad, but I have something special planned."

Celeste rolled her eyes and threw the covers off. "Every time you tell me not to be mad, I end up being mad."

"Not this time. This time I nailed it."

Her eyebrow rose again.

"Just trust me, Lovebug." I grinned at her, confident about

my plan since Mr. Hendricks texted me he was feeling better this morning. That had to be a good sign.

After we both showered (Celeste wouldn't let me shower with her), we found Mrs. Aguilar in the kitchen with a big breakfast spread on the island. I had asked her to cook us breakfast, but this seemed a little overboard. She grimaced at me when I sat down.

Before I could ask why, I heard the brisk taps of my father's dress shoes thundering down the hall.

Fuck, I thought.

He rounded the corner, two women in skintight, skimpy dresses following. They barely looked older than me. It took everything in me not to roll my eyes. He must have foregone his bachelor pad a few blocks away that he thought I didn't know about. Both women smiled seductively at me as they rounded the island to sit on my other side and grabbed plates. As if I would ever be tempted by my father's sloppy seconds.

My father, however, shot me a look of pure loathing. "What are you doing here?" he demanded.

"Technically I still live here," I reminded him sarcastically.

"Not you," Benedict replied. "Her." His gaze zeroed in on Celeste.

She blinked at him, eyes wide and alarmed, before glancing at me. It sickened me how she withered under his scrutiny.

"Obviously Celeste is here with me, Benny," I goaded him. "She *is* my girlfriend."

The dangerous way his eyes narrowed should have alerted me that I was now in bed with a shark, but his mere existence was enough to piss me off. I wasn't gonna back down at this point.

"She is not welcome here, Wesley. Get her out of my sight."

My hackles rose. The fucking prick was hardly ever here. Celeste had slept in our penthouse more in the last six months than my father had in the past three years. As far as I was concerned, she was far more welcome here than he was, and I suspected Mrs. Aguilar would agree with me if asked.

If it weren't for my desire to give Celeste the surprise later today, I would have taken my anger out on his jaw again. Pure love was the only reason I was able to grind my teeth together and keep my true thoughts in my head. Without breaking my furious glare, I stood up and grabbed Celeste by the elbow so we could leave. Her eyes were still wide and scared, uncomfortable with the exchange.

"I won't forget this, Wesley," came my father's hard voice just as we reached the door.

"Neither will I," I shot back over my shoulder. From the corner of my eye, I saw Celeste shudder at the venom in my tone.

The ride to the hospital was as tense as a mistress at a vow renewal. Neither of us said a word, though mine was mostly due to the temper that continued to spike. The more I thought over that asshole's words, the more infuriated I became. He acted as if Celeste was dog shit under his shoe, unworthy to be in his precious penthouse, when the exact opposite was true. If he was on fire, I wouldn't summon the saliva to spit on him. Sadly, though, I knew without that I was going to pay for the whole thing somehow. Even if those women were high end escorts (which was a huge possibility), Benedict Madden III was not the kind of man to let go of a grudge.

Celeste's silence could have been due to any number of things. Hopefully by now she had learned that my father's shitty manners and pompous attitude had nothing to do with her, but I strongly suspected she was taking all of his words to heart. Nothing I said could ever get through to her that his opinion was worthless at best and that I didn't give a flying fart in space what came out of his mouth. Celeste had noble dreams of us reconciling at some point in the distant future, which was a direct reflection of her love and kindness. While admirable, her visions were also a complete fantasy. I had no reason or intention of reconciling with anything he had done. Some people were simply rooted in evil, and no amount of patience, understanding, or compassion could change that.

Mr. Hendricks was sitting upright in a clean robe when we arrived. It looked like he had a fresh shave, his beard now trim and tidy, and his hair had been cut. The whole effect made him look ten years younger and much healthier than he had in a long time. Celeste and I both brightened at the change, the urge to smile too great to ignore. She happily threw herself into his arms and beamed.

"How's my sugar bee doing?" he asked. "Better than last night, I hope?"

I couldn't help but laugh. Throwing my girlfriend over my shoulder like a ragdoll in front of her father wasn't exactly my finest hour. But hey, it got my point across, didn't it?

Celeste and her dad discussed how school was going briefly before she asked hesitantly, "Where's Desiree? I haven't seen her in a few weeks."

Mr. Hendricks' face quickly soured. "She said she had to head back to River's Run this weekend to help Hillary get ready for prom. How come you're not going, by the way? That's an important rite of passage, sugar bee."

She frowned. I could tell from the way her mouth was

puckered that Celeste was trying to hold back what she really wanted to say. "I'd rather be here with you, Daddy," she promised. "There will be other dances."

He scratched his jaw as he considered her answer. "Or you could give this ol' man some joy and let him see his only daughter all spiffed up."

At that, Willow walked in, followed by a glam squad with a rack of designer dresses. They all grinned at her mischievously.

It was probably the corniest thing I had ever done or would ever do in my life, but I got down on one knee in front of my girl, holding a single light pink peony that Willow had discreetly handed me upon her arrival. "Celeste Renee Hendricks," I drawled, my voice as smooth as butter, "will you be my date to prom?"

Tears filled her eyes as Celeste beamed down at me. "You want to fly back to River's Run just for a dance?" she finally laughed tearfully.

I shook my head, standing up and handing her the flower. "We're gonna have our own prom right here."

If I didn't know any better, I would say Doug had some water rimming his eyes, too. Celeste merely looked confused.

"Here? At the hospital?" she asked.

Willow stepped forward. "There are some other teenagers here for treatment who can't attend prom because they can't leave the hospital. After Wesley suggested it, we invited all of them to attend, too! The hospital staff has arranged everything, thanks to Wesley's generous donation. All of the girls have a selection of dresses to choose from and we have professional hair and makeup artists here. The boys have real tuxes to wear! We even picked a theme and decorated."

Celeste's astonishment was adorable. As if I hadn't shown

her yet that I was willing to make her every dream come true. What I wasn't expecting was her mouth to quiver and more big, fat tears to leak from the corners of her vivid green eyes as she turned to her dad and whispered, "Will you be there, too?"

If Mr. Hendricks was surprised, he didn't show it. Instead he smiled at her and replied, "I'd be happy to chaperone your prom, sugar bee. But I gotta tell ya—you've already got the best date there."

Now it was my turn to get emotional. All I had ever wanted was this guy's approval and it meant the world to me that I had it.

"Why don't you come pick your dress, Ms. Hendricks?" Willow suggested.

"Wesley, you better go get settled, too," directed Doug. He gave me a pointed look.

I shrugged. "I've got plenty of tuxes."

"That wasn't what I was talking about, young man," he replied. "I don't want any more photos of you with that wild mane to grace my mantel."

Everyone in the room laughed, including me. My hair was always long enough to pass my chin, but it tended to crest out in untamable waves. It never bothered me, but more than once Nana and Mr. Hendricks had suggested I needed a haircut.

"We could also use your help with the rest of the set up since the staff here still has patients to mind," Willow advised. She and Celeste were flipping animatedly through the rack of dresses as the salesperson from Saks described which designer and style she chose. It should have been Mrs. Hendricks helping Celeste decide on a prom dress, but at least Willow was a better replacement than Desiree. That bitch probably would have insisted Celeste needed to be covered from neck to toe in a wool shroud.

Pulling Celeste close, I whispered, "Is this okay? I didn't want you to miss your prom."

She wrapped her arms around my neck, delicately weaving her hands in my hair and pressing her body close. The scent of jasmine, her preferred body wash and lotion scent, wafted around me and I knew I was home. Right here in her arms was where I was meant to be.

"This is perfect, Wes," she murmured in my ear. "I'm so grateful my daddy can be a part of it."

I gave her a quick kiss on the forehead and headed up to the rooftop terrace where we were holding the prom. The hospital had a designated conference center up there with movable walls. There was a small outdoor area where the patients who were able to go outside could rest with tables and a small garden. I helped decorators hang pale blue lights along the perimeter wall before adding some glittery fish that the patients too young to participate in the prom had decorated. The theme was 'Under the Sea' because I wanted Celeste to remember how fun her birthday had been.

With the help of some hospital staff and parent volunteers, the inside was transformed into a water wonderland fit for Aquaman himself. A makeshift dance floor was marked off with a row of tables to dine at circling the corner. One of the parents had a friend who was a DJ and agreed to provide music for free. He was busy setting up his equipment on the edge of the dance floor. There was a photo booth area along with the stereotypical stage for the keepsake prom picture that had blocks identifying the year and the theme. More shimmery fish hung from string at the ceiling along with tissue paper designed to look like seaweed. Long banquet tables were being set up for the food offered. Due to some of the dietary restrictions of the other patients, different tables would have different options to ensure everyone could have something to eat.

All in all, things were shaping up pretty well for the Prom Do-Over as I dubbed it in my head. It would be nice to have other teens here, too, even if it was hard to swallow that they might not all be here a year from now. I knew my girl wouldn't want to dance in a huge room alone and it definitely meant a lot to Willow when I suggested it for the teenagers hospitalized here.

It took several hours, but when everything was ready, I was pretty sure it would give Smithson County High a run for its money. Prom Do-Over knocked it out of the park and then some. And according to my watch, I had just enough time to clean up and change into my tuxedo.

I felt bad for using the bathroom in the employee lounge, but Willow insisted it was fine. There was a shower and everything, so after another quick clean up, I stared harshly at my reflection in the mirror. Combing my hair felt like the right thing to do, but I didn't even own a brush. I dialed Phillip in a panic and asked him what I should do. I could practically hear him roll his eyes on the other end of the phone before agreeing to send one of the stylists in to help me.

A few minutes later I recognized one of the ladies from Mr. Hendricks' room as she strode through the door. Introducing herself as Kaila, she shoved me into a chair and set to work on taming my unruly hair. I lost track of how much product she used to slick my hair back before using the clippers to even out the baby hairs on my neck and around my ears. She frowned as she scrutinized her work and asked if I would be open to cutting my hair.

"Not a chance," I huffed. Why was everyone harping on my hair all of a sudden?

"Well in that case, you look downright handsome! You and Celeste are gonna be pretty as a picture!" she cooed.

That's what I was hoping for.

CHAPTER 26
PROM PERFECTION
CELESTE

THE LADIES from the salon were some of the sweetest people I had ever met. They reminded me of butterflies with how they fluttered around me as they fawned over my hair and makeup. Each one gave me step by step instructions on how to properly care for my hair type as well as how to properly do makeup with my skin tone. I had never had so much attention before and as cliché as it sounded, I truly felt like a princess. All of the products they used were included in the fee Wesley paid them because of course they were. Wesley always thought of everything.

Picking out my dress was much more difficult than I imagined, primarily because of the lump in my throat. More than anything, I longed for Mama to be here to tell me what color would look best or which neckline was appropriate. In some ways it almost seemed like a waste of time because no matter what dress I put on, Wes would tell me I was the prettiest girl in the room. I wanted to really knock him off his rocker, a gown that had a real "wow" factor.

In the end, the personal shopper from Saks who brought the dresses was helpful in identifying not only the style I preferred but the appropriate cut for my body type. There were matching shoes for every option, too, so I didn't need to agonize over footwear. Daddy hummed with approval when I stepped out wearing a pale blue gown with ruffles on the A-Line skirt. There was glitter along the bodice that shimmered as I moved. My hair was twisted and curled into an elegant bun on the back of my head, with soft curls that dangled around my face. A headband of the same glittery blue had been woven into my tresses to add a bit more sparkle.

The heels might match the dress perfectly, but they were far too tall and made me feel like I was walking on a tightrope. I had no intention of keeping them on all night, but there wasn't enough time to properly hem all of the ruffles in the dress I selected so I had to make due with them. At least I could get a photo with Wesley where he didn't tower over me for once.

The final result was rather stunning, I was reluctant to admit. I didn't recognize myself in the mirror, but then again, I hadn't been able to do that for several months. All the makeup helped put some color back on my cheeks and erased the permanent crease in my forehead from all the frowning I sported nowadays.

Marla and Nana joined Daddy while I was getting ready and all three of them had tears freely flowing when I exited the bathroom. Marla clapped her hands in delight.

"Sugar bee, you are gonna take that boy's breath away," Daddy sputtered.

Nana nodded in agreement. "You look just like your mama." She lost control then, bursting into a crying fit that nearly bowled her over. Marla wrapped an arm around her, swiping the tears from her cheeks and smiling.

"Come on, y'all can't make me cry after all the work they

put into makin' me look like this!" I cried. Now I finally understood why those silly pageant girls always waved their hands over their faces when they won.

Willow came back into the room with two male nurses and explained they were going to help Daddy shower and get ready so he could go upstairs with me. While he looked frail climbing out of bed and needed the nurses' help to stand upright, he was able to walk into the bathroom with them without much assistance. It buoyed my spirits tremendously.

"Now let's get a few pictures before Wesley gets here!" Marla exclaimed. "Trust me, someday you'll have a daughter who will want to see your prom dress!" She winked at me.

By the time I got done modeling my gown, then taking pictures with her and Nana on her cell phone, Daddy was showered and in clean clothes. He even donned a button up shirt with a clip on bow tie for the occasion. Marla whispered that his goal was to stay out of his wheelchair for as much of the night as he could.

A loud knock on the door interrupted the conversation and Marla squealed with delight. "That'll be Wesley!" She rushed to answer the door.

More tears streamed down her cheeks as she came back around the corner, this time with Wesley close behind. Forget my outfit—Wesley in a crisp black tuxedo with black satin lapels and a black satin pocket square should be the outfit of dreams. The effect was dazzling since the jacket was clearly tailored to fit every muscular contour on his body. For once, his shaggy scruff was slicked back away from his face except for one stray curl that fell down just into his eyes. My favorite megawatt smile was in full force, and I idly wondered if the blue of my gown now looked frumpy in comparison to the bright cobalt of his eyes. He was magnificent, my prince charming here to take me to the ball.

Judging by the way he stopped dead in his tracks at the sight of me, however, the feeling was mutual. Wesley slowly let his gaze start at my feet and wind slowly, seductively up my body, lingering just a fraction more on my hips, then my breasts, before finally settling on my face. The heat from his gaze made my skin tingle, and I knew I had to be blushing redder than a tomato. If my family noticed, they didn't comment.

Nana let out a wolf's whistle. "You sure shine up like a new penny!" she commented.

"Give her the corsage, Wes! Go on!" Marla urged. Her cell phone had become a permanent fixture in her hand, taking photos of every second of the process.

Wesley grinned sheepishly at me as he pulled out a plastic box holding a corsage made of white orchids and calla lilies out from behind his back. His fingertips caressed my wrist as he slid it on, the fire in his eyes telling me just how much he was affected by my attire.

"You're perfect," he breathed, barely loud enough for me to hear.

I shook my head slightly, still dazed by how incredible he looked. The long diamond earrings dangling from my ears swayed. "Not hardly."

Gingerly, he tilted my head up with his fingers so I couldn't hide from him. "For my whole life."

Warmth coated my insides and my knees quaked. This boy would be my undoing.

"Now it's not prom night unless we get three dozen pictures in, y'all, so get over here and pose!" Nana interrupted. Thank goodness, or I would have been lost in the depths behind Wesley's eyes.

How Marla managed to have any storage left on her phone from all the photos was beyond me, but when she finally deemed them enough, Daddy and Wesley escorted me upstairs. Daddy stayed in his wheelchair with Willow and one of the male nurses present. Willow assured us that she would try to remain as inconspicuous as possible for the duration of the party.

"Don't be silly," Wesley replied easily. "You should enjoy tonight just as much as the rest of us. You worked hard to pull this off." All the while his fingers remained tightly intertwined with mine.

I was rendered speechless when we arrived on the top floor by the grandeur of the event and the number of guests in attendance. There were more than thirty people out on the dance floor, some wearing masks or tubes for oxygen, and several more were seated at tables around the room. A professional photographer encouraged one girl to smile next to a four foot tall seahorse and two boxes that read "Under the Sea: Emory Hospital Prom" with the year. And although I had little experience in the matter, I would hazard to guess that the DJ behind the turntable was an honest to goodness professional. Sea creatures made out of glitter and paper mâché were scattered throughout the room along with a mural of ocean life on a banner hung behind all the food tables.

The biggest giveaway that this was a hospital prom and not a real one was the number of nurses in scrubs and doctors in white lab coats that stood around the perimeter. Everyone was smiling, however, talking animatedly and laughing. Some were even dancing with patients. It melted my heart like ice cream in July to see so many sick kids happy. Wesley changed all of their lives and probably didn't even realize the impact it made.

"May I have this dance?" Wesley asked sweetly, pulling our joined hands up to his mouth to softly kiss my knuckles.

We weaved in between the other dancers as Tim McGraw's "One of Those Nights" came on the speakers. Aware of my daddy's eyes drilling into the back of my head, I kept Wes an arm's length away from my body. He glanced my daddy's way and chuckled, but maintained the distance.

It was the perfect night and the perfect prom, better than I had ever imagined a school dance could be. I was so grateful not to deal with Hillary and her groupies, who surely would have crashed my good time had we been back in River's Run. Daddy smiled and laughed the whole time, talking with Willow, the hospital staff, and other patients. He even took photos with Wes and me at the photographer's set up where he managed to stand upright rather than sit in his wheelchair. Other than his smaller frame, no one could look at that photo and guess that he was sick. I already knew that silly photo at "Prom Do-Over" as Wes called it was one of my most prized possessions.

I saw Willow steer Daddy's wheelchair over to the DJ. They spoke briefly to him for a moment before Daddy grinned and came over towards the dance floor. As the song changed, Daddy stood out of his chair to join us.

"Sorry, son, but this one is for Celeste and me," Daddy said. Wesley smiled and nodded, stepping over to the side to watch us. I recognized the open chords to Heartland's "I Loved Her First" and it was impossible not to cry again. Mama and I always talked about playing this song at my wedding back when I was a little girl who dreamed of her big day. Daddy's arms came around my shoulders as mine wrapped around his waist in what was more of a hug than a dance. We slowly turned in circles with his head resting on the top of my hair as the song sang about a father watching his daughter move on with the love of her life.

The impact of his cancer stabbed me in the chest yet again as I realized Daddy wanted this dance with me now because he would never have it at my wedding. Even though he couldn't be there when the time came, it didn't mean I couldn't have the father-daughter dance I deserved.

I had to wonder if Daddy was also crying because his voice sounded thick and gravelly when he said, "Wes is growing into a good man, sugar bee. Might need to get his temper under control so his fists stop doin' all the talkin,' but I'm proud as hell of him. I hope you know that."

A watery chuckle broke loose. "Yeah, he's been more than good to us, Daddy. We're lucky I met him at the creek that day."

He nodded against my hair. "I'm proud of you, too, sugar bee. You have your mama's heart, but it's so much more than that. I can't believe the young lady you've turned into. I'm so grateful for every second of this life I spent as your daddy. D'you hear me? I wouldn't trade a single minute of it."

We were both openly crying now, there was no way around it. I ceased spinning and instead pulled away enough to look Daddy in the eye through my tears. The crinkles around his eyes were just the same as I remembered, his smile warm even while tinged with sadness.

"I just want you to always know that *you* were my greatest blessing, okay?" Daddy whispered thickly. "No matter what happens down the road, it was and has always been you, sugar bee. I love you, Celeste."

Sobs were choking me now, everything so blurry through my tears that I could no longer see. I crushed myself against Daddy's chest and managed to blubber out, "I love you more than anything, Daddy." I felt a gentle hand on the middle of my back and knew without looking that Wesley had stepped forward to console me. His soothing presence wrapped around me like a blanket, even with my father right there.

"You just remember your promise to me, Wesley," Daddy said.

"For my whole life, sir," he replied.

Exhaling sharply, I turned to look at Wes, smearing makeup all over my face as I scanned his features. He gave me a reassuring smile. The word choice was definitely intentional.

"Well, now, I didn't mean to ruin your evening, kids," Daddy coughed and took a few steps back, hastily wiping his eyes as he settled into the wheelchair Willow pushed forward. "If it's all the same to you, I'd like to go rest in my room. Enjoy yourselves."

As they navigated through the other prom goers, Wesley laced his hand through mine. "Wanna get some air?" he offered kindly.

Considering I was still a wailing mess? Absolutely.

There was hardly anyone out on the terrace now that the temperature dropped. I reminded myself that it probably wasn't safe for any of the patients to be outside when there was a chill in the air. Too many brightly lit skyscrapers meant stars were nearly impossible to see here in Atlanta, a feat that surprised me the first time Wesley pointed it out, but now as I looked up at the sky I felt a surge of pity for the city's inhabitants. They were missing so much beauty and they didn't even know it.

Wesley came to stand behind me, wrapping his arms around my waist. "We decided not to name a prom king or queen since it wouldn't be fair to all of the kids in there, but you're prom queen in my book," he whispered. Laughing, I shook my head at how foolishly insignificant something like a prom queen felt at that moment.

I wasn't sure how long we stood like that, quietly enjoying each other's company and lost in thought. It felt like quite some time had passed by the time I finally came back to the present.

I smiled. "Can we leave yet? I think all this crying has tuckered me out."

"Of course, lovebug. Anything you want."

"Let's just pop back in and say good night to my daddy, okay?"

We wove back through the dancers, hand in hand, and took the elevator down to the next floor. It sounded like someone was howling when I stepped across the threshold of Daddy's room, however.

We both raced down the short hallway into his room and found Nana bawling her eyes out, rocking forcefully on the couch, with Marla trying to comfort her. Silent tears ran down Marla's face, too, and my heart bottomed out of my chest.

"Where's Daddy?" I demanded.

My question made Nana wail louder.

It was Marla who answered, though. "He had another one of his seizures shortly after he got back," she whispered. "It was a really bad one, so Willow called for Dr. Hassan. An alarm started going off that his heart was in distress and the doctor said they needed to get him into surgery immediately. They wheeled him out about an hour ago."

Numb. My whole body went numb.

I couldn't breathe, couldn't hear, couldn't even think. Why hadn't I come back down here with him? How could this happen when he had been feeling so good all day?

"Desiree's on her way," Marla added, her voice low.

"How long will he be in surgery?" Wesley asked.

"We don't really know just yet," Marla replied. "Everything happened in such a rush, with all kinds of beepers and things goin' off. Couldn't even really understand what they were saying. Willow said she would come back soon with an update for us."

Wesley nodded before gently guiding me onto the couch next to Nana. As soon as I sat down, I instinctively wrapped my arms around her and continued soothing her the way Marla had been.

It might as well have been lifetimes that passed while we waited in that position. There was never a way to accurately describe how time flows while you're waiting in crisis. It was just different, an experience I wouldn't wish on my worst enemy. The perpetual waiting, with different scenarios running on repeat in your head, was enough to make you go crazy. So you just wait a little more. It was all you can do.

Nana's sobs eventually quieted enough that her body was no longer shaking, but the three of us stayed clustered together on the sofa. Wesley stood on my other side, as frozen as a statue. A piece of my heart actually broke as though there was a permanent change to my internal structure. Fear that deep in your core will do that to a person.

None of us reacted when Desiree, Hillary, and Jeremy stormed inside. Hillary was wearing a blood red silk dress that showed more of her boobs than I would have thought acceptable at a school dance. Somewhere in the back of my mind the old Celeste scoffed at the idea that *I* was going to be the one with the bad reputation, but the new, heartbroken version no longer cared.

Desiree was also dressed up in a frilly cocktail dress and sky high stilettos as though she had been chaperoning the prom back in River's Run. For once, she didn't say a word to anyone other than to ask if we had any news. When Marla shook her head, Desiree simply began to pace back and forth across the room. The clacks of her heels became my metronome, and I zeroed in on the sound to keep myself focused on something rather than the sheer terror that solidified in my chest.

By the time Willow came in, I was semi-certain I had gone stark raving mad. My mind had become a loop of regrets, cycling through all of the things I should have done differently, all of the ways I should have taken better care of my dad, all of the moments I missed because I was too selfish to stay with him. Did school really matter that much in the grand scheme of things? It was so much wasted time that could have been spent up here with Daddy…and now I realized how fleeting all of that time was.

"Dr. Hassan assessed Mr. Hendricks' condition and felt the tumor removal can no longer wait. He is going to remove as much as he can while the cardio surgeon monitors Mr. Hendricks' heart…it looks like he had a mild heart attack tonight in conjunction with the seizure. I will keep you updated, but honestly, Dr. Hassan and his team expect this surgery to last more than eighteen hours. It's extraordinarily complex and they need to take their time. You may want to try and get some rest." She added that last sentence half-heartedly, likely knowing how tall an order her suggestion was. Willow nodded to Desiree before leaving the room.

Marla sighed, and I felt the weight of the world on her

exhale. We were all suffering from the kind of exhaustion that takes root in your soul. "Welp, you heard the woman. We are gonna go and try to get some sleep while we wait."

Nana seemed to be out of it, standing up on autopilot without really seeing the world around her. Marla continued to hold her with one arm around her shoulder.

"Yes, I think we'll return to the hotel and change out of these clothes," Desiree said. She gestured to Hillary and Jeremy to follow them out the door.

Only I was left sitting on the couch, unable to move. It no longer felt like I actually resided in my body. I didn't know where to go or what to do.

Wesley knelt in front of me, gently cupping my face with both his hands as he scanned my eyes. He didn't say a word, for which I was grateful as I was no longer capable of speech, but he also wasn't going to leave us there. This time rather than throwing me over his shoulder, Wesley scooped me up with one hand behind my back and another under my knees, carrying me across the threshold like a married couple. I let him because that was easier than thinking. As carefully as I could, I burrowed into his chest, recognizing on a subconscious level that my body was trembling but not giving two shits about it.

I couldn't remember how I got there, but somehow I found myself in Wesley's cavernous bathroom. A small voice in my head hoped that Mr. Madden wasn't there because there was no way he had forgotten his earlier statement of me being unwelcome, but I was also too dazed to care. Wes was gentle and kept his eyes on my face as he reached around to unzip my dress, letting it cascade in its ruffled glory on the floor. The dress had a built-in corset, so I didn't have a bra on, but he tenderly pulled my panties down next.

Hot steam billowed out from the glass shower as he pushed me inside. Wes made quick work of removing his own clothing, leaving them in a rumpled pile on the floor. He joined me in the shower, placing me just under enough of the water that I received the heat. My body finally stopped shaking. Methodically, he removed the bobby pins and headband from my hair until it all finally dropped loosely down my back. Only then did he direct me under the water, tipping my head back to let everything wash away. He grabbed my loofah from its place on the wall and began gently scrubbing my body. The whole time his blue eyes stayed trained on my face, watching every reaction I had.

Except, I had nothing to give him. All the makeup and hair spray and other remnants of the night streaked down my skin as I prayed to a god I didn't believe in to wash me away right with it. I didn't want to live in a world without either of my parents.

The inability to move continued, and once Wesley washed my body and hair, never once lingering longer on one body part versus another, he scooped me back up into a bride's hold and took me to his bed. We were both naked as he tucked the heavy duvet around us, but I couldn't register the feeling of his skin against mine. He wrapped his entire body around me, legs and all, until the safety and warmth of his Wesley cocoon broke me.

Floodgates unleashed within me, more tears and pain than I thought possible. There was no way the human body could withstand the onslaught of grief I experienced. I welcomed the darkness, wanted to dive in with open arms, if it meant I no longer had to operate without my daddy here. A doctor was cutting into his brain like the meat back at the diner, and I found myself desperately wishing I could trade places with him. My daddy deserved to live, and if God needed a sacrifice, he could take me instead.

Wesley held me the entire time, gently humming a tuneless song that nonetheless made me aware of his presence. His grip remained tight as if he knew that any slack would mean I utterly shattered. It was the only thing that grounded me enough to maintain a sense of reality. My soul was already moving on to the next life where it could join my parents.

THE HARDEST GOODBYE

CELESTE

At some point I must have fallen asleep because when I jerked awake sometime later, the sun was brightly pouring in through the windows. Wesley forgot to darken the glass before we went to bed, which was unheard of, but I only rolled over so that I was facing him and tugged the duvet higher over my head.

In the muted light filtering through the covers, Wesley looked more angelic than I could ever recall. His shaggy hair swept down across his forehead, curling every which way, and it was all I could do not to brush it aside so that I could drink him in. Lips slightly parted, he let out a contented sigh and gripped me tighter. Even in sleep he couldn't bear to let me go.

The limited space between us made me *very* aware of the rigid morning wood he sported. As delicately as I could, I allowed one finger to trace along the side of his shaft, once again in awe of how thick and hard he became.

Suddenly, all I wanted was to forget everything. Let the world fade away until the only things that existed were our two bodies and how they joined together perfectly. Every time he brought me to release before, I had lost myself and I craved that oblivion like a crackhead craves his next fix. The numbness still filled my chest, making me brazen and desperate, and I let my hand firmly grasp Wesley's shaft and move. Pressing my boobs further into his body, I began sucking on his neck in the way I remembered got the biggest reaction before.

"Whoa, hey!" Wesley's hands cupped my shoulders and forced me back to look at him. He was trying to fight his arousal, judging by how far dilated his blue eyes had become, and while the rational part of my brain knew I should stop, I just couldn't. I needed to feel *something*. It didn't matter what it was as long as I remembered that I was alive and gave me a brief reprieve from the darkness.

"Please, Wes," I whimpered. "Please, I need this. I need you." My hand resumed its ministrations on his dick.

He tipped his head back and groaned. "Celeste, that feels so good. I don't wanna stop you, but I don't want you to hate me later."

I scoffed. There wasn't anything he could do that would make me hate him. Hate was too strong of an emotion for me to handle right now.

"Please," I begged, my voice pleading and frantic. It must have worked because he let out a frustrated growl and shoved me on my back, kissing me harder than he ever had before. I reveled in the pain, thrusting my hips up to meet his, mewling like a cat in heat. Within seconds Wesley kissed his way down my chest, across my collar bone, and then onto my harden nipple. Our hands were clasped, pushed above my head, and I squeezed to the point of pain when he used his teeth to nip at the sensitive flesh around my nipples. My entire body felt tingly, ready to combust with the fire burning through my core.

Wesley laved his tongue further down. He swirled playfully around my belly button and I felt his smile against my abdomen when I cried out in protest. I parted my legs even more, my hips rising to meet his tongue. My hands were finally free as he wrapped his arms around my thighs to draw my pussy closer to his mouth. Quick flicks of his tongue drove me to madness, although it could have been the triumph at being right. Now that Wesley's mouth tasted every inch of my flesh, I was more alive and aware than I had ever been before.

The orgasm was right on the cusp and I was anxious to fall over the edge. Leaning forward, I tugged on his hair to bring his mouth back to mine, my tongue warring with his in a desperation taking permanent root inside me. As Wesley adjusted his legs to prevent all his weight from resting on me, the head of his cock slipped inside my slick folds.

Both of our eyes shot open at the intrusion; it was the first time his cock touched me there. Alarm bells were going off in the back of my mind, but I was too determined to chase any feeling at this point to consider what they meant.

"Do it," I breathed. "I want you to."

Wesley's eyes were so far blown there was no blue left. A tick in his jaw indicated how much effort he was using to try and restrain himself. "Celeste, I don't have a condom. I didn't plan this."

I shook my head. I didn't care. Excuses had no effect on me at the moment. The high I chased was dissipating like smoke with every second he stalled.

"Just do it. I want you so much, Wes. We love each other, right?"

After a long moment Wesley offered me a soft smile. "Yeah, we do. I'll pull out, okay? As long as you're sure you want this."

It wasn't really a matter of wanting to have sex as much as it was the knowledge that it was going to happen, and I knew deep down I was always meant to lose my virginity to Wesley Madden. I had loved him for so long. Life had forever changed when he came into the picture. Our souls recognized their other halves.

"Yes, Wesley," I breathed. "I want this."

My favorite megawatt smile burst across his face. It was more dazzling than the sun and had the power to burn me deeper than the light ever could. He kissed me deeply, his fingers seeking my clit and circling the swollen bud. My pussy was so wet that I could feel it dripping down my thigh.

Bracing himself on one arm, Wesley guided his cock to my entrance. Physics didn't seem to be on my side because there was no way something that size could fit inside me. All of the girls in the school bathrooms made it sound like losing your virginity hurt, so I inhaled sharply, preparing for the sting.

The crown of Wesley's shaft pushed inside and we both gasped at the sensation. It wasn't entirely unpleasant, but it didn't bring all kinds of pleasure like Maggie's stupid magazines made us believe. My muscles clenched around him, trying to dispel the intrusion.

"I'm gonna try to go a little further in, lovebug," Wes whispered. "You're doing so well."

"I love you," I replied softly, which made him smile.

A few more inches made their way inside. "I love you, too."

Okay, *now* it hurt. I turned my head away rather than let him see me grimace, knowing he would insist on stopping rather than hurting me. Pain meant I was alive. Pain was *good*.

Gently, Wes' hips began to rock forward, easing out before pressing forward. Each thrust went a little farther, stretching me more and more, the pain sharp, but growing more tolerable. It took several tries before he was finally fully sheathed inside me. We both laid together, awestruck at what we were experiencing together. And as I looked up at him, the boy who had been my saving grace time and time again, I knew I would never forget this moment. All the feelings I longed for came rushing back and I couldn't stop the tears from falling.

"Oh my god, am I hurting you?" Wesley asked in a panic.

"No!" I could have swallowed sandpaper with how gritty my voice sounded. "I just can't believe this is happening!"

In typical Wes fashion, he pulled me closer and lightly peppered my face with kisses as he continued to thrust in and out of me. With each kiss he murmured some term of endearment, telling me how beautiful I was, how special I made him feel, how lucky he was to love me. It was the sweetest, most poignant experience of my life. His fingers returned to my clit as his thrusts grew bolder and he grew more confident in his movements. Out of nowhere, an orgasm ripped through me, curling my toes and rolling my eyes back into my head.

"Fuck, Celeste, you're so goddamn gorgeous when you cum!" Wesley panted. His hips were plunging so hard into mine that I knew they would bruise. I welcomed the reminder that I was alive enough to feel something as powerful as love, so I gripped his backside and pulled it tighter against me.

Wesley gasped. "No, Celeste, don't!" But it was too late. I could already feel Wesley's cock jerking inside me as he came to release without a condom.

We were both frozen in place for a long time. Neither of us knew what to do or how to proceed now that we had unprotected sex. I winced when Wesley withdrew from me, his cock coated in a mix of cum and blood. The hollow feeling that returned the instant his body left mine hurt far worse than the loss of my virginity. Now that it was over and reality crashed back around us, I was too ashamed of my poor actions to even look at him. My daddy was on an operating table, on the verge of death, and my recourse had been to sleep with my boyfriend? What kind of fool followed that logic?

I didn't say a word as I rolled out of bed and power-walked down to the bathroom, locking the door behind me so Wesley couldn't enter. Sex ed taught me enough to know that there was no way to wash the deed out of me, but I sure as hell was willing to try.

Water so hot it scalded me seemed like the appropriate baptism for my sins. I didn't make a peep as I harshly scrubbed my skin, spending extra time washing my private areas as though it would change what happened. By the time I was done, my skin was a lush pink, blistering and raw.

With a towel wrapped around my torso, I brushed past Wes waiting at the door, refusing to look at him or address the elephant in the room. The walk in closet was set up with most of my clothes, so I made a beeline in there to dress.

Wesley followed hot on my heels. "Hey, we need to talk about this!"

I held up a hand to stop him, still refusing to meet his gaze. "I need to get back to the hospital. That's the only thing I need right now."

"Damn it, Celeste, don't do this! Don't shut me out because you're scared!"

There was no answer I could give that would satisfy him so I remained silent. Now wasn't the right time anyway. We both needed to process the enormity of what we had done before we could safely talk about it.

Besides, it wasn't like unprotected sex *automatically* meant a baby. There were couples who tried for years and couldn't get pregnant. It was way too soon to start worrying over things that could happen when there was enough actually happening to suffocate me. Daddy might even be out of surgery by now.

"Fuck!" Wesley roared. Out of my periphery, I saw an object fly through the air before it smashed into the full length mirror hanging on the wall. "Don't you dare ignore me over this, Celeste! You owe me more than that!"

"Owe you?!" I screamed. "Is that how we're gonna play it now? You do something for me and it means I *owe* you?! Guess you really are your father's son!"

That was shame turning my insides to stone. It was the lowest blow I could possibly give him and I was appalled I had even said it, but I was also way too freaked out to take it back.

Wesley blinked like he was seeing me for the first time. "I'm gonna shower," he finally said, "and hopefully when I get out, the real Celeste will be here. Because my Celeste would never intentionally hurt me like that."

Mama was right, I realized. Hurt people really did hurt people. I would have gladly stepped into a black hole if it meant I could escape the shame and guilt swirling through me.

Well, genius, you wanted to feel something, huh?

What should have been an intimate, romantic memory with the boy I had loved for most of my adolescence was now tainted. Neither of us would ever look back on this moment without remorse and anger, and Wesley had every right to hold a grudge. And the worst part of it was that nothing could be further from the truth. The similarities between Wesley and Mr. Madden began and ended with their last name.

Thank God the mirror had shattered because I was too despicable to look at right now.

Pounding so hard the walls rattled came from the other room. Wesley, freshly showered and angrier than a thundercloud, beat me to the door and opened it to Marla and Nana's frantic faces.

"C'mon, the hospital called! He's outta surgery and we need to get there pronto!" Nana yelled.

My heart leapt into my throat. Hope was the most dangerous drug there was and I was riddled with it. Wesley didn't even look at me as he swept from the room, whipping out his cell to call for his driver to meet us downstairs.

I wanted to say something to him, but a car ride with my nana and my mama's best friend was not the appropriate setting to discuss my nonexistent virginity. It was almost a blessing that they were both so preoccupied with Daddy's surgery that neither of them noticed Wes and I sitting on opposite sides of the car, our bodies both angled away from one another.

There was a bevy of activity on Daddy's floor when we arrived, with a nurse shouting and a bell-like alarm going on. As we rounded the corner from the elevators, I realized everyone was running into Daddy's room.

For once, the movies got it exactly right. Everything shifted into slow motion as I went into autopilot. Although I could see the nurses and doctors' mouths moving, only white static echoed around me. Dr. Hassan was there, his face blurry, as he pointed towards a monitor on the wall with a long, straight line. My daddy, white as a ghost, lied flat on his back on the hospital bed, an oxygen mask over his nose and throat, while a nurse performed CPR. I already knew it was futile in the way that everyone knows the day will pass into night. Merely fact. While my daddy's body might occupy that bed, there was no longer a living soul dwelling in it.

This wasn't the peaceful exit most people dreamt of. This was chaos and pandemonium, with nurses and doctors hectically trying to draw life back into a corpse that refused to accept it. It was like my mind was playing tricks on me as I drew parallels between my daddy's death and my mama's, and suddenly it was my mama on the hospital bed with a different doctor trying to revive her. My vision went back and forth between the two extremes, recalling in minute detail every aspect of both. Their passings were both so distinct and vivid, yet utterly and inconceivably the same.

A hurried body knocked into me, damn near bowling me over, and time snapped back into the present. I could hear Nana's gasping sobs behind me as Dr. Hassan barked orders for someone else to take over compressions and to inject something in Daddy's IV. They hadn't accepted what I already knew—Daddy was gone.

Numbness washed over me again, settling in next to my old pal, Grief. They were gonna be like another layer of skin for the foreseeable future.

"It's no use, sir!" the nurse performing compressions cried.

Dr. Hassan sighed heavily. "Time of death, 1904."

And that was it. The end of my daddy's life was reduced to a number. Just another question on the hospital's tedious forms. It had no consideration for the life we led, or the father he had been, the husband I could remember admiring as a little girl, the savvy businessman, or the man who was so warm and caring that he built his mother-in-law a cottage on his land just to take care of her. What did any of the doctors or nurses care that Daddy had been a real *person*? To them, he would never be anything more than the patient in the VIP room. Forgotten by the end of the night.

It was such a hollow, bitter pill to swallow that I could actually taste the bile rising in my throat. All of these people were gonna go home to their houses after this without any change in their lives. Yeah, they'd probably say it was a bad day at work, but for them, it was a job. A way to earn a paycheck. For me, they represented the worst day of my life. I hated every single one of them with more intensity than I would have thought possible.

Desiree burst into the room, shrieking like a hyena. "You killed my husband!"

Using that magical verb had a ripple effect around the room. Two nurses flocked to her side and Willow materialized out of nowhere with a cup of chamomile tea meant to calm Desiree's nerves. Dr. Hassan was apologizing profusely and explaining that he believed Daddy suffered a large stroke after returning to his room, how it was an unfortunate side effect with high risk surgeries, but they did everything they could. It was all the same pandering I heard after Mama died.

Wesley's body barreled through the room like a bullet, colliding with Dr. Hassan and pinning him against the wall. Both of Wes' hands wrapped around the doctor's neck as he bellowed, "YOU WERE SUPPOSED TO SAVE HIM!"

His hands were too tight for the doctor to reply. One of the nurses ran to the hallway and called for security while the other people in the room tried to pull Wesley off. Throwing one arm back when a male nurse tried to yank him off Dr. Hassan, Wes sent the man crashing into a medical cart while blood spurted from his nose from the impact.

With a bellowing roar reminiscent of a wildebeest, Wesley knocked over the room's computer, breaking the top of the laptop away from the bottom, then grabbed Willow's tablet and chucked it across the room at one of the windows. The screen shattered on impact, though thankfully the window remained intact.

I was too stunned to move, let alone cry. While I had seen every shade of Wesley's temper, this was a rage so deep it was nearly black. He looked like an entirely different person, his hackles raised and his fists clenched to the point that the veins popped out on his hands. Never once looking at me, Wes tore from the room, the echoes of more items crashing ricocheting off the walls.

"How could he do this to me after I lost my dear husband!" Desiree wailed, draping an arm across her forehead and regaining the attention of most of the hospital staff. One of the nurses ran to an intercom on the wall and directed security to call the police.

"No!" I shouted. The threat of Wesley's arrest broke through my detachment enough to run into the hallway. I was likely the only person who could calm him down.

Metal, plastic, and papers were everywhere. Several nurses were huddled together on the back wall behind the desk. Wesley acted like a cornered lion, screaming himself hoarse and swinging at anyone who dared get close enough. Three security guards were trying to trap him, their arms outstretched and ready. One sported a bloody nose, which may have been why none of them charged him.

Four police officers in tactical gear raced down the hallway, hands already on their holsters. They pressed forward, making the hospital security guards step back, and screamed at Wesley to put his hands up. Rather than complying or settling down, Wes turned around and tore a framed painting off the wall, then smashed it onto the floor. Glass shards shot out everywhere, causing all the officers to shield their eyes.

Wesley used this to his advantage and broke through their line to run for the elevators. All four cops and three security guards were immediately hot on his heels. The burliest one managed to gain on him enough to tackle him to the ground. Wesley reared his head back to head butt the officer. Blood spurted from the guy's mouth as he swore every cuss word in the book.

After that, none of them were gentle with him. Two officers pinned Wesley's head down while another sat on his legs. The cop who straddled him pulled Wes' hands behind his back and cuffed them.

I found my voice and shot forward. "Please don't arrest him, sir!" I cried. If my tears moved them at all, not a single officer showed it. "He's just upset!"

One of the cops hauled Wesley up to a standing position. "He's also a menace with a one way ticket to downtown."

As I started to protest, Wes let out an exasperated sigh. "Don't worry, babe, I'm just doing *exactly* what good, ol' Benny Madden would do." There was only darkness in his eyes as he glared at me, and the tiny fraction of my heart that remained from my daddy's death was pulverized.

"Come on, you!" One of the cops shoved him forward while a nurse quietly asked the security guard and the police officer with blood on their faces to sit down so she could help get them cleaned up.

Helpless. I was totally helpless. This was normally a situation where I would immediately go to Daddy to sort out. Quite frankly, I didn't need Wesley's jarring reminder that he was no longer with us—it was already a pain embedded in my DNA. As I watched the officers surround him to get onto the elevator, I saw fat tears roll down Wesley's cheeks. Grief had finally introduced himself to Wesley Madden.

CHAPTER 28
SETTING THE WORLD ON FIRE

WESLEY

Cops really were a bunch of useless fucking pricks. Not a single one of them read me my rights and they all scattered like a cluster of cockroaches when they discovered who my father was. They still kept me in a jail cell where I could hear bits of a distant conversation about whether or not they were going to transfer me to a juvenile detention center. Apparently, the fact that it took four grown men to overtake me had them reconsidering...like the pansies they were.

It didn't matter anyway because all I could see, feel, or hear was rage. This was unlike anything I had ever experienced, and I couldn't stop picturing Mr. Hendricks on that bed. When Dr. Hassan didn't give an update until frickin' *Desiree* came into the room, offering an apology to the bitch who couldn't even be bothered to be there while Celeste, his only daughter, got a front row seat to their failed attempts at revival, I just lost it. I had been bankrolling the operation for almost a goddamn year and they couldn't even say something to me first?!

Celeste had to be losing her mind right now, and every

fiber of my being yearned to go to her. What I said to her was unfair and watching her recoil like I slapped her was a memory that would haunt me forever. Our earlier argument seemed so stupid in comparison; of course she had been freaking out. We lost our virginity without any kind of protection—what teenager in this day and age was that reckless?

But I couldn't regret our actions or even call it a dumb decision, really. Celeste and I were inevitable, as much as the Earth's axis would turn and circle the sun. The love I felt for her defied logic and reason, so why wouldn't our first time having sex be the same?

But I needed to get to her and fix it *NOW*. The longer I was stuck inside a jail cell, the longer her depression had to convince her my ugly words were true. I knew her well enough to know that she would believe them, especially when I had already delivered the sucker punch to the gut right after she got the wind knocked out of her from Mr. Hendricks' death.

And if I were being honest, Doug's death wasn't something I couldn't face. He was the first man I ever respected, someone I genuinely looked up to and loved as a family member. Fuck, in the few years I had known the Hendricks family, there had never been a time when he hadn't shown up for me, hadn't given me advice, hadn't tried to talk me down off the ledge of fury I constantly found myself on. For all intents and purposes, Mr. Hendricks was my dad, too, and although I knew this day was coming, it hit me like the collapse of a brick building.

"WHERE IS HE?!" a voice roared. "WHERE IS MY SON?!"

"Here we go," I muttered.

"YOU!" My father came into view, his black Tom Ford suit making him look every inch the villain I knew him to be. "What have you done, boy?!"

As I opened my mouth, he waved it off. "No, not a word out of you! It's gonna cost me a fortune to get you out of this! A goddamn fortune!"

"I need to get back to Celeste!" I screamed.

Benedict's smile was evil. "Oh, you're never going to see that girl again, do you hear me? As soon as I can sort this out, you're going straight on the plane to Montmeri, and that's final!"

My hands shot forward and rattled the bars on my cell. He was too far out of reach for me to strike him like I wanted, but I knew it wouldn't help my case at all if I assaulted someone else at the police precinct. "I NEED TO GET BACK TO CELESTE."

"You can't!" he yelled right back. "They've filed a restraining order against you after your ridiculous outburst!"

"Wh-what?" I asked, my voice quiet as fear choked the life out of me.

He nodded, a smile so vindictive and cruel twisting on his face that he almost resembled a snake. "Her family took out a restraining order. Your precious, little girlfriend never wants to see you again!"

That couldn't be right. It had to be Desiree's doing—Celeste couldn't really be that angry with me, could she? Yes, what I did probably scared her, although she had seen enough of my fights at school to know how violent I could get.

"We're about to go see the judge, so for Christ's sake, keep your fucking mouth shut and let me get you out of this. My son, behind bars…you disgust me." Disdain dripped from his words, but I didn't even hear them. My heart was too busy shattering.

They led me in handcuffs down to a small office where a judge, a few officers, my father, and one of my father's attorneys waited. A court clerk of some kind read me my rights and explained this was my arraignment, meaning I was officially charged with crimes and the judge determined if it was safe enough to let me out on bail. The judge then read off my crimes in a monotone voice as if he were merely reciting a recipe for the millionth time. Charges included vandalism, assault, and…attempted murder?!

"I did NOT try to kill anyone, for fuck's sakes!" I yelled.

"Wesley!" my father snapped.

The judge, an older Caucasian man with wispy white eyebrows and a receding hairline, pursed his lips in a frown. "Young man, there are several witnesses who attest to you choking a doctor against a wall. He had to have medical attention!"

As soon as I rolled my eyes, I knew it was the wrong call.

"Since you clearly don't have any remorse for your actions or the extensive damage you've caused, I am going to set bail at one million dollars!" the judge rasped.

My father looked murderous. "Fine. We'll pay it."

If the judge was affronted, he didn't show it. Our attorney stepped forward, holding out his arm to guide us through to an enclosed office where an officer glared at me while he removed my handcuffs. Benedict went up to a glass window and signed a check. The receipt gave us a court date three months away for my first hearing.

The attorney led us out through a maze of hallways to a

black SUV waiting in an alley behind the jail. Clearly my father wanted to avoid the press, although for once, we agreed. The last thing I wanted was to see my mug shot plastered all over the tabloids.

All of that paled in comparison to my new reality. I needed Celeste like I needed the trees to keep providing air. She was my life source, the very essence of who I was, and without her, I couldn't survive. Fuck a restraining order. That had to be Desiree's dumbass idea anyway. There was no way my girl would have done that to me.

Except...I couldn't forget the tortured look on her face when I delivered my final blow at the hospital. Why the fuck had I said any of that? Her dad had literally just died right in front of her, and all I could do was kick her while she was down? I certainly didn't see any Boyfriend of the Year awards in my future.

When I pulled my phone out of my pocket to call her, Benedict yanked it out of my hand faster than a lightning strike. "Hey!" I protested.

"You no longer have phone privileges," he sneered. "Come on, we've got a plane to catch."

"I'm not going to that school, Benny. You can piss off," I replied. Turning on my heel, I started to storm away from him, down the alley to the main street.

A firm hand clamped on my shoulder and pressed harshly. It was one of my father's bodyguards, though my father was right next to him. "You're either going to Montmeri or I take you back inside and revoke your bail. Good luck talking to anyone from a jail cell."

It was my worst fear come to life. I had no choice but to follow them, my brain whirling a thousand miles an hour to formulate a plan to get me back to River's Run. Celeste needed me now more than ever. She had barely survived her mom's passing, and that was right after I came into her life.

Animosity prevented me from even making eye contact with my father as we settled into the back seat of the SUV. His bodyguard climbed into the front passenger, nodding at the driver that we were ready. A soundproof partition rose between the front and back so that they couldn't overhear whatever my father was about to say.

"I've already spoken with the headmaster at Montmeri," Benedict said. "You will not have access to any computers, tablets, or phones. I made sure you had a room to yourself, so don't even think about sneaking onto another kid's stuff. If you try to contact that family in any way, I will know about it. Not only will you violate the restraining order and get in more trouble, but I will revoke the bail and my attorney. You're looking at serious jail time, Wesley, maybe even a trial as an adult. From now on, you do as *I* say and forget that girl ever existed."

The injustice of it all burned my throat to where I couldn't speak. To my surprise, a tear trickled down my cheek as I kept my eyes focused on the window. If I thought my heart shattered before, this must be what it felt like to have my heart ripped out of my chest and shredded in a blender. My entire world was in shambles after one of the best mornings of my life. How could everything change in a millisecond?

"You're also going to earn back every cent of the money this is going to cost me with a fifteen percent interest rate," my father continued. "The gravy train stops now for you, boy. You wanna act like a hotshot, it's time to earn a hotshot paycheck and be grateful for the doors I've opened for you."

Arguing was futile at this point. He had me under his thumb well and good, and he knew it.

I sighed heavily. "What do I need to do?"

The Grinch-like grin I received in return told me everything I needed to know. I was royally fucked.

CHAPTER 29
TRIPLE THREAT
CELESTE

Seven Weeks Later…

MAMA ALWAYS USED to say that trouble comes in threes. The first month after my daddy passed taught me that trouble just set up shop when it found a comfortable place to land. After I watched the police escort Wesley onto the elevator in handcuffs, I returned to the hospital room to find a new level of chaos had been unlocked. Desiree's crocodile tears were gone, and instead she was barking orders to everyone. Daddy's body had been covered with a white sheet as staff arranged to transport the body back to the Smithson County morgue for the funeral home to pick up.

Nana started a huge argument when she realized that Desiree's instructions didn't include burying Daddy next to my mama, which had always been his wish.

"You, old woman," Desiree hissed, "are done with this family. Consider this your notice to vacate my property." She then proceeded to say that Daddy had a new Will and Testament drawn up after they got married that named Desiree as the sole heir to his property, his belongings, and…The Comfy Cushion.

If I lived a thousand years, I could never forget the light that died out in Nana's eyes upon learning her daughter's restaurant—her legacy—was left to a total stranger who had no passion or interest in the business.

After that, everything went up in smoke. Desiree claimed to have sole custody of me. "It was Doug's last wish for Celeste to have a proper mother after his passing," she sniffed. "And that means things are gonna change around here."

While some part of me registered how horrific the scene had been, at the time I was still too numb to process any of it.

Desiree had us all fly back to River's Run together. I was by myself in business while she stayed in first class with Jeremy and Hillary. Marla and Nana had left the hospital without telling me their plans, so I alternated the entire flight between mourning my daddy, worrying over Nana, and praying that Wes was okay. I didn't let myself think on him too much or I would have come apart at the seams.

It wasn't until several days passed that the panic really set in. Upon our arrival back home, Desiree confiscated my cell phone, stomping her sharp stiletto against the screen to break it. Wesley could have tried the house phone…but it never rang. I couldn't get out of bed, and I don't remember eating. At some point the dehydration set in, making the tears stop.

Hollow.

I was hollow. A shell of the girl who had once been the beloved daughter of Doug and Rachel Hendricks. That Celeste was foreign to me. Her memory disappeared when her boyfriend left her on the day her daddy died.

Marla came with several boxes and packed up all of Nana's belongings. She came up to my tower to tell me that Nana was moving to a retirement community in Florida, near the beach. Nana would write to me as soon as she was settled, and she was really sorry she couldn't be here for me with Daddy's passing.

Or so Marla said. I didn't see her face because I was too grief-stricken to do anything other than stare at the ceiling until the roaring in my ears subsided. First my daddy, then Wes, then Nana. People certainly deserted me in threes, though I doubted that was what Mama meant.

When I didn't respond or react, Marla quietly climbed down the stairs and left. The tower was stifling, no longer the happy refuge of my childhood. All the happy photographs mocked me, my dead parents' faces smiling down at me in a permanent reminder that I would never see either of their faces doing so in real life again. I couldn't bear it for another second, and I shoved as much of my clothing that would fit into a backpack and went out to Nana's cottage, locking the door with a deadbolt behind me.

And there I stayed. Desiree came out and pounded on the door after the eight day mark so that I could attend Daddy's funeral with her. She had a scratchy black lace dress for me to wear with a high neck and skirt that brushed my ankles. I didn't say a word in protest, though, nor did I say a word during the entire service. The same preacher man as Mama's funeral presided over the affair. At the luncheon afterwards, I managed to sneak out the back door and sit on the ground, leaning against the building to count the passing clouds.

I couldn't take another person offering me their condolences. Their pitying looks knowing I was the orphan with no family to care for me. Nana hadn't come to the funeral, which could have been Desiree's doing, but it hurt either way. Why did I have to tell her that I needed her when my daddy died? She knew with my mama.

Enough time passed for the sun to crest the skyline by the time Maggie found me. She didn't say anything, just sat on the ground next to me. After a moment, she wrapped an arm around my shoulders, pulling me in to rest my head against her neck. It was the soft contact, the gentle touch that I hadn't felt since that fateful morning in Wesley's arms, which made the tears finally come.

"Wes should be here," I cried.

I could feel her nod against my hair. "I know, Cee. I'm sure he wants to be."

When Desiree, her kids, and I all returned home that evening, I made a beeline for Nana's cottage and collapsed onto her bed. It was one of the few places that didn't hold a memory of Wes and therefore the only place where I could breathe.

Days went by. I never fully slept, but I didn't leave the bedroom either unless it was to use the tiny, adjacent bathroom. Showering was pointless. School had no appeal whatsoever. Maggie came twice, but I refused to answer the door.

What happened to Wes that he didn't come back for me? Abandoning me was the opposite of what I expected him to do. I kept replaying the awful things we said to each other over and over again like a broken camcorder until I wanted to vomit. He couldn't really believe I likened him to his father, could he? I regretted it as soon as I said it, but then to have my traitorous words spit back at me when he was being arrested made me doubt his faith in me. Had I broken his heart beyond repair? Was this a breakup? We had never had a real fight before, so I didn't know what the protocol was for reconciling.

As time crept on, though, it became abundantly clear that the only thing I had to reconcile was my life without Wesley Madden.

I imagined Daddy and Mama reunited in some kind of beautiful Afterlife and wanted nothing more than to join them. Were they looking down on their only child, yearning for me like I did for them? Was I worrying them? Or would they welcome me with open arms? I didn't want to disappoint them in death, but I saw no hope towards making them proud in life. The future no longer existed; that kind of potential was terrifying.

As the days turned into weeks, I knew people were starting to get more concerned. Maggie stopped by every day after school. She alternated between yelling at me to snap out of it, reminding me that only my daddy died, I was still living. Other days she would curl up in a ball next to me, never saying a word, just letting her presence do all the talking.

Marla came by, too, giving me updates on the regulars at The Comfy Cushion. While I was surprised she stayed on now that the restaurant technically belonged to Desiree, I knew Marla didn't want to leave her best friend's life's work in the hands of a jealous rival. I wished I had the heart to thank Marla for all the sacrifices she had always made for my family—for me—but I couldn't do it. Misery was too potent as company.

Now, seven weeks after my daddy's death and The Last Day, as my mind had come to call Wesley's abrupt departure, Marla and Desiree both came into the bedroom, presenting a united front I had never seen before. While Marla's face was kind and full of concern, Desiree's was full of poison. Her makeup was still flawless and her dress still molded to her body in a way that should have been considered improper. How could I have changed so much and she so little?

"Celeste, honey," Marla whispered carefully as she edged onto the bed beside me, "we need to do something. You've gotta get out of this bed."

Unbidden, tears started sliding down my nose. I made no move to wipe them away. What did it matter anyway?

"We mean it, Celeste!" Desiree barked. She crossed her arms over her chest.

Marla frowned at her tone, but didn't say anything to contradict her. "Honey, when's the last time you showered?"

Two full minutes passed before Marla sighed and said, "Fine, then I guess we'll do this the hard way." She abruptly grabbed the hem of my t-shirt and yanked it upwards, pulling it over my head.

"HEY!" I shot out of bed, using the t-shirt to cover my chest. "It's none of your business, Marla!"

She stood up, clashing her hands into fists that rested on her hips. It was normally the position that made me quiver because I knew it meant I was in for a real scolding. Now I couldn't even muster up the energy to care.

"You will shower and you will eat a plate full of food or so help me, I will have you committed to the hospital!" Marla demanded.

I snorted. "You can't do that!"

Desiree stepped up shoulder to shoulder with Marla. "But *I* can. You live under my roof and are in my care, and this unseemly behavior ends today."

The entire exchange already deflated me. It was more effort than I had expended in months.

Sinking back onto the mattress, I couldn't look at them as I admitted, "There's no reason for me to shower. I just want to be left alone."

"Well that's just too damn bad," Marla tutted. "Get in the shower and I'll fix you something to eat."

As if to prove her point, she went into the bathroom and turned the water on. The bathmat made a smacking sound as she threw it on the floor.

"Celeste…?" Marla's voice suddenly went higher, cresting like it was on the verge of breaking. She came out of the bathroom holding the small garbage can from under the sink. "Have you been emptying the trash?"

I snorted again, bending down to root around in the backpack I had carelessly tossed under the bed and find clean clothes. "Of course not. Why?"

The strange octave remained. "Why aren't there any pads or tampons in the trash?"

What?

My mind finally caught up with Marla's, making me gasp and drop the socks I had been holding. Desiree's eyebrows rose to meet her hairline, and she brushed past Marla to enter the bathroom, throwing open the two drawers and solitary cabinet under the sink as if she needed to see the evidence for herself.

"There aren't any tampons in this bathroom!" she screeched. "What have you been using?"

I stared at them both in dumbstruck horror. The realization was too frightening and overwhelming to put into words. My mouth went dry as my heart pounded an unfamiliar rhythm to the panic coursing through my veins.

"Desiree," Marla whispered, equally as astonished as me, "I'm gonna run out to the store and grab us a pregnancy test."

Trouble came in three's? Seemed like I had the worst triple threat of them all.

PART TWO

"Until we have seen someone's darkness, we don't really know who they are. Until we have forgiven someone's darkness, we don't really know what love is."
-Marianne Williamson

CHAPTER 30
TICKETS TO THE STRUGGLE BUS AIN'T CHEAP

CELESTE

Ten years later

"ORDER UP!" Jesse called through the window, slamming his meaty hand down on the bell.

"Heard!" I hollered back over my shoulder. Continuing to pour the coffee into Mr. McInworthe's mug, I flashed him a smile. "Will that be your usual, sir?"

Lines crinkled around his eyes as he smiled back at me. "Gosh, you're as pretty as your mama."

It was a sentiment most of our older crowd felt the need to deliver weekly. Each and every time made my heart skip a beat. Ten years had passed since my daddy died, thirteen years since Mama's passing, and any reminder of them still ripped the wounds fresh and raw. Working at The Comfy Cushion had become my penance, an endless criminal sentence for which there was no parole.

The best thing I could do in these circumstances was focus on my work...and there was a lot of it. Over the past decade, The Comfy Cushion had slowly crumbled around us. All the other staff left until there was just me and Jesse, with Marla occasionally helping when I needed to go to an appointment. Desiree had successfully managed to alienate most of the food vendors to where we no longer had fresh, locally sourced produce and the quality of our food had gone downhill. No matter how many ways I tried to cut back on expenses or find better alternatives, the red line hung precariously over our profit margin. The patrons we had most days were regulars who remembered my parents and wanted to honor them, but made no secret of their disdain for Desiree.

The bell tinkled over the door as another customer entered. Without looking up, I called for them to go ahead and sit anywhere.

"Girl, you better get over here and give me frickin' hug!" squealed a voice I recognized.

"MAGGIE!" I raced around the corner and threw my arms around her. She jumped like a giddy little girl as she tightened her hold on my waist. "Why didn't you tell me you were coming back into town?"

When we were nineteen Maggie and I had gone to a party near the Army base a half hour away as a joke and Maggie met Sergeant Ezekiel Hayes. As a third party bystander, the chemistry between her and Zeke was palpable the moment they locked eyes. However, even I wasn't prepared for her to tell me a week later that they had gotten married. Nor could I fake a smile when she immediately followed her announcement with the news that he received orders to South Korea and she was going with him. Yet here we were going on seven years later and somehow she seemed just as happy and in love as I could ever hope for.

Since then, they had moved back Stateside to his current duty station in Fort Lewis, Washington, where he had risen in rank to Sergeant First Class. Maggie and I video chatted daily, but it had never come up that she planned on visiting.

"Since Zeke is deployed, I figured why not come home and visit for a spell?" Maggie laughed. "It's better than rattling around the house by myself for no good reason." Only I could have detected the undercurrent of sorrow in her laugh. She was scared.

"He's gonna be okay," I whispered.

She nodded, refusing to meet my eyes. "I know. He's good at what he does. It'll be fine."

We both migrated over to the counter. Maggie slid onto one of the vinyl barstools as I rounded the counter, grabbing a glass to fill with Coke for her. She was still one of the only women I knew who could have a diet consisting of sugar and anything deep fried, yet remain the same weight as high school.

Meanwhile, I had become every woman's worst fear. If I so much as looked at anything with butter or flavor, I gained five pounds. Curves rounded out my shape in a way they never had a decade ago, but with how much I worked, I was far too tired at the end of the day to care much about it.

"How's Iris?" Maggie asked.

"We'll know in a few minutes. She should be here soon," I replied tightly.

Maggie spun around on the stool. "At least this place is still open." It was an olive branch, meant to lighten the mood, but it only served to deflate my spirits even further.

"Barely," I hissed between clenched teeth. "She's gotten worse lately."

"Honey, tickets to the struggle bus ain't cheap. It's gonna get worse before it can get better."

The bell over the door tinkled again before I could

respond. Desiree walked in, her hair curled into an elaborate bun and large sunglasses obscuring her face. Her head did a sweep of the patrons before a deep frown settled on her face.

"I see you're not doing anything to improve business like we discussed, Celeste," Desiree chided. She clucked her tongue, lifting her sunglasses onto her head. "It would be a shame to see your mama's pride and joy close down because you didn't make enough of an effort."

Storm clouds were forming in Maggie's eyes, which never promised anything good.

"I'll come up with some new marketing ideas to run by you," I offered.

My stepmother smirked. "Be sure and do that."

Ever since I graduated high school, I spent all of my time at The Comfy Cushion. Desiree loved to remind me that it was *her* restaurant, and that I was lucky to be allowed to work there. Slowly, more and more of the responsibilities fell on my shoulders. As the other few waitresses quit and Marla opened her bakery down the street, I was left to run the place by myself. Desiree had never even learned where things were located. She rarely came in other than to berate me for the profits being down. There was never enough money to fix any of the equipment that was quickly falling into disrepair, nor would she invest money into digitizing our systems. The Comfy Cushion lagged further and further behind, and our reputation for great food had long since died out.

Desiree stepped around the counter to the cash register, pressing the button to open the drawer. She grabbed all of the paper bills that were inside and stuffed them into her wallet.

"What are you doing?" I asked incredulously.

"We're gonna do some shopping in Savannah after class is over." She glared at me for daring to question her.

It took sincere effort on my part not to roll my eyes. "And how am I supposed to make change for customers?"

"Go to the bank like a normal person!" snapped Desiree. She threw up her hands in impatience as if the answer was obvious.

"Desiree, I don't have anyone to watch the restaurant so I can go down to the bank." Talking to her often felt like talking to a toddler. She could rarely understand anything that didn't directly impact her.

Like now. Shrugging, her curt response was, "Then put up a sign and close down for twenty minutes."

Maggie sniggered at my facial expression, which had to indicate the murderous direction my thoughts were taking, but thankfully my stepmother was too distracted by counting the money to notice.

And so it had gone for eight long years. The moment I graduated high school, Desiree told me I had to start earning my keep by working at the restaurant. Everything I earned went right back into her pocket as "rent" for living in Nana's cottage. She said it wasn't right for me to live there for free any longer if I was legally an adult. A stipulation that wasn't passed along to her two children. Marla had to help me out to pay Jesse's salary more than once when there just wasn't enough profit from the restaurant to cover it.

Somehow Desiree continued to have money to burn. Credit cards came to the house by the dozen, and she was constantly shopping. While the bills piled up, repairs or updates down at The Comfy Cushion were ignored, and the house my mama and daddy worked so hard to fix up fell by the wayside. The whole thing made me sick to my stomach. Most nights lately I stayed up, tossing and turning until the wee hours of the morning, trying to get the math right to keep something afloat. It was like watching a slow motion train wreck of my parents' legacies going up in smoke.

Having Hillary back at home made it far worse. She took a gap year after high school. In her case, that meant she moved to Las Vegas and tried to live a champagne lifestyle on a drug store beer budget. She came home with her tail between her legs, wallowing in self-pity, before Desiree convinced her to go away to college. Hillary was accepted at Georgia State and then immediately pledged to a sorority to live in their house. She spent five years there, attending all kinds of parties and pageants, but never completed enough credits for a degree.

My stepmother was far more concerned with Hillary getting her M-R-S degree, however, and foamed at the mouth when her daughter started dating William Thornton-Belle-mere IV, the son of a Georgia congressman. After a year, they were engaged, and Desiree took out a second mortgage on the house and the restaurant, then sold two acres of land that had been in Daddy's family for generations to pay for an extravagant wedding at the Thornton-Bellemeres' country club. On the night of the rehearsal dinner, William was found with his dick in one of the bus boys at the restaurant. It caused a scandal that sent shockwaves through Atlanta society, and he fled town.

The scandal really hadn't impacted Hillary at all, other than a few people questioning how she didn't notice William was gay, but she had come back to our house carrying on as though life was over. Desiree's solution had been more shopping and a fancy new car. Like anyone in River's Run would be impressed that Hillary drove a Mercedes.

I knew Daddy would want me to help them and treat them like family, so that was what I continued to do. Hillary's sorrow might have been ridiculous to me, but to her it was very real, and I empathized with her for that. She had always been decent to Iris, too, which made it easier to keep my opinions to myself as far as she was concerned.

Right on cue, the bell chimed over the door for the third time and my daughter walked in. With her bright blue eyes and long, blonde hair, she was the spitting image of her father. So much so that when she asked at four years old why we didn't "match" like other mamas and daughters, I dyed my hair blonde and had maintained it ever since. Iris was the rainbow at the end of the storm, my light and only source of pride. Getting pregnant at sixteen should have been a nightmare, but instead became my saving grace. It was that tiny, squalling baby looking up at me with all the trust and love in the world that pushed the dark clouds away. And while I remained heartbroken at every milestone that I couldn't share with either my parents or her daddy, Iris made my life worth every tired morning and sleepless night.

"Hey, pipsqueak!" Maggie cried, crouching down to scoop Iris into a hug.

"Aunt Maggie, you're here!" Iris screamed. Her delightful laugh was a balm to my soul, pushing my irritation with Desiree out of my mind.

"Come along, Iris, and get changed," my stepmother instructed. "We need to leave soon for your class."

Our family dynamics were strange, and honestly varied depending on Desiree's mood. Taking it one day at a time was best.

It still surprised the hell out of me that Desiree took my pregnancy in stride. We had all met with Mr. Hildebrandt, the superintendent, and agreed for me to be fully enrolled in distance learning after the doctor confirmed how far along I was. As soon as I completed all the necessary credits, I would have my diploma. Never once did Desiree pressure me towards adoption, something I never could have considered, but she did maintain strict rules about eating a balanced diet, practicing prenatal yoga, and attending all my doctor's appointments. Her rules about Wesley never wavered; he was not informed of my pregnancy. Desiree and Hillary showed me a magazine article when I was six months along that had a photograph of Wesley attending a London movie premiere with a model on his arm. I cried every day until Iris was born over that betrayal.

On the day my daughter came into this world, Desiree and Marla both took me to the hospital. They each held my hand and coached me through childbirth. Desiree told the doctors I was not allowed to have any pain medication, that women had been giving birth naturally for thousands of years, but I was so delirious with pain and fear that I didn't voice an argument. Shortly after they placed Iris in my arms, Desiree sent Marla away to get me some food, then gently took the baby from me. She sat on the edge of the hospital bed, gazing softly at Iris's tiny pink bundle, before leveling me with a cold stare.

"You know, because you are a minor and in my charge, that means Iris is technically my daughter, not yours," Desiree stated.

Ice filled my lungs. What was she talking about?

"As long as you continue to do as I say, minding your manners and remembering where a hussy like you stands in society, I will let Iris know you're her mother," Desiree went on. "But the moment you become defiant will be the last time you ever see your daughter. D'you hear me, Celeste? If I ever catch you trying to contact that Madden boy again, Iris will disappear. That's not what you want, is it?"

How could a voice so honeyed drip nothing but venom? Fear settled into my heart like a dead weight.

"I won't do anything, Desiree, I promise." It was an easy promise to make, given the alternative. Iris had been alive for all of thirty minutes and was now the axis upon which my world spun. There was nothing I wouldn't do for her.

"Good, then we have an understanding," Desiree had agreed.

While she never helped with Iris as an infant, the more independent Iris became, the more Desiree threw her weight around. If I dared to disagree or question anything, Desiree would nonchalantly ask if I was being defiant. The gleam in her eye always told me that she remembered the threat; there was nothing nonchalant about her question.

Thankfully, Iris never caught on or seemed confused, and I knew better than anyone that a child could never hurt by having more people love them. Desiree and my stepsiblings all doted on Iris, constantly praising her and showering her with gifts and attention. When Iris was a toddler, Hillary and Desiree forced her into tons of beauty pageants. I was vehemently opposed, but bit my tongue. However, when Iris started dance lessons as her beauty pageant talent, we all discovered she had an incredible gift for ballet.

Hearing all the praise from dance instructors turned Desiree's head, and pageants were dropped in favor of more dance instruction. Now, at only 10-years-old, Iris was the youngest ballerina ever to dance with the Savannah Ballet Company. Having her daddy's height and lithe figure certainly helped. She attended dance classes five days a week in Savannah as well as private lessons twice a week that I knew firsthand cost a fortune. Desiree included their fees in my "rent." It was all worth it, however, to watch my baby girl shine.

Right now at The Comfy Cushion, Iris nodded. "I'll go change." Instead of heading back to the office, however, Iris came over and wrapped her arms around me. "I love you, Mama," she whispered.

No one had prepared me for how much those four words would knock the wind out of me. The first time I heard them, I burst into tears, scaring poor Iris in the process. All the stress from the diner and the house melted away every time she said it.

"Hi, Rainbow," I murmured back, smoothing her blonde hair away from her face. "You have a good dance class, m'kay? I love you."

"Come on, we don't have all day!" Desiree snapped. She waved impatiently towards the door. "Go get your leotard on this instant!"

Iris flashed me an apologetic smile as she pulled away. "I'll show you my report later, okay? You're gonna be proud of me."

It was Maggie who chimed in. "We're always proud of you, pipsqueak. Now go break a leg!"

Waving, Iris dashed back towards the office to change into her dance clothes. Desiree huffed impatiently again. "I'll be waiting in the car," she informed us. "Make sure you get this place cleaned up, Celeste. It looks more like a barn than a restaurant."

Maggie's jaw dropped. "That woman is the devil incarnate. How you still put up with it is beyond me."

I shrugged. "She does right by Iris. That's all that matters."

My best friend bit her lip, a tell that she was holding back on saying more. It was a topic of conversation we had exhausted too many times.

"I'm so glad you're here." I reached across the counter to clasp her hands in mine. "How long are you planning on staying?"

She shrugged. "We'll see how things go with my mom. She's between boyfriends again, so she's back to being Mom of the Year. I can only handle that for so long." We both chuckled. Her mom was constantly cycling through relationships.

Just then, Bob from the garage down the street burst through the front door. "Poor Miss Shirley died!" he announced to The Comfy Cushion patrons.

As the few people in the dining room tittered over the new gossip, I tried to mask the pain creeping up my spine. I hadn't seen Wesley's great aunt since Iris was born. Her health took a turn and she was confined to bed most days, with a live in nurse caring for her round the clock. Most of the town had forgotten all about her. I felt instantly guilty that I hadn't checked on her in all these years. I was too afraid she would see Iris and make the connection to Wesley.

Because one thing was certain. Not a day had passed in over ten years where my dreams weren't filled with shaggy haired, blonde boys and megawatt smiles.

CHAPTER 31
THE PAST ALWAYS CATCHES UP WITH YOU

WESLEY

SLAM!

My right fist connected with the bag.

PFFT!

My left fist sent an upper cut to match the first.

It didn't matter how many times in how many ways I beat the punching bag. Rage was my natural state and had been for years. Visualizing my father's smug face on the center of the bag always took the edge off, though not enough to fully make the anger go away. I had often wondered if competing in an MMA tournament would finally make the hatred dissipate, but unfortunately, all of my contracts prohibited me from doing anything that might mar my face.

And by contracts I meant the numerous modeling gigs my agent booked. So far I had done ad campaigns for Calvin Klein, Dolce & Gabbana, Tom Ford, and Betsey Johnson. If I wanted to venture out, I could have my pick of runway shows to model in, but I found fashion shows tacky. Hell, I found all of it weird, but if someone wanted to pay me $8 million to snap some photos of me in funny clothes, I would be an idiot to pass that up.

Modeling helped me earn my own money, which had more than paid my way through college and paid my father back all the money from my Emory Episode. Now I was on the verge of joining Madden Enterprises as assistant general counsel in our legal department. My bar exam results were still pending, but I felt confident that I passed. Studying came easy for me, thanks to Celeste.

"No, not Celeste!" I muttered under my breath. If I started thinking about her now, my day would be ruined.

"Talking to yourself is a sure sign of madness," Phillip said, breezing into the room with a tablet in hand and an Airpod clipped to his ear. He had been my official assistant since I started college. It was difficult to manage accelerated classes on top of modeling gigs and the never ending social functions my father required me to attend as his consort. Tabloids loved me because I often had other hot, young models on my arm. The girls liked the exposure. I liked that it gave old Benny boy the impression that I had moved on.

Moving on was impossible, though. Celeste's ghost had become my shadow, haunting my every waking moment and encompassing all of my dreams at night. She was never going to be someone I got over because soul mates weren't meant to pass you by. Nothing was ever going to convince my father otherwise, however.

Once, after I started my Bachelor's program at Princeton, I found Maggie on Facebook and begged her to tell me how Celeste was doing. She read the message, then blocked me, thereby further breaking my heart. If Maggie wasn't willing to give me the time of day, there was no way Celeste was ready to. They were two peas in a pod, and as much as it killed, I had to accept that I had essentially disappeared right at the moment Celeste needed me most. My final words to her still lived rent free in my head, the guilt often constricting the oxygen in my lungs.

So I did the only thing I could do: I focused on working hard to be a man that would be worthy of her whenever I had the chance to win her back. Double majoring in business and economics at Princeton, I managed to graduate suma cum laude in only three years. Then it was on to law school at Harvard. Combined with the international photo shoots and the charity I anonymously founded for neurological cancer research, life kept me busy enough that I appeared on the outside as a functioning human being.

Inside, I was anything but.

"What's on the agenda today, Phillip?" I asked with a sigh.

He snorted. By now we had spent enough time together that we could read each other like a book. While I wouldn't necessarily call him a friend, Phillip had definitely earned my respect with the work and dedication he provided for all aspects of my life. Working myself to death seemed to have improved his impression of me, too.

"You have orientation, followed by a board meeting this afternoon. And I need your answer for the shoot in Rio," he stated.

I punched the bag again in my frustration. "Jesus Christ, my father owns the fucking company. I've been coming to his business meetings since I was barely old enough to walk. I seriously have to attend orientation on my first day?"

He shrugged, which was his habit when he agreed with my assessment but didn't want to risk badmouthing Madden Enterprises. No matter what, Phillip would always remain loyal to my father.

I gritted my teeth. "Fine. Hold off on Rio. I have no clue what I'll be doing that far out. Anything else?"

"The nurse called. Shirley passed away early this morning." Phillip looked grim, no doubt assuming the news would set me off.

My already too small of a heart shrank further. Great Aunt Shirley had been my last link to River's Run, to what I considered my real life, which was why I paid for a private nurse to care for her the past eight years. My schedule was far too demanding to visit, but I called her on the phone as often as I could. As the years passed, her mind was gone, often confusing me for her dead husband or dead son, but I tried to make her smile as best I could. She took me in when nobody else would, and if not for her generosity, I never would have met Celeste. I owed a lot to her.

Hearing of her death brought up so many mixed feelings and memories...sadness, regret, belonging. She gave me something no one else had ever given me before—a home. I loved her for it. I should've made more of an effort to visit. Poor aunt Shirley went to the grave without ever truly knowing how much she meant to me.

"It looks like she's made you the executor of her estate," Phillip added.

"Guess today won't be my first day after all," I commented.

"Wesley, with all due respect, you can't seriously be thinking of—"

"Of what? Putting my first day at my father's corporation on hold because of a family issue requiring my attention?" I snarled. "Pretty sure they aren't gonna fire me. Benedict won't even notice."

It was true. I hadn't seen or actually spoken to my father

in almost three years due to our conflicting schedules. Well, that and the fact that I actively avoided him at all costs.

My mind was made up. Aunt Shirley deserved more in life than what I had given her, so the least I could do was go down in person to settle her affairs. Maybe I'd even get a chance to say goodbye in some small way.

Phillip's eyebrows contorted as he grappled with his response.

"Just spit it out," I ordered. I already knew what he was going to say.

"What about her?" He didn't need to use her name for me to know who he meant.

Exhilaration and anxiety were currently dancing in my chest. I wanted to see Celeste more than I wanted to take my next breath. Perhaps this was my chance to finally make things right between us. It could be a sign that our timing was finally right.

"Guess it's a good thing my charming personality is still intact." I winked at him.

Slowly unwinding the hand wrap from my workout, I turned towards the window, effectively dismissing him. All of downtown Atlanta was visible from the apartment I purchased a few blocks away from my father's building, but in my mind's eye, the only thing I could see was a young girl with a wild brown mane of hair and a shy smile.

"I'm coming home to you, lovebug," I whispered.

CHAPTER 32
THE WELCOME WAGON
CELESTE

Spending time with Maggie was nearly impossible over the next two days. One of the grill tops stopped working and without money for an electrician, the repairs fell on me. I watched every YouTube video I could find at night after the restaurant closed, but nothing I tried did any good. The grill top unit would have to be replaced or worse—the entire appliance might need to go.

It was therefore incredibly tempting when she arrived on Friday morning, arm in arm with Marla, and sang out, "We're going to a masquerade tonight!"

Wait—a what?

"A masquerade? Did we go back in time?" I quipped.

Marla laughed as she came around the corner and untied the apron around my waist. "I'm taking over for the day."

Maggie grinned. "It's a costume party over in Savannah! Some big charity auction, party-thing hosted by an anonymous bigwig. I won tickets on the radio this morning!"

I snorted. "Nobody listens to the radio anymore, Mags."

She shrugged. "That's probably why I was able to win the tickets. C'mon, I wanna go! And I can't go alone! Poor Zeke would hate to learn you let me go into Savannah by myself at night."

Well, Maggie had me there. Zeke wasn't the sort of man to put hands on a woman, but being on the receiving end of his disappointment was akin to disappointing a saint. Tourists might believe the propaganda that Savannah was a safe city, but anyone who lived in the area knew otherwise. A solo woman downtown at a party was not the best choice.

"I don't have anything to wear to a costume party," I argued.

"Then it's a good thing we now have all day to get ready," Maggie countered, crossing her arms over her chest. Her obstinance would be my undoing someday.

"Marla, I feel so guilty!" I cried.

She waved a hand at me to dismiss my sentiment. "You deserve a night off, honey. You're working yourself to death."

A costume party *did* sound fun. It had been so long since I had a night out. I was either at The Comfy Cushion far later than I should have been or at home helping Iris with her schoolwork. Still, as a mother, it wasn't like I could just up and leave her for the day.

"What about Iris?"

"She's gonna have a slumber party with her favorite auntie tonight, of course," Marla explained with a smile. Friday was the one night of the week where Iris didn't have a class or some sort of ballet commitment. Our usual routine consisted of her hanging out at the counter of the diner, just like I used to do, then heading home to watch a movie in our pajamas. It wasn't exactly groundbreaking but it was our ritual just the same. I didn't want to disappoint her by skipping it.

"Nope, we're not doing this!" Maggie stood up and

walked around the counter to me, firmly placing both hands on my shoulders to stare me down. "Get out of that head of yours, Celeste Hendricks. You are *allowed* to have your own adult fun. It doesn't make you a bad mom."

If only it was that simple to turn my brain off. I was an overthinker; the more you pointed it out to me, the more my brain overthought it.

I sighed heavily. Money was a sore subject since I didn't want to outright admit to Maggie how much Desiree took from me, but I also knew she would offer to pay for whatever I needed if I raised it as an argument. Zeke didn't make a ton of money from being in the Army, but he certainly made enough to provide for the two of them. Every now and again Maggie would go work at a salon to keep up with her cosmetology license, but it bored her to tears to perform the same haircuts all the time, so it never lasted long.

"C'mon," my friend said, clearly believing she won the battle. "We're gonna go thrifting and find some fun costumes!"

Three hours later, we were in our third thrift store in Savannah. Nothing I found would satisfy Maggie, who wanted me to be some sort of provocative vixen—something I most definitely was not.

"How come you can be an old lady and I can't?" I whined. Her muumuu dress, beige orthotic shoes, and frizzy gray wig were hilarious.

She rolled her eyes like the answer was obvious. "Because no one is gonna wanna bang you tonight if you look like a grandma!"

That brought me up short, colliding into a display of handbags. "I am NOT having a one night stand," I hissed at her through clenched teeth.

"You're right. Hopefully you'll start a relationship!"

"Maggie…" She knew this was a dangerous topic for me. I hadn't dated anyone other than Wesley, and despite all the years between us, I didn't think I was ready to date again. Certainly not as a solo mom working a million hours a week.

Her brown eyes were warm but firm as she assessed me. Maggie stayed by my side through Wesley's disappearance, through my pregnancy, and then as a teen mom. She never once complained that we had to stay in so I could be home with Iris or protested when all our movie nights turned to animated Disney cartoons for my daughter to watch. When we were in the newborn stage, she was one of the few people who ever watched Iris so I could get some sleep or take a shower long enough to wash my hair *and* body. Even though I never told her the full details of what happened at the hospital or the horrible fight Wesley and I had the morning my father died, she didn't question my decision to cut him out completely to preserve what was left of my heart. Maggie had been just as aggrieved when candid tabloid photos of Wesley with models and celebrities appeared in the papers. After all, he had been her friend, too.

"Cee, you know I love you more than my own family. I have respected every decision you've made in your personal life, whether it made sense to me or not." She grimaced before continuing. "But it's time to let him go. There's a reason the rear view mirror is smaller than the windshield."

How could I tell her that letting go hurt too much? That I was so used to numbing everything and everyone out just to function, that I wasn't ready to stare down the future knowing Wesley wasn't in it? Grief had permanently altered me as a human being, and I was in so deep now that I couldn't tell if it was from the death of my parents or losing the person who mattered most to me. Life kept dealing me a shit hand, so I just accepted it was the way it was.

"It's not that simple," I settled on as a reply.

Her brow furrowed. "Then it's time to roll out the welcome wagon for your vagina."

We both burst out laughing.

"I don't even wanna think about how dry and dusty you must be down there!" she giggled.

When I could take in enough air, I wiped the tears from my eyes. "There's something wrong with you, Mags! I already said, no one night stands!"

She nodded. "Then we'll have to settle for a one night blowie." Her grin told me how determined she was to make that happen before the night was through.

However, I was distracted by a mannequin visible just over her right shoulder. Pointing to the dress on it, I asked, "What d'you reckon?"

Maggie squealed. "Sir, we'd like to try this on!" she called out to the store attendant.

Ten minutes later I was being laced into a corset-style top on a dress that barely came mid-thigh. If I danced with any kind of enthusiasm tonight, everyone in the vicinity would get quite the show. My friend might have also become a sadist because she seemed to relish my agonized cries from how tightly she laced me in. Pretty sure my tits were closing in on my throat from how high the corset shoved them upward.

"There!" she declared. "Check yourself out!"

I stepped out of the dressing room to look in the three way mirror. The dress was a pale blue, like a color you'd expect to see for Easter. Iridescent tear drop pearls were woven into the material, giving all of my movements a shimmering effect.

The sweetheart neckline combined with the tight corset definitely made the girls perkier than they had been since I had Iris, but in a way that made me feel sexy. A frilly petticoat created volume at the skirt that flared out at the waist, making the length almost indecent. It reminded me of my prom dress, only way sexier.

"I can totally do your hair and makeup!" Maggie clapped gleefully. "Ooh, and shoes! We need some stunners to pull off this Cinderella motif you've got going on!"

Still mesmerized by the reflection staring back at me, I was barely paying attention when I declined. "It's a masquerade, right? I want to wear something as beautiful as this over my face."

Anonymity was the only way I would be brave enough to wear a dress like this.

"We also need to wax your welcome wagon," whispered Maggie mischievously.

CHAPTER 33
SAVANNAH SURPRISES
WESLEY

PHILLIP SOMETIMES DESERVED MORE than the obscene amount of money I already paid him, and pulling off a last minute charity gala for my foundation was probably one of those times. When my father raged about me missing my first day on the legal team, Phillip was able to smooth the whole thing over by providing information for my foundation's event in Savannah that dozens of celebrities and politicians accepted invitations to attend. It was already established in my Madden Enterprises contract that obligations to modeling companies and *Cure, Rise, Hope,* my foundation, took precedence over anything my father might want.

What Phillip failed to mention was that this last minute event was actually a costume party.

I groaned. "I don't want to wear some cheesy costume!"

Phillip shrugged. "Then wear your tux with a mask and a top hat. You can be the Phantom of the Opera." He continued to clack away on the keyboard next to me on our first class flight.

Long gone were the days when I used Benedict Madden III's private plane.

It wasn't the worst idea to add a mask to my tux, but I wasn't going to tell him that. My hope was to remain as anonymous as possible tonight so that I could slip away and head out to River's Run. We were going to meet with the attorney early tomorrow afternoon to look over Aunt Shirley's final Will and Testament, but I couldn't stomach knowing how close I was to Celeste and not seeing her.

If all of the rich, conceited pricks who normally attended these functions sank their claws into me, I would never leave. Some of those fuckers could drone on and on for hours without saying anything worthwhile.

I liked that Phillip included a number of tickets at a cheaper rate for regular people to purchase. Those all sold out immediately. My guess was that he selected a venue that had some sort of VIP area to separate the society people from the rest. Maybe I could mingle with the non-celebrity guests and avoid everyone altogether.

"Find someone from a local salon who can give me a temporary new look," I ordered. "I don't want to be recognized."

Phillip paused his typing, raising an eyebrow at me.

I sighed. "Just do it. I need a night off from being Wesley Madden, heir to the Madden fortune. I'm too wound up over everything else going on."

Thankfully that answer satisfied him, and Phillip nodded before going back to his computer.

Technically it wasn't a lie, either. Law school had been hard work, but it wasn't what I really wanted to do with my life. Hell, corporate law was my least favorite out of all my classes. If I really had to practice law, I would rather do something like criminal or family law, something where I might have a happy ending down the line. Arguing with other egotistical jackasses in a board room over the various ways to make my billionaire father even more money wasn't exactly how I envisioned my life going, but then again, nothing had been so far.

Grief was funny like that.

I accepted my father's job offer because I had become so numb to him over the years that I no longer fought it. We both knew I still hated him with a burning passion—wouldn't spit on him if he were on fire—but he kept me under his thumb for so long when I served my probation as a teen that it was second nature to me now.

He had to pull all kinds of strings to let me go to Montmeri, the international boarding school in France, while I was facing criminal charges like attempted murder. A whole team of lawyers worked around the clock on my defense, citing my youth, my mental state, and my history as a "troubled kid." It took nearly a year to reach a plea deal that satisfied the judge, winding up with me on probation until I graduated high school. If my father or my probation officer ever reported poor behavior on my part, even bad grades, I would be sent to prison. That was enough to set me straight and keep my head down.

That, and the fact that I couldn't access the girl I loved.

A flight attendant came over the intercom and announced we were beginning our descent into Savannah. Phillip snapped the laptop closed, preparing to stow it in his briefcase.

"I have a hairstylist and makeup artist meeting us in your suite," he said.

Perfect.

By the time the charity gala started, I was unrecognizable. For the past few years I had worn my hair cropped at the sides, with longer, controlled waves at the top. Gone was the shaggy scruff that Cel—that certain people used to prefer. The hairstylist who arrived adjusted a dark brown wig that we slicked back to resemble the Phantom. Rather than wearing a mask that covered one side of my face, I added a white mask that covered the top half, only exposing my mouth and jawline.

The hairstylist, whose name I couldn't remember, had bright pink hair and a mouth lathered in sparkly lipstick, kept shooting longing looks at my dick. When she was done, she leaned over my chair, exposing her cleavage until I could stare right down her shirt, and asked if I was satisfied with my experience. Her breathy voice only added to the invitation she was clearly extending to me.

Fuck that.

"Yep, we're all good here," I said, standing upright so abruptly that she fell back on her ass. I didn't even offer to help her up, just swept from the bathroom into the bedroom of the suite and firmly closed the door. I locked it for good measure.

Women tended to throw themselves at me because money and power made their brains go funny. It was like they couldn't actually see me as a person beyond me as a figurehead for my father's corporation. Kinda gross, to be honest. Especially since I was a giant asshole to most people and nothing about my behavior should have been attractive, let alone indicated I was interested in fucking.

Nope, there was only one girl in that department. And if I played my cards right, I just might catch a glimpse of her before the weekend was over.

"Guests have started arriving," Phillip called through the door. "Are you ready?"

I sighed. I would never be ready for one of these things. "Be out in a minute."

Heading over to the bar cart tucked into a corner of the room, I poured myself a double shot of whiskey. Galas and parties didn't make me nervous, but being so close to *her* did. Just knowing that I was close enough to jump in a car and go made me want to do it. The temptation was nearly bowling me over.

A masochist, however, I was not. I needed to get it through my head that she might very well reject me. And for all I knew, the restraining order had become permanent. I was too chicken shit to actually check the records during law school because learning that truth might have killed me. Dear old Dad certainly never let me forget about it any time I even hinted at wanting to write to her.

This was how to drive a man crazy. Keep his girl an arm's length away.

Pouring another double, I threw the shot back and headed for the door.

A costume party benefiting *Cure, Rise, Hope* was the perfect idea, not that I'd ever tell Phillip. That jackass let every compliment go to his head. Costumes always established a warped sense of freedom at these events, and with the booze flowing and a different DJ in the VIP lounge, the main dance floor, and the roof top deck, there was plenty of opportunity for people to melt away as their inhibitions reigned.

The best part? None of the goons from my father's society bothered me all night. My disguise was working perfectly so that I could wind through the dancers with ease. No one paid me any attention. Which suited me just fine because my nerves led me to down shot after shot. Alcohol was making my head fuzzy.

What surprised me, however, was that one woman on the main dance floor caught my attention. Her blonde hair was piled into an elaborate mess of curls on her head, sprinkled with blue sparkles that matched the light blue of her dress. It was short, almost showing her ass, but definitely drawing my attention to her long legs. I couldn't stop my mind from wondering what might be in store for me underneath a costume like that. A traditional masquerade mask with lace, beads, and pale blue feathers obscured her face.

She seemed to be with only one friend, a woman dressed up like an old lady, including a walker and orthotic shoes. The juxtaposition between the two was quite comical, but I couldn't shake the feeling that I had met them both before. It was an eerie sense of déjà vu that I hadn't ever experienced, leaving me unsettled and drinking far more whiskey than I should have been. That was the only reason I hadn't yet left for River's Run. I was an asshole, but I wasn't going to drive drunk. And I refused to be left in that tiny town without a vehicle to get myself back out.

The more that I watched them from my corner of the bar, the more my smile grew. They both were having fun, laughing and dancing to every song, shouting the lyrics to what must have been their favorites. Whiskey made me bolder than ever, and for once Phillip's advice to move on from Celeste sounded appealing. There was no way I ever would have those thoughts sober, though, which was the only reason I hadn't yet acted on them.

Still, the stiff drink in my hand was playing with my head.

I had to talk to her, even if it was just a hello. It didn't have to turn into anything more than a conversation, right?

My costume wasn't the only phantom hallowing these halls tonight. Celeste, in all her ghostly, gorgeous glory, haunted me as I resolutely set my drink down and headed over.

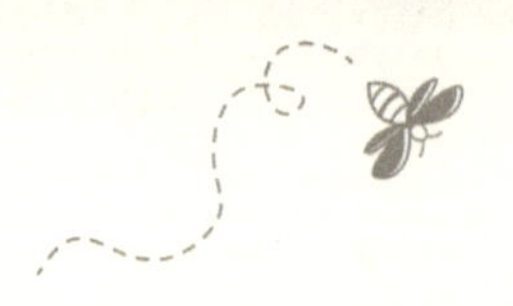

CHAPTER 34
CINDERELLA AT THE BALL
CELESTE

IT HAD BEEN a long time since I had this much fun. Maggie had a way of bringing out my joy, making me forget all the stressors that were constantly weighing me down, so I could just be a carefree woman out on the town. What did it matter that my mama's legacy was literally falling apart around me? Why did I care that my shattered heart no longer operated? Who else paid attention to the love of their life ghosting them on the worst day of their life? Certainly not me!

Music thumped loudly around me, the bass high and settling in my bones. Hours of standing on my feet at The Comfy Cushion day in and day out had prepared me to dance the night away now. Even in the too high heels Maggie forced on my feet, I barely felt a thing as I swayed my hips to the rhythm of the beat. Iris would have been proud of my skills.

I was simply proud that I managed not to break an ankle in a pair of heels that laced up my ankle with glittery, glass beads. Cinderella, indeed.

Maggie's costume caused more than one rowdy pack of guys to buy us a round of drinks. Everyone thought it was hilarious to see a grandma get down on the dance floor. I had a delightful buzz, and even though I declined every offer to dance, all of the attention was flattering enough to forget my misgivings over my too-short dress.

"Yo, that man at the bar hasn't taken his eyes off you for a second!" Maggie shouted in my ear. She nodded her head over my shoulder, directing my attention to a man in a tailored tuxedo with a white mask covering most of his face. He donned a top hat and a swordsman cape with his costume, but that wasn't what made my heart flutter. It was the intensity of his smolder that instigated the goosebumps erupting down my arms and made my thighs clench together. No one had looked at me like that since Wesley.

The worst part? I didn't exactly mind.

There was something about the man that seemed familiar, but as much as I wracked my alcohol-addled brain, I couldn't place him. Back in the day, The Comfy Cushion was a hotspot for tourists, so it was possible he had been one of our earlier patrons. Yet he didn't look any older than me.

Our eye contact prompted him to guzzle the rest of the drink in his hand before sauntering over.

He didn't say a word, simply held out a white gloved hand as if presuming I had already agreed to dance with him.

I rolled my eyes at Maggie. She returned my look with an evil grin, glancing suggestively at his waiting hand.

"Welcome wagon!" she mouthed.

After we found our costumes earlier, Maggie had dragged me to her old salon, where she was still good friends with the owner. They let us use one of the spare booths so Maggie could do our hair and makeup before squeezing me into the waxer's appointments. My skin was smoother than silk on all areas of my body, much to Maggie's delight.

Her reminder now only made me flush. I glanced at the man, who did not seem to mind my hesitation. His hand never wavered as he waited patiently for my acceptance.

Wesley's face burst so clearly in my mind when I slid my hand into this stranger's that I stopped short. It wasn't my first hallucination of him, but definitely the most intense.

The man smiled. Clasping my hand firmly, he led me further onto the dance floor. Everyone parted for him easily as though he had the god given right to be in the middle of the throng. Right as we reached the center, the song changed over to a slower melody. "I Will (When You Do)" by Avery Anna and Dylan Marlowe started playing, their crooning challenge to one another echoing the challenge in my heart. I couldn't cheat on someone who hadn't been present in over ten years.

So why did it feel like I was?

Maybe because there was something about the stranger in the mask that reminded me of Wesley. His eyes had the same power over me, though it was impossible to tell their true color in the smoky lowlights of the room with a mask and hat shadowing his features. The tiny bit of hair I could see underneath his top hat was so slicked back with hair product that it looked nearly black. He was taller than I remembered Wes being, but then again, memories faded with time.

The stranger spun me out, then back in, stopping me just before I collided with his chest. He dipped me back low and his head fell into my cleavage. I could feel his warm breath between my breasts as I slowly returned upright, his nose grazing my skin the entire time. Just to get my bearings, or perhaps to tease him as much as he was doing to me, I turned so that my ass was pressed into his groin, wrapping one arm up around his neck. The man leaned down, letting his mouth meet my earlobe. He briefly nipped it before murmuring, "You are a vision."

It was so low I could barely make out the words, but they sent lightning straight between my thighs. All of the drinks were hitting me at once. Desire flooded my senses, the tequila coursing through my veins amplifying the sensation.

Just once, I wanted to forget Wesley Madden like he had forgotten me. Just once, I wanted to throw caution to the wind and do something reckless like every other woman did in their life. Days were flying by in a monotony of dark grays and black; the trajectory of my life on a loop for which there was no escape.

But this masked stranger, with his hungry stare, and impressive dance skills made me see color for the first time in years. Suddenly, I was back at the Georgia Aquarium, eyes wide to the brilliant fish and sea creatures around me. It was the same sort of sensation, where the real world was a muffled backdrop against the bright joy surrounding me. I wanted to feel like that again. Weightless and carefree.

So I chased that feeling. I leaned up and kissed the masked stranger.

The moment our lips met, all I could see or feel was Wesley. Memories of our last kiss consumed me, bringing back all of the love and bliss I used to feel in his arms. My eyes shot open, and I gasped in surprise.

For his part, the man looked equally as startled. His gloved hand brushed his lips in the wonder I knew was echoed in my own expression.

"No names. Just tonight," I panted before launching myself at him once more. This time, his lips opened to greet me, his tongue sweeping through my mouth as though committing the taste to memory. Strong arms wound around my waist, sealing off any air between us, and I had the errant thought in the back of my mind that it had been years since I last felt this safe. It was a ridiculous thought—this man could very well be a serial killer for all I knew—but the omniscient assurance that he was going to make me happy overrode any concern of danger.

Maggie's whoop of delight behind me drew my attention, hyper aware of the hundreds of people around us. The man offered me a small smile, keeping one arm encircled around my waist before steering me away from the crowd. We reached a darkened staircase that led up to the VIP lounge, and with a simple nod to the bouncers, the velvet rope opened to us. However, rather than leading me towards the dancers and bar area in the VIP section, the man kept a firm grip on my waist and pulled me towards the outdoor balcony overlooking downtown Savannah.

Party goers were decidedly more drunk in this part of the event. An outdoor bar was lit up with blacklights and neon painted boards created alcoves for couples to have a veil of privacy. Another DJ was set up in the corner, but the dance floor consisted of people gyrating on one another. There was far more skin exposed with these dancers than the ones inside.

The man went to the corner of the bar and grabbed two glasses with a glowstick inside the drinks before returning to me. He placed one in my hand. Rather than guiding us towards the rest of the revelry, we headed towards a wood wall with slashes of neon paint glowing ominously in the blacklights. With a forceful shove, a panel of the wall opened to a narrow hallway of sorts as the hotel's typical lattice privacy fence stood on the other side. Once he pushed the temporary wall back into place, we were enclosed in darkness, the bass from the music still rattling the floor. Stars were just barely visible overhead as they mingled with the street-lights below and the blacklights to my left.

Our glasses clinked, a sign I interpreted as an instruction to drink. Knocking back the alcohol burned my throat far more than anything I'd tasted yet. The man pulled my drink's glow stick, a neon blue that gave off very little light, from the glass and swirled it around the swell of my breasts. Alcohol dribbled down my cleavage, and before I could suck in a breath, the man's tongue was there, licking the alcohol off my skin as his hands crept up the backs of my thighs. I leaned back against the lattice fence of the hotel, using the branches of whatever flowery shrub that grew there to support myself, as my knees were quickly giving way to his attention.

A long finger slipped down the corset, circling my nipple. The rest of the man's fingers pushed their way in, forcing my tits up and over the steely ribbing, so that his tongue could work its way around my erect nipple. I moaned, the sensation sending a flood of lust between my thighs.

"Shh," he urged me in a whisper.

But there was no way anyone could hear my cries over the loud music pounding through the speakers.

The man directed his attention to my other nipple while a hand crept up to my panties. Despite my better judgement, Maggie insisted I wear a thong tonight, claiming a sexy costume demanded sexy underwear. The scrap of lace at my entrance should have dissolved from the wetness pooling there, and when the man's fingers swept across, he groaned around my nipple.

Without warning, two fingers were shoved inside me, plunging deep. My muscles clenched tightly at the foreign intrusion. I hadn't ever even used a sex toy for fear of Iris discovering it, so my body was no longer acquainted with the feeling of penetration. Now, though, instinct propelled me forward, letting my knees fall open as a hand snuck down to meet his and pick up the pace. His thumb joined my index finger on my clit, swirling rapidly as the two fingers pistoned in and out of me. One of his digits curled, hitting the elusive G-spot Maggie alluded to, and I saw stars. If this was what she meant I had been missing, I would kill her for downplaying its significance.

Kisses were trailing across my breasts as the man sucked hard enough to pucker the skin. There would be marks for weeks, some part of me realized, but I was lost in the growing pressure low in my belly. When the man's mouth worked up to my neck, licking along the edge of my jawline before nibbling on my earlobe, it only took three little words for me to shatter.

"Cum for me," he whispered.

I detonated. The orgasm barreled through me as the stranger in the mask nuzzled into my neck. I clung to the vines for dear life as ripple after ripple of pleasure left me shaking. His thumb continued to circle my clit, working me down from my high.

I didn't stop to think as I dropped to my knees. His belt was unsnapped in the blink of an eye and his massive erection unfurled from his boxers. Letting my jaw relax as much as possible, I took as many inches in my mouth as I could. I loved the way his cock tasted and how good it felt hitting the back of my throat.

He let out a guttural cry, bracing himself on the fence behind me as I worked more of his dick down my throat. I was a snake, unhinging my jaw, willing to cut off my own oxygen supply if it meant I could continue sucking on him like a lollipop. My hand cupped around his balls, applying a light pressure of massage. Tears were starting to leak out the corner of my eyes from how hard I fought my gag reflex, but I couldn't stop.

The stranger took charge, thrusting his hips forward to fuck my mouth. He set a rapid pace, and the tears fell in earnest. I couldn't breathe, I was choking as his rigid shaft stretched my throat to the max, and as I hummed my approval, he spasmed ropes of cum in my mouth.

By the time I finished swallowing, which was difficult from how sore my throat was, the stranger pulled me up by the elbows. It was too dark to see his facial expression and I was too shy to break the silence. He placed a chaste kiss on my mouth before looping his hand through mine. We both took a moment to rearrange our clothing, then exited the way we entered.

Back inside the light of the hotel, I offered him a shy smile, grateful the lacy mask still obscured my face. His breath caught at the sight of my smile. Without another word, he tugged at my hand, leading us towards the elevators. I snagged a shot glass off a passing waiter's tray and gulped it down. If we were going to his hotel room, I needed all the liquid courage I could get.

Once we reached the elevator, the man swept off his top hat. His gloves had long since gone, probably when we were out on the balcony. Dark tresses fell down in a silky sheet around his face, and he swept off his tuxedo jacket in one fluid motion. The moment the elevator doors closed, the stranger descended on my mouth like he needed the oxygen in my lungs to function.

I swore on Mama and Daddy's graves I would never drink this much again, but everything about this strange man's touch set me on fire. I grinded against him, chasing relief between my legs that could dull the throbbing ache that formed there. The air charged with the current between us and I welcomed the feel of it. We only had tonight after all, so I needed to make it count.

The elevator doors opened on a suite rather than a hallway, something I was far too drunk to notice in the heat of the moment. As soon as the stranger pulled me inside, he began stripping out of his clothes, carelessly tossing them on the marble floor. The back wall was made entirely of glass looking out on the Savannah harbor. It was the kind of lovely view that normally would have held my attention for hours. I so loved the water.

My companion had other ideas for the view, however. We collided again, the primal need to physically connect taking over our actions, as he pulled me back towards the window. He shoved the corset down, breaking the metal ribbing inside the fabric, then pressed my breasts together with a gleeful moan. Sinking onto the sofa facing the window, I climbed on his lap to straddle him. My nipples were aching to be touched, and he pulled one into his mouth with a ravenous sigh. I let my head fall back, enjoying the drunken stupor and unearthly pleasure flowing through my body. One of my hands slid under the skirt to push my thong to the side.

"Have a condom?" the stranger panted. His rigid cock was straining so hard against his pants that it was going to break through the zipper. I would have guessed he was in agony based on the growling timber of his voice.

I shook my head. There weren't exactly pockets in a dress this tiny.

He nodded. "Hold on."

Setting me on his side, the man rose and jogged down a

long hallway, where there were several other closed doors. He darted inside one.

I was left feeling foolish with my tits hanging out and the euphoria quickly wearing off. Righting the corset as much as I could, I wandered over to the kitchen and poured myself a glass of the red wine chilled in a galvanized bucket. The taste gagged me—I was not a wino—but I hoped it would help enough to take the edge off the anxiety I started to feel.

This whole night had been reckless and wild and I hoped I never forgot it. Every woman needed just one night to go to a party in a pretty dress and pretend to be someone she wasn't. Cinderella without her curfew should be a life goal for every woman over the age of 21. And whoever the masked man was, he came right at the moment when the universe knew I needed to let go.

I didn't realize I stopped at the couch again, wine glass in hand, until the man's firm chest and warm presence met my back. Two arms circled my waist again, pulling me close, as he nuzzled into my neck. My hair must look similar to a bird's nest by now, but all the hair spray and glitter Maggie applied would keep it in place until Doomsday. That didn't stop him from winding one stray curl around his finger and whispering, "Ready?"

I shuddered at the way one simple word sent a bolt of electricity to my core. Instantly, my panties were wet and the wanton freedom came surging back. It was time for the masked man to liberate me.

Rather than respond, I turned my head and opened my mouth to him, guiding his hands back to the sweetheart neckline of my dress. He freed my swollen breasts immediately, then continued downward to pull the skirt up around my waist. The thong was all but useless now, far too small to capture the arousal pooling there. It snapped with one hard yank and the man's fingers went straight to my clit to pinch the tingling bud.

I cried out, more from shock than actual pain, and the man hummed his approval. The rustling of a condom wrapper came from behind and he pushed between my shoulder blades so that my torso was hanging over the back of the couch. I had a momentary lapse of panic where I realized for all intents and purposes, I was basically a virgin, having only had sex one time a decade ago, but before I could find the words to convey that to him, the crown of his cock met my entrance.

"You're so tight!" he growled. He began strumming my clit like a guitar string, deftly working his fingers to loosen the muscles that refused to let him in. I inhaled sharply and let out a long, deliberate exhale, urging my body to relax like it had out on the balcony. Long fingers caressed my tits, kneading them to add the small bite of pain with my pleasure that allowed my pussy to welcome him in.

I was stretching so much that it reminded me of giving birth. There was no way a human cock was this big, nor could I take that much inside me. Standing on tiptoe in the high heels, I angled my ass up to give him deeper access.

That somehow flipped a switch, and he slammed into me hard. My knuckles went white from gripping the back of the sofa. It felt so incredible that my whole body could have gone white and I would have begged him for more. Hitting it from this angle gave him a direct line to my G-spot.

"More! More!" I could barely form the words because my brain was so muddled.

He pounded into me, moving one hand into the curls piled on my head and pulling my torso back upright.

The effect was instantaneous. Crests of an orgasm sent shockwaves through me, over and over like I had been storing them up in all of my years of forced celibacy. Eyes rolling into the back of my head, I slumped forward, totally spent.

With a guttural yell of triumph, the stranger followed, coming so hard that the condom moved. He let out a contented sigh before collapsing on top of me.

Feeling and awareness were slow to return to my body. I started flexing my toes and fingers, letting the blood circulate, before bending my knees. The man came down from his own post-coital high and stood upright, taking his still semi-hard cock with him.

My dress was in shambles, with the tulle of the floppy petticoat bent and sticking out in all directions. There would be no salvaging the corset top as it had torn in his haste to free my tits from their jail. What had once been an elegant mass of curls was now tumbling down the back of my neck, with bobby pins sticking into my skull. I welcomed their sting because it brought me back to reality with a vengeance.

"Here." The man threw his button up shirt from earlier over my shoulder. "I'll go grab you some sweatpants."

There was no way a pair of his sweatpants would fit me, but I appreciated the kindness all the same. I needed to right myself and get the hell out of here to face the inevitable shit-storm my mind was cooking up. Not to mention Maggie and her game of Thousand Questions before we could go home to River's Run.

It was in this sort of mindless daze that I buttoned up the shirt, not paying an ounce of attention to the fact that my entire lower body was on full display. When the man returned with a pair of dark gray sweatpants, I didn't hesitate to bend over and pull them on, causing him to gasp.

"Sugar bee?" he asked incredulously.

On my eighteenth birthday, Maggie and I had gone out and gotten tattoos, as most kids determined to prove they were adults did. While I intentionally selected the outside of my hip to prevent anyone from ever seeing it (there was no way Desiree would have forgiven me for a tattoo), it was still a momentous occasion that I used to honor my daddy. I had missed him more than ever on that birthday and getting a minimalist design of a bumblebee landing on a pile of sugar felt oddly fitting.

No one had ever seen it before, though, not even Maggie. I had been too tearful afterwards to show her, so we returned home where I could cuddle toddler Iris and watch Mickey Mouse while I bawled my eyes out.

Letting a random, one night stand—someone who couldn't ever possibly mean anything to me—not only see the tattoo but recognize what it represented rattled me. It was better than any other form of sobriety, and I darted to the elevator in a mad scramble. The sweatpants were still too long for me to properly move in, but thanks to the glossy floors, I slid into the elevator more than I walked.

"Hey, WAIT!" the man yelled behind me.

It was only as the doors closed on him that I realized he had removed his mask, revealing an angular, clean shaven face that would have made angels weep. It was the kind of face that belonged on billboards and commercials, and without the conscious part of my brain to make the connection, I surprised myself by talking to my mirrored reflection as the doors closed between us.

"Wes?" I breathed.

CHAPTER 35
HOME SWEET HOME
WESLEY

WAKING up with a hangover wasn't something I had done in years. I did my fair share of partying in college, before I realized all the alcohol in the world couldn't chase away the ghost of lost love, and the tabloids always had a field day with it. Headlines frequently labeled me as a partying bad boy and grossly exaggerated the damage and alcohol involved. But even those days had nothing on the migraine putting my brain through a blender now.

Phillip breezed in, throwing open the heavy curtains to reveal bright sunshine outside. Literal birds chirping type-shit.

I threw a pillow at his back as hard as I could. The corresponding grunt was only mildly satisfying.

"Go away!" I groaned and fell back into the pillows, an arm stretched over my eyes. I needed an IV with the heaviest painkiller we could find.

Phillip snorted. "If we don't leave in the next half hour, we'll be late meeting the attorney in River's Run."

It was my turn to snort. "I can get us out there in under thirty minutes if you just let me drive!"

"A driver is already arranged and waiting down in the lobby," Phillip countered. The tablet was once again out as he swept through emails and the calendar. "Not that you asked, but the costume party garnered around $500,000 in donations. It was a great turn out for such a last minute affair."

Affair. Why did that send a trickle of unease down my spine?

I sat upright, still squinting at the bright-ass sunshine, and realized how sore I felt. "Did I fall or something?"

Phillip glanced up at me and blushed, immediately diverting his eyes back to the tablet.

Confused, I clambered out of bed and into the immense bathroom, turning on the light to face the floor to ceiling mirror on the wall. Yeah, I was naked, but Phillip had seen me naked for years. That wouldn't have even gotten a reaction out of him at this point in our relationship.

No, it was definitely the bright red lipstick smeared all around my dick. Thanks to all the modeling shoots, my pubes were groomed regularly and kept at nearly transparent levels. But now that only served as more canvas for the desecrated artwork trailing down my shaft.

What. The. Fuck.

I had never been so blacked out drunk that I hooked up with someone. It just wasn't in me. Celeste was the only woman I ever wanted my dick in, and now that the evidence alluded to someone else getting up close and personal with the junk in my trunk, all of last night's dinner came hurling back up. I barely made it to the toilet in time.

Phillip poked his head through the open doorway. "Are you ill?"

"Please tell me I didn't have a one night stand last night."

He grimaced. "I swore I'd never lie to you."

I sneered. "You lie to me all the time."

My assistant shrugged. "Only when necessary."

"This is necessary!" I snapped, throwing my hands up in exasperation.

He gave a noncommittal nod in response. "Should I let the attorney know we need to reschedule?"

I sighed, the bile rising back up in preparation to puke again. "Nope. Just let me empty my stomach real quick."

Thank god fancy hotels had large toilet bowls.

After a quick shower, where Phillip informed me I still smelled like a distillery, we were on our way out to River's Run. The only reason I wasn't jumping out of my skin with nerves was the guilt building a summer home in my chest. Bits and pieces of last night floated back. I could vaguely recall a bombshell with blonde hair mesmerizing me on the dance floor. Mr. Hendricks' nickname for Celeste kept rolling around in my mind, though I couldn't figure out why. I hadn't heard or thought of "sugar bee" since I was a teenager.

"Mr. Sanderson assured me that everything is very straightforward," Phillip said. "Shirley didn't have much in the way of assets." He sat across from me in the modified Range Rover, letting one of the Madden goon squad members drive us, and had a laptop balancing on his lap. "You should know, your father is still incredibly pissed and instructed you —in no uncertain terms—to be back on a plane to Atlanta this evening. He needs you to head over to Tokyo with him in the morning."

I craned my head back, the ibuprofen still doing nothing for my splitting headache. "My dad can go fuck a cactus, Phillip, with my compliments," I replied, irritated. The last thing I needed right now was to have my father breathing down my neck when I already felt lower than the fleas on dog shit.

How could I have slept with someone and not remember? Fuck, how could I have slept with *anyone* who wasn't Celeste? Capturing sand with a fishing net would have been easier than trying to recall memories of last night, but I needed to know how bad it had gotten if I was ever gonna make it right. All I knew how to do was fuck things up with her.

Assuming there was still anything to fuck up.

We rode in silence the rest of the way. As the large houses morphed into small trailers with miles of forest and farm-land in between, my anxiety started to rise to the point where I struggled to control my erratic heartbeat. My throat was closing up, making it difficult to swallow--not that I could have swallowed anything with a mouth as dry as sandpaper.

I knew the second we crossed into Smithson County. Even the air was different out here, purer, with a strong Georgia pinewood scent. Maybe it was a blessing or a curse, but the attorney's office was located a couple blocks over from The Comfy Cushion so we didn't have to drive by. I'm not sure that I could have stomached seeing it yet.

Mr. Sanderson's law office was just a small room in the front of his house. Phillip was so aghast when we pulled up to the one story colonial that I had to stifle a laugh. I expected nothing less in River's Run.

A receptionist that I strongly suspected was Sanderson's wife led us into his office with a promise to return with coffee. Old Mr. Sanderson had been practicing law since Georgia representatives signed The Declaration of Indepen-dence. I could tell why Aunt Shirley trusted him. He was cordial as he went through her will line by line, clarifying things that nobody asked about. I don't think he knew I was a recent law school graduate.

Shirley left everything to me, including her house, her savings account, and her little Buick Lacrosse. In her final will, which Mr. Sanderson stated she completed two years ago, she included a note to me about how proud she was of the man I had become. It brought tears to my eyes that I quickly blinked away. No one had said that to me since Mr. Hendricks died.

Phillip directed the driver to take us over to Shirley's house once we were done with Mr. Sanderson. We needed to look at the condition of the place so I could decide what to do with it. Part of me wanted to preserve it just as she left it. A time capsule to commemorate my life with Celeste. But I also knew there was no point in keeping it. Even if I were to return to River's Run permanently, Aunt Shirley's place wouldn't be where I wound up.

Still, nostalgia hit me hard as we pulled into the driveway. The same porch swing hung near the living room window and the same boxy shrubs offered the only semblance of curb appeal. Curtains were drawn, which was unusual in the daytime, but I assumed the nurse had closed them before she left. I paid her a bonus for providing such diligent care to my aunt.

"Wow, it's like a time machine," Phillip commented when we stepped inside. Just crossing the threshold sent me back thirteen years, to the angry, scared little boy who hated his father and desperately wanted someone—anyone—to love him. I suppose nothing had really changed. Except I had found someone to love me and lost her anyway.

Everything inside was exactly how I remembered. Even the magazines on the coffee table looked the same. Aunt

Shirley's favorite armchair in front of her old tv was so indented from her years of sitting in the exact same spot that there was probably no salvaging it. A sofa that was probably new in the 1970's was still centered under the bay window. The whole place was clean, even if it was extremely dated. It would need a lot of work to appeal to buyers if I chose to sell it.

My legs automatically took me upstairs to my old room. The door was shut, probably for Aunt Shirley's safety since she had been so confused for the last few years, but I wasn't prepared at all for how I felt from opening it. All of my memories, all of my belongings that dear, old Benedict refused to let me claim, all of Celeste's photographs...everything remained exactly as I left it. Hell, it wouldn't have surprised me if her scent still lingered.

Sinking onto the bed, I leaned forward and braced my elbows on my knees. The erratic heartbeat returned, along with my upset stomach. It wasn't until I noticed the small drops of water sliding down my forearms that I realized I was crying.

Being surrounded by all these memories *hurt*. A bitter resentment grew in my chest at all the years I had lost. Celeste and I should have gotten our first cars together. We should have attended all the school pep rallies with Maggie. I should have had a stack of college application and acceptance letters on the desk to my right. We would have walked at graduation *together*. It was all just so unfair.

The injustice of the past was what set me off. I stood up and threw all my weight in a punch to the drywall. When the hole didn't take the edge off, I threw the lamp from the desk. Then I picked up the small desk chair and swung it into the tiny mirror that hung beside the door. Even the shattering glass did nothing to alleviate the pain. As a last resort, I yanked on the string lights that still hung across the ceiling, polaroids flying everywhere, and then I smashed all the bulbs with my boots for good measure. I was just about to flip the mattress when Phillip cleared his throat in the hallway.

I couldn't look at him. He was suddenly a living reminder of how my father held me hostage in that godforsaken boarding school, and with the rage coursing through my body, there was no telling how I would take it out on him.

"You won't be returning to Atlanta tonight, I take it?" he asked quietly.

I swiped a hand through the sweaty tangles of hair on top of my head. "Not a chance in Hell," I agreed.

CHAPTER 36
INVITATIONS
CELESTE

"Oh my god," I grumbled, stirring a packet of Splenda into my fifth cup of coffee. "Why didn't I think about the morning after?"

Maggie grinned over the rim of her own mug. "Because you don't have enough experience going out."

We were at The Comfy Cushion, and for once I was grateful for the lack of customers. I could barely make my legs function let alone serve a dining room full of people. Desiree had pursed her lips with a fierce glare when she arrived to pick Iris up for all her dance stuff in Savannah, but then glanced at Maggie in a way that let me know we would speak about everything later when we didn't have an audience.

Marla came around from the kitchen carrying three plates of eggs, toast, and bacon. On an ordinary day it would smell divine, but right now, the very thought of food was enough to turn my stomach.

"So tell me about this party," Marla began. "Was it hopping?"

Maggie snorted out a laugh. It had been nearly three in

the morning by the time we made it back to River's Run, crashing in Marla's spare bedroom like girls at a sleepover. Had Iris not woken me up a couple hours later, the restaurant wouldn't even be open right now.

"It was...fun," I hedged. It had been fun, and thrilling, and wild...all things that were long gone from my vocabulary. Yet it felt strange conveying any of it to the two of them. Maggie had already peppered me with questions on the way back to River's Run, but I managed to dodge them all. It was hard to believe last night had really happened. That was the part of the story everyone missed out on; how did Cinderella really feel when she woke up the next morning and realized it had all been the equivalent of a fever dream?

"Celeste had way more than just regular fun, wouldn't you say, Cee?" Maggie prompted me. The twinkle in her eye promised mischief that I couldn't escape. "You were just about to tell me about your mystery man, after all."

Busted.

Marla blinked at me in surprise. "Mystery man? Did you meet a fella?"

I rolled my eyes at her old fashioned expression, then pushed the food around on my plate to buy myself some time. "Not exactly," I finally replied.

Now Maggie was laughing in earnest. "Disappearing with a guy for a couple hours doesn't count as meeting someone?"

With the right force, even an old butter knife could break the skin. Why was Maggie outing me like this?!

"I never asked his name," I admitted.

Both of the women hollered, though Maggie's was more with glee while Marla was clearly in shock. Her mouth hung open as she gaped at me.

"Celeste Renee Hendricks, did you have a one night stand?" Marla gasped.

Sighing, I turned back to the coffee pot to refill my mug. Nothing could have prepared me for this conversation, and I didn't know how to continue because I remembered so little of it. For being such a lightweight, I sure pounded back drinks last night like I had the liver of a Marine.

The stranger in the white mask, though, stood out to me clear as day. What I couldn't understand was why he reminded me so much of Wesley when the elevator doors closed. Maybe it was just triggering memories because Wes was the only other person I had ever slept with. Maybe I was simply wishing it had been him, because let's face it, if I had to choose a partner, he was the only one I would have wanted. And yet, I did want someone else last night. Someone with dark hair and a gravelly voice who whispered sweet nothings in my ear.

I involuntarily shuddered.

"What's done is done, so there's no use harping on it," I decreed.

Maggie shook her head. "No, ma'am, that is not how this is gonna work. I need details. What happened? You disappeared into the VIP area with him and then scampered back in different clothes later."

This time Marla definitely gasped as she gaped at me.

Yeah, there was no version of this story that wasn't gonna make me out to be the harlot Desiree used to accuse me of being. "We agreed not to exchange names. We were both pretty wasted and things just...happened." It was a lame excuse, certainly not a story I would have ever accepted from Iris if the roles were reversed, but I didn't know what to say.

Marla smiled softly. "You know, your mama and I used to

go down to the docks in Savannah and get wild." Her eyes were lost in another time and place. "She was so much fun. Never feared anybody. You couldn't have scared her off with a shotgun pointed at her chest! Rachel used to think the stories were what made it worth it. 'I'm too young for regrets,' is what she'd tell me."

I smiled. That definitely sounded like something Mama would say.

"So you don't know anything about him?" pressed Maggie. "You can't find him or see him again?"

Shrugging, I replied, "It's not like I want to, Mags. He isn't —" I cut myself off, biting down hard on the inside of my cheek until I tasted the bitter tang of blood.

"He isn't Wesley," she finished for me. "Honey, you don't have to cut him out of your life. You *chose* to do that without giving him a chance to explain."

We had been over this so many times that I felt like a broken record. "He's had ten years' worth of chances that he didn't take. He left me, Maggie, right when I needed him most. It's as simple as that."

Marla's eyes darted between the two of us, and she hesitated before saying her piece. "Celeste, I love you as if you were my own flesh and blood. But I was also here to see how that boy loved you. I'm willing to bet there's a darn good reason why he didn't come back for you."

Tears sprung up unwittingly, making me briskly swipe my cheeks. "Guess we'll never know, will we?" I countered.

Thankfully one of the guys from the mechanic's shop stepped inside, the bell twinkling through the restaurant. He greeted me with a request for coffee before settling into his favorite booth.

Work was the distraction I always needed. Neither one of

them was going to let me off the hook any time soon, and none of the answers I had to give them would satisfy them anyway. The truth was I had no idea why I acted so recklessly last night, but I couldn't bring myself to regret it. All I wanted was the time and space to figure out why that man reminded me so much of Wes. Memories were hazy at best, and it wasn't like the lights were on or anything that could have made his features stand out. He had dark hair while I was fairly certain Wesley still sported light blonde locks, although it had been a while since I scoured the internet for his modeling shots. It was too painful seeing all the tall, thin models and celebrities he was rumored to be dating.

And yet, for the rest of the day, Wesley was all I could think about. I saw him in the face of everyone who walked by The Comfy Cushion. His megawatt smile beamed up at me from every table I greeted. Even picking up orders from Jesse in the window reminded me of the food Wesley used to make as he poured over my mama's recipe book like a fiend.

He was definitely present in my daughter's face when she burst inside late in the evening and triumphantly waved a flyer over her head.

"Mama, I was invited! I was invited!"

I smiled at her eagerness, despite being clueless to what she celebrated. "Invited to what, honey?"

Desiree and Hillary swept in behind her. My stepmother cast a long, calculating look around the empty dining room. It instantly sent me on high alert because nothing good had ever followed a look like that.

"Iris was invited to audition for the Boston Ballet School," Hillary explained. She gripped my daughter's shoulders in a possessive way that made me grit my teeth.

Desiree smiled. "And she's going to get it because she is

the very best!" Both of them smiled down at Iris, who grinned at their praise.

My heart sank, however.

"That sounds expensive…" I hesitated. It was a war between wanting to encourage Iris' dreams while also being realistic about our financial situation.

My stepmother snorted in derision. "Yes, I can see why that would be concerning since you still haven't managed to get more business. This place is turning into a dump!" She waved her arms around, gesturing to the empty tables. Every worn surface, every torn cushion, all the cracks and divots stood out like sore thumbs. She was right. It *was* turning into a dump.

Hillary let out a dramatic sigh. "What would poor Doug say if he were still alive?" She shook her head sadly. "He worked so hard to make this place a success and it's gone downhill so fast."

Shame burned a hole straight through my chest. Daddy must have been rolling in his grave to see how I let things go. No matter what I did, I never worked hard enough to make a difference. It was all my fault.

"He certainly never took a night off to go drinking in Savannah," commented Desiree with a seething look in my direction.

Iris watched their commentary volleyed to me with wide eyes. Her good news was shadowed by my failure, and I was crushed to ruin this moment for her. I needed to redirect the focus back on her.

"So tell me about this audition!" I gushed.

That was all the prompting she needed to launch into an excited tale of the Boston Ballet School's prestigious history, how her dance instructor had filled out the nomination form, and how she wanted to attend more than anything in the world. It was quite an honor, I gathered, for Iris to be invited to audition at such a young age. The school had direct ties to the Boston Ballet Company, which was considered one of the top ballet companies in the United States. Iris would be given opportunities to participate in the Company's shows by attending Boston Ballet School.

Keeping a mental accountant's ledger running, the zeroes just grew and grew the more she talked. There was no way I could afford something like that even if the restaurant had been steady. We were already too far behind on all the bills as it was.

Hillary procured a pink bag that I recognized from one of the ballet boutiques in downtown Savannah. All of their merchandise tended to be on the costly end of the spectrum. It was nothing any of us should have been able to afford.

"And because we want to wish you luck, Gigi and I got you this!" chorused Hillary, holding out the bag with a flourish.

Iris squealed. Inside were two new leotards, one a soft sage green and the other a pale shade of lavender, a floral chiffon skirt to match, and two sets of knitted leg warmers of the same colors. As she withdrew the final item from the bag, the receipt fluttered out onto the floor. I picked it up only to grip the counter for support. The total read $468.

"Can I talk to you for a minute?" I whispered hastily to my stepmother.

Her eyes narrowed dangerously, but she stepped far enough away that I could continue to whisper without Iris overhearing.

"Desiree, how did you get the money to pay for this?" I held the receipt up to her face as proof. "This is too much!"

One fake eyebrow arched and served as my only warning. "Excuse me," she hissed, "but how I spend my money on *my* daughter is none of your business!" The emphasis on Iris being hers was intentional—my second warning. She could take my daughter away in the blink of an eye because Iris belonged to her.

Like always, I deflated. Iris was the ultimate weapon and Desiree could rule me with an iron fist if she so chose. Nothing was worth putting her in jeopardy.

My stepmother sneered at me. "Don't you ever question me like that again. I could have you out on the street with the snap of my fingers." Her face leered at me in disgust before returning to Iris to preen over her new dance attire.

Hyperventilating wasn't going to get me anywhere, but it was hard to keep the panic at bay. While we never got along, Desiree had never outright threatened me like that before. She had to be furious with me over going out last night. Any time I exercised any kind of freedom or independence, she tended to lash out. Though it was never this severe.

Instead of freaking out, I did what any other mother would do. I plastered a smile on my face, blinked away the tears, and returned to my kid. Iris only needed to see how proud I was of her accomplishment.

CHAPTER 37
MEET YOUR MATCH
WESLEY

SOMEHOW THE GYM was still the one place where I found clarity. All of my modeling contracts required me to maintain a certain physique, and I'd be lying if I said my muscular build didn't get me more attention. No workout ever replaced the feel of hitting a man square in the jaw, though. Punching the bag only got me so far.

It had long slipped my mind that I still owned a gym in River's Run. Phillip left last night in a huff, mumbling under his breath about how my father would make me pay for my actions, and after tossing and turning down on Aunt Shirley's lumpy couch, I went for a run and stumbled upon my old stomping grounds.

There was no one inside, but my code still worked. I didn't even know who managed it or if we had any members. Everything was clean and organized, so someone had to maintain it.

An empty gym was perfect. I stripped down to my shorts, foregoing the wraps for my fists, and beat the bag until my knuckles split. My Airpods blared my workout playlist, Keith Urban's "Stupid Boy" reminding me how badly I had fucked up. She *had* laid her heart right in my hands...and I dropped it.

A movement in the corner of my eye gave me pause. There was a small area towards the back that was set up as a class studio, with mirrored walls on two sides. A girl with light blonde hair pulled into a tight bun wearing a leotard and tights was spinning in pointe shoes. Classical music tinkled out of a miniature speaker she tucked into the corner next to her bag.

She didn't stop as I approached. Not until I was only a foot away with my arms crossed at my chest. There weren't any other adults inside, meaning the girl was in here all alone. A huge liability issue, by anyone's standards. She couldn't have been more than ten or eleven years old.

"What do you think you're doing?" I asked.

The girl stopped gracefully, slinking down flat on her feet. "Practicing," she answered calmly. Her brilliant blue eyes didn't betray an ounce of fear.

I turned around again, double checking for a parent I might have missed. "By yourself?"

"It's a solo piece," she informed me. "I don't need anyone else."

What was with this kid? For all she knew, I was a child predator about to kidnap her into my windowless van, yet she was ready to square up like Mike Tyson.

"You got a name?" I didn't remember most of the people in town, but a name might give me a place to start.

She leaned back on one foot, clearly sizing me up from head to toe. "Not sure why you need that," the girl finally replied. "You're not from around here."

It was so reminiscent of Celeste's first greeting that I

almost laughed out loud. "Technically I used to be. I've been away for a while. How did you get in here?"

The girl shrugged. "My mama has a code to the building. I need somewhere to practice and no one ever comes in here."

"Why don't you just go to your dance studio?" I asked.

She rolled her eyes and turned to face the mirror again. "Because my dance studio is in Savannah and I can't exactly drive."

Damn, her sass was enough to shut me up. It was like talking to a mini version of myself at ten years old. Lord bless her parents because that attitude had to be a hand full.

"Well, I own this gym and I can't let you be in here without a grown up."

That got her attention. She rounded on me, hands on her hips and a mean mug that made me take a step backwards. "If you really owned this gym, you'd know that I come here to practice every day. When my mama's stuck at work, this is the only thing that makes me happy."

The girl clamped her mouth shut after that last remark. Maybe she figured she told me too much, but if anything, she spoke in a language I understood. I knew all too well what it felt like to have a parent too busy working to notice you. At least she found something that made her feel good. That was already a jumpstart on me.

But the lawyer in me couldn't let her be here unsupervised. "Look, I get that you've been coming here for a while," I began, "but for safety reasons, I can't let you do that without an adult here. What if you got hurt?"

It was her turn to cross her arms over her chest. "Just talk to my mama. She only works down the street."

Patience wasn't really my thing, so I bit back the snarky comment on the tip of my tongue. She was just a kid, even if she did have a mouth on her that would land her in trouble one day. For some reason, I pictured Mr. Hendricks dealing with a little girl like her and had to hide my smile.

"My workout is done, so let's go talk to your mom, okay?" I suggested. "Otherwise I'm gonna have to call the sheriff on you for trespassing."

Her eyes widened at the threat, then narrowed in a glare. "Forget it. I'll find somewhere else to practice." She huffed over to her bag and withdrew a pair of sweatpants that she aggressively yanked on over her leotard.

I watched her as she walked to the door, muttering under her breath what I hoped wasn't some kind of voodoo curse on me. Guilt hit me hard in the chest. I remembered what it felt like to be that kid, the one with nowhere to go and no one who cared either way. At least dance was a healthy activity that gave her an escape. What kind of asshole would take that from her?

Right as she was about to step outside, I called out, "C'mon, tell me your name!"

"Iris," she called back over her shoulder.

"Do you wanna meet here tomorrow?" I offered. "I can do my workout and you can get your dance practice in."

She rounded on me. Her blue eyes lit up with hope, then skepticism as she regarded me coolly. After sizing me up, she slowly nodded. "Be here at six a.m. sharp!" Iris instructed.

I chuckled after her as the door closed. Whoever her mama was, I hoped she had the patience of a saint.

It wasn't the time to ruminate on the girl, however, because it was time to face my past. I needed to shower and look presentable before heading over to The Comfy Cushion. Picking up my cell phone from the floor next to the weight rack where I left it, I saw six missed calls from my father and groaned. Each voicemail got progressively worse, with him going so far to threaten cutting me off completely. As if I would shed a tear over no longer being associated with him or Madden Enterprises.

Now that I had my own nest egg from modeling, he had nothing to touch me with. I could continue leading the same lifestyle—albeit with fewer private jets and yachts—and be just fine. And while being an attorney wasn't my dream job, it was certainly one that could pay the bills. I didn't have any real debt, so let him cut me off. I'd get myself straight.

The phone buzzed in my hand again. Instinct told me to ignore the call, but I knew my father would just keep at it, so I might as well get it over with. I adjusted the volume as low as I could before I hit the green button, though.

Sure enough, his angry scream belted in my ear. "WHY ARE YOU IN THAT WASTELAND OF A TOWN RATHER THAN ON THE JET TO TOKYO?!"

My jaw hurt from the way my teeth ground together. "Gee, Benny, it's good to hear from you, too."

"Don't give me any of your horse shit, Wesley! You were hired to do a job and I expect you to fucking do it!"

He tended to forget how many days of my life I wasted in his corporate offices, watching mediocre white men over-paying themselves without doing any actual work. I knew for a fact that I had more schooling than half his board members. Rich people only supported rich people. There was no actual need for me; this was nepotism at its worst.

"I guess something else came up," I sighed. We were just going to keep talking in circles. I wasn't sorry for skipping out and I couldn't care less about getting fired from a corpo-rate job I hadn't technically started.

Benedict lowered his voice, the contempt thick enough to

choke a horse. "You get your ass on the next flight to Japan or I will rain hell down on you."

I snorted. That was the best he could do? "Not gonna happen, Pops, but thanks for playing. Bye now." And I hung up.

It took several minutes of visualizing painful ways for Benedict Madden the Third to die slow, gruesome deaths before I was in the right frame of mind to leave. Glancing back towards the classroom area, I texted Phillip to look up business properties for sale in River's Run.

Phillip called rather than text back. "Do you have a particular kind of business space in mind?"

"Yeah, something big enough for a dance studio."

CHAPTER 38
THE ICK
CELESTE

SSUNDAY MORNINGS WERE ALWAYS the slowest point in the week at The Comfy Cushion. Most people in River's Run practiced some brand of Christianity, and they would judge you quicker than a rooster over which church you attended. Mama and Daddy had some sort of societal free pass on account of being local business owners, which had thankfully been passed down to me when I took over at the restaurant. Neither of my parents ever set much in store by the church, and I had not been required to attend as a child.

Desiree considered herself a Methodist and went to church most Sundays. For the first several years of Iris' life, Desiree forced her to go, too, despite my objections. Four years ago, a boy in her Sunday school class told Iris she was a bastard because she was born out of wedlock and would therefore never be allowed in Heaven, sending her into a crying fit that left her shaking in bed for the rest of the day. After that, Desiree agreed that Iris no longer needed to go to church with her.

That left Sunday mornings as the restful start to my week. Without Desiree breathing down my neck, it was easier to prep food and plan the menu. We also opened an hour later since nobody ever rolled in until after their church services ended. I always allowed Iris to go over to the town gym to practice her choreography while I got everything ready for the day. She usually practiced for a couple hours, returning in time to have lunch with Desiree and Hillary after church ended, before heading into Savannah to meet with her private dance instructor.

Iris confidently informed me on the drive into town that she needed to increase her individual practices if she was going to be ready for Boston. It weighed on me as she left that I still hadn't found a good opportunity to talk with her privately about Boston not being a possibility at the moment, but I was a coward, and like all cowardly mothers do, I let her walk down the street with her precious dreams still intact.

It was incredibly surprising then, when only a half hour later, Iris marched back inside The Comfy Cushion with an indignant huff and ranted, "Men, I tell you!"

Jesse barked out a laugh behind me in the kitchen while I stood at one of the tables where I had been refilling the salt and pepper shakers, totally dumbfounded. I was used to Iris' habit of speaking older than her years—it was inevitable when she was surrounded by adults or much older kids in her ballet classes most of the time—but I had no idea what would have made her snarl such a thing.

"Iris?" I prompted as she continued to stand by the door, stewing.

She stomped her foot. "Mama, I can't practice at the gym anymore! There was a man inside who said I can't be there without an adult! Can you believe that?"

Biting on my cheek to hide my smile, I shrugged instead. "It does sound like a safety concern."

Iris rolled her eyes, then dramatically threw herself into the booth in front of me. "Then why have you been letting me do it all this time?"

I laughed at her theatrics. "Because up until now, no one has ever called us out on it. We'll find somewhere else for you to practice."

She shook her head sadly. "It won't be the same. I need the smooth floor and mirrors."

"We'll figure something out," I ventured. I moved on to the next table, spinning the silver tops off the shakers.

Iris didn't look convinced. "It's okay. He said he'll meet me there tomorrow morning so I can practice before school while he works out."

I turned sharply in her direction. "He did what, now?"

The alarm in my voice didn't faze her. "He's not a weirdo or anything, Mama. I think he just felt sorry for me."

A knife of guilt stabbed my heart. I never wanted anyone to pity Iris, but with a solo parent household where I had to work all the time, the reality was that she went without more often than not. As far as I knew, scientists hadn't yet given mothers the ability to be in two places at once.

"Be that as it may, I'm not sure how I feel about you meeting a strange man in the morning. We don't know anything about him."

Iris shrugged. "He said he used to live here. Maybe you already know him."

My chest tightened a little. "Did he tell you his name?"

She shook her head, but that didn't alleviate my anxiety. First, I had a one night rendezvous with a man who brought all of Wes' memories to the surface, now my daughter was meeting a man who used to live in River's Run in the gym that her estranged father owns? I hadn't done statistics in a long time, but I knew those odds weren't great.

I didn't want to alert her to my rising anxiety. It didn't mean anything. People were moving out of River's Run pretty steadily now that the canning factory closed down a few miles out of town. Jobs were scarce in Smithson County. Wesley Madden was an international celebrity. He had no reason to come back to River's Run, Georgia.

Except that wasn't really true, I thought as I stared at my daughter's profile. She was the spitting image of her daddy, with the hot temper to match.

It wasn't that I didn't want them to meet someday. In my dreams, I somehow turned The Comfy Cushion into such a success that I had the money to take Desiree to court and get full custody of my daughter, then we would find her daddy together. Wesley deserved to know the truth—deserved to know Iris. As long as Desiree held all the cards, however, my hands were tied.

Speak of the devil. Desiree, Hillary, and Jeremy, much to my dismay, walked in with all their church finery on. Jeremy and I never had the contentious relationship that I shared with Hillary, but after Wesley left, he became a bit...different. I'd find him watching me all the time in a way that unsettled me. After Iris started kicking in my belly, he begged me nearly every day to feel her movement, keeping his hands on my stomach far longer than was necessary. I even caught him once going through my laundry, though he never told me outright what he was looking for.

Jeremy moved into a small apartment over the pharmacy a few streets over after he got a job as a night security guard for one of the historic sites out in Savannah. He didn't come over often, to the house or The Comfy Cushion, but when he did, there was always a gleam in his eye as he watched my every move. Like a predator stalking his prey. It always caused me to grow flustered, then break something. His attention gave me the ick.

"We'll have our usual," snapped my stepmother. She slid into a counter barstool and pulled out a compact mirror to check her hair. "And make sure Iris has enough water for dance. You never check."

Sometimes I wish I had the ability to stand up for myself. I had never once forgotten to provide Iris with water for dance practice. Even though it broke my heart that I could never be the one to take her or participate, I tried to be as involved as possible. Handwashing her dance uniform, helping her stretch every night before bed, binding her toes when her point shoes led to blisters and cracks—I had done it all. And her talent continued to astound me every time she practiced her routines for me at home. She was so dedicated to ballet. I yearned to feel that passionately about anything anymore.

Iris caught my eye and gave me a small smile of comfort. She knew that I had never forgotten. I always made a bag of healthy snacks and had a gallon size jug of water ready.

A few other patrons started to trickle in, a sign that my restful morning was over and it was time to get back to the work week grind. I did my best to ignore Jeremy's stare as I served up eggs, pancakes, and other breakfast platters to guests, but sure enough, feeling his creepy eyes on my back made me spin around too fast and knock over two glasses of lemonade I had just placed on a table for Mr. and Mrs. Windman.

"Celeste!" Desiree barked after I hastily apologized and mopped up the spill. I returned behind the counter to swap out my now wet apron for a spare one. "If you cannot keep my guests happy, why do I let you work here?" she hissed.

My shoulders slumped. It was growing harder with each passing day to remember my mama's way of dealing with difficult people. Turns out you could only kick a dog for so long. I was too scared of losing Iris along with my parents' legacy to bite back when Desiree got out of hand. It grew worse with each passing year.

"I'm sorry, Desiree," I replied. "It won't happen again."

"It's okay, Mama," Iris piped up. "Everybody makes mistakes." Her sweet face frowned at our exchange.

I offered her a small smile, grateful that she would try to stand up for me when I couldn't stand up for myself. It was moments like this that I saw my mama's personality coming out in her.

Desiree sniffed. "Yes, well, your mama makes a lot of them." She slid off her barstool, grabbing Iris' dance bag off the counter. "Are you ready, dear? We don't want to be late."

Iris shot me a quick look of apology. It embarrassed me to no end that Desiree and Hillary always talked about me like that in front of my daughter. Nobody should ever talk poorly of someone's folks right in front of them.

Hillary and Jeremy both got up, too, though Jeremy waited for the other two to walk out with Iris.

"You need someone to take care of you," Jeremy said, his voice low and sinister. "Don't you think it's time you gave up the solo mom thing?"

My eyes widened in surprise. As if I had a choice in my circumstances and being a solo mother wasn't forced upon me. Jeremy never said anything to me about my relationship status before, and I wasn't sure how to respond now. The leer he sported made me apprehensive to even acknowledge him.

He grinned at me, letting his eyes fall to my cleavage. While my V-neck was stretched and showed more of my figure than I would have liked, I never felt as dirty as I did right then with Jeremy.

"See ya later, *Mama*," he said before sweeping out the door.

God, I needed a shower and an antibiotic after that encounter.

"Oh, and Celeste?" Desiree poked her head back through the front door, ensuring everyone in the restaurant heard her. "Someone will be stopping by later to get some things from you. I have a new investor since you've failed to make any profit here."

Scratch that—I needed a hot shower, an antibiotic, and a bottle of whiskey.

CHAPTER 39

MAKING AN ENTRANCE
WESLEY

I WASHED everything on my body three times over before I could get out of the shower, and I still wasn't entirely convinced I was clean enough. Smelling good, looking apologetic, and turning on the charm to a hundred were the three key factors I could control about this meeting. Going to The Comfy Cushion made me want to throw up—as in my bubble guts were actually audible from how hard my stomach churned—but it had to be done. The only way to conquer your fear was to face it.

Most of the clothes I owned were given to me by all the fashion houses who courted me for contracts, but I always asked Mrs. Aguilar, who was now my housekeeper, to include what I called undetectables—regular jeans, simple shirts, and hoodies. Clothing that wouldn't catch a paparazzi's eye. Not that I needed to worry about that in River's Run. Normally, however, when I arrived in larger cities, my celebrity status meant there was at least one slimeball with a Canon following me.

Celeste was going to get the real me, though. A simple white t-shirt and plain jeans, with a beat up pair of black

Chuck's. She always preferred my natural hair, so I resisted the urge to put in the massive amounts of styling cream I normally used and just let my length on top do its thing. While my reflection looked entirely too pale, it was the me that I remembered and liked. I hoped that would be enough for her.

Since Phillip and the driver left with the Range Rover, all I had to drive was Aunt Shirley's old Buick. Which was actually now my old Buick, technically. It took me more than twenty minutes to find the keys, and I prayed the damn thing would even start. The engine took a few tries to start up, but it finally turned over and I backed out of the driveway at a pace that matched my frantic heartbeat.

The outside of The Comfy Cushion was a bit more run down than I remembered. Paint peeled from the sign overhead and all of the windows needed a good scrub. The bricks on the exterior would have benefited from harsh power washing. There weren't nearly as many cars parked out front as there had been the last time I came in, especially for it being a Sunday afternoon. Less of an audience, though, which would make it easier.

What if she wasn't even there? Maybe she left for college and never looked back. Maybe I was getting myself worked up over nothing because The Comfy Cushion had been passed on to new owners. Nana must be really getting on in years, so maybe Celeste took her to a quiet, little seaside town to spend her days in tranquil bliss.

Doug's old, rusty pickup truck was in its usual spot out front. None of my imaginings could be true if that was the case.

Peeking through a corner of the window, I tried one of the breathing techniques my old MMA coach taught me to help me get a handle on my nerves. It didn't work for shit then, and it didn't do a damn thing now. There was only one table with an older couple. I could just make out the vague outline of Jesse back in the kitchen. No Marla or Celeste.

A woman came from around the counter with her long blonde ponytail swinging. I didn't recognize her from the back, but it was only natural for there to be new workers after ten years.

Okay, it was now or never.

Pushing open the door to The Comfy Cushion made two things happen simultaneously. Recognition of the blonde bombshell behind the counter as my one night stand from Savannah and shock that she and Celeste Hendricks, the love of my life, were one and the same.

Everything after that was a total shitshow. Celeste didn't initially look up as she greeted me from behind the counter, encouraging me to sit anywhere I'd like. She grabbed a coffee pot from the warmer and came around the counter. It was then that she finally made eye contact with me…and dropped the pot of coffee on the floor. Glass sprayed everywhere, along with hot coffee all over her shoes, shins, and the bottom of her jean capris.

"Shit!" she screamed, rushing to the back of the kitchen.

Fuck, I guess we were going off the script in my head already.

"Celeste!" I hollered. I didn't think twice before following her behind the counter and into the kitchen. She was already in the back prep area, running cold water onto a cloth and slipping out of her canvas sneakers.

"Please tell me you're not hurt!" I cried. I snatched another rag from the shelf and fumbled with it under the water in the sink, crouching down to lay it across her leg.

She jumped backward, kicking at me with her other foot. "Don't you dare touch me, Wesley Madden!" Celeste yelled.

After a full minute of trying and failing to roll up the bottoms of her tight capris, she growled in frustration and sped out of the room. I stayed right on her heels. If I let her out of my sight, she would probably bolt for the hills.

Inside her dad's old office, Celeste was already stripping out of the capris. I had a momentary glimpse of the curve of her ass and luscious hips in a pair of black panties before she shrieked at me.

"GET OUT! GET OUT!"

Dogs would howl at that pitch. I turned back, slamming the office door behind me, but kept my hand on the doorknob. This was the only way in or out, so she'd have to face me one way or another.

"You better not be out there, Wesley!" she screamed through the door.

I rolled my eyes. "Like I would leave at a moment like this!"

"Why not? Leaving's what you're good at!"

Okay, I definitely deserved that. At least now I knew we were gonna be duking it out right away. This was where the heavy groveling part of my plan commenced.

"Lovebug, I have a good reason for being gone. You have no idea how sorry I am, and if I live to be a hundred, I'll never make it up—"

"You don't even deserve to speak to me!" Celeste raged through the door. "Get out of my restaurant!"

The door handle rattled as she tried to pull it open, so I held on for dear life.

"No, ma'am!" I called back. "You aren't leaving this room until you agree to hear what I have to say!"

"HOW DARE YOU?!" she roared. "You no good, slimy—"

"Hey, Wes," Jesse said, standing in the doorway to the kitchen. He didn't seem surprised to see me or hear our heated exchange. This was just life back to normal for him.

I gave him the man nod. "Hey, man, what's up?" The office door gave a violent shake and I added my other hand.

Jesse nodded towards the office. "Don't really sound like she's too happy."

Leaning backward to hold the door, which now rattled as though being attacked by a wild bear on the other side, I shrugged and shook my head. "Women, am I right?"

He snickered. "I'll leave you to it, then."

That earned him another man nod. "Yeah, say hi to your mama for me."

Pounding now erupted from the door. Celeste couldn't pull it open so I guess she settled for beating it down. She was still calling me all sorts of names, but I expected nothing less.

"Celeste, you *have* to talk to me," I yelled.

"Like hell I do!" she shouted.

"Lovebug, we both know you don't have anywhere else to go right now! This is the only way out of there."

A brief pause and then, "Fine!"

As soon as the door swung open, Celeste's fist came flying out. She wasn't forming the fist correctly and we were too far apart for her to actually get much power behind it. Even still, I dipped my head to the left to dodge the hit and smirked at her.

"You've literally watched me train with an ultimate fighter," I scolded.

"Oooh, you!" She stomped her foot, then brushed past me and down the hallway. Apparently, she was too angry to finish her statement.

It wasn't until she was two steps ahead of me that I realized she had swapped out her jean capris for a pair of Daisy Dukes that made me bite my knuckles and pray for mercy from a god I didn't believe in. She must have slid on a pair of flip flops in the office, and when I followed her back into the kitchen, held out a broom and dustpan for me to sweep up the mess out front. Celeste went over and started filling the mop bucket with soap and hot water.

Being allowed to clean up had to be a step in the right direction. Metaphorically and literally.

By the time I got into the dining room, the couple who had been in the booth was gone. I really hoped they hadn't stiffed Celeste on the bill. Sweeping all the glass, I became acutely aware when she came back out in the dining room. It was like the electric charged air right before a lightning storm. We worked in silence for several minutes to clean up the mess, including wiping down the barstools and the base of the counter that got splashed.

Finally, when there were no remnants anywhere, I opened my mouth to speak but she beat me to it.

"What are you doing here, Wes?" Celeste wouldn't look at me, gazing obstinately at her feet.

It gave me a moment to note all the changes since I had last seen her. Blonde hair, almost similar in shade to mine, was the biggest difference, but she had also gained weight in all the right places. Her body was now like an hourglass and I couldn't wait to feel it pressed up against me to fall asleep at night. We probably wouldn't be at that point for a while, though.

"Celeste, I've been trying to come home to you for years," I eventually said.

She snorted and leaned down on the counter with both

arms. "Is that what you call all those pictures in magazines and stuff?"

"I was earning money for us—"

"No, don't you dare say that to me!" Her voice cracked, from the tears gathering in her eyes or the swell of sorrow leaking into her voice. "There is no 'us' and there hasn't been in a long time, Wesley."

Under normal circumstances, seeing tears run down her face would have me equally choked up or madder than a hornet's nest cut down from the pinewood. Now, however, it did the exact opposite. Her reaction gave me hope, because people who don't care don't have the emotion to spare when a person from their past barges in. Celeste might not want to feel anything for me anymore, but she did, and that gave me something to work with.

"I came back in town because Aunt Shirley passed," I said quietly.

Celeste nodded, sparing me a quick glance before darting her eyes away again. "Yeah, I heard. I'm sorry to hear it. She was a real good lady."

"Yeah, she was somethin' special," I agreed. "Her funeral will be on Thursday if you'd like to come."

I didn't want to push my luck any further. "I'm staying at her place, if you'd like to talk. But lovebug, I'm not leaving this town until you do. And I'll come back here every day just to prove myself to you." Holding up a hand in farewell to Jesse, who stood watching us with unveiled interest from the kitchen line, I resisted the urge to plant a kiss on Celeste's forehead and exited out the front door.

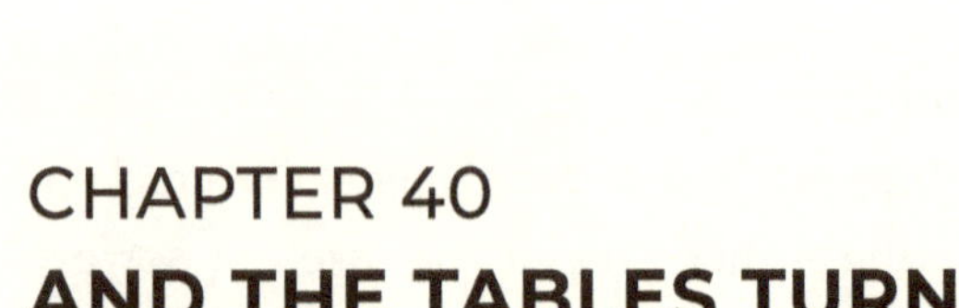

CHAPTER 40
AND THE TABLES TURN
CELESTE

THE OXFORD ENGLISH dictionary didn't have a word to convey the emotional gamut running through me. All of the warning signs from the past two days led me to his arrival and I ignored every single one of them. Look how that turned out. I'm sure Mama and Daddy were having a good laugh at my expense while whatever guardian angel they sent after me was shaking her head in dismay.

Wes looked *good*. He always had an incredible body, but it was obvious with the bulging biceps and round shoulders under his t-shirt that the past decade was spent concentrating in the gym. Reading between the lines of Maggie's vague reports over the years, I knew he had done some shirtless photo shoots in exotic looking places, and from just one encounter with him, I could see why. His hair was shorter now, no longer the shaggy mess hanging around his face, though I supposed now he no longer needed the shield from the world. He had gone ahead and made it his own.

And those blue eyes. The clearest cut sapphires to ever exist. Just looking at them again made me want to go back in time to when his presence was the safest place in the world to be. To do everything with him all over again, just to experience the joy, love, and craziness packaged as the Wesley Madden experience. He had been the greatest love I'd ever known, then let me freefall into darkness when he disappeared.

However, seeing him in The Comfy Cushion—no matter how sexy—meant a world of trouble. Iris was bound to notice a man who looked identical to her sitting in our restaurant and calling me "lovebug." Or worse, Desiree would see him and I'd lose Iris forever. That was a chance I couldn't take. No one was going to take my little girl from me.

The only way I could see to prevent that from happening was to go over to Ms. Shirley's house after closing up tonight and let him get everything off his chest. I remembered all too well how immovable a stubborn Wesley could be, so if he needed to say his piece and then get on with his life, I would let him. But he needed to immediately leave River's Run afterwards and never come back.

Just the thought of hearing him out made me breathless and twitchy. There was no way I could tell him about Iris. Unless Wesley had an entirely new personality, learning he had a daughter going on eleven years old was going to send him through the roof and he would be a battering ram to fight with Desiree over her. No, it was far better to end the war before it began and leave Iris out of it.

"Jesse, I'm gonna head back to the office for a spell," I called out. "Let me know if anyone comes in."

"Sure thing, boss," he replied as he scrubbed his prep space.

Back in Daddy's office with the door firmly shut, I allowed some of the emotions to rise to the surface. I missed Wesley so much. He hadn't just been my first love, he had been my first friend. Someone who knew me inside and out, and accepted me anyway. Wes was the one who saved me from my own darkness, who brought laughter back into my life. He was the reason my daddy had a full year after his cancer diagnosis, a year where he received the best possible care in the world.

But we also hurt each other so deeply that day. I was grown enough now to recognize how poorly I treated him. Obviously, I had a reason to panic after having unprotected sex, though truth be told, if Iris was the outcome at the end of that choice, I would have made the same choice in every lifetime. Yet I could forgive myself for being a dumb kid. I didn't think I could ever forgive him for promising to be there and then abandoning me. Nothing had ever kept us apart before. Not a single one of Mr. Madden's threats ever swayed Wesley in the slightest. So what could have possibly done it then?

Wracking my brain for the answer to that question only served to circle my thoughts. There wasn't a good reason, it was as simple as that. The Wesley I thought I knew and loved wasn't real, and whatever promises this current Wesley spewed out would be just as empty and meaningless as those had been.

I needed to guard my heart as carefully as I guarded my daughter. Walls were going up and staying there.

A knock resounded through the room as Jesse said, "Boss, there's somebody here for you."

I hastily swiped the tears from my face and vowed to never again cry over Wesley Madden. "Be right there," I said. It was time to grow up. My fairytale ending had disappeared when Prince Charming left.

Out in the dining room, I received the second shock of my day. Thankfully, I wasn't holding anything hot this time.

Benedict Madden III, Wesley's father, was standing in The Comfy Cushion. His tailored black suit and black shirt made him look like the Harbinger of Death, complete with the menacing scowl and dark eyes. Just seeing him made a shudder run down my spine.

"What do you want?" It was hard to be polite to him. The insults of never being good enough for Wesley were as fresh now as the day he uttered them.

The smile he gave me was malevolent. "It's a pleasure to see you, too."

"Wesley isn't here," I replied quickly. It was habit to protect Wes from his father, even after everything that happened.

"No, Desiree sent me. I bought this…diner…from her and I'm here for our meeting. Where is she?" The way he paused on *diner* while casting a judgmental eye about the room set my blood to boiling. We might not have white glove service like the restaurants he frequented, but that was because my parents built this place from the ground up on a dream and hard work.

Right on cue, my stepmother sauntered through the door, a triumphant sneer on her lips. "My apologies, Benedict," she drawled. Somewhere throughout the day she had changed into a black wrap dress with a low neckline. It looked like she had her eyelashes redone, too. She batted them coyly at Mr. Madden. "I do hope you can forgive me."

Thank God she didn't have Iris with her.

The way he appraised her figure would have made a cat throw up. "Where is this recipe book you kept telling me about? That's what I paid to see."

Excuse me?!

"My mama's recipes are NOT for sale," I said vehemently. "And neither is our restaurant. There's been some mistake."

Desiree's eyes flashed in my direction. "You failed, Celeste. This place isn't going to be a burden on my family any longer so that I can indulge in your childish dreams to be like your mama. She's dead, and The Comfy Cushion along with it."

I was too stunned to speak. I knew Desiree could be cruel—downright evil, really—but this was on a whole other level. Her true colors were bleeding through and it made my stomach bottom out. "Indulging" in my dream? From the thriving restaurant she ran into the ground with her greed and poor decisions?

"Go get the book," she commanded. An eyebrow rose in challenge, the proud smirk on her face gloating at her right to order me around.

"No, I won't." Mama's recipes were what made The Comfy Cushion so special. They were what used to make people drive hours out of their way just to stop by. Our menu varied constantly as she tried something new, and guests loved that, too. There was magic to her cooking, magic that couldn't be recreated by just anyone.

Mr. Madden scoffed at us. "Is this how you do business, Desiree? I offer you half a million dollars to put this pile of garbage in my stores and you can't even pony up? We're done here." He turned on his heel towards the door.

"No! NO!" Desiree was frantic, skittering after him on her stilettos with her arms failing. "I'll get the recipes! Don't you worry, Benedict! You'll have them, I swear it!"

Mr. Madden paused in the doorway. "You have three days or the deal is off." The door bell's chime after it closed seemed to mock the drop in temperature as his presence lingered.

Desiree rounded on me with pure hatred burning in her eyes. She crossed the dining room in two strides and slapped me hard across the face. My head flung backward, a hand clamping on my now throbbing cheek.

"You'll produce that book by the time he returns or you'll never see your daughter again."

Somehow, the slap hurt less than the threat.

CHAPTER 41
A CHANGE IN PLANS
WESLEY

As SOON AS I stepped out of The Comfy Cushion, a firm hand clamped down on my ear and jerked my head down several inches.

"The nerve of you, Wesley Carter Madden!" Marla howled.

"OW!" I yelled. "Let go!"

Marla scoffed. "Oh yeah, I'm sure that hurts a tough guy like you! C'mon, you big baby!" She wrenched my ear forward, forcing me to follow.

For as little as Marla was, she sure knew how to bring a man to his knees. My coach should hire her.

We charged down the sidewalk together with her fingers squeezing the cartilage out of my ear. A block down, crossing the street, we came to an abrupt halt outside a storefront that had a painted window declaring it *Marla's Sweets*. A small black bistro table with two chairs sat on the sidewalk in front and a chalkboard sign listed the day's pie and cupcake flavors.

Inside, the bakery smelled heavenly, and a large glass display held slices of pie, cupcakes, and cookies. Another large chalkboard on the wall behind the counter listed prices and advertised that custom cakes were available for order. A few other bistro tables lined the opposite wall, with navy shiplap and a light-colored wallpaper decorating the space. Black and white checkered tiles added the final touch. The place was quaint, clean, and a hundred percent Marla.

Good for her.

Thankfully, she let go of my ear when we walked inside. "Since when do you own a bakery?" I asked.

She glared at me. "Since Desiree fired me eight years ago after Celeste graduated high school and took over The Comfy Cushion. Don't change the subject."

"What subject? I came out of the diner and you *attacked* me!"

"Just like you needed!" Marla countered. She went behind the display and pulled out a white plate with a slice of rhubarb pie, shoving it towards me with a fork. "Here, it's your favorite."

I sighed as her aggression left me defeated. "No, it isn't." But I took the plate from her anyway, setting it down on one of the small bistro tables lining the opposite wall and falling into the chair.

Marla looked just as affronted now as she had every other time she offered me a slice of pie.

"How about we start with what the heck you're trying to pull?" she asked.

"I needed to see her!"

"Did not!"

"Did, too!"

"Did not!"

I spread my arms wide in invitation. "I can do this all day."

Marla's fists rested on her hips. "Me, too. I've had a lot longer to practice!"

Well, she had me there.

"This is a waste of my time," I concluded angrily. "I need to figure out what I'm going to say to Celeste."

"Like hell, you do!" The scowl on Marla's face would have stopped me in my tracks when I was younger. After some of the pricks I dealt with in law school, it would take a lot more than a dirty look to make me back down now.

"Let me tell you something, Wesley Madden, it's not like Celeste is the only one you left behind when you skipped town." She dared me to contradict her. "You left behind the rest of us who loved you, and I know for a fact that Doug taught you better than that!"

Shame weathered my resolve. What Marla was really getting at was her own pain. She missed me, too, and hadn't deserved my silence. And while that was true, I spent all of my time concentrating on Celeste. Marla wanted her apology, too.

"I wouldn't have stayed away if I had any other choice," I insisted. "The hospital pressed charges on me after I choked that doctor and I was on probation for a while. My dad sent me to boarding school overseas as a way to punish me. I never meant to be gone like that."

The explanation softened her somewhat as her hands loosened at her sides.

"You have to help me," I pleaded with her. "Celeste has to forgive me!"

She frowned, then came around to sit across from me. As gentle as a woman like Marla could manage, she clasped her hands in mine on top of the table and stated firmly, "No, she doesn't, Wes."

"Oh, fuck all!" I hollered. I bolted out of the chair and started pacing like a baited tiger. "Do you have any idea what I've been through, Marla?"

"What *you've* been through?!" Fuming, Marla stood up and poked me hard in the chest. "What about what *she's* been through? You show up here after ten years without so much as a postcard and you think you can just waltz into her life with an 'I'm sorry' that'll make it all go away?! Good Lord, boy, I thought you were smart!"

Her accusations stung because they were true. "How did you even know I was in there?"

"Because your assistant hired me to bake desserts for Ms. Shirley's funeral luncheon and I knew if you had a hand in it, that meant you were gonna come down here and stir up trouble!"

That wasn't an entirely unfair assessment, which pissed me off even more.

"Celeste deserves—"

Marla cut me off. "Celeste deserves more than all the stars in Christendom after everything she's been through, you included! Unless you brought them with you, the best thing you can do for her is to leave her alone."

I slumped back against the register. My worst fears were being hurled at me as a solution.

"Things have changed here, Wes." Marla finally relented, her tone sad and apologetic. "You can't barge into her life like a hurricane after all this time."

"Then what can I do?" I asked. A note of desperation crept in. "I don't want to keep living without her."

Marla leaned forward, cutting straight to the chase. "You don't even know her anymore, Wesley. Start there."

She was spot on, like always. I wasn't the same person I

used to be, so how could I expect any less from Celeste? But that meant we needed to grow back together because I knew in my heart that she was meant for me. It was the only truth I had ever known. Even the brief few minutes I had spent in her atmosphere earlier reconfirmed that in my soul.

And if that wasn't enough proof, surely the fact that my only experience with a one night stand just so happened to be with Celeste meant something. The very Universe wanted us to be together! We were magnets, fighting our attraction only to wind up paired anyway.

It didn't matter what had changed for Celeste or for me. When two souls were forged together, nothing could keep them apart. I waited ten long years for a sign that our days apart were over. Now that I had my first taste of her, there was no going back. I was going to make her forgive me or I was going to die trying.

CHAPTER 42
MISTAKES WERE MADE
CELESTE

My mind was racing as I played out all the different scenarios in my head of what could happen. The injustice of it all was too much.

I had done everything Desiree had ever asked of me, without complaint, since the day my daddy died. In all the years she left The Comfy Cushion to me, I never once called off sick or closed the restaurant for my own personal reasons. Only on rare occasions when Iris had a recital and I was permitted to go. Any time Iris was sick and I needed to be home with her, Marla had closed her own business to help ours.

Acting as though all of my sacrifices, all of my hard work, were merely a whim she entertained and not the means by which her household functioned was the worst kind of insult. I was breaking my neck to keep a roof over our heads and all she did was remind me of the ways it wasn't enough. There were so many important moments for my daughter that I missed because I wanted to keep the peace, because the restaurant was the only link I had left to my parents since Desiree took over our house.

And now all of it had been for nothing. What was worse—all of it was going into the hands of a man I had hated for half my life. Mr. Madden wasn't even going to maintain the integrity of The Comfy Cushion. He wanted to commercialize my mama's handwritten recipes so that he could install a fast food version in all of his stores.

I might not know much about business, but I wasn't sure that half a million dollars was the right price for all that.

How the heck had Desiree even contacted him? Did he know about Iris? For her to have spent so many years keeping Wesley in the dark about our daughter, it seemed odd for Desiree to involve Wesley's father in anything.

But wait—what if this business deal was the real reason Wesley was here? My stepmother had been manipulating me for so long in so many ways, I wouldn't put it past her to shove Wes into the equation. That would ensure my emotions were muddled and I was no longer thinking clearly, therefore far more willing to give up Mama's recipes. Desiree didn't know I had given the book to Marla for safekeeping and I prayed she didn't find out.

My fury only continued to grow the more I speculated on Wes' involvement in their scheme. It was the deepest form of betrayal, a pain that made the past ten years pale in comparison. There was only one way to find out.

"Jesse," I called out. "We're closing up early."

"Sure thing, boss," he said jovially. He was the most easy-going man I had ever met.

The thing about living in Southern Georgia is that thunderstorms roll in on the drop of a dime. By the time Jesse and I had everything shut off, wiped down, and back in its place, dark clouds were surging across the sky with cracks of lightning and booms of thunder that were loud enough to wake the dead. A torrential downpour broke out, with rain pelting so hard and fast, I couldn't see the playground across the street.

Flooding was quite common during rainstorms like this, so it was really a blessing in disguise. We weren't going to miss out on any business by closing up early, and my stepmother wouldn't be caught dead out in the mud and rain, so she wouldn't come looking for me if I were out too late. The downside, however, was that I also didn't want someone to notice my daddy's truck parked over at Ms. Shirley's house. I was going to have to run there and hope like hell I didn't catch my death of cold on the way.

Waving goodbye to Jesse, I took off down the alleyway, pushing under the loose board in the fence to cut through Old Man McInworthe's backyard, and over onto Ms. Shirley's street. My clothes were soaked through the moment I stepped outside, my long hair plastered to my face. I looked like a half drowned house elf.

Ms. Shirley's house hadn't changed a bit since I last visited. Her car was parked in its usual place in the driveway, but no matter how hard I pounded on the door, no one answered. A light shone in one of the rooms upstairs, which meant Wes had to be inside.

"You're not ignoring me that easy, Wesley Madden!" I muttered to myself.

Following along the side of the house, I unlatched the gate and let myself into the backyard. There I found Wes shirtless, in a pair of black sweatpants, strumming on an acoustic guitar on the back deck. Rain pelted the metal awning overhead and canceled out the music notes.

My brain short circuited when he jumped to his feet, displaying a six pack set of abs that definitely hadn't been there when we were kids. His eyes set my skin on fire as he quickly descended the steps towards me.

"Why did you come here?" I screamed. It was hard to hear anything over the thunder and rain. "What's the real reason?"

"You!" Wesley shouted back. He was now drenched, too, great, big droplets of water gliding down his nose. "It's always been you!"

My heart strings tugged. They wanted me to break down my walls and believe him, but I couldn't. There was no way this was real.

"You're lying!" I choked back tears. "This has to do with The Comfy Cushion and your dad's stupid deal!"

Wesley looked dumbstruck. "What? What deal? You're not making any sense!"

"Just forget it!" I yelled in frustration.

I turned to leave and his hand gripped my elbow. It left my skin tingling from his touch.

"Let go of me," I demanded.

Why did he have to be so handsome? Why did my traitorous heart have to skip a beat just from being in his vicinity? Why did I still have to want him so badly after everything we had been through? I was fairly certain now that he was the mystery man from the costume party in Savannah, and if that was the case, my body ached for the bliss he gave me then.

Whether it was ten years or ten thousand, my heart wanted him in this life and every life thereafter. Time didn't matter when two souls were meant to be one.

He took a step closer to me so that we were standing chest to chest. With every angry, heaving breath, my breasts pressed against the solid muscle of his torso. I had to crane my head back to even look at him. There was a vague hum of silence as though Mother Nature herself paused the racket to hear his answer.

"Never," he breathed.

Something inside me unleashed, and I launched myself at him in the same moment he descended on me like man starved. I hated him. And I loved him. And that made all the difference in the world.

Our lips crashed in a tidal wave, the storm raging around us finally matching the passion blazing within us. In seconds he had my back pinned against the fence, both arms clamped around my thighs as they wrapped around his waist. We were soaked to the bone as the rain poured down in waves, but I didn't care. I doubted Wesley did either.

In one fluid motion, Wesley had my t-shirt off and in the mud at our feet. The cotton of my cheap, white bra was all but sheer now under the water and I swore I heard Wesley mumble, "God yes!" before he sucked one breast in his mouth, bra and all.

With a strangled cry, we lurched away from the fence. Wesley didn't hesitate to carry me up the deck stairs and into the house. We crashed onto the kitchen table, which trembled beneath us, but thankfully did not break. He laid me out like I was his last supper, his blue eyes roving every inch of my body with undisguised lust. Lights flickered and then the power cut off, leaving the only light from the open back door where lightning flashed every few seconds.

"Do you have any idea how perfect you are?" he whispered. Steady hands unzipped my jean shorts, peeling the wet fabric slowly down my legs. Even my panties were wet from the rain. It didn't stop Wes from leaning down and inhaling between my thighs.

My pussy clenched with need. Just having his eyes on me

was enough to drive me crazy. I wasn't sure if I wanted him to devour me or to grab a butter knife from the counter next to me and stab him. Maybe both.

The shifting light from outside cast planes on Wesley's face that cloaked one side in shadow, the other side in stunning clarity. It was the perfect juxtaposition for how I felt about him as he was both the good and the bad in my life. Right now, he was so sexy that I just wanted him to fulfill every fantasy I had played out over the past ten years alone.

My panties followed my shorts, only this time when they slipped off my feet, Wesley crumpled them up and stuffed them in his pocket. His face returned to my pussy, his tongue tentatively licking up my slit.

"I almost forgot what you taste like," he whispered. Lightning flashed and I had a momentary glimpse of the sorrow in his eyes.

But I didn't want to acknowledge that. "Shut up and do it."

"Are you gonna hate me for it later?"

"Who says I don't hate you already?"

The sound he emitted sounded like a mixture of a growl and a groan. I didn't have time to analyze it, however, before his mouth parted my lips and sucked my swollen clit.

All of the neurons in my body fired off at once. Wesley had some sort of instinctual map that laid out all of my pleasure centers so he could wring my body out like a sponge. He suckled on my clit while pinching my inner thigh, giving me small stings of pain to lace my pleasure. When his tongue flattened out to lick the arousal dripping between my cheeks, I may have seen the Almighty.

Suddenly, Wesley started peppering heavy, wet kisses up

my body. I had an internal moment of panic that he would notice the stretch marks on my belly from Iris, but that fear was negated as he nipped and licked every inch of my stomach. He yanked on my bra, indicating that I needed to take it off, but I must have moved too slow for him because both hands pulled the bra cups down to bare my chest to him. Cool air danced around my nipples in a delicious sensation before Wes wrapped his tongue around the right, then the left.

"Suck," he commanded and put his thumb in my mouth.

His other hand returned to my pussy, thrusting a single digit inside. I did as he ordered. My cheeks hollowed out as I let my tongue swirl around his thumb. The heat in his gaze was an atomic bomb, and I couldn't ignore the thrill it gave me to know I could still affect him like that.

After a moment, he withdrew his thumb and abruptly returned to my pussy. He sat down in the chair, spreading my legs like he was ready to feast. With one quick jerk, Wes had my ass hanging off the table so my knees could hook over his shoulder. All I could see was the top of his head as he descended between my legs in a ravenous swoop.

The thumb I sucked on was now swirling my asshole. Rational thought gave up the driver's seat, and I didn't protest as Wesley's tongue invaded my pussy while his thumb pushed inside the back door. Slowly, as I relaxed and adjusted to the intrusion, he worked his thumb in and out of my ass in rhythm to the way his tongue laved my pussy. The sensation was unlike anything I had ever imagined. My fingers laced into his hair, all but burying him between my thighs. Wesley moaned his approval.

As the pace increased in my ass, Wes returned his mouth to my clit. It was the final straw, and I nearly blacked out from the orgasm that tore through me. My thighs bracketed his head and he lapped at my cum like a dog.

After several minutes of riding out my pleasure, reality came crashing down on me again. This was a mistake. I wanted to *talk* to him, not desecrate poor Aunt Shirley's kitchen table.

Wesley sensed the change in my demeanor because he stood up and backed away slowly with his hands laced around the back of his head. It gave me a delectable view of his rigid abs, round biceps, and the deep V that highlighted the path to his best feature. He had no business looking like that when I looked like a busted can of biscuits.

Which reminded me that those lumpy biscuits were now fully on display.

"Do you have a change of clothes I can borrow, please?" I asked. My arms wrapped around my chest to cover my tits and I crossed my legs to cover my lady bits.

The look he gave me was so infused with vulnerability and longing that I had to turn away. "I'll be right back," he said.

CHAPTER 43
END OF THE BALL
WESLEY

SEEING Celeste materialize in Shirley's—my—backyard looking like a literal wet dream would be permanently imprinted on my mind until the day I died. I had zoned out completely, mulling over Marla's advice, and then Celeste appeared like I manifested her into being. She was breathtaking with the rain cascading down her face, long hair trailing down her back, and those tiny damn jean cutoffs that made me jealous for hugging her ass so tight.

Something just came over me the moment I touched her. The same pulse of intensity charged the air between us, more powerful than any storm ever could be. While the lightning might have illuminated the sky above, the real electricity surged the second Celeste and I made contact. I couldn't hold back any longer. Kissing her was more important than inhaling my next breath.

On the other side of our antics, now that the rush of heat, lust, and serotonin died down, I was terrified of what awaited me downstairs. I didn't even bother to change my own soaked sweatpants, just grabbed a cotton t-shirt and pair of gym shorts for her. Celeste Hendricks was my personal hurricane, and I would happily drown if it meant being in her presence. I just didn't want her to hate me for it.

Back in the kitchen, I allowed myself to drink her in as she scrambled into my clothes. The round curves of her body were fuller now compared to when we were teens, sexier, and I loved the change. No model I worked with could ever hold a candle to Celeste's beauty. It probably creeped her out to see me ogling her like a pizza, but damn it, I was a glutton for punishment.

"That wasn't why I came here," she finally said after wringing out her long, wet hair in the kitchen sink. "I need to talk to you."

I nodded. "Yeah, okay."

Celeste glanced at me and her cheeks flamed. "Can you please put a shirt on or something?"

Now she was just stroking my ego. "No." I crossed my arms and leaned against the doorframe. "I'm pretty comfy the way I am."

She rolled her eyes. "In your wet pants?"

"Lovebug, you don't have to beat around the bush if you wanna get me out of my pants."

The pink in her cheeks turned red. Her shy smile, my favorite, returned as she whispered, "Some things never change with you."

I grinned, loving that I could tease her like I used to. I would take this reaction any day of the week. And it gave me hope that our future together was possible. We could work through this. If I could only convince her to give me a chance.

"What do you wanna talk about?" I asked.

That lit the fire in her. I could tell from the way she bristled, standing straighter and holding her head high.

There's my girl, I thought.

Celeste stared me down, gauging my reaction. "Are you here because of the deal with The Comfy Cushion?"

"What are you talking about? What deal?"

My father was a savvy businessman, I had to give him that. He could sense a good deal from five miles away and he was typically three steps ahead of the competition. While I knew Madden Enterprises invested as a silent partner in other companies, buying a small town diner wasn't really something I could imagine on his radar.

Celeste didn't respond, just continued staring me down. Hostility rolled off her in waves and I desperately wished I knew how to fix it. It aggravated me that she wouldn't explain. She came here to talk, didn't she? How were we going to fix anything if she shut me out?

"I've been wanting to come home for a while," I finally told her to break the silence. "I've missed you so much."

"Home?" she repeated. Except it was a loaded question, meant to be used as ammunition. "This isn't your home. You don't belong here, Wesley."

Okay, so we were doing this with the gloves off. "My home is anywhere *you* are," I argued. "You're all I've thought about since the day I left."

"You have a funny way of showing it," she countered, crossing her arms over her chest. I tried not to smile at how good it looked to see her in my clothes again. *Focus, Wesley.*

"Do you know how many times I tried calling you at the diner? The number changed and I'm pretty sure mine was blocked at some point because all I ever got was a dial tone—"

"*THAT'S* your effort?!" she screeched. "After the way you left, you thought a phone call where I worked was gonna fix everything?!"

I ground my teeth before slamming the palm of my hand into the wall beside me. Red was all I could see. "Maybe if you hadn't put a fucking restraining order on me, I could have done more!"

To my surprise, she laughed in response. It was a bitter, resentful sound, not her usual soft giggle that softened me. "I had a bit too much on my plate to get a restraining order, Wes. I don't even know how to do something like that."

That had to be a lie. We were in court; I *heard* the judge talking about it…

Except I had blocked out so many memories from that part of my life. It was the lowest I had ever been. One of my psych classes in college suggested that our brain would remove traumatic memories to protect us, which made sense to me at the time. Now that I actually tried to visualize it, I couldn't recall ever seeing the court papers for a restraining order. Nor could I distinctly remember the judge using the words "restraining order."

I shook my head. None of that mattered now. "I never wanted to leave you, Celeste. We made promises to each other, promises I've done everything in my power to keep."

Celeste scoffed and paced towards the door before rounding in on me. "Stop doing this! You don't get to come back here and bringing up feelings and memories that—"

"So you *do* feel something for me?" I interrupted. I knew it!

She threw up her hands and stormed towards the back door again. I was right on her heels.

"Why are you running away from this, lovebug?" I shouted. Catching her in my arms, I spun her around to face me, practically nose to nose. "I know you still love me. And if

I have to spend every day for the rest of my life making the past ten years up to you, I will."

Tears streaked her face as she ripped herself from my grasp. "You don't even have a clue what I've been through the past ten years! The way I've struggled while you've been out living the high life!"

"Lovebug, I was earning that money for you just as much as me! You can take it all, I don't care! Everything that's mine is yours anyway!"

She snorted in disgust. "Because that's always your solution to everything, Wes! Just throw money around, that'll fix our problems! Take the Benedict Madden approach."

My comeback died out in my throat. It never occurred to me that I was doing the same thing as my father, but she was right. I might be less of a dick about it—sometimes—than he was, but the results were the same. Money was a means to an end. There was always a dollar amount that was just right and opened whatever doors I wanted it to.

Celeste eyed me sadly. "I need you to leave River's Run, Wes."

"You need me to go or you want me to go?" The distinction mattered. This wasn't the way any of this played out in my head, and I wasn't going to go down without a fight.

"I don't have the luxury of wanting anything anymore," she said quietly.

"What does that even mean?" I asked in confusion. We were talking in riddles and I was missing a big clue.

Outside, the rain started to die down. Thunderstorms never lasted long here. Celeste glanced out the back door. "I should go," she said, hitching her thumb over her shoulder.

"No, wait! Just tell me how I can fix this!" Defeat was not an option. Now that my addiction was back in full force, the only way I was leaving her would be if she told me directly she wanted me gone. Something about the way she acted made me question what was really motivating her behavior. Celeste wasn't angry or upset about how hard I just smashed on her pussy, but wasn't going to talk to me about what it meant for our future?

"I know you were the girl at the hotel!" I called out after her. She was almost to the gate, the rain gone and lighter clouds rolling in.

She smiled sadly over her shoulder. "Cinderella can't stay at the ball forever, Wes. Neither can I."

CHAPTER 44
THIS AIN'T IT
CELESTE

Leaving Wes' house left me with more questions than answers. While he seemed genuinely confused over Madden Enterprises' deal with Desiree, his excuses on everything else were weak at best. A restraining order—really? I was only sixteen and Wesley hadn't done anything to me to warrant protection. Everything that happened at the hospital happened to the doctor and security guards, not me. It hadn't even scared me because I was so used to his temper.

I was grateful the rain stopped, but I no longer thought going home was the best option. Desiree was the epicenter of all my problems and I didn't have the energy to confront her. I was always welcome to stay at Marla's so that was where I headed. It was doubtful Desiree would even let me speak to Iris until I gave her Mama's book, anyway.

Letting myself in through the door behind her bakery, I climbed the stairs to Marla's apartment and only remembered that Maggie was staying with her after a loud rendition of "Dancin' in the Country" by Tyler Hubbard blasted out the front door. Maggie was in a pair of pajama shorts and a tank top at a kitchen sink full of soapy water and dishes, singing at the top of her lungs while she danced along to the music.

"Hola, chica!" she called over to me. At the sight of my crestfallen face, she dropped the plate in her hands back into the water, thereby spraying all the counters with suds. "Oh my god, what happened? Is it Iris?"

The dam wall broke. Tears flowed freely and before I knew it, Maggie had me nestled onto the couch with a glass of red wine in my hand and her arm snuggling me against her shoulder.

"Spill," she commanded like only a best friend could.

"Wes is here!" was my tearfully inarticulate response as I succumbed into a sniveling mess.

It took several minutes of her stroking my hair while I cried it out before I could even explain to her what had happened. By the time I calmed down enough to get all of it out, including the fact that Wes was my hotel mystery hookup, Marla had closed up the bakery and joined us, making me regale the story all over again. Maggie was left gaping at me like she wanted to catch flies while Marla pursed her lips in a way that told me she was holding back what she really wanted to say.

"Just spit it out," I sighed. She wasn't going to be able to relax her face until she said her piece.

Marla huffed before refilling her own wine glass. "I talked to Wesley earlier. After he left The Comfy Cushion. He's pretty determined to make things right between y'all."

"And you believed him?" I asked incredulously.

Maggie grimaced, a very un-Maggie-like expression. "He did reach out to me a few years ago when I started my social media accounts…and I may have told him to leave you alone." She held up her hands in a placating gesture. "I thought it was best because of how freaked out you were over Iris!"

This was all the opposite of what I expected them to say. I assumed both of them would assure me I had done the right thing by telling Wesley to leave town. Instead they were both acting like I overreacted.

"Did y'all miss the part where his daddy is buying my parents' restaurant?" I reminded them. "How am I supposed to forgive him for that?"

"You're supposed to hear him out," Marla replied. "You're making assumptions and it's gonna cost you."

I jumped up, too infuriated with the situation to sit still. Wine was also spurring me on, but that was a whole other issue.

"He's the one who left me! On the day my father died, in case y'all forgot! Wesley Madden is the love of my life and *he left me.*"

Maggie's mouth curved into a triumphant grin. "You said 'is the love of my life.' Present tense."

Sputtering, I snarled, "Semantics!"

Marla shook her head. "I agree with Maggie. Celeste, you're letting your pain make the decisions for you. None of us know what really happened. Y'all were kids in a very bad situation. Both of you deserve to hear the truth." She shot me a pointed a look. "Including Iris."

The very thought of it had me sinking back onto the couch in defeat. "Desiree will take her from me," I whispered.

Marla shrugged. "Seems to me that Wesley has more than enough money to pay for a lawyer and get her back. Wouldn't that be a chance worth taking if it means you get the family you always wanted?"

If only it were that simple. "Assuming, of course, Wesley

forgives me for not telling him about Iris from the beginning. He's gonna be madder than a rattlesnake when he finds out."

Both of them paused to consider that.

"Doesn't mean you shouldn't tell him," Maggie finally admitted.

Deep down, I knew she was right. I just wasn't prepared to face all the feelings that came with it. My daughter meant more to me than anything, and it was a huge risk to lose her permanently and hope that Wesley would fight Desiree for custody. It was something I had always wanted to do, but never had the funds to pursue.

"Your parents never wanted this life for you, Cee," Marla said quietly, thereby starting the tears flowing again. "They both worked so hard to provide for you, and baby girl, this ain't it."

Her words echoed in my head long after they all went to bed. Maggie invited me to share the spare bedroom with her and have a "real sleepover" like when we were kids, but I needed the space.

As moonlight filtered in through the windows, casting shadows that danced on Marla's hardwood floors, I tossed and turned with indecision. Ultimately it didn't matter what kind of life my parents wanted for me. They left me, whether it was their own choice or not, and I had to deal with the consequences. Feeling guilt-ridden that they might not be happy with how things played out wasn't really going to get me anywhere.

The fact was that I hadn't thought about how drastically different my life could have been in a long time. Being a teen mom wasn't something I would have wished on my worst enemy, but it would not have been nearly as hard with Wesley's help. I had a feeling that Iris would have had him wrapped around her finger from go, and it certainly would have helped to share the emotional toll of parenthood with her dad. I always wanted them to meet, I just figured it would have to wait until Iris turned eighteen.

Marla was partially right—pain and fear were making my decisions for me, something Mama and Daddy never abided by. I could visualize Mama next to me as clear as day, a ghostly figment of my memory, with her wild brown waves and soft hazel eyes. She would rest her hand on my knee and gently remind me, "Be brave and be kind. That'll take you far in life."

Suddenly I missed her and Daddy so much that my bones ached. None of what had happened was fair to any of us, but maybe this was my chance to make it right.

"After all," Mama's memory reminded me, "life always comes full circle."

She was right, of course. I just didn't want the circle to break.

CHAPTER 45
REVELATIONS GALORE
WESLEY

"Will you be returning after the funeral or have things developed further down there?" Phillip asked in his usual clipped tone.

I wrenched my torso upward, holding the 25 pound dumbbell with both hands above my head to complete the inclined sit up. My abs burned in a way that reminded me of the punishment I deserved. Yesterday was such a shit show, I doubted I would ever work my way back into Celeste's good graces.

"Oddly enough, Phillip, when I pay someone to work *for* me, I don't let them tell me what to do," I ground out. Only one Airpod was in my ear in case that ballsy little girl from yesterday showed up, but I had thrown myself into an arduous workout routine the moment I set foot in the gym. Phillip claimed he only needed to discuss the final funeral arrangements with me, which would take place later this afternoon, however he started grilling me the moment I tried to end the call.

He sighed into the phone, a weary sound that I imagined my guardian angel repeated a lot. "Wesley, I'm only trying to manage your affairs. Your father is furious and with this setback for your start date with Madden Enterprises, you could accept the offer to go to Milan this weekend for the Armani shoot."

Flames erupted in my muscles as I tried for one more rep. I had long since lost count. "I'm not leaving River's Run without her, Phillip," I snapped. "Which reminds me, I need you to answer something for me, and I need you to be honest. Is my father buying The Comfy Cushion?"

Phillip's hesitation said everything.

What a motherfucker!

"Get me all of the information you can on that deal immediately!" Admitting defeat with my ab routine, I laid back against the bench, willing the pain to eat me alive. "And I want a copy of the restraining order Celeste had on me in my inbox within the next twenty minutes."

"Sir?" Phillip inquired, sounding confused.

"The restraining order. From when I was sixteen," I prompted him.

My assistant sounded puzzled. "I'm not sure what you mean, but I'll get all the court documents from your case sent over to you straightaway." A click let me know the call ended, and my workout mix resumed. Dan and Shay tried to tell me how not to think about a lost love, but if they couldn't stop, how could I?

Going through the motions of my familiar routine, I let my mind wander as my body acted on muscle memory. Something about Celeste's whole demeanor yesterday was totally off. I still felt like I was missing a core piece of information.

Yet she didn't seem ready to give up on me. The chemistry was still there. Even as a stranger at the charity gala, I was drawn to her like a moon orbiting its planet. It didn't matter how long I had to stay here in River's Run if it meant I could make things right with her. Home was wherever she laid her head at night. And while her words might have been pushing me away, her actions told me how badly she wanted me to stay.

The door opened and the fiery blonde girl stalked in. She had a bookbag slung over one shoulder and street clothes on, but her hair was pulled back in a tight dancer's bun.

"Sorry, I'm late," she said. Her head was held high with her chin out, yet I could faintly detect how close to tears she was. "I don't have enough time to practice this morning. Can I please come back after school?"

"What are you practicing so much for?" I asked.

Her answer surprised me. "Because if I become the prima ballerina in a major dance company, I can take my mom away from here."

I wiped a towel across my face to get rid of the sweat. "You don't like River's Run?"

Iris shrugged. "It's fine, I guess. But Mama never smiles anymore and she has to work so much that she can't ever see me dance. I want to see her in the front row someday, smiling at me like she's proud of me."

Her sadness was so deep and profound, my heart crinkled a little bit. These were an adult's problems trapped in a little girl's body.

"Not sure if I can come back later this afternoon, but I'll do my best," I offered. "I'm about to head over to The Comfy Cushion. Wanna come with me?"

She gave me a small, shy smile that was so reminiscent of Celeste, I almost did a double take. "Yeah, I'm heading there, too."

Iris waited by the door for me to gather my stuff before

we headed out together. The sun was just starting to creep over the tree line across the street. A lone truck drove down the street, the driver honking and waving as it passed. That was the thing about small towns; friendliness was a way of life.

I noticed Celeste through the window of The Comfy Cushion, pouring hot coffee into the mugs of the two old men who ran the mechanic shop. God, her beauty still knocked the wind out of me. Even the changes like the blonde hair and wide hips were such a turn on. She was literally perfect.

Iris led the way inside, walking right up to the counter. What happened next made my stomach bottom out and time stand still. I watched, horrorstruck, as Celeste squealed at the sight of her and ran out from behind the counter to catch an excited Iris in her arms. Celeste looked moved to tears, stroking Iris' head and rocking her as though she couldn't pull her close enough. For some strange reason, the sight pulled at my heart strings.

"Oh, baby girl, I missed you so much! Does Desiree know you're here?!"

"Hold the fucking phone!" I exclaimed.

Celeste jumped like she touched a fork to an outlet. "What are you doing here?"

Iris smiled at me. "Oh, Mama, this is the man from the gym I told you about."

But Celeste wasn't eyeing her daughter. Her green eyes were wide and fearful while those glorious lips formed a perfectly round O as she took in my horrified face. I couldn't even handle blinking at the moment.

"Wes, I can explain..." she started, trailing off with uncertainty at the end.

Poor Iris' swung her head back and forth like she was

watching a tennis match. "What's wrong, Mama? Do you know him?"

Imitating Flynn Rider from *Tangled* wasn't on my list of things to do today, but incoherent noises were all that came out. I was about to freak out, and everything else was background noise.

"Please don't do this in front of her!" Celeste held up her hands in a placating gesture. Like a caricature of myself, the sound muted in the back of my throat while my face remained frozen in a now silent scream. Celeste gave a very confused Iris a hug and promised to explain everything after school before sending her out the door.

It was then that I realized the handful of diners were all staring at us as though we were a circus sideshow. I didn't argue when she grabbed me by the arm and yanked me back towards the office.

"Wes, I can explain," she said again. Her back pressed against the door with one hand on the knob as though she was preparing for a quick getaway.

I nodded too vigorously for what the moment called for. It seemed I was no longer in control of my limbs. "Uh huh. Yep. You said that." Only it came out in a high falsetto that pierced my eardrums.

Pacing sounded like a clever idea, so I began to briskly walk the length of the room. A total of six steps in either direction. Celeste remained silent, watching me apprehensively. She chewed on her bottom lip warily in a way that I would have found cute in any other situation.

"So you have a daughter," I finally stated.

She was going to split her lip in half if she chewed any harder. "Um...*we* have a daughter."

There are moments in your life, as clear cut as a diamond, that permanently alter your state of being. In the blink of an eye, everything you ever stood for, worked for, and wanted shifts, and there's no going back. This was one of those moments.

"We have a child?" I asked. "An actual, living, breathing child?"

Celeste's shoulders sank. "Yes," she replied. She still regarded me carefully, taking one small step forward while maintaining a hand on the door.

Roaring filled my ears and I found my fist punching a hole into the drywall. It was only after I noticed the blood on my knuckles that I realized the roaring came from me. "ARE YOU FUCKING KIDDING ME?!"

She winced like I had physically slapped her. "Please don't be like this," whimpered Celeste.

"Don't be like what, Celeste? Furious that I've been a father for a decade and I'm only finding out now *on accident*?!" I screamed. "Livid that you kept such a giant secret from me?"

The whole thing sounded like some sort of cosmic joke. While the night of losing my virginity had been spank bank fodder all these years, I had never once considered the repercussions of our foolish decision to have unprotected sex at sixteen. It completely slipped my mind in comparison to the larger problems thrown at me during that time in my life. And while I had been ruminating for the past 48 hours on Celeste's strange behavior, it hadn't occurred to me that another life would be so influenced by our decisions.

It was a heady realization of new responsibility to drop on your lap before nine in the morning!

"Does she know who I am?" I settled on asking. There

were so many questions buzzing around in my head that I didn't even know where to begin.

Celeste wilted, staring at the ground while she shook her head. For some reason this revelation was a kick in the gut. Not only had I never had a chance to know of my daughter, she never had the chance to know of me. Although, even in the few minutes I spent with her, I could already tell Iris wouldn't have let go of her interest to meet me.

Too many emotions were at war within me, all trying to bubble to the surface. I wanted to know everything. I wanted to build a time machine so that I could go back and do every single thing differently. I wanted to have Celeste suddenly laugh that her prank had worked; now that we were somewhat even with our betrayals, we could move forward.

But as I watched the tears continue to stream down her cheeks, I accepted the fact that none of those things were true.

"She—you—" I sputtered, trying desperately to gain some sort of ground on all the feelings swirling around. "She has brass balls bigger than Texas!"

Celeste's lips pressed together in a firm line as she fought back a laugh. "And where do you think she gets that from, Wes?"

Oh my god—it was my worst nightmare. We created a female version of me!

"I need to go…I think. Yeah…" My voice trailed off in confusion. I swept past her and went to the back door to exit. I didn't want to be seen by anybody, even if there were only a few patrons at The Comfy Cushion in that moment.

"Wesley, hold on! We need to talk about this!" Celeste cried desperately. She followed me out to the doorway and stood there helplessly.

I only got three steps away before I rounded back in front

of her. "Celeste, I've dreamed of you carrying my child since I was old enough to fantasize about sex. And knowing that I missed out on that dream is something you're just gonna have to give me some time to process."

A sob broke free from her throat, and for the first time ever, the fact that I was the cause didn't bother me. She had taken something so precious from me that I could never get back.

Time.

CHAPTER 46
PAIN...SO MUCH PAIN
CELESTE

ROCK BOTTOM SHOULD AT LEAST COME with complimentary ice cream. If you're gonna find yourself in the gutter, the least the Universe could do was give you a sweet to make you feel better.

The look on Wesley's face as he left haunted me. Getting hit by a semi might have caused less damage because while the body can physically heal, your heart never fully recovers. That was a lesson I had learned the hardest way possible and now here I was inflicting the same pain on another person.

Shame.

Regret.

Those were the only two thoughts on my mind as I slowly returned to the front of The Comfy Cushion. Jesse eyed me sadly as though he knew something was up, and the fellas from the auto shop wouldn't make eye contact with me as they shoved a twenty dollar bill in my hand. I moved on autopilot through the rest of my morning, agonizing over the best way to approach the situation. Would it be better to give Wes his space? Should I force him to talk to me?

And worse—what could I do about Iris? If she was able to

come to the restaurant after school, she would have a million questions after the bizarre episode she witnessed this morning, and while I would love to tell her everything, I was already skating on cracked ice with Desiree. I didn't want to challenge her any further.

However, there was also Wes to contend with. He had obviously met Iris and formed enough of an impression on her that she trusted him enough to come here with him. She mentioned before that he was going to meet her at the gym in the mornings so she could practice dance in the fitness classroom. How could I prevent him from saying something to her? It would get even uglier if I asked him not to speak to her because of Desiree. He always hated my stepmother.

As if I spoke her into existence, Desiree stormed in wearing a tight black dress and large sunglasses. She whipped them off her face with a smirk, scanning the now empty dining room in triumph.

"Still no customers," she tsked. "Hardly seems fair letting poor Mr. Madden buy the place. He's clearly getting ripped off."

"If that was the case, there's no benefit to buying it in the first place," I countered, surprising myself. I always tried to bite my tongue around Desiree.

Except I was sick of doing that. My mama raised me to be kind, but she also raised me to be fair. It had become second nature for me to take everything lying down, and I had become a version of myself that I didn't recognize anymore. Maybe it was seeing Wesley again as a reminder of who I used to be. Maybe the imminent threat of losing my daughter and my parents' legacy all at once was the straw that broke the camel's back. Maybe I was just too exhausted to deal with yet another go round. But it was time for things to start changing.

"If you're here for the recipe book, you're not getting it," I stated flatly.

Her eyes flashed.

"Over my dead body will my mama's words make that devil man more money," I added. The conviction made my voice sound a lot surer than I felt. Desiree wasn't going to back down.

So I wouldn't either.

She gave me a menacing smile that made my veins turn to ice. "Oh, didn't I mention? He's going to buy the house and all our land, too. Excuse me—*my* land," she clarified.

Our house and the six acres beyond had been in the Hendricks family for over a hundred years. We even had a cemetery further back on the property with relatives buried during the Civil War. And now Desiree was going to throw it all away? I never understood why she married Daddy in the first place, but to squander our family's land was downright cruel.

"Madden Enterprises needs a new warehouse location and it turns out, we are the perfect spot for it," Desiree continued. "However, he's willing to let the house remain so long as you provide those recipes."

It was a fool's bargain; nothing to gain and everything to lose. Having the house there would hardly matter when our backyard became a parking lot for whatever industrial monstrosity Mr. Madden built. A hatred stronger than I had ever known filled my chest. I never considered myself a violent person—Wesley was the hothead, not me—but now I could finally understand why words fail and fists spoke.

"I'm not giving you her recipes," I repeated firmly.

Desiree's face contorted in fury. "Then I suggest you make peace with the fact that you'll never see your daughter again! You're no longer welcome in my home!"

She stormed out of the restaurant, letting the door clatter loudly behind her. All of the adrenaline left my body the moment she stalked from view and I sank to the floor, shaking uncontrollably. A sob tore from my throat, then another, and another.

"Yo...I'm gonna call Marla," Jesse said nervously as he peered around from the kitchen.

He could call the Pope for all I cared. Everything was spiraling out of control, and I felt the darkness taking hold again, a darkness I thought I escaped after Iris was born.

But I hadn't really escaped it, I just built a small glass cage around my mind to preserve what was left of it. And that's the thing about glass—it shatters. After the fallout with Wesley and the desperate ultimatum from Desiree, my cage was pulverized. All the things I loved were being taken from me and there was no way out.

"Hey now, darlin'," Marla hushed me. I had no idea when she arrived or where Jesse went, but as she wrapped her arms around me, tears obscured my vision and a caterwauling wail broke free. Both of our bodies trembled from my pain.

"Here," I vaguely heard her say. "Take my phone and call Wesley."

"No no no no no!" Impossible as it seemed, I cried harder.

Marla continued to stroke my hair and gently shush me. I had a momentary flashback to just such a moment with Nana, where I was equally gutted and broken, and I had the horrific thought that this was always going to be the state of my life. While I had a childhood full of happiness and love, life came crashing down hard the moment Mama died, and it had never quite gone back.

Maybe that's what life was all about. Maybe it was just storm after storm, a never ending current of bullshit, including dashed hopes, discarded dreams, and lost love. Or perhaps each person only got a certain quota of happiness in life. With two incredible parents who doted on me, I used mine up before I really had a chance to know what it meant.

That thought only served to make me cry harder. I didn't think it was physiologically possible at that point.

A new set of arms firmly grabbed me, one arm hooking under my knees and the other tugging on my back. I was lifted like I weighed no more than a plate of grits. My vision was far too blurry to see who held me, but the sudden warmth and overwhelming sense of safety didn't make it hard to guess.

"I've got you, lovebug," Wes whispered in my hair. "I'll always get you."

CHAPTER 47
THE RECKONING
WESLEY

I HAD no fucking clue what was going on, but when Jesse called me from Marla's phone, he only got out two words. "It's Celeste." I ran back to The Comfy Cushion like the world was on fire.

Seeing her break—really, truly break—in my arms like this was enough to convince myself that she was never leaving them again. Yeah, I was pissed off about Iris. About the time I lost and couldn't get back. We were gonna have to work through that. But love meant forgiveness, which was a lesson only Celeste taught me. And I could summon a whole lot of forgiveness watching her fall to pieces.

This was beyond anything I'd seen before. I always thought her worst was discovering the extent of her dad's cancer, but this was a million times worse. Celeste's body shook so hard that her teeth were chattering. I doubted she was even aware of it, though. The sounds emanating from her mouth were inhuman. Incomprehensible. I gripped her harder, clutching her to me so she didn't fall out of my arms.

"Her daddy's truck is parked out back," Marla said.

One of the strangest things I had learned when I first

moved to River's Run was that people often left their keys in the ignition of their vehicles. Nobody worried about theft in a town where everybody knew everyone. For once, I was grateful for it because I didn't have to hunt Celeste's truck keys down when she was unable to give me directions.

We flew to my house. I didn't want to bother with stop signs and pauses when I already knew there wouldn't be anyone on the roads anyhow. Once there, I carried her inside and straight up to what had once been Aunt Shirley's room. My aunt had been confined to the den downstairs for the past several years, so no one had slept in the bed in a long time. All the dust in the room reflected such. It normally would have made Celeste pause to see a room so filthy.

Now, she only continued to wail.

I cradled her in my lap like a child, both arms fiercely pinning her to me. Hot tears were coating my neck and, in an instant, the collar of my shirt was soaked, but I didn't care. The only way out was through. Celeste needed to let all of the pain out.

It might have been minutes or it might have been hours before Celeste's crying died down. Her body started to relax against me and I realized she cried herself to sleep. As gently as I could, I settled her against the pillows, only darting out long enough to grab the blankets from the couch downstairs where I had been sleeping. Her face was red and blotchy, her breathing deep and even. She would be out for a while.

Grabbing my phone, I stepped out into the hall to call Marla and find out what was going on. Storming out after our fight earlier wasn't the right thing to do, I could admit that, but this reaction seemed a bit excessive, and Celeste wasn't a drama queen. Something else had to have happened.

"Is she okay?" Marla answered on the first ring.

"She cried herself to sleep," I whispered, glancing back over my shoulder to Celeste's sleeping form. "What the fuck happened, Marla?"

She sighed heavily, the defeat evidenced in the sound. "Desiree took Iris. And she's selling The Comfy Cushion to your daddy."

I was momentarily stunned as I tried to piece together how those ideas were linked. "What do you mean Desiree *took* Iris?" I demanded angrily. "Where is my daughter?"

Marla's sharp inhale was piercing. "Celeste told you?"

"Yeah," I said. "But I think I might have already known." It was all there, clear as a bell. Iris could have been my twin. The blonde hair, the blue eyes...the fucking attitude.

Lord help us all, I thought.

"Why would Desiree take Iris? That has nothing to do with a business deal," I continued.

"Because Desiree holds Iris over Celeste's head like a pawn." The anger in her voice coiled through the phone and sent a shiver down my spine. "She's been doing it her whole life."

"Her whole life...?" I trailed off uncertainly, some of the puzzle pieces starting to fit into place. "But she doesn't have the right to do that."

Marla replied, "Of course Desiree does. Iris belongs to her, after all."

"What? No, she doesn't. That's—"

Celeste rolled over fitfully, jarring my attention. I promised Marla I would call her back later and ended the call. Celeste continued to fidget in her sleep, jerking erratically with whatever nightmare she faced. I settled in beside her and pulled Celeste in my arms. It quieted her enough that she stilled, nestling into the groove my neck to sigh contentedly.

"We'll get through this, lovebug," I promised her.

⁂

It was well into the night before Celeste roused from sleep. I only managed to doze, too nervous of her waking up and spiraling downward again. As she lifted her head from my chest, her eyes were bloodshot and swollen, tears still welling in the corners. Blinking hard, she turned to me in astonishment and said, "How did I get here?"

I would have laughed if it weren't so sad. "Lovebug, I had to come get you." Attempting to keep my tone light so as not to spook her, I added, "You were in a rough way."

Celeste nodded curtly and flung the covers off to stand. "I have to go."

"Go?" I repeated, throwing the blankets onto the floor in my haste to follow her down the hall. "It's the middle of the night. Where are you gonna go?"

For some reason, my question brought her up short and another sob shuddered from her throat. I really did need to work on my tact.

"You're right," she added. "I don't have anywhere to go. I have nothing." She should have been dehydrated with all the tears she shed earlier, yet there were more trailing down her cheeks.

I pulled her to me, tucking her under my chin and stroking her back. "You have me," I whispered. "I know it's not much, and I'm sorry for that, but I'm here."

The tension in her body lingered for another minute or

two before she finally sank into my embrace, wrapping her arms around my waist and squeezing me close. The fight left her, which was the closest I'd felt to a victory with her in a long ass time.

"I can't go home anymore," she finally replied, pulling away from me to wipe her eyes. "Desiree is selling the house and all our land to your father. Along with The Comfy Cushion."

My jaw clenched as my teeth ground together. *Fucking Benny boy strikes again!* He had nothing to gain from such a deal other than another way to manipulate me. This was about his anger over my refusal to start at Madden Enterprises until I had things settled down here. Using Celeste to get to me was always his favorite method, after all.

"I'm not gonna let that happen," I vowed angrily. "He's only doing this to get back at me."

Her sigh let me know she felt the weight of the world on her shoulders. "It hardly matters when I'm the one who has to deal with the outcome," Celeste reminded me. She started down the stairs and I followed.

"Goddamn it, Celeste, quit walking away!" I yelled at her back. She almost reached the front door.

"Why? You taught me how!" she argued, throwing her hands up as she rounded on me. "And the only explanation I got doesn't make a lick of sense!"

"It hardly matters when I'm the one who has to deal with the outcome." I threw her own words right back at her. Because sometimes you just have to throw gasoline on a fire, like a dumbass. I folded my arms over my bare chest and glared at her.

"Oh my god, you cannot be serious right now!" Celeste yelled. "You *left* me!"

"And you hid my daughter from me for her entire life!" I screamed back. "Don't you think that makes us even?"

My accusation hit like a slap across the face. She stepped backward, mouth hung open, and stared at me as though she had never really seen me before.

Fighting with her wasn't going to make things better, so I let my temper deflate a bit. "You were the one who taught me that you have to love someone through their biggest mistakes. Or was that all a lie?"

Celeste opened and closed her mouth like a goldfish, weighing her response. "I'm sorry that I hid her from you. I wouldn't have if I had any other choice," she finally admitted.

But that only deepened my frustration. "It's the same for me! My father has been controlling things from the moment I got arrested. Even now, all of this business with your family is about manipulating me! I'm sorry that you keep getting caught in the crossfire, lovebug, but we owe it to ourselves and each other to save this! To have the life we always wanted!"

Her eyes flashed. "What life? This isn't living, Wes! Desiree has my daughter, my home, and my parents' business in an iron fist. I have no hope of getting any of it back! You have no idea how hard I've been working, day in and day out, since Iris was born. I'm in that restaurant from sun up to sun down every single day, without a break, because that's all that I have left of my mama and daddy that she hasn't taken from me!" A sob caught in her throat and it killed me. I hated to watch her fall apart again, yet I couldn't help but think this was a far more therapeutic version of what happened earlier. At least now she was voicing her feelings.

I stepped up to her, cradling her soft, wet cheeks with

both my hands. "Celeste, that was all before me," I assured her. She looked like a feral cat, cornered and terrified, but desperate enough to take the chance of listening to me. "It shouldn't have taken me so long to come back to you. I can admit that. I was scared of how I hurt you and scared of not being worthy of you. I've been busting my ass just as much to build a life you deserve, without any of my father's strings attached. And I've done it. So I'm here now, and I'll stay here now. For my whole life."

More sobs broke free and she leaned her forehead against my chest. "Wes," she said tearfully, "we're such different people now. I don't know if I can love you again like before."

I nodded into her hair. "You're right," I agreed. "We're not the same and our love won't be the same. It's going to be stronger now because of everything we've been through."

Celeste pulled away, taking all the warmth with her. "It's not that simple."

"It's not that hard either," I retorted.

Silence stretched between us like an empty vacuum. There was no way her stubbornness could beat mine, and I suspected that all of her protests had more to do with how broken she felt rather than how honest she could be with me. Hell, she probably wasn't even being honest with herself at the moment.

Forcing her hand wouldn't help the situation, though. "Tell me about Iris. I need to hear the truth from you."

She winced again. "What is there to tell? Desiree has her and I'll likely never get her back."

This wasn't making any sense. I frowned at her. "What does Desiree have to do with it? Iris never should have even been around that bitch."

She pulled her long, blonde hair over one shoulder and

moved to the living room. Sinking down on the weathered sofa, Celeste looked like she aged ten years overnight. Everything about our situation was beating her down, covering the radiant light I knew she emitted.

"Iris was born on February 8th. When I was still at the hospital, Desiree told me that since I was a minor, she was the legal adult who had custody of Iris. She said she could take her away from me any time she wanted, especially if I didn't do the things she asked. That if I tried to talk to you in any way, I would never see Iris again. Desiree had already made Nana move out, so I didn't want to call her bluff."

All I could see was red as her words sunk in. Desiree lied, and that was the reason I missed out on one of the most precious moments of my life. Thank God I didn't look good in prison orange or that bitch would be eviscerated.

"None of that is true," I told Celeste through clenched teeth. "Just because you were a teenager doesn't mean Iris belongs to her. Unless you signed legal custody papers, Iris belongs to you and has always belonged to you. Desiree has no right to take her from you."

Celeste blinked at me like I sprung a second head. "What?" she squeaked out.

My rage was too great to fence in and I started pacing the room. "I graduated from Harvard Law School, Celeste. I promise I know what I'm talking about." Too infuriated to hold back, I punched the wall closest to me. The resounding crack did little more than split my already callused knuckles. "Why didn't you ever consult an attorney?" I inquired.

She whimpered. "Because I don't have any money! Desiree told me that I had to earn my keep by running the restaurant or else she wouldn't allow me to live in Nana's cottage anymore. Sometimes Marla or Nana have to help me out just so I can pay Jesse, otherwise we wouldn't be able to stay open."

It was the wrong thing to say to me. I exploded like a volcano. "YOU MEAN TO TELL ME THAT FUCKING WOMAN HAS BEEN STEALING FROM YOU?!" Breathing like a wounded bull, I made to punch the wall again until Celeste darted in front of me.

"Stop, Wesley! You can't keep lettin' your temper do the talking! I'm just trying to explain what I've been through," she finished.

"That doesn't matter, Celeste!" I seethed. You mean to tell me that you haven't seen a penny of the money you *earned* after working like a slave in that diner for TEN YEARS?!"

She flinched at the storm in my voice, choosing to remain silent rather than add to my fury.

The reproach hung heavy between us, however, which stopped me from breaking anything further. My mind flipped through a thousand facts at once to make sense of the chaos around us. One thing was certain. We were getting our daughter back immediately.

"Right," I finally said, hands on my hips. "So we're gonna get Iris back, and then we're gonna get married. I'll figure out a way to stop my dad from doing all this. Hell, all I really have to do is show up and he'd probably let it go anyway. Let's just—"

"Hold up, Wesley Madden," interjected Celeste. "I am *not* marrying you!"

I blinked at her like I was stupid. Hell, I must've been because I could have sworn I heard her say she *wasn't* marrying me. "Yeah the fuck you are," I replied firmly. "Father of your baby, remember?" My finger drew an air halo over my head as if she had forgotten to whom I was referring.

She rolled her eyes and stood up to leave again. "That's not how it works anymore, Wes. You're in the wrong century."

I huffed in exasperation as I trailed after her. She threw open the front door and ran down the steps like her feet were on fire. "Celeste, you love me! I *know* that you love me! So yes, that's exactly how it works! It's not like we wouldn't have gotten married if I had been here for everything."

She rounded on me with the grace of a dancer, and I had the fleeting thought that Iris got all her ballet talent from her mama. The idea brought me a ridiculous amount of giddy excitement.

"Why can't you understand?" she shouted. "I'm not the girl you think I am! I'm not who I used to be! If you got to know me now, you wouldn't still love me, Wes. Nobody could." Her voice broke on the end, a pitiful squeak as her jaw clenched to prevent tears.

Desiree truly broke her spirit. She took my sweet, kind Celeste and offered her a world filled with cruelty, loneliness, and despair. Petty, jealous women like Desiree, and probably Hillary too, if she were anything like her mother, were the worst sort of people.

There was nothing I could say now that would convince Celeste otherwise. She needed time. The more, the better.

"Believe what you wanna believe," I argued, "because my truth still stands. I love you, I've always loved you, and I'm not going anywhere. We're getting our kid and getting the fuck outta here! Period!"

Celeste was on the brink of madness. She threw up her hands and screamed into the night sky. "I'm not leaving River's Run, Wes! This has always been my home!"

This woman was going to be the death of me. Not even

ten minutes ago she was insisting that she had nowhere to go and nothing left, yet she wasn't going to take my offer to get us out of here.

I sneered. "Your home? So that your entire fucking life can pass you by while you live out your parents' dream rather than your own? Hell, do you even know what you want out of life, or is everything just supposed to stop because they're gone?"

It was a low blow.

The lowest blow I could deliver.

She crumpled like I struck her. In a way, I had. Regret immediately washed over me. No matter how angry I became, she didn't deserve this.

Therefore, she surprised us both greatly with the venom she threw back at me. "Oh, like you're so much better?" Celeste screamed. "Have you *ever* had a friend, Wesley? A real friend, outside of me? How could you when you don't know how to do anything other than throw your daddy's money around to control the situation? You're a Madden through and through, and it makes me sick!"

Flashing red and blue lights came around the corner as a sheriff's car came flying around the corner. Brakes screeched as it came to a stop…right in front of my house.

Fuck.

Chief Hillsborough himself climbed out of the vehicle, his skin even more wrinkly in his old age. The glare he fixed on me set off warning bells in my head. There was still an outstanding warrant for what I did to his stupid shed. And although he always suspected me, there was never any proof. Hillsborough was far too gleeful any time he was called for one of my fights back in high school.

Now, he looked downright victorious. "Gettin' a whole lot

of calls down at the station about a domestic disturbance," Hillsborough stated. "Figured as soon as I heard the address that it had to be our…celebrity." Only he made the word sound like a dirty expletive.

Celeste blanched before turning abruptly on her heel. "I need to go, Sheriff," she said. "Nothing happened. I'm sorry about the racket."

"That's not the way we heard it," countered the sheriff. "A neighbor phoned it in that the fella laid hands on the woman. I take that kind of thing very seriously around these parts."

It had already been the longest day of my life, so I was fresh out of fucks to give for this prick. "Look, man, you heard her say that nothing happened clear as a bell. I don't know what else to tell you. It won't happen again."

He stepped up to me like he wanted to square up, sending my temper flaring. "I don't like your attitude, boy. What are you doing back in my town, anyhow? I thought we got rid of the likes of you."

My jaw clenched. "I came for Ms. Shirley's funeral."

The sheriff eyed me suspiciously. "And yet, I can't recall seeing you there this afternoon," he snarled.

"Because there is someone who will always be more important to me," I replied evenly. It might have been the answer to Chief Hillsborough's question, but it was Celeste to whom I spoke. Our eyes held over his shoulder, and I watched as a tiny fraction of hope sparked to life in her face.

"You missed her funeral?" Celeste asked on a sharp inhale.

"What kinda man misses his kin's funeral?" Hillsborough glared at me as though I had mortally wounded him.

Wasn't this guy due to kick the fucking bucket? Where

was all that "divine intervention" bullshit when you needed it?

Celeste shivered as though doused with icy water and turned back towards her daddy's old truck, parked at the end of the driveway. "Everything's fine, Sheriff. Thanks for checking on us!"

We both watched her drive away like her ass was on fire. My heart went with her.

"Seems to me like I better take you in for questioning," the sheriff said as soon as her taillights trailed out of sight. "I don't let anyone put their hands on a woman in my town."

I sputtered like a fish out of water. "You can't be fucking serious! She just told you that everything is fine here!"

As impossible as it seemed, Hillsborough took another step closer, his rotund belly pushing against me. "That's not the way I heard it."

The accusations from earlier pounded through my head. *You don't know how to do anything other than throw your daddy's money around to control the situation!*

Would it hurt as much if it weren't true? Was I turning into my father, despite all my attempts to the contrary? I wanted to emulate Celeste herself, or even Mr. Hendricks. This was a test. A test I was going to pass.

"Fine," I said coolly, holding out my hands, palms upward. "Let's go talk down at the station."

If he was surprised, he didn't show it. Spinning me around, a harsh *clink!* filled the air as he clamped handcuffs on my wrists.

"Shouldn't you be reading me my rights, old man?" I taunted him.

Hillsborough only jerked me towards his squad car in response.

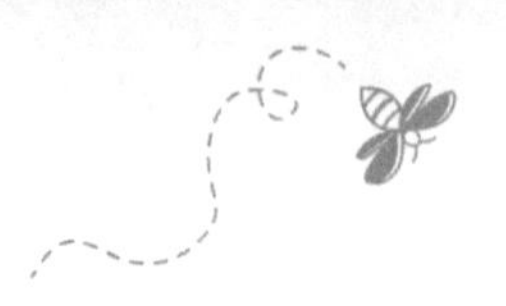

CHAPTER 48
THE UNEXPECTED
CELESTE

I COULD BARELY SEE the road through my tears, but I could probably drive through town while blindfolded. The brakes squealed as I hastily pulled into a parking space behind Marla's apartment. Maggie's rented car was nowhere to be seen, so she must have been over at her mama's place for the night. For once, I was grateful for her absence because it meant I could go to bed without playing a round of Twenty Questions.

Exhaustion hit hard and I didn't bother to turn on a light as I sank onto the mattress to pull off my shoes. What I didn't expect was the mattress to rumble underneath me.

"OH MY GOD!" I screamed, jumping three feet into the air as another voice shouted with me.

Marla came flying into the bedroom, flipping on the light with a metal baseball bat in hand.

"Is this how you greet an old lady?!"

"NANA?!" I cried. My breaths were still coming out in heavy pants as I waited for my pulse to return to normal.

Nana sat up in bed, her gray hair disheveled and her

signature scowl intact. "Were you expecting the queen of France?"

"You scared the dickens outta me!" Marla sighed. She leaned the bat against the doorway and came to sit on the edge of the mattress next to Nana. "I called her and told her you needed her, Celeste. It's time for everything to get settled, once and for all."

I sighed in exasperation. "How did you afford the ticket to get here, Nana? You're on a fixed income!"

She rolled her eyes. "You sure know how to roll out the welcome mat, don't you, girl? Get on into these arms for a hug!"

Nana smelled like peanuts and Downey fabric softener, and it wasn't until the combination hit my nostrils that I realized how much I missed the smell. I felt like a little girl again, running into Nana's arms when the thunderstorms got too loud for my liking. She held me so tight until they were over, just as she did now.

"It's so good to see you," I whispered.

"Sure would be nice to see my son-in-law," Nana commented. "I don't suppose you brought him with you."

Now it was my turn to roll my eyes. "Wesley and I aren't married, Nana, you know that."

"I know it's not every day you land a man who was on the cover of GQ magazine," she snapped back. "Do NOT let him slip by again."

It was such a Nana argument that I couldn't help but laugh. If there was a southern version of the grandmother in *Mulan*, it was Suzanne Moffitt.

Shrugging one shoulder, I joked, "I'll take my chances."

Marla gasped. "Didn't y'all work things out?"

I shook my head. It was too late to have this conversation without sleep to clear the fuzziness in my brain. "It's not that simple, Marla. The last thing I need is to focus on romance."

"Yeah, 'cause nothing good ever comes of that!" Nana replied sarcastically.

Pursing her lips into a thin line, Marla stared at me for a full minute before answering. "Celeste, I love you," she began. "So it's high time you start listening. Get your man, get your kid, and live your dang life!"

"Let me start by getting some sleep first, alright?" I snatched the extra pillow from the bed. "Sorry I scared, y'all. Good night."

I settled onto the couch with a fluffy blanket and contemplated everyone's advice from the past 24 hours. Wesley's accusations stung. But they stung because they were so true. It was too painful to consider what I wanted from life because it would only lead to disappointment when I didn't get them. Operating on autopilot was second nature because when you're too numb to feel anything, nothing can happen to you. Except when nothing can happen to you, it means nothing ever happens. Was that the life I was going to settle for? Did I want Iris to get that kind of message?

Yet how could I be expected to jump into a committed relationship with Wesley after ten years' worth of separation? Sharing a child meant we needed to co-parent, not end up together. And while the lovestruck teenager he left behind wanted nothing more than the fairytale ending, the level-headed woman I was now wanted consistency, reliability, and peace. Three things I had yet to see from Wes.

I did believe him about Iris and my custody issue with Desiree. Come first light, I was heading over to Desiree's and getting my daughter back. We could figure out where to go from there.

It wasn't much of a plan, but it was enough for me to fall into another weary, fitful sleep.

* * * * *

Habit woke me up in just a few short hours as the first rays of sunshine pierced the sky. Given the situation, I refused to open The Comfy Cushion. It was a knife to the heart to make such a choice, however. Mama rolled over in her grave the moment Desiree threatened our restaurant, and I amused myself by imagining her ghost smiting my stepmother during one of her laser treatments.

I was too much of a coward to face Nana and Marla again, so I splashed some cold water on my face in the bathroom and tiptoed out the door. I always kept a spare set of clothes and toothbrush down at the diner because of how many times I ended up staying in town when the work ran too late. Sending a quick text to Marla so she didn't worry about me when she woke up and found me gone, I drove to the restaurant and let myself in the backdoor.

The lights remained off so that patrons knew we weren't open, but I could easily move around in the dark. My clothes were kept in the bottom drawer of Daddy's old office and I didn't pay attention to the shadows in the room as I shimmied out of my jeans. So when a hand shot out of the darkness to clamp around my throat while another wound around my waist to pull me backwards, the scream stifled as the hand squeezed my vocal cords shut.

"This is how I've always wanted you," a man's voice whispered in my ear. His breath was foul and sour, reeking of alcohol and rotten food. "At my mercy, with your body ready for me."

I bucked against him, thrashing my body as much as I could to break free. This wasn't Wesley, this was a dangerous presence that made the hairs on the back of my neck stand up and fear flood my body.

Something long and hard pressed against my lower back. No matter how hard I tried, I couldn't break free from his grip.

"It's so sexy when you fight me," the man breathed. With a violent shove, he pushed me forward, pressing my torso down on the desk and knocking all the paperwork to the floor. Cold air hit my ass as the man yanked my panties down. "I bet he hasn't taken your ass yet. Wesley Madden is an idiot. Real estate like this is meant to be painted."

My blood turned to ice as I recognized the voice. Only one person ever said Wes' name with that mixture of hatred, jealousy, and reverence—my stepbrother, Jeremy.

A door slammed towards the front of the restaurant and Jeremy froze. Loud, rapid footsteps echoed from the dining room, making him curse under his breath.

"Don't worry," he murmured in my ear. "I'll be back for you. You're not gonna ignore me anymore, *Mama*."

In the next second, Jeremy was gone.

My body trembled so hard that my teeth chattered and I fell to the floor in the fetal position. Jesse flipped on the light switch and darted over to me.

"Oh my god, Celeste! What happened?!" He grabbed an old tablecloth from one of the shelves lining the wall on his left and carefully draped it over me, preserving some of my modesty. It did nothing to shield the chill. "I'm calling 911!"

His words sounded like an echo in the back of my mind. The entire situation was too much when I was already too raw to face my demons. I blinked slowly before letting my eyes close so the darkness could finally swallow me whole.

CHAPTER 49
GLORIOUS TRUTH
WESLEY

CHIEF HILLSBOROUGH COULD SUCK START a Glock for all I cared. The man was entirely too gleeful about putting me in the cell at the Smithson County jail, to the point where he moved his desk over so that he could grin at me over the rim of his coffee cup afterwards.

He made it really hard to regret setting his shed on fire. My one phone call kept getting pushed back because he was "busy" with paperwork, yet all I had seen so far was him dismissing the other deputies on duty and refilling the old Keurig several times. I didn't want to give him the satisfaction of knowing it was getting to me however, so I let him keep digging himself a hole. If he wasn't aware of my educational background or the strings I could pull, he could find out the hard way.

After what felt like an eternity, I was permitted to call Phillip.

"Where are you calling from?" he asked instantly.

My back teeth ground together. Hillsborough eyed me suspiciously over the top of his computer monitor.

"I need you to come bail me out of Smithson County Jail,"

I replied. "Just bring a blank check."

The traitor snickered. "And what have you done now?"

I rolled my eyes. "Can you just do what I pay you for? Please?"

"Alright, alright. I'm sorry. I'm already on the way there because we have an even bigger problem."

That piqued my interest. "What do you mean? What did you find out?"

"Wrap it up, inmate," the sheriff called. Malice lit up his face as he said it. The fucking prick.

"Prepare to make a generous donation," I advised Phillip before hanging up.

Hillsborough shook his head. "That kinda thing isn't gonna work around these parts. We don't care about your dirty money." He firmly gripped my shoulder to steer me back into the cell before angrily slamming the iron grate.

I glared at him, but wisely kept my mouth shut for once.

Within an hour, Phillip arrived. By that time, several other deputies and clerks had also shown up, which proved to be beneficial when Chief Hillsborough tried to deny my bail.

"B-but, sir," the clerk stuttered, "that's a million dollar check. That more than pays Mr. Madden's bail and fees."

The sheriff silenced him with an evil stare. "Are you questioning me?"

"Look," I finally yelled out from my cell. "I am sorry for what I did. I take full responsibility for your shed and what happened last night, Chief. All I'm trying to do is get my girl, get my kid, and leave River's Run. Let me out and I will pay for everything to be replaced."

Hillsborough assessed me critically from across the room. He slowly approached, hand on his duty belt near the badge on his hip. "You're prepared to take care of Celeste and Iris now?"

I nodded emphatically. He couldn't possibly know how badly I wanted that.

"Then it sounds like you've finally grown up, boy," Hillsborough said. "Ain't no reason to be leaving your hometown if you can finally act the way a man is s'posed to."

You could've knocked me over with a cotton ball. My jaw audibly dropped as I gawked at him like an idiot.

Another deputy opened the door for me so that I could join Phillip and Hillsborough at the front of the jail. My eyebrows were stuck on my forehead.

"Would you quit lookin' at me like I'm the anti-Christ?" Hillsborough snapped.

"All this time, I thought you hated me!"

He rolled his eyes. "I didn't want some punk kid raising hell in my town," Hillsborough explained. "But then Doug Hendricks died still believing in you. I've watched for years as his poor daughter suffered under the hands of that woman he married. If you're willing and able to get Celeste and Iris away from her, then I reckon you're all right. Nobody deserves to be treated the way they have been."

The fact that even a douche canoe like Chief Hillsborough noticed how poorly my soulmate and my daughter were being treated made my blood boil. Not nearly as much as the call that came through the radio perched on the desk, however.

"All units respond. B and E at The Comfy Cushion. Possible SA. Victim ID'd as Celeste Hendricks..."

I was out the door before anyone could react, Phillip close behind. We tore down the county highway toward The Comfy Cushion faster than was legal, three sheriff cruisers hot behind me. Sirens blared, but I couldn't really hear them. The dispatcher's voice kept playing on loop in my head. *"Possible SA. Victim ID'd as Celeste Hendricks."*

"Tell me what you know," I screamed at Phillip, although I already had a sinking feeling in my gut of what he was going to say.

"There was never a restraining order," Phillip said. He pulled a large manilla folder out of his briefcase and flipped through all the paperwork it contained. "Technically there shouldn't have even been any charges against you. Turns out they were all going to be dropped, but your father paid the judge to keep them, then paid him again to put you on probation. Probably so that he could have some leverage over you."

"FUCK!" I slammed my hand repeatedly on the steering wheel, nearly causing the car to swerve off the road.

My assistant scowled. "There's more, but I'll tell you when you aren't in a position to kill me."

If Celeste's life weren't in jeopardy I would have skidded to a stop in the middle of the road and smacked him until he spit it out. Right now, there were far more important things. I wouldn't be able to process a word he said anyway until I knew that she was all right.

And whoever the motherfucker was who had done this to her, he better hope the cops found him before I did. That was the only chance he had of living through the night.

❦ ❦ ❦ ❦ ❦ ❦

Outside the diner, Main Street turned into a scene out of *Criminal Minds*. There were squad cars, an ambulance with a pair of EMT's, and two fire trucks. What they were doing, I hadn't the faintest idea because there wasn't so much as a flicker of a flame. Maybe everybody on duty just wanted to feel needed.

They wheeled Celeste out on a stretcher with a thick gray blanket wrapped around her shoulders. Her eyes were closed, her lips pale and trembling. Although there was no visible sign of trauma from where I screeched to a stop, that didn't mean she wasn't injured. My desire to incinerate the bastard increased tenfold.

A sheriff protested when I dove under the caution tape they strung up along the street, but I ignored her in my haste to get to Celeste.

"Tell me everything," I demanded the paramedic wheeling the stretcher.

"Are you family?" he asked quizzically.

"Duncan Thompson, I beat your ass in tenth grade for talking shit about her and that's gonna look like a toddler's tantrum compared to what I'm about to do to you!" I'd never wanted to tear a man's head clean off his body until today. "What the fuck happened?!"

I stepped back long enough for them to adjust the wheels and load the stretcher into the back of the ambulance before clambering in after them. Celeste's hand was ice in mine; no matter how hard I squeezed, she did not give me a response.

"She's been out cold since we arrived on scene. You'll find out more at the hospital," was all Duncan the Dumbass offered.

"Hey you!" I screamed up to the driver. "FLOOR IT!"

Everything happened in lightspeed once we arrived at the hospital. A doctor and three nurses flew out to greet us, barking orders and ushering Celeste into a room. The words "rape kit" were used, making my heart drop to my stomach.

It was all I could do to sink into a crouch on the floor outside her room and wait. Part of me wanted to pray to God, like Nana always talked about, because I figured right now it couldn't hurt. But I didn't know how to begin and he'd probably think I sounded like a whiner anyway.

Phillip arrived shortly after, asking me how she was doing. I couldn't form coherent words to answer him, and for the first time ever, my assistant hugged me. It was oddly comforting. Somehow, Phillip's strength gave me strength, and I was able to draw a shaky lung full of air for the first time that morning.

He stepped away to call Marla for me. I couldn't handle being the one to tell her something else happened to Celeste. When he stepped back, he said she was on her way.

A nurse came out at around the two hour mark to let me know that they believed Celeste's system crashed after the traumatic shock of her "incident." Right now there was nothing to do but wait because Celeste had to wake up on her own. Her pulse was low, but steady.

I thanked the nurse and turned to Phillip in a daze. "Give me your news. I need something else to focus on right now or I'm gonna drive myself crazy."

He pursed his lips. "I doubt what I'm about to tell you will prevent that." Withdrawing the manilla folder from his briefcase again, Phillip flipped to whatever document he was searching for. "So I have a friend who works for LexixNexis, the legal site for judgment orders, and they pulled some paperwork for me. Doug Hendricks didn't leave anything to Desiree. The house, the land, everything that he owned went to Celeste. And get this—The Comfy Cushion has actually belonged to Celeste since her mother passed away. It was left to her in trust with Doug and a woman named Suzanne Moffitt…any idea who that might be?"

"That's Nana," I replied distantly as my mind whirled to track all of this information. That meant that this whole time, Desiree had been leeching off my girl and Celeste didn't even realize it. Desiree had no legal right to any of it. Given the number of times we had seen her speaking to Mr. Hendricks' attorney at the hospital in Atlanta, I had a tough time figuring Desiree was unaware of this information. If anything, she must have gone to great lengths to keep the truth hidden from Celeste.

"What's more, Doug Hendricks had a three million dollar life insurance policy. Turns out, the Hendricks family land is worth far more than we thought. Guess who was the beneficiary?"

"GOD FUCKING DAMN IT!" I roared. Kicking a chair down the hallway, several hospital staff members poked their heads out of rooms and the nurse's station to check on us.

Phillip raised a hand. "So sorry! Everything's fine!" he called out to them with a fake smile plastered on his face.

No, everything was decidedly *not* fine. Celeste had been killing herself at that diner for years when she should have been enjoying every moment she could with our daughter. Iris could have the dance studio of her dreams to practice in.

"And let me guess—somehow Desiree Hendricks was the one who received every penny."

Snorting, Phillip nodded. "And blew through it. A gentleman at the bank was very accommodating in giving up Desiree's financials. She's insulted just about everyone on their payroll, apparently. The woman doesn't have two nickels to rub together."

I scrubbed a hand down my face. "Of course she doesn't."

How many more times could my world get flipped around in 24 hours? All of this changed everything, and judging by the paperwork in Phillip's hand, we were accumulating the paper trail necessary to take her down.

Phillip's face contorted as he opened his mouth to say something, then second guessed himself and shut it. His fingers were tapping out a rhythm on his hip, one of his tells that he had news he was reluctant to share with me.

"Out with it," I snapped at him. We didn't have time for games.

"Bank statements also show Desiree has been receiving a monthly payment of twenty-five thousand dollars...since roughly the time Iris was born."

The entire world was gonna go up in smoke with my rage. Wrath like I had never experienced before made me murderous. It was difficult to breathe and control myself enough to reply, "Take me to him. *Now.*"

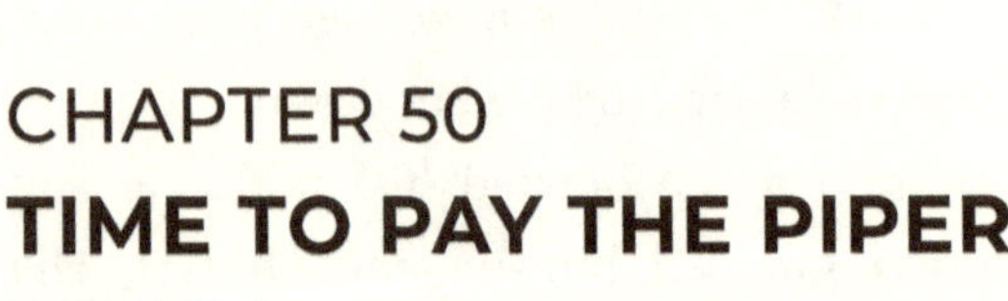

CHAPTER 50
TIME TO PAY THE PIPER
WESLEY

THE PLANE RIDE to Atlanta could go down in the record books because I had never zoned out so much during a flight. Nothing could cool the rage burning through me. A small part of me—the little boy inside who still wanted to believe his father loved him—tried to rationalize the money away. I had no concrete proof that Benedict Madden sent that money every month, but my gut told me I was right. Desiree didn't know anybody else who would front that kind of cash.

We went straight to Madden Enterprises when the plane landed. I realized on the way there that I was still wearing the navy sweatpants and tight gray t-shirt I pulled on to sleep in the night before, but it wasn't like confronting my father while wearing a suit would change the outcome. His secretary informed us he was in a board meeting and could not be disturbed. I walked right past her into the boardroom and proved her wrong.

Sixteen of the executives for our company sat along the long wood table, including Denny Carmichael, technically my boss in the legal department, and Elle Fielding, the only female and head of public relations. She was the mastermind behind all those paparazzi shots and TMZ reports because she very quickly realized how much our stock went up any time there was a Madden scandal in the newspapers. I got played like a fool my entire life.

For some reason, that fact, along with her presence for this moment, irked me today. I had to give her a show for the world to see.

"Wesley, we're in a meeting!" my father yelled. He sat at the head of the table with a stack of papers in front of him. A screen behind him cast stock numbers and revenue charts for the board to discuss.

"Tell me it isn't true!" I roared. My hands were already in fists at my sides, veins popping out along my forearm in restraint from knocking Benedict's teeth down his throat.

My father cleared his throat, glancing around the room at the congregation of eyes on us. "Let's schedule a meeting later. You're clearly too emotional to talk right now."

Way. Wrong. Answer.

"Did you know about my daughter?!"

Gasps broke out among the board, with whispers following. Elle's eyebrows receded into her hairline as a triumphant gleam hit her eye.

My father turned a particularly hideous shade of puce. "Could you all excuse us for a moment, please?" he asked pointedly.

The room cleared in a matter of seconds, with the head of PR shooting me a meaningful stare on her exit. I hope she blasted this shit on every gossip blog within the next five minutes so that my father couldn't blow off this conversation.

Benedict stood up and walked over to the bar cart, helping himself to a thumb full of scotch. "This kind of behavior won't be tolerated, Wesley," he growled. "You get entirely too worked up over things. You always have."

"Yeah, Dr. Phil's special is coming up," I quipped. "Now what about my daughter."

My father's eyes darkened. "You should be thanking me. I saved you from ruining your life."

Even though I expected it, the confirmation still left me dumbstruck. Instantly, I was a ten year old kid, watching his only parent leave the day before his birthday because dear old dad forgot and didn't care. Benedict Madden had no regard for me. He truly didn't understand what he had taken from me.

That's why I didn't hesitate to throw the first punch. Hell, I didn't even reconsider the second or third. It wasn't until I realized my father was huddled in the fetal position on the floor, blood trailing down the side of his head, that I thought *maybe* I had gone too far.

Maybe.

But then I remembered that I wasn't there when Iris first entered the world. I never got to change a diaper or see her first steps. I missed her first day of school, her first dance class, her first recital. I never got to comfort her during a thunderstorm or check her temperature while she was stuck at home with the flu. She went to bed every night without a dad to tuck her in and scare away the monster in the closet.

And suddenly the ass whooping I gave Benny boy paled in comparison.

It took longer than I would've expected for security to arrive and pull me off him. Phillip might have blocked the door, though I had no proof. One of the officers moved to put me in restraints until Elle Fielding stepped inside.

"Just take care of Mr. Madden," she instructed. "I'll handle him."

The officers picked Benedict up, his face bloody and bruised, and slung his arms over their shoulders. They dragged him from the room while Elle pierced me with a speculative stare.

"You're not fucking spinning this for some story," I barked at her. "That bastard knew I had a daughter and he kept her from me!"

Elle shared a look with Phillip. "And how much would you like to make Benedict Madden pay for that?" she asked.

"What?" I snapped. This was the last answer I expected.

She stepped forward and slid a flash drive across the boardroom table to me. "You're not the only one who has suffered under the hands of Benedict Madden," Elle told me quietly, examining her fingernails as she spoke. "It's high time he was brought to justice."

I turned to my assistant, holding up the flash drive. "What do you know about this?"

Phillip shrugged. "I've worked for your father my entire life. He's the kind of guy who makes a lot of enemies."

Nodding, I replied, "Then let's knock him down a peg or two".

It would take us hours to comb through everything on the flash drive. Elle had been amassing information on Benedict's discretions against women, most of whom worked for him. Several former employees made allegations of sexual harassment and sexual assault, only to become suddenly radio silent. There was a thread to be unraveled in all the accusations, and my father was at the center of it.

Somehow Elle managed to get several classified financial

documents, too. It looked like my father engaged in dirty dealing across the board, including fraud, tax evasion, and bribery. And we weren't talking chump change; there was a paper trail for a quarter of a billion dollars that seemingly vanished into thin air.

"Get this over to our friends at the attorney general's office," I ordered Phillip. "Make sure they're attorneys that aren't on his payroll."

He nodded. "What are you gonna do?"

"I'm heading back to River's Run. It's time this thing ended once and for all."

CHAPTER 51
SUGAR BEE
CELESTE

A HOSPITAL ROOM slowly came into view as I first cracked open one eye, then the other. Marla and Nana were both sitting in chairs to my left. Nana had her knitting needles out where it looked like she was creating a fuzzy green tent.

"What happened?" I croaked.

"Oh, baby girl!" Marla wiped a tear from her cheek. She grabbed one of my hands and squeezed. "Let me get the doctor. We've been waiting for you to wake up." She swept from the room.

Nana leaned over. "You gave us a scare. That British guy called us and said we needed to get down here as soon as possible."

It hurt to swallow, which I realized belatedly stemmed from the way Jeremy choked me. An involuntary shudder ran down my spine at the memory. That's why I was in the hospital.

The doctor came in, followed by Marla and Cassie Heddings, the only female deputy in the Smithson County Sheriff's Department. They both asked me to recount the attack, with the doctor pausing to examine my throat, ears, and scalp during the parts of the story where I relayed how he held me down and where he put his hands. Nana and Marla both offered to step out of the room and give me privacy. I declined because I needed their strength. Nothing had actually happened, I assured all of them, but I emphasized how closely Jeremy came to going past that point. He had every intention of sexually assaulting me.

Deputy Heddings promised they were going to issue a warrant for his arrest along with a restraining order. He wouldn't be able to come within fifty feet of me. Everyone told me how brave I was, Marla and Nana while choking back tears, and finally left the room so that I could get dressed. As always, Marla was one step ahead and brought a change of clothes for me. My outfit from The Comfy Cushion was being admitted into evidence.

When all of my test results confirmed I was safe to leave, the three of us walked out to Marla's car. I didn't want to acknowledge my surprise and disappointment that I woke up to Wesley's absence. Now that he was back in River's Run, it just seemed natural for him to know when I needed him, just as he always had.

"We need to go get Iris," I insisted. "She should be in school by now, so unless Desiree is guarding the building, no one can stop me."

Marla nodded as she slid into the driver's seat. "I'll try Wes again on the way."

"What do you mean?"

Nana scoffed. "D'you really think we weren't gonna keep him updated after he left? He stopped answering his cell phone a couple hours ago, but maybe by now he's done with his own emergency."

"What emergency?" I asked.

"We aren't sure," Nana explained. "Said there was some-thin' he had to take care of before he could come get you."

Maybe this time he'll actually come back, I thought.

"If we're getting Iris," Marla said, "we are telling her the truth about Wesley." Her tone was firm, brooking no argument.

She wouldn't get any from me. It was time for Iris to know the truth.

After signing her out of school, my sweet girl flew into my arms, encasing me in a bone-crushing hug while she sobbed into my chest.

"Mama!" Iris cried. "Desiree said I would never see you again! It's been awful! She said that you stole from her? And that you've been lying to me? What is going on, Mama?! I'm so scared!"

I tightened my hold on her, tears streaming down into her dancer's bun. "Baby girl, none of that is true. Let's go so that I can explain. You don't need to be scared."

It took more than an hour and a few slices of Marla's famous lemon meringue pie to calm Iris down. We were all settled into a table at Marla's Sweets, which she had refused to open, saying today was a personal day for us to get every-thing sorted out. Nana inhaled all the treats Marla set down in front of us, and got Iris to laugh by teaching her the proper way to sneak food into a purse.

"Baby girl, there's so much I need to tell you and I'm not sure where to begin," I admitted. "I think we need to start with the man you met at the gym. He's...well, he's someone pretty important."

My daughter nodded solemnly. "You mean my dad? Yeah, I'd say he's important."

The rest of us shared the same expression of shock. "You *knew*?!"

Iris' eyes widened. "You keep that box of photos in the back of your closet, Mama," she explained. "I know you always tell me not to go through your stuff, but I needed a baby photo for a school project a couple years ago and I found a bunch of pictures with him in them. There were never any other boys, so I figured he had to be my daddy... you wouldn't've kept his photos otherwise."

Of course Iris would make that deduction. She noticed things and read people, just like her father always had.

I was still so stunned that she knew. "Honey, why didn't you say anything?"

Iris shrugged, picking at the corner of the table. "Because I knew you would tell me when you were ready. I didn't wanna hurt you."

Her maturity broke my heart. I wanted a time machine, something that could take me back so I could make different choices.

Except wishing things were different wasn't going to bring change. Actually making different choices would. It was time to make my Mama and Daddy proud.

"We're going to Boston," I blurted out.

Iris broke into a wide smile. "Really? So I can audition for The Boston School of Ballet? You mean it?"

Her excitement gave me confidence in my suddenly emerging plan. "Yes. That's exactly what we're going to do."

Nana hummed her approval next to Iris. "I think I'll go, too."

Marla and I simultaneously dropped our forks.

"You *will*?!" I asked incredulously.

She nodded. "Life's too short to keep missing out on family. Being here just reminds me of that fact."

My eyes felt watery at her admission. Life *was* too short. We were all done missing out, myself included.

Hours went by before the door flew open. Wesley stormed in, his eyes an electric blue that locked in on mine. Nobody else in the room existed as he strode straight towards me, snatching me out of the chair to clutch me to his chest. As soon as my feet found the floor, Wes cupped my face in his hands and planted a firm kiss on my mouth.

It was the kiss that set me free. I realized the power of a kiss, the power of love. Because that's what Wesley and I had —love.

Just as abruptly, Wesley turned to Iris and pulled her into a group hug with the two of us.

"Hey there, Rainbow," he said to her. "I'm your dad."

She rolled her eyes but hugged him back. "Yeah, duh... except...why are you calling me 'Rainbow'?"

Wesley looked directly at me as he answered. "Because 'Iris' means 'rainbow'...and you're the rainbow at the end of our journey."

Leave it to Wes to know exactly why I named her the way that I did. Only him. My eyes were shining with tears as I hugged both of them tighter. I had my family back.

We all sat down to catch up on what happened over the past ten years. Wesley scooped Nana up and twirled her in a circle before swearing, "It hasn't been the same without you, Nana."

She shrugged. "Well of course it hasn't. Nobody can hold a candle to me!"

Everyone around the table, including Wes, shed tears and laughed until our bellies ached. It wasn't until my phone started blowing up at the end of the school day that the outside world disturbed our peace. Desiree sent text after text demanding to know Iris' whereabouts, which Wesley ordered me to ignore.

We couldn't, however, ignore a snarling Desiree when she burst inside, her face twisted in fury.

"Iris, get away from that man, NOW!" she yelled.

All of us, Marla and Nana included, jumped to our feet and stood in front of Iris, forming a human shield against my stepmother. Wesley drew himself up to his full height, well over six feet, so that he had to stare down his nose at Desiree.

"You will *never* talk to my daughter again," he barked. It was so forceful that the hairs on the back of my neck stood up.

Blood drained from Desiree's face. She froze, staring at Wes in horror.

Wesley stalked towards her until they stood nose to nose. I could see the tension in his spine as he tried to hold back from unleashing his full temper.

"Your games are over, Desiree," he said. Pulling a cell phone out of his back pocket, Wesley checked something before shooting us a maniacal grin over his shoulder. "You see, I went to law school with the man who is now the assistant to the attorney general of Georgia. I had him double check a few things for me that just didn't sit quite right when Celeste said *you* wouldn't let her tell me about my daughter. That *you* are the reason I wasn't able to support Celeste during her pregnancy, that I didn't get to see Iris being born…you get the idea.

"As it turns out, you haven't been very honest with any of us, have you, Desiree?" Wesley began to circle her, like a lion taunting a gazelle before striking. "Who *really* owns The Comfy Cushion?"

My stepmother began to quake. Her knees visibly clenched together as she forced herself to stay upright.

I, however, had no clue what he was getting at. "Someone else owns the diner?" I asked.

Wesley nodded, though he kept his eyes trained on Desiree. "The Comfy Cushion was left, in trust, to Celeste Hendricks after Rachel Hendricks died, isn't that right, Desiree? Even your husband never actually *owned* The Comfy Cushion, did he?"

A lightness settled in my chest. Something that felt like the burgeoning of a new hope. If what Wes said was true—and I had no reason to believe otherwise—that meant Desiree didn't have the right to sell it.

"I'm sorry, I can't seem to hear you, Desiree," Wesley continued. "Did you have more to confess?"

Nana exhaled a shaky breath behind me. "We better sit down, sweet pea," she stage-whispered to Iris. Both of them dropped into chairs at the table.

It didn't faze Wesley. "Doug Hendricks didn't leave you his house or the Hendricks land either, did he? That was also left for Celeste Hendricks, according to his last Will and Testament! Which you knew—your signature is right here on this prenuptial agreement, isn't it?" He held out his phone and pointed to whatever document he opened.

Phillip and Chief Hillsborough slowly came through the door, with a few more deputies visible through the windows. To my surprise, Wesley gave the male nod to the sheriff, who returned the gesture.

"Let's tell everyone how you really hit the trifecta, though,

Desiree." He slid his phone back in his pocket. "What happened to Doug's life insurance?"

Desiree's lips were pursed in such a thin line they almost disappeared from her face. There was nothing but hatred in her eyes as she ground out, "He was my husband. That money should have been *mine!*"

Wesley nodded angrily, his arms crossed over his chest. "But it wasn't. You accepted a payout of three million dollars that belonged to his beneficiary, none other than Celeste Renee Hendricks."

"Mama!" Iris gasped. Nana stared at the two of them like it was a live episode of *Fear the Wicked*. Even the sheriff raised his eyebrows. That was quite a sum. How like Daddy to ensure, even in death, I was provided for and wanted for nothing. He knew that as my stepmother, I would have provided for Desiree, too. Family is supposed to take care of family.

As her nostrils flared and her hands clenched into fists at her side, Desiree remained silent, shooting eye daggers at Wesley. She made no move to deny the accusations.

It was too much for me. I pushed past Marla, approaching my stepmother with caution. She already proved she wasn't above hitting me. "How could you do it?" I asked in a whisper. "How could you take everything from me?"

Desiree turned her hateful gaze on me. "I took what I deserved. You never mattered to me at all."

My bottom lip quivered, but I refused to let her see me cry. Desiree Stanbrooke wasn't going to get another tear from me.

"Mrs. Hendricks, you're under arrest," Chief Hillsborough said. He stepped behind her, placing the handcuffs on her wrists as he rattled off her rights and listed the charges against her. Desiree's eyes remained on my face until the sheriff led her outside and into the waiting cruiser.

Wesley immediately turned and pinned me to his chest again. "It's all over now, sugar bee," he murmured.

Hearing that nickname on his lips broke through the dam, setting the tears free. He kissed the top of my head, gently rubbing a hand along my spine. "I can't believe you did that."

He drew back just enough to tuck his fingers under my chin, lifting my gaze to his. "I promised your dad that I would take care of you."

A warmth joined the lightness as my heart filled with hope. "You did?"

Wes smiled. "The morning she found us in your tower together. When he pulled me inside to have 'The Talk.'" He couldn't help but laugh. "Doug asked what my intentions were and I told him, point blank—'I'm going to marry your daughter.' Part of me always wondered if he already knew he was sick, because when I swore on my life that I would provide for you, he said, 'No. Swear on *my* life.' That was why we did everything we could to make his final days special for you, Celeste. You were his sugar bee, and now you're mine."

I let out a shaky laugh because I could imagine the entire exchange clear as day. It sounded exactly like something my daddy would have said. And exactly how I would have expected Wes to respond.

"Well, we'll have to see what happens after we get settled in Boston," I offered.

He raised an eyebrow in challenge. "Oh, you're gonna marry me. It's just a matter of when."

Rolling my eyes, I let go of him to rejoin Iris, Marla, and Nana at the table. "And what makes you so sure?"

"Because I'm the only one on this earth who has his blessing." Wes smiled at us, sending a rogue wink Iris' way.

"And mine!" she instantly piped up with a grin.

"Thanks, Rainbow," he replied.

"Mine, too," Nana added. Marla nodded silently beside her.

I couldn't help but offer a shy smile to all of them. This was how family should be.

"C'mon." Wesley held out a hand. "Let's go home and get some rest. We all need it."

Iris jumped up to join him. "I have so much I want to tell you!"

They both turned to me expectantly from the door. I gave Marla and Nana a quick hug, promising to return first thing tomorrow morning, before joining my daughter and her daddy for our first night together as a family.

CHAPTER 52
THE TURNING POINT
CELESTE

THE SHRILL CRY of a phone ringing was not how I wanted to wake up. After the three of us talked for hours in the living room at Aunt Shirley's old place, Iris, Wes, and I had gone to bed. Wes made up his old room for Iris, showing off the photographs I decorated with all those years ago. Iris asked for backstories on each and every one, which took another couple of hours.

While I offered to take the couch, Wesley flat out refused for us to sleep apart. He told me it would be too hard for him to sleep if he couldn't reach out and touch me to know that I was safe. Since I was still frightened over the prospect of Jeremy returning to finish what he started, I agreed, and we collapsed into Aunt Shirley's old bed in sheer exhaustion. The only reason I was able to keep the nightmares at bay long enough to fall into a deep sleep was Wesley's presence. He cocooned me in his arms, tucking my head under his chin, and we were both out cold as the adrenaline finally leveled off.

Now, however, the vibrations on the nightstand combined

with the piercing ringtone abruptly brought me back to the land of the living.

I didn't even check whose phone it was as I hit the green button and whimpered, "What is it?"

"Celeste!" Marla's voice was frantic. "Get down here right now! Right NOW!" She hung up before I could respond.

"Wesley, we have to go!" I scrambled out of bed, snatching clothes out of a random dresser drawer without any consideration for fit or size.

For how tired he must have been, Wesley didn't hesitate to jump up and join me. He went down the hall to shake Iris awake. I suspected he would struggle to let her out of his sight from now on.

As we loaded up in Shirley's old Buick, dark smoke billowed in the sky as a large fire truck sped down Main Street…towards Marla's place. My heart sank.

"Wow, this is bad," Wesley commented as we got closer. Even from a few blocks away, the bright flicker of flame was evident licking the sky. Only it was further down the street than Marla's.

The Comfy Cushion was on fire.

"Nononononononononono!" I launched myself out of the car before Wesley could bring it to a full stop.

Several fire trucks circled the building, blocking off the street. Although there were dozens of firefighters, I couldn't see anyone combating the flames. The entire structure was on fire. Even from the other side of the road, the heat was enough to burn my face.

"Why aren't you doing something?!" My lungs hurt, the ashes in the air infiltrating my airway. I tried to grab the hose from one of the trucks and immediately felt a strong set of arms wrap around my waist, carting me backwards. "No!" I screamed. "They have to save it! THEY HAVE TO SAVE IT!"

"They can't, sugar bee!" Wes sounded anguished. "They can't save it!"

"What…?" My voice was barely above a whimper.

Wesley watched as the center of the roof caved in, the flames soaring higher with the newly added fuel. Iris stepped in between us. Our whole family watched in silent horror as my parents' legacy literally went up in smoke before our eyes.

A movement in my peripheral caught my attention. Desiree stood on the opposite corner, a malicious smile on her face. Despite the early hour, she was dressed in a sleek little black dress with black stilettos.

My feet moved on their own accord. My stepmother didn't even flinch as I approached. "What did you do?" I ground out through clenched teeth.

Desiree shrugged one shoulder. "I always win, Celeste," she said. "In one way or another."

"You're fucking pathetic, Desiree!" Wesley's voice cut over the flames. Or maybe it was just his sudden presence at my shoulder.

Her evil grin widened. "That may be. But it was worth paying bail to see your faces now."

More sirens wailed behind us as two sheriffs pulled up. Wesley ran over to meet Sheriff Heddings in one while Desiree continued to stare at me with the same harsh smile.

I turned back to The Comfy Cushion just as the final vestiges of the walls crumbled to dust.

Their descent was the perfect allegory of my life. That restaurant symbolized everything my parents had ever worked for. I devoted everything to their dream, even when I had nothing more to give. And now that was gone, too.

All I could picture were the moments with Iris that I missed out on because of the restaurant. I barely got to attend so much as a parent teacher conference because we never had help. Yet I couldn't bring myself to regret a single moment of it. Working there kept my parents' memories alive. I never felt as close to Mama as I did in that kitchen, nor could I better imagine Daddy anywhere other than in his office.

"Mama!" Iris' voice was distant. It was only after I sucked in a harsh breath of air that I realized it was distant because of how hard my feet were running.

Wesley

Punching a woman didn't sound like the worst form of rock bottom. Some would argue that hitting Desiree didn't even count since she was half-woman, half-spawn-of-Satan.

I was livid at this turn of events. Phillip and the sheriff both assured me on the way back to River's Run that there was enough evidence to lock Desiree away for a long time. Usually that meant bail would be set too high for her to afford, especially since all her bank accounts were frozen. Dear old Dad intervened one last time on her behalf, however, and fronted the money for her to get out. Since even Desiree wasn't stupid enough to believe there was anything other than an orange jumpsuit in her future, she decided it was worth it to find one last way to make Celeste pay.

Only she didn't have the balls to do all the dirty work on her own. Jeremy Stanbrooke was found a few blocks away, badly burned from his escape. They both wanted to ensure the fire caused total devastation; there would be no chance to rebuild. So Jeremy lit everything internally while Desiree set fire to the exposed wood on the exterior of the building in order to spread as much fire as they could in the least amount of time.

I could have strangled both of them with my bare hands and smiled in my mug shot.

By now, half the town stood on the sidewalk, gawking at the crumbling ruin and the ensuing chaos. Nana was absolutely beside herself. Iris and Marla were doing everything they could to console her, but the loss of her deceased daughter's restaurant really did a number on her. There was nothing any of us could do or say in that moment to make it better.

That was why it took me so long to realize I didn't know where Celeste was. When Nana began her heartbreaking wails, I assumed Celeste went to get something from Marla's to help comfort her. However, it had been almost an hour without any signs of her, and I was starting to panic. What if Jeremy and Desiree had a third person acting out with them? We had no idea where Hillary was or if she had any involvement.

I didn't want to cause the others the same panic, so rather than voicing my concerns, I simply started whipping my head around to scrutinize the faces of everyone lining the street. Iris noticed, though.

"She went to her special place," Iris called over to me.

"Her special place?"

My daughter nodded. "I've never gone with her, but she said it's the perfect place to go and think. It has to be nearby because she doesn't drive there."

I hugged Iris, still awestruck over this perfect miniature of me that Celeste created. "I'll be right back," I assured her.

Following the dirt path, I walked past the playground, behind the baseball diamond, and into the foliage on the creek bank. The path was as worn as always, like time hadn't actually passed. I suppose time never really did pass in a place like River's Run.

My girl sat on the lowest climbing branch of our old tree, her shape barely visible in the dim light of the morning. Everything was darker this morning as the world mourned with her. Celeste would never be the same after this. I already knew that, given the gravity of the situation. It wasn't fair. But then again, nothing Celeste dealt with had ever really been fair. That was what made her kindness so much more beautiful.

Neither of us said a word as I climbed up and settled in beside her, one leg dangling over each side of the branch so that I could lean against the tree trunk and watch her. Her long blonde hair was different, but otherwise she was exactly the same as my first meeting with her in this very spot. What was that saying Celeste always credited to her mother? "Life always comes full circle" or some damn thing.

When I met her, I was a scared, angry teen who wanted nothing more than to watch the world burn. My father never taught me what love was or how a family was meant to treat one another. Although Celeste had been sad over the loss of her mom back then, she also still had so much joy and love in her heart. She was the first person to show me what life could be.

Celeste Hendricks took that scared, angry teen and welcomed him into her heart. She forever changed my life.

It was jarring to see us on the other side right now. I was fully prepared to be a man worthy of her father's blessing, taking care of Celeste and Iris—hell, even Nana and Marla, if they'd let me, because this was our family. Right now they all needed me to be strong. Everything was about to change.

"I've measured my life inside that restaurant," Celeste suddenly said, her voice cracking from her tears. "It was all I had left of Mama."

"I know, sugar bee," I whispered. Wrapping my arms around her, she settled in against my chest and continued to stare down into the creek, numb and lost.

We sat like that for a long time before either of us found words to say. Celeste needed to find some way to accept the situation, and I would set up shop in that tree with her until she did.

"So what happens now?" she mused.

I kissed the top of her head, stroking her hair. "Now we build the life we always wanted. We learn to love each other again in the ways we need. We teach Iris what a real family is, and watch her grow. This next part of life is where we get to be happy."

Celeste turned her face towards me, the hope apparent in her watery eyes. I couldn't believe how beautiful she was, the same as the day I met her right in this very tree.

"Really?" asked Celeste.

Her lips, even dry and cracked as they were, tasted like heaven. It reminded me of the Kane Brown song because I truly didn't think I could dream up a more perfect soulmate if I tried. I wanted to love her and protect her for the rest of my life, starting with this kiss.

I tried to give her my full "megawatt" smile as she always called it when I promised her, "For my whole life."

And she smiled back…because she knew.

EPILOGUE
FIVE YEARS LATER

Celeste

"Turns out you were right, Mama," I said. "Life really does come full circle." Leaning forward, I brushed a stray leaf from her gravestone. It was the first time I'd been back to River's Run in five years and while I felt like everything about my life was different, my hometown stood the test of time. The pain was gone and I was able to traipse through all my old haunts without any of the dark clouds following me. My therapist would be really proud of that when I told her.

Visiting Mama and Daddy's graves was the first thing on my to do list the moment we hit the county line. Wesley wanted to come with me, but I made him promise to give me some time alone with them first. We had a lot to catch up on.

Daddy was finally buried right beside Mama, where he should have been all this time. It probably sounded crazy to everyone, but I swear I felt one of their family bear hugs when the final shovel full of dirt landed. Like some part of my soul could finally be at peace knowing they were reunited and happy together once more. By now, the grass had long since grown over and both graves looked like they naturally belonged…just like how they had looked in life.

"Marla's doing great things with our recipes," I added. "Finally getting all the recognition she's always deserved."

As clear as if he were standing next to me, I felt my Daddy's approving smile. He always wanted Marla to succeed on her own rather than be stuck in our restaurant. And so she had.

Marla's Sweets and The Comfy Cushion had joined forces in the rebuild after the fire. It was now one giant restaurant and bakery, filled to the brim with home-cooked meals that stuck to your ribs and fresh desserts that went straight to your heart rather than your stomach. It had been featured on The Today Show, The View, and in dozens of magazines. Wesley and Phillip connected Marla with a great attorney who brokered a deal to get her pies into grocery stores around the country. She was working on a highly sought after cookbook, and well on track to become a household name.

Although Marla took a while to come around to it, I had wholeheartedly agreed with the decision to rename the place. Marla finally relented after a lot of deep conversations with Nana, Maggie, Wes, and me, and so Hometown Heaven was born. A little bit of Mama, a little bit of Marla, and a whole lot of Daddy's business savvy. The perfect combination.

Business was booming and had been since the day Marla reopened. I cried in bed all day over the fact that I wasn't strong enough to be there for the event, but everyone assured me that I deserved the time away to heal. At that point, healing was all I could really do. My friends and family were in my corner, just as they had been from the beginning.

Desiree and Jeremy's trials lasted more than a year. When the guilty verdict came down after only three hours of deliberation, I blacked out on the bench in the courtroom. Both faced 25 years in prison, though Jeremy's was without parole. He was also required to register as a sex offender. The district attorney assured me she would continue to fight against Desiree getting parole, which was enough of a promise that I pushed the worry from my mind. It would only drive me to madness anyway.

Mr. Madden's trial, on the other hand, took a lot longer. He paid several flashy attorneys to defend him, but in the end, all of the proof Elle Fielding accumulated through the years was too much for the judge to ignore. He was found guilty of more than 26 counts of fraud, embezzlement, tax evasion, conspiracy, and more. Ultimately, Wesley's father was sentenced to 35 years in federal prison and ordered to pay close to $1 billion in restitution and fees. Wesley turned off the tv in disgust and spent two hours alone in our home gym after the reporter announced the verdict.

To this day, nobody had seen or heard from Hillary. I speculated once that she probably still had enough friends out in Vegas to start over out in the desert again, but I also hadn't lost a minute of sleep worrying about it. She wasn't worth it.

"Mama! Mama!" Joshua's animated trill came from behind me. I turned just in time for my son's sticky toddler arms to wrap around my neck as he buried himself in my arms.

Iris was close behind, rolling her eyes. "He's such a mama's boy. Acting like I'm not over here being the best big sister ever."

Wesley came up beside her, resting an elbow on her shoulder. "That's why it's us against them, Rainbow." He turned his megawatt smile in my direction, the same bright smile that made him look every inch the angel I knew him to be, and it was hard not to melt into a puddle. "Can't wait to see whose side the new recruit will be on."

I laughed and rubbed my protruding belly. "We'll know soon enough." Ever mimicking me, Joshua leaned down to rub my baby bump before slapping a slobbery kiss on top.

All three of us cooed.

"Just wait, Joshy! I've gotta show you the ropes of this big sibling thing!" Iris bent down to scoop him up, twirling him in a circle so that he giggled and screamed in delight.

Wesley held out a hand to pull me up. "You okay?" He still had small pockets of anxiety whenever there was something he couldn't fix for me, but we were working on it.

Therapy had become my best friend in the past five years. After heading to Boston, Wesley and I both went to intensive individual sessions three times a week. We took Iris for family sessions, too, so that we could work through her overwhelming feelings of reconnecting with a father she had never known. It was hard—so much harder than any of us anticipated—but in the end, it was the best thing for all three of us. After a year's worth of therapy, self-care, bucket list trips, and watching our daughter live out her dreams on stage with the Boston Ballet, when Wesley proposed, I said yes.

Neither of us wanted a big wedding. We booked a cruise down to Turks and Caicos with Nana, Marla, Maggie, and Zeke, who had become a close friend of Wesley's by that time, and got married on the boat with our favorite people surrounding us. Nana loved every second of it and spent the entire vacation talking about the hot pool boys that she wished were actors on one of her soap operas so she could watch them shirtless each day.

Iris gave me away in Mama's wedding dress.

With Wesley's encouragement and the suggestion of my therapist, I finally enrolled in college. Earning my BSN to become a registered nurse was probably one of the hardest things I had ever done, especially when Joshua surprised us with his arrival halfway through, but I didn't regret it for a second. I was fortunate enough to work in the oncology department at the Boston University Medical Center, caring for patients like my daddy. Every one of them reminded me of him, and it brought me that much more closure over his loss. I loved my job. So much so that I applied for a master's program to become a nurse practitioner. The letter burned a hole in my pocket at that very moment because I wanted to open it with Mama, Daddy, and Wes.

Wesley was a changed man. Though his temper rose every so often, he had finally learned how to manage it so that walls weren't broken and objects weren't thrown. It made him a formidable lawyer now that he had made the switch over to criminal prosecution. Wes said inspiration hit after everything we went through with Desiree and Jeremy, and he loved nothing more than giving bad people what they deserved. Evidently, he was good at it because after only a few years, the city placed him in charge of the district attorney's office. Rumors swirled that he would become the Attorney General of Massachusetts, but every time I asked him, he groaned and said that he would rather dry hump a cactus on national tv.

I took that as a "maybe."

Most importantly, Wes and Iris had grown so close they were practically inseparable. He attended every dance recital, every exhibition, every school event, and routinely took her on Daddy-Daughter Days. Usually they were just expensive day trips, but Iris came back beaming every time.

He had been so worried the day the doctor confirmed that I was nine weeks along with Joshua. What if Iris felt like we were replacing her? "I missed out on all of this stuff with her," he whispered to me in bed at night. "What if she thinks my excitement means I love the baby more than her?"

Thankfully, that hadn't happened because Iris was more excited over the prospect of a sibling than we could have reckoned for. She wanted to go to every doctor's appointment with me and immediately framed every ultrasound photo. Maggie helped her plan a huge gender reveal party for us, and the memory of Iris crying while jumping up and down screaming, "I KNEW IT!" over the blue ballons that escaped the box could go down in the record books as one of the happiest of my life.

Joshua ended up being the world's most cheerful child, and we were all smitten and wrapped around his little fingers from the moment he opened his eyes. Wesley was exactly the kind of hands on daddy I dreamt he would be, only sharing Joshua with Iris. "You got to carry him for nine months already," Wes griped. "It's my turn now."

Life had turned out better than I had ever hoped for. The future finally became something I welcomed with open arms and a blissful heart, filled with promise and excitement. I loved my family, my job, and our home, so even if it was a rejection letter in my pocket, everything was going to be okay. It just meant I was already exactly where I needed to be.

"So?" Wes prompted me. "Can we open the letter now?"

I smiled. He grabbed a squirming Joshua from Iris and both of them grinned at me like they were in on a secret.

Hastily, I pulled out the envelope and withdrew the letter.

"UMass Boston is pleased to welcome you to the Fall semester of the Nursing Master of Science program," I read aloud.

Iris and Wesley both whooped and hollered. Joshua set off in another round of giggles as Wesley tossed him up in the air and caught him. "Say, 'good job, Mama!'" Wesley crowed. He handed Joshua off to Iris, who continued to dance and spin with him so that my husband could plant a firm kiss on my mouth. "I'm so proud of you," he whispered in my ear.

Longing flooded me and I deepened the kiss. Having someone around to tell me that they were proud of me was one of the things Wesley and I had identified in therapy as a way to provide reassurance. It built up my confidence and reinforced the belief that I was worthy of love...basically a way to reprogram my brain after everything Desiree put me through. Wesley never forgot. Even if it was something as simple as trying a new recipe, he made it a point to tell me how impressed he was.

Iris came over and wrapped her arms around me. "I love you so much, Mama! This is so exciting!"

My heart soared. "Yeah? It's going to be a lot of work. Between school and the new baby, I don't want to take away from you."

Her smile was identical to mine, the only time she ever resembled me instead of her daddy. "You always put me first, Mama," Iris assured me. "I know that will never change."

Tears of joy sprung at my eyes, but I wiped them away before they could fall. "I love you, baby girl." She ran back to Wesley and Joshua, the three of them still carrying on like we won the lottery.

Tearful laughter was the best kind, I discovered. "We did

it, y'all," I whispered to Mama and Daddy's gravestones. "Thank you."

"C'mon, let's head back over to the restaurant and share the great news with Marla!" Wesley called over his shoulder, steering the kids towards the Land Rover idling on the lane.

There was already a waiting area full of people when we arrived at Hometown Heaven. Cassidy, the hostess, proudly informed us that there was a 90 minute wait.

With the big remodel, this updated version of the restaurant was larger than before. White marble counters replaced the old Formica, including the new bakery area on the left side of the dining room. Two large, glass bake cases fenced in a large marble bar top with twirling metal barstools. One bake case displayed breakfast pastries that were baked fresh daily and the other displayed dessert items like Marla's famous pies, cookies, brownies, and more. The flavors and variety changed each morning. Marla modeled Daddy's old practices and sourced locally as much as possible, getting fresh fruits, flour, and the like so that everyone along the Florida-Georgia line wanted to come taste their produce for themselves.

The bakery side of the kitchen opened behind the counter so that people waiting in the lobby and sitting at the bar top could watch as bakers, expertly overseen by Marla's watchful eye, worked to replenish the cases, fill orders, and provide items for diners. They were able to create the most beautiful designs with dough. It was like watching an artist create an edible masterpiece.

New metal tables with marble tops congregated in the center of the dining room. Since the wooden tables were burned in the fire, Marla hired Old Man McInworthe to build large booths around the outer perimeter. Fluffy cushions lined all the chairs and booths, this time in a matching gingham print. There were no longer any barstools as the countertop was long gone, but several servers' stations led back into the kitchen.

Jesse was now the back of the house manager, supervising all of the cooks Marla could afford to hire. Mama's recipe book was kept under lock and key in what was now Marla's office. She was the only one permitted to look through it when the menu changed seasonally.

The best part of all was how many jobs she was able to offer to the community. Hometown Heaven was able to employ ten people full time and six people part time. Wesley helped set up a tuition program as well so that the employees could further their education at an online college or any number of the colleges in Savannah. All of them so far had done so, which I knew would have meant the world to Mama and Daddy.

"My baby girl is finally here!" Marla cried as she looked up from the butcher's block table in the bakery area where she was kneading pie dough. She wiped her hands on the apron around her waist as she scrambled around the counter to us.

Iris immediately enveloped her in a hug, Joshua all but diving out of Wesley's arms in his haste to get to Grandma Marla. Her smile brightened the room. She moved on to Welsey, then me. As the closest thing I had to a living parent, Marla's hug felt like coming home. While she visited us in Boston and traveled with us on some of our family vacations, this was the first time I came home to River's Run to see her. It was a pivotal moment for both of us. I blamed my tears on my pregnancy hormones. She didn't have that excuse.

"Looking good, Celeste," she said warmly, cupping her

hands around my belly. I was only 21 weeks along, but I already popped enough for there to be a noticeable bump. "Are we still good for tonight?"

I grinned. "I can hardly wait!" We were going to have a family gender reveal dinner after she closed down the restaurant early. Iris already had the envelope. Marla was also going to take the kids to her house for the night. It was really Ms. Shirley's old house, which Wes gave to her as soon as we signed the deed for the Hendricks family home. He agreed that we didn't need two houses in a place like River's Run and Marla had more than earned the right to have a place of her own. I couldn't have agreed more.

Like Mama always said, when you have more than you need, you build a bigger table, not a taller fence.

Wesley

Celeste looked radiant in a floral sundress, her bump just noticeable in the flow of the skirt. Every day she made me fall in love with her all over again. Whether it was watching her be a fantastic mother to our children, hearing about her compassion for her patients, or tasting the homecooked meals she insisted on making us every night for a family dinner, there was always another reminder of what a lucky son of a bitch I was to call her mine.

I meant it when I vowed to love her for my whole life. Celeste Hendricks, now Celeste Madden, *was* my whole life. She brought me everything I ever needed and more.

We weren't religious people, so I had no idea if there was

a heaven, but I'd like to believe that wherever Mr. Hendricks was, he rested easier knowing I kept my promise. If I could be half the man and father he taught me to be, then I would call myself a success.

"Let's get going," Nana bemoaned. "I hate these old lady dresses y'all force me to wear at these shindigs."

Celeste's eyes sparkled as she glanced my way, clearly repressing a laugh. Nana was never satisfied unless she got to wear sweatpants and oversized t-shirts. That would never change. She even made us promise to bury her in them. Since it was technically a party, we asked her to dress up in something a little nicer and she had been loudly grousing about it since we walked through the door. Now that the party was winding down, it seemed Nana reached her limit.

"Me, too," Iris whined. "I'm ready to go back to Aunt Marla's." Joshua was already snuggled into her lap, fast asleep.

It was hard to believe that in a few months' time I would have a second little girl to love. I might need to build a bunker if she was as tenacious and outspoken as our first-born. As soon as Marla read the doctor's note aloud with the ultrasound photos to match, Celeste and I both swooned. Iris was elated and loudly declared that her baby sister was going to be a dancer just like her. I certainly hope so. Watching Iris dance was my favorite pastime.

"Alright, let's head on back," Marla agreed with Iris and Nana. The two servers who volunteered to stay and help immediately stepped forward to start clearing the table as one by one our friends and family left. Everyone stopped to give us one last hug and congratulations on their way out the door, including the recently retired Chief Hillsborough and his wife.

Maggie and Zeke flew in for the occasion and shuffled out after Marla and the kids to help her get them settled at her place for the night. Celeste and I hadn't had a moment alone in quite some time, so tonight was a real treat.

"So another girl," my wife gushed as we walked hand in hand out to the car. A soft breeze blew, the temperature quickly dropping now that the sun was going down. Days were starting to get longer. Summer would be here before we knew it and we could go on our annual summer vacation. This year we were going to Greece so that we could enjoy the beaches of the Mediterranean and Celeste could stay off her feet. I didn't want to force her to walk all day when she would be that far along in her pregnancy, but I still wanted to spoil her with a trip to a new place. I promised Mr. Hendricks I would give her the world and ever since I got her back, I kept that promise.

"What should we name her?" I asked after we pulled out onto the county highway leading back towards our house. Distracting her was my main intention because I knew she was apprehensive about returning and facing the horrible memories of what Desiree had inflicted on her. Hopefully, my surprise worked in my favor.

Her long hair had returned to its natural brown, as wild and untamed as my girl. It danced now across her face with the wind from the open window. Therapy had done wonders with helping Celeste reconnect with the person I always knew her as: a sweetheart with more kindness in her pinky toe than most people had in their entire being. She smiled constantly now, for which I was grateful, and her work at the hospital gave her a sense of purpose that I knew she couldn't have achieved if we stayed in River's Run. Everything worked out exactly the way it was supposed to, even when it meant we had to start over in Boston.

"What name would you pick?" asked Celeste, my favorite shy smile tugging at her lips. Her skin glowed in the setting sun, and I had to catch my breath once more at how beautiful she looked.

"Annie Marla Madden," I answered immediately.

She chuckled in surprise. "That was fast!"

I shrugged, flipping on the blinker to turn onto the dirt road back to the Hendricks family home. "It's the name I picked out when I first realized I loved you."

Celeste sat up straighter, peering at me quizzically as if she didn't believe me.

"Well, okay, 'Marla' is something I'd choose now, not back then," I admitted. "I just always saw you reading classic novels where the women had names like 'Anne' and 'Elizabeth,' so my thirteen year old brain thought that was what we should name our daughter."

I could tell she was fighting a smile.

"Annie," she mused. "I like it."

I parked the car and went around to Celeste's door to open it. Phillip had been in charge of the contractors here for the past several months who worked around the clock to restore everything to the original design from when Celeste and I were kids. The exterior had a fresh coat of paint, new shutters, and a new porch railing. Gardeners had returned the yard to its floral glory, the colors muted in the dim twilight. String lights hung from the large tree back to the corner of the porch. A soft glow illuminated the old tire swing Phillip's team managed to salvage.

Celeste stopped short at the sight of the house, her jaw

hanging open. "Is it just me or does this look..." Her voice trailed off and I let the uncertainty hang in the air.

Weaving my fingers through hers, I led her inside through the front door. Candles and white roses were on every surface of the foyer, the living room, and the kitchen beyond. Everything had been restored so that no traces of Desiree or her children remained. I also asked Phillip to incorporate some of the elements of our home in Boston, so there were already large portraits of us and the kids on the walls. The effect was cozy and welcoming. Exactly how I wanted it.

Celeste's face was priceless. Silent tears streamed down her face while her free hand covered her open mouth. Eyes darting everywhere at once, she tried to drink it all in.

"Wes..." she finally gasped.

"I didn't want anything here to trigger you," I explained softly. "This has always been your home, and she never had any right to take it from you. We can gut the place and renovate it completely, if you'd like, but I wanted you to start with it being as close to home as you remembered. I only want you to be happy," I finished.

In response, Celeste threw herself at me. The salt from her tears tasted bittersweet on my tongue and I groaned. She grabbed both of my hands and placed them on her breasts, already engorged from pregnancy, and shimmied the straps of her dress off her shoulders. It fluttered to the floor in a silky puddle, leaving her hard nipples in the palms of my hands. She didn't have on a bra or panties.

"Goddamn it, woman, you're gonna keep getting pregnant if you keep doing this to me," I wailed, my mouth descending on one of her nipples. My tongue circled around the peak while my other hand reached down between us to find her drenched.

Celeste wasted no time. Within seconds, my belt was undone and my jeans were sliding down my legs. We both almost fell as I stumbled out of my boxer briefs, cock ready to cut steel. She yanked my shirt violently over my head in our frenzy. Hands caressed everywhere; I needed to feel every inch of her skin.

It was rare for us to have time alone like this. Between both kids, Nana, and our jobs, sexy time was often reduced to a scheduled ritual once or twice per week that we had timed down to six minutes tops—the longest amount of time we could ever count on before life got in the way. Right now, getting to really explore her gorgeous body, to lavish her with all the attention I always wanted to give, was my idea of perfection.

I scooped her up, bride-style, and carried her over to the couch, placing her on the arm and then pushing her back to lay against the throw pillows at an incline. Looping both knees over my shoulders, I kneeled between her legs and entered the pearly gates of heaven when I tasted the sweetness waiting for me between her thighs. My tongue speared her, causing her thighs to clamp so tightly on my head that I could no longer hear. Unless she gave me a brain aneurysm, I wasn't stopping.

I moved my attention to her clit, suckling on it like a mint. Three fingers replaced my tongue, working in and out in a heated frenzy to stretch her walls for me, and her thighs squeezed harder. I lapped at her release when a tiny orgasm rippled through her.

Celeste yanked hard on the roots of my hair, drawing my attention away from her sweet pussy. Once she made eye contact with me, she swung her legs over my head to clamber off the couch altogether, pulling at my shoulders so I would sit down. Instantly, she straddled my lap, sinking onto my erection with a cry worthy of a Viking raider. I let her set her own rhythm, too entranced by the sight of her giant titties bouncing in my face. My mouth settled on one to pucker the skin in wet, languid kisses, leaving hickeys in their wake. The caveman in me roared with delight over marking my territory. Like her last name, wedding ring, and my baby growing inside her wasn't enough. None of it ever would be.

Her moan went straight to my dick. Taking the other nipple in my mouth, I sucked and nipped, snaking my hand under the bump to rub her clit. It was the equivalent to dropping the atom bomb because an orgasm strong enough for me to feel ripped through her. Pussy walls gripped my cock so tightly that I saw stars as I thrust my hips to pound my release inside her.

Dazed and happy, Celeste slumped against me, both of us a sweaty, spent mess. "I love you so much, Wesley," she murmured against my neck.

"For my whole life, sugar bee," I whispered back.

This was the life my father tricked me into believing I didn't deserve and would never have. I was the lucky bastard who got to grow old with the love of my life by my side. Celeste and I would get to retire to this very home, the house that Mr. Hendricks left for us, so that we could rock out on the old porch swing while our grandchildren and great-grandchildren played in the yard around us. We'd line the walls with more photos of our adventures around the world, reminiscing about all the lives we changed as a nurse and prosecutor.

I wish I could go back and tell my thirteen year old self how remarkable things would be. That all the anger and the hatred would one day go away, letting so much love and joy filter in through the cracks. I would thank Mr. Hendricks all over again for guiding me in the right direction for the kind of husband and father I wanted to be.

For now, I sighed contentedly, nuzzling my wife's hair and gently rubbing her belly where our little Annie was cooking. This was life as it should be.

The End

ACKNOWLEDGMENTS

Writing acknowledgments doesn't get any easier as I write more books, so we'll just have to chalk this section up to being as awkward on paper as I am in person. There are so many people to thank, and I apologize now if I leave anyone out.

First and foremost, a giant thanks to my Barnes & Noble crew. Sometimes I think I would go crazy if it weren't for you guys. Jeannie, thank you for continuing to embrace the chaos of the indie author world. I know how weird it all sounds, and yet you keep rolling with the punches like it's no big deal. You're the best manager a girl could ask for!

To the rest of my B&N peeps: Peri, Autumn, Carmen, Paige, Mady, Tiegan, Staci, Ahmru, Jackson, Roman, Talia, Maraya, Ally, Max, Ben, David, and "Little" Sam. Thank you for making my "day" job so fun and rewarding. The way y'all continually show up for me is such a blessing. Let's party in the break room later!

Lea, my amazing editor—we did the damn thing! This book truly took us through the wringer, but we came out on the other side with a pretty spectacular story to show for it (if I do say so myself). I love getting to work with you. Thank you for your patience, understanding, and support.

Kate at Y'all That Graphic, you've reached queen status! The way you swooped in at the last minute to not only save the day with a last minute cover change, but then you created two gorgeous covers and an entire line of marketing graphics in just a few HOURS. I cannot recommend your services enough! We will definitely collaborate again on future projects!

To my Booktok Book Club family, thank you for giving me something to look forward to at the end of every month. Sometimes it's the only thing that keeps me sane. It's definitely the best reason to take a break from the stories in my head and enjoy someone else's plot for a while. Our book club is the best book club, hands down!

For my Samantha Gail Starlets, who always give me a reason to keep going. I hope you've enjoyed seeing the growth of our group as much as I have. It's rewarding to connect with new readers, and I value each and every one of you.

There are some authors that I simply have to acknowledge because their mentorship has been invaluable in writing this book:

Jenn McMahon, you were always there any time I needed to vent. Thank you for reminding me I'm not alone in the indie world.

Sara Massery, while I might have forced my friendship on you (LOL), your advice is so appreciated. I definitely could not do this without you as a sounding board.

Not to be dramatic, but Melanie Harlow and her Harlot Authors group changed my life. I've never had so many women I admire and aspire to be all in one place to make suggestions and provide feedback.

And lastly, B. Celeste, without whom this book would not have been written. While it might have been a seemingly errant conversation to you, your words of encouragement came at a time when I needed them most. I am forever in your debt.

And finally—even though I hope they never read this book—Jack, Tristan, and Cael, you continue to be my beacon in the darkness. I'm sorry for the late nights, early mornings, and quick dinners, but y'all motivate me to work harder and aim higher. You deserve all the world and more. I love you so much!

Let's all be like Celeste and spread more kindness, please!

-SG

ABOUT THE AUTHOR

Samantha Gail is a former Probation Parole Officer who supervised sex offenders before deciding she needed more happily ever after's and decided to write books instead. Her work falls into multiple genres, primarily thriller, romance, and fantasy. She currently manages a bookstore and writes when she's not spending time with her three children and three fur babies.

ALSO BY SAMANTHA GAIL

Pay the Price

Epoch: Book One of The Hourglass Saga

www.ingramcontent.com/pod-product-compliance
Lightning Source LLC
Chambersburg PA
CBHW061852310726
48972CB00004B/996